THE
STRANGER
NEXT DOOR

ADAM SOUTHWARD

ACCENT

First published in 2021 by Headline Accent
An imprint of HEADLINE PUBLISHING GROUP

1

Cataloguing in Publication Data is available from the British Library

ISBN 978 1 4722 8513 3

Typeset in 11.25/15.25 pt Bembo Std by Jouve (UK), Milton Keynes

Printed and bound in Great Britain by Clays Ltd, Elcograf S.p.A.

Headline's policy is to use papers that are natural, renewable and recyclable
products and made from wood grown in well-managed forests and other
controlled sources. The logging and manufacturing processes are expected
to conform to the environmental regulations of the country of origin.

HEADLINE PUBLISHING GROUP
An Hachette UK Company
Carmelite House
50 Victoria Embankment
London EC4Y 0DZ

www.headline.co.uk
www.hachette.co.uk

For Kerry, Isla, and Daisy,
who keep me happy and loved in these crazy times.

After

My stomach heaved. I coughed, hacking up smoke and soot, wheezing with the effort, my eyes watering in protest as the first body bag was zipped and tagged. The paramedics didn't look at me. I wasn't hurt. Not badly. I heaved again.

The stretcher caught on the kerb, the wheels snagging, lurching to the left before righting itself. The paramedics yanked it free, cursing as they pulled it on to the road.

Smoke billowed from the rear of the house. The firefighters ran in and out, unpacking more equipment, rolling hoses across the front lawn, shouting at each other with controlled urgency. The noise swept over me. I couldn't process it. Just another wave of chaos.

I resisted the urge to run to the ambulance, to jump inside and beg. My legs were frozen, rooted to the ground. The grief was overwhelming; the relentless build-up of the last few weeks seizing my every muscle.

A second stretcher appeared, a second body bag, wheeled more carefully, missing the kerb. The paramedics lifted this one easily into the vehicle. The bile caught in my throat this time. I coughed again, my saliva thick with ash.

How did it come to this? How could it? This was my house, my family, destroyed by reasons too hurtful to contemplate. I sank to the ground, hugging my knees to my chest, thoughts spinning with pain as the shivers took me.

The air was electric, the storm gathering pace. The rain hadn't arrived yet, but the wind howled through the street, taking my breath with it. Jake barked from a neighbour's garden — he'd got out, scared but unhurt, not even a mark on his golden fur. A firefighter had taken him to calm him down. His barking cut through my shock, keeping me from the brink. Beyond, there was only darkness.

I shook my head, blinking to clear my vision and my mind. The curtains were still drawn in Ashley's windows, untouched by the blaze. I pictured the neatly made bed, patterned with hedgehogs — Ashley's favourite — and the patchwork quilt rolled up at the end. It would fall on to her dolls' house, knocking the delicate figures over. Ash moved them around inside the dolls' house every day, a wonderful cycle of disorder in which only a child could delight.

My Ashley. Perfect. Vulnerable, as all children are.

I turned to Nancy's house, standing untouched, separated by the flawlessly trimmed hedge and picket fence. Nancy's house would never be the same, either. It might not burn, but it was damaged beyond repair. Some wounds would never heal.

The shivers increased. A paramedic sauntered over, pulling a silver blanket from his bag. I took it but refused to move. He backed away, promising to return.

Thoughts of Matt spun out of control, refusing to settle, refusing to make sense. Imogen and Matt Roberts, the perfect couple. My perfect husband, and now what? I knew it would get worse before it got better, but I struggled to tear myself away from this moment, where time had stopped, a period of respite between the pain of before and the pain yet to come.

There was a roar as the first police car entered the road. It was followed by a second. They disappeared from view behind the fire trucks and the sirens stopped. The doors opened, slamming shut a second later. My heart missed a beat.

I'd expected to see them, but it didn't reduce the shock. Or the fear.

Three short months.

And it still wasn't over.

Matt

Three Months Earlier

Matt drew several deep breaths, savouring the smell of cut grass and a multitude of other garden scents, of tree pollen and shrubs and wildflowers. The tension of the last few months seeped away. He could feel it in his shoulders and neck, a distinct shift in his posture. *So this is what relaxed feels like.* The physical relief was palpable, and he allowed himself a smile. London was behind them, and the country sun beat down as he turned to Imogen. She squinted, pecking him on the lips.

'See,' she said. 'I was right.'

'As usual.'

It *was* a great house. Old and detached with four bedrooms, a hundred-foot lawn and a block-paved driveway. He'd viewed it only once, trusting Imogen to make the final decision. Now they were moving in, it was even better than he remembered.

'Have we really bought a house in a private country estate?' he said.

'Village community,' said Imogen.

'What's the difference?'

'The price, I think,' said Imogen.

It had been rather high, on their financial limit, but he'd convinced himself they'd manage – and they didn't have a whole load of options, given the timescale. His new job paid quite well, all things considered, plus the cost of everything else would be lower outside London. Besides, it was perfect for Ashley. The primary school on the main road was highly rated, and they already had a place for her, starting in the autumn term.

'You did well,' he said, nudging her gently in the ribs.

'I know,' she said. 'These places never come on the market. Can you believe it?' Her dark hair fluttered around her face and she swept it out of her eyes, tucking a few strands behind her ears. Her smile was infectious and Matt grinned, reaching out to her.

Imogen squeezed Matt around the waist, her hand fidgeting like it always did when she was nervous or excited. He suspected a little of both. He was nervous too, but he hid it better. More practised, perhaps. They looked left and right at the neighbouring houses, then back to theirs – standing proud in prime position at the end of the cul-de-sac.

'Number thirteen,' she said. 'It's lucky we're not superstitious.'

There were only thirty-one houses in the community, bordered by a natural treeline and a security gate on to the main road. Tucked into the northeast corner of the village of Albury in Surrey, it was as idyllic as it got. Paintings were made of such villages, stories were told. People retired in places like this to get away from it all.

Matt knew he was lucky to live here. Lucky to get a second chance.

'What do you think the neighbours are like?' said Imogen.

5

'I'm sure we'll find out,' said Matt. 'But probably just like us. Perfect in every way.'

Imogen gripped him a little tighter. 'It's nice you think that,' she said.

They enjoyed a few moments of silence, arm in arm, before a scream erupted from the car.

'Mummy! Daddy!'

Ashley was bouncing in her seat, hammering on the window, her pigtails bouncing around her face, her brown eyes wide with excitement.

'Somebody's awake,' said Imogen, breaking away. She opened Ashley's door, trying but failing to stop Jake leaping out. He barged past Ashley and sprinted off into one of the neighbours' front gardens, sniffing a small cherry tree before cocking his leg against it.

Ashley stretched, blinking several times before dancing over to Matt, burying her head against his stomach. Matt pulled her into a hug, gripping her small shoulders, reaching around to tickle her gently on the neck. She giggled, writhing away, but still too tired to escape. He wondered what she thought about the move, what questions might be bubbling around in her tiny head. She seemed to take it in her stride, her normal happy self – she was a perpetual daydreamer, often lost in her own little world, which was almost certainly a good thing. A more inquisitive personality might have asked more awkward questions by this point.

'Is that our new house?' she said, yawning. She looked puzzled. 'I thought it would be blue.'

Matt stared down at her, her skinny body wrapped in denim dungarees and pink trainers, white socks pulled up to her knees. His chest tightened, a warm squeeze reminding him of what he had, what he could have lost. But he'd fixed it, *would* fix it. Just a few more loose ends, and everything would be sorted.

'Blue?'

'I had a dream,' she said. 'It was blue.'

Matt laughed, ruffling her hair. 'That,' he said, pointing to one of the upper front windows, 'is your bedroom. Want to go and check it out?'

Ashley's eyes widened. 'Yes!'

'I'll open up,' said Imogen. 'Can you grab Jake?'

Matt nodded, emptying the boot of the car on to the driveway, keeping an eye out for the removal lorry. He scanned the road, taking in the mature leafy green gardens and the neatly trimmed hedges. He hadn't paid much attention to the outside of their old house in Bermondsey – they always had at least one broken fence panel and a tree in need of lopping, weeds sprouting all over their driveway – but things were clearly different here, with each house exquisitely manicured. He suspected most of the neighbours were retirees with nothing to fill their time except hedge trimming. Perhaps they'd do his as well. Either that or he'd have to find a gardener. He certainly wasn't going to do it himself.

He turned back to the car as his phone rang.

'Happy moving day!' It was Shelley, the editorial director at the *Guildford Press* – his new boss.

'Shelley, hi,' he said, not expecting a work call. He didn't start for another week, taking the opportunity for some time off to unpack and wade through all of the moving paperwork.

'Chill out,' she said, 'I can hear the tone in your voice. This isn't work, it's just a welcome to the area. Making sure you haven't changed your mind, et cetera.'

Matt smiled. 'No. Not changed my mind. I'll be your new editor, right once I've finished unpacking my entire life's belongings. Though the lorry hasn't arrived yet, so this might be it.'

She laughed. 'Don't worry. If they don't turn up, I have a blow-up bed you can borrow.'

'Good to know,' he said.

'Just one thing,' said Shelley. 'HR tell me they're still waiting on a reference, from your previous director, a Mr ... let me see ...'

'Mr de Vries,' said Matt. Damn. He'd hoped one reference was enough.

'That's him,' said Shelley.

'I'll chase it,' said Matt. 'You'll have it asap.'

'Brilliant,' said Shelley. 'In which case, see you soon, Matt. And welcome – you'll love it in Surrey. I promise.'

Matt tucked his phone into his pocket and forced away the faint unease that threatened his good mood. It would all come together. He'd work hard, and he'd try to make Imogen happy. She'd given up a lot to be here.

He'd promised he would make it worth her while.

'Do you remember the first time we did this?' said Matt, checking his watch. They'd been unpacking for almost three hours, and he was ready for a chilled glass of wine, or at the very least a warm one. His romantic suggestion of spending the first night sitting on boxes with takeaway pizza had been quickly dismissed by Imogen, who said she couldn't relax until they'd made some headway. She'd barked orders until Ashley was in bed and all the essentials were unpacked. Jake was confined to the utility room until he calmed down, after which he lay in front of the fireplace, watching them both and yawning.

Imogen kept insisting unpacking was fun. Matt reluctantly played along, knowing that if it was left to him, they'd be sitting on boxes until they grew old and withered, their belongings preserved forever in bubble-wrap and cardboard.

'We had less stuff the first time,' said Imogen, shoving a box across the floor with her foot.

They'd moved immediately after their wedding, fifteen years ago. Matt remembered the stress of not only planning the big day but also coordinating the house, which was to be ready on their return from their honeymoon. Their new life together in London would be sealed.

'We had *cheaper* stuff,' he said.

Imogen shrugged. 'Stuff is stuff. It's not . . . you know.' She kicked another box, turning away.

Matt paused, watching her linger in the doorway, facing away, through the kitchen-diner towards the garden. She'd loved their little garden in London, the outdoors, getting in touch with nature – she told him it was a necessary contrast from the clinical confines of the hospital. She used to drag him for long walks in the parks, out of the city for a few hours and into proper countryside. She'd sometimes take her trainers and go for a jog. Matt would make an excuse, feign an injury, trail behind. They used to run together, years ago. He couldn't remember the last time they did.

He watched her now, the way she wrapped her arms around herself, holding her body tight. Perhaps they could again.

'It's not what makes a home,' he said.

She turned, her face breaking into a surprised smile. He walked over, slipped his hands around her waist.

'But I know what will,' he said.

'Oh?' Her voice was soft. Not sad, but thoughtful.

'You and Ash,' he said. 'That's all it'll take. We don't need stuff.' He kicked out, catching the nearest box with a dull thud.

Imogen chuckled, her breath hitting his cheek. She sighed. 'You mean that? You really mean it?'

'I mean it,' he said, staring into her eyes, not blinking, not flinching. She had to believe he really meant it, or all of this was for nothing.

She held his gaze for a few moments before leaning in, kissing him firmly on the lips, causing a warm rush of excitement, of longing. He pulled her body against his. She tensed, for just a moment, before relaxing, pushing her arms against his chest, her fingers creeping up to undo his top button.

'I believe you,' she said, breaking away.

'Good, then—'

But she shook her head, putting a finger to her lips. She kept her eyes on him, tiptoeing across the wood, biting her lower lip in the playful way that meant trouble. She stopped at the foot of the stairs.

'Come on,' she said. 'It's nearly midnight. Work's over. Time for play.'

They lay on the mattress, catching their breath, Matt's feet still tangled in the sheets. Imogen reached over and grabbed her wine glass from the floor. She sipped at it, her face glowing.

Matt watched her lips, followed the curve of her neck down to her body.

'Poor thing,' she said. 'Did I break you?'

'Nearly,' he said, pushing himself on to his elbows, 'but I'll survive.'

She passed him the glass and swung her legs off the mattress. 'Good, because there's plenty more work for you tomorrow. The kitchen door sticks, and so do the French doors. The dishwasher's broken, oh, and there's something wrong with the boiler.' She winked and jumped up, grabbing her robe from the chair, slipping it on.

Matt laughed and sank into the pillow, listening to the shower start up. The door to the en-suite clicked shut and Matt closed his eyes, absorbing the sounds of the new house – the vibrations of water against the bath, the creak of pipes expanding, the whistle of the breeze through the window frames, and the most striking thing of all – the silence outside. He raised his head off the pillow, straining to hear the sound of a car, or a siren, or a group of teenagers shrieking on their way to a party.

Nothing. Not a peep of human activity. It would take a little getting used to.

He slid off the mattress and went to the window overlooking the back garden. He flicked the light off so he could see more than just his own reflection.

The gardens were dark, most of the houses darker still. Over the back fence was another row in the estate, all of the buildings silent and sleeping. Beyond was the main village, and then countryside for miles. He looked at the garden to the left. In the dim moonlight he could make out a large patio with a long table and chairs, ordered and neat.

To the right, the other neighbour's garden looked more overgrown, not messy, just mature, large clumps of black hiding the lawn underneath. His eyes moved towards the house and he jumped – there was a figure near the back door. He squinted. An old man, wearing a bathrobe. He raised his hand to his mouth. Matt saw the ember of a cigarette glow bright orange, then fade.

Matt checked the time: 1 a.m. He didn't know why the sight of the man had surprised him; he'd expect to see people in London this late. He leaned in against the window and realised the man was facing his way, staring at the house. He wondered whether to wave but decided it would look ridiculous, plus he was naked, albeit most of him was hidden beneath the windowsill.

The neighbour took another long drag of his cigarette before stubbing it out on the ground, the ember dying in a shower of sparks. He paused, staring at Matt's window. Matt could have sworn he saw the man shaking his head, before he turned and disappeared into the house.

Matt didn't mention it to Imogen. She'd tell him not to stare into people's gardens, which, at this time of night, would be fair enough. He took a quick shower and they both collapsed on the mattress, sleep taking them quickly.

Matt found himself restless, in and out of the same, strange dream for hours – walking barefoot through his neighbour's garden, late at night, high walls on each side, darkness at the end. He broke into a run, but it was never-ending. He stopped, his legs locked, unable to move another step. He turned around to find the old man in front of him. The man took a long drag of his cigarette, then flicked it through the air. It landed by Matt's feet and extinguished.

12

The dream played on repeat until the early hours, when the silence of the countryside was broken by the sounds of his family. The welcome, noisy sounds of a young girl wanting her breakfast, and a dog wanting the same.

Imogen

I waited until Matt fell asleep before I slipped out of bed and sat on the toilet, staring at the wall. The black and white mosaic tiles stared back – the tiles Matt had already said he'd replace with something more modern. I supposed I'd chosen the house, so he got to choose the tiles.

The insomnia was biting. My mind was racing, exhausted. My parents were right. They'd said moving was one of the most stressful things you could do in life. More than the other stuff. Moving away from them, our friends, from our hometown, only added to the pressure. Were we sure we needed to go?

Yes, I was sure.

An emotional rush. A sense of loss, or perhaps a premonition, something primal. A flicker of unease.

But we'd done it, hadn't we? A perfect new beginning. The unease would be transient, the sinking feeling would rise. The simmering would dissipate and happiness would return.

It was just moving nerves. Matt was convinced of it.

I was trying. God, I was trying.

I put my mood down to the stress, the wine, the sex. The

relentless positivity and smiling. *Yes, dear, it's perfect, and so are we. Let's unpack, eat, drink, fuck like we're newlyweds again.* I was exhausted.

Focus on the future.

That meant not hiding in the bathroom all night. I tiptoed back into the bedroom, pausing at the door. I stared at Matt. He was out for the count, snoring with the annoying nasal hiss he saved for when I was too tired to complain.

I crept along the side of the bed, discovering the creaky floorboards, wondering why it mattered. If Matt woke up, we'd talk, we'd cuddle, we'd get frisky again and pretend we were fine. Matt was trying, too, I had to remember. This wasn't easy on him, either. His enthusiasm hid the weight of the responsibility he carried.

Past Ashley's room, I poked my head in. Fast asleep, duvet tucked around her shoulders, mouth hanging open. She was still too young for any of this to really affect her. That's what I hoped, anyway.

The ground floor was alien in the dark, unfamiliar shadows, the dust still hovering. I heated some milk and stirred in hot chocolate. It was my comfort drink, the one my dentist told me I shouldn't have in the middle of the night. But that was my old dentist. The new one might be more forgiving.

The garden was black, the sky lit with stars. I followed a few, trying to remember the constellations, racking my brains. What were you supposed to do? Use Orion's Belt as a marker, trace the rest of the hunter's body, working outwards. Matt had taught me that, lying on a beach in Brighton at 3 a.m., the alcohol making the sky spin until I couldn't even find a streetlight without heaving. Matt had held my hair while I threw up on to the damp sand. I fell asleep in the taxi on the ride home. The stars were worth it, though. It was the only thing I remembered from that night.

My gaze fell. Our garden was huge. I loved it. You didn't get gardens like that in London, not where we'd lived, anyway. The grass stretched away into the pitch-black, the magical secrets of the garden hidden from us mortals. The neighbours' houses were out there somewhere, beyond the hedgerows, full of strangers. Full of opportunity.

The dregs of the hot chocolate were sickly sweet. I licked the inside of the mug, imagining Ashley scream, 'Mummy, you're *not* allowed to do that!' I smiled, ran my tongue over my lips, and placed the evidence in the dishwasher.

Matt's phone was on the worktop, on charge. The LED was flashing. Message. Email. Some banal social media notification. Or something else.

My stomach sank, just a little. It would fade, and there was really nothing for it to get itself in such knots about. I was clear on that.

I wouldn't be here otherwise. I wouldn't be trying this hard.

My heart fluttered, but I resisted. The phone would be locked, and I didn't know his passcode. Why should I? I didn't need to know it.

It was the dead of night, Matt was asleep, and trusting wives don't check their husband's phones.

Matt

The first few days passed in a frantic blur, the grotesque quantity of their material possessions laid bare as they struggled to shift them around the house, shoving toys into cupboards, clothes into wardrobes, pushing shoes under the stairs. Several boxes were hidden in the shed, perhaps ready for next time.

Matt ducked into the study while Imogen took Jake for a walk, something she did frequently to clear her head. Ash went with her, wanting to explore the village and look for sweet shops. 'I'll bring you back some bon-bons, Daddy, and perhaps some liquorice, if you're good.'

Being good had dropped a little way down Matt's list at the moment. He spun back and forth on his swivel chair, staring at the laptop screen. The early evening sun had dipped below the window-line, causing him to squint. Fitting blinds was a long way down the list.

The two paragraphs of text stared back at him. They weren't quite right, but they'd have to do. Tinkering with it wouldn't help matters. He had the headed paper, and the envelope ready to post. His gut sank with what he was doing. He'd already been offered the job. They wanted him. But the reference was the final hurdle, one which he'd hoped in vain would magically appear from his previous employer, no questions asked.

Except it was a personal reference, and the silence said it all.

His eyes drifted to the wedding photo Imogen had unpacked on to his desk, angled so he could see it from any position in the room. He smiled, both at the photo and the gentle nudge to his memories.

Their wedding had been lavish, Imogen taking her parents' offer of a blank cheque at face value. Matt felt out of place for much of the day, scared to touch the bouquets, each costing more than his shoes, or ruffle the napkins that had each taken ten minutes to hand-fold. To be fair, Imogen didn't care for any of that stuff either, but told him it was part of the *experience* – for the guests, not for them. Regardless, Matt drifted through the day in quiet contentment, watching Imogen beaming. She was happy, so he was happy. He couldn't have wished for more.

She bought him a leather-bound writer's notebook as a wedding gift, which he intended to keep in the top drawer in this very study. He'd never used it, scared to mark the soft material. Once used it would become just another notebook. Imogen had written a note on the first page: *Stay faithful to the stories in your head*. She'd taken it from a novel, although Matt could never remember the name of it. She added her own note below: *Write your dreams. I hope I'm in them*.

And she was. But fifteen years is a long time, and things were different now.

He huffed, struggling with the closing sentence, deleting and re-typing it a couple of times. Would they check? Did anybody check? He shouldn't have to do this. He was innocent of any wrongdoing – had sworn it was all a misunderstanding, a lie – but they'd closed the door and that was that.

Imogen believed him. That was all that mattered.

Except he still needed the damn reference.

His fingers danced over the keys, interrupted as his phone buzzed, shuffling across the desk. He checked the caller ID and closed his eyes for a second, taking a deep breath before answering.

This was all he needed.

'I can't,' he said, picturing his bank balance, the glaring red of his overdraft, the mess of credit card accounts.

A moment of silence. 'You promised.'

Matt sighed. 'I've just moved house. You know that. I don't have it.'

A grunt. 'I'm not asking for much. Just the usual.'

Matt closed his eyes, clenched his jaw. 'It all adds up. I simply can't right now.' He paused. 'I'm sorry, I really am. Maybe in a few months.'

He listened to the rapid breathing on the end of the phone.

'I need it by the end of the week,' came the reply, 'or I don't know what I'll do.'

'Look, I—'

The line went dead.

Matt stared at the screen for a few moments, waiting for his pulse to settle. It was an old threat, tired, worn out. He was certain of it.

Almost certain. The flutter in his chest said differently. But what could he do? He was being truthful, and he was damned if he'd let some empty threat distract him. There was no money left in his accounts, threat or not.

He tried to put it out of his mind, returning to the document he'd been working on, scanning it over one last time before hitting the print button. He took a deep breath and signed at the bottom, using long, sweeping handwriting, and folded the page carefully. He sealed the envelope, and with it, that period of his life. The period where he'd nearly come unstuck; nearly lost everything.

He tucked the envelope into the side pocket of his work bag, carefully out of sight.

This time would be different.

Matt took a deep breath, stretching his back, casting his eyes across the lush gardens to the front of the house. The spacing between the houses was generous, assuring privacy, the low fences bolstered by mature shrubs and trees overhanging the gardens and road. Through a small gap he spied Imogen, back from her walk. She was at the neighbour's house to the left, standing in their front garden with Ash and Jake, chatting to a dark-haired woman dressed in a floral blouse and long pink skirt, apron tied at her waist.

Imogen said something and the woman laughed, waving her hands animatedly.

Matt had been expecting this. Getting to know the neighbours was something Imogen had been looking forward to. She'd made a point of stressing how important it was, that the faceless anonymity of London wouldn't be acceptable here. It would be good for him, she'd said. Time to work on his people skills.

Perhaps, but Matt didn't need to address it quite so rapidly. He stepped back from the window, keeping out of sight until Imogen broke away, heading home.

He watched her stroll up the garden path, swinging Ashley's hand in hers, the optimism flooding back again, sweeping aside the nagging doubt.

His beautiful wife and daughter. He didn't need anything else.

Matt

'I think we need a new coffee machine,' said Imogen, pouring a cup down the sink. It was Saturday morning and she fussed around the kitchen, examining her freshly baked lemon drizzle cake from every angle.

Matt agreed, but it was another item on the *can't afford* list, as far as he was concerned.

'What does the bottom of it look like?' said Matt, eyeing the cake and his watch. 'I still have time to nip to the shops.'

'It's not funny,' said Imogen. 'First impressions count.'

'What's her name again?'

'Nancy,' said Imogen. 'Number fifteen. She's lovely, and, well . . .'

'You want to make a good impression,' he said, 'I get it. Although if she judges us by your cooking, I think we're screwed.'

'You could have helped.'

'Then it would be even worse.'

'Mum,' said Ashley, 'are we going yet?'

'Not until this afternoon,' said Imogen. She passed Ashley the paint brochure. 'Why don't you pick a colour for your bedroom?'

'I don't know why you're pretending,' said Matt. 'Neither

of us can cook. We almost put it in our wedding vows – *until starvation do us part.*

'Because,' said Imogen, waiting until Ashley was out of earshot. 'Because while you're in the office all day, I'll be here. Until I get some work sorted, I'll be surrounded by these people day in, day out. It's important to me, Matt.'

Matt nodded. He understood, though still felt she was trying too hard. He had to keep reminding himself this wasn't London, where you could get on with your life and ignore everyone around you.

'How old is she?' he asked, feigning interest. 'We're not doing dinner, are we?'

Imogen shrugged. 'A little older than us. I don't know. I'm going for tea, Matt. You don't have to be involved.'

Matt smiled his relief. 'Husband?'

'No idea. A daughter. Teenager. Ruby, I think.'

Matt stared at the cake, nodding, thankful he had a list of things to do at home.

'I think it looks tasty,' he said, 'honestly.'

Imogen poked the cake a few more times before throwing him a desperate look.

'The bakery's open until one,' she said. 'Go and fix this.'

Imogen headed to Nancy's a couple of hours later, with Ashley in tow and a boxed cake from the village bakery. Matt remained at home with Imogen's task list.

It gave him a chance to catch his breath, take a mental break from the over-excitement of the move, the very deliberate enthusiasm with which he and Imogen were throwing themselves

23

into the days ahead. He loved her for it, the way she fussed around the house, organising, *nesting*, even getting to know the neighbours – giving it a sense of permanence that he worried might be lacking.

But no, he needn't have worried. Imogen was true to her word, and he would be to his. This was going to work, and the other problems . . . well, he'd deal with them.

He gave the boiler a wary look, rocking it back and forth, watching the gas pipe twisting, something he was sure it shouldn't do. He couldn't get at the fixings without taking the cover off, so he gave up and called the village plumber, who promised to pop over in the next day or two. Matt had a brief sinking feeling about the cost of a major plumbing repair, wondering if he could just take the advice and do it himself. He checked it off his list and moved to the dishwasher, examining the door. His phone buzzed on the worktop.

'Rob, hi,' he said, jamming the screwdriver into the hinge. Rob was a joint friend, although closer to Imogen – they'd gone to university together; now he lived somewhere in south London with his eccentric Serbian girlfriend. Rob was a writer, unpublished, as yet, and frequently asked Matt for editing advice, despite not appreciating the world of difference between a newspaper editor and a fiction editor.

'Hi, Matt. How are you? I just called to see how the move went.'

Matt wiggled the screwdriver. 'It went great, thanks. Imogen's out at the moment. I can get her to give you a call back?'

'Ah, it was you I was hoping to catch. Do you have five mins? I'd appreciate your editor's eyes on something.'

'Umm.' Matt wrenched the screwdriver out and dropped it on the worktop.

'Imogen suggested you might take a look,' Rob continued. 'I'm submitting a manuscript to a big agency and I want to nail it. If I emailed you my letter and synopsis, would you give it a quick review? Just sense-checking, really.'

Matt stared at the dishwasher.

'Imogen said you had a week off? I know you'll be mega busy unpacking, but . . .'

'Yeah,' said Matt. 'That's the thing, Rob. I have to go into work Monday.'

Impossible, even if the reference arrived over the weekend. The thought of it caused an unpleasant lump at the back of his throat, visions of it being rejected, queried, *What is this, Matt? Mr de Vries says he never offered such a reference. In fact . . .*

Matt shook the thought out of his head. It would be fine. Ninety-nine percent of the time it was just a formality.

'Sorry,' he added. 'Plus my boss has sent me a bunch of stuff to read beforehand. I'd love to help, but I'm snowed under. I'm in the middle of it now.'

'Oh,' Rob's voice was full of disappointment. 'Oh, well, of course.'

'I'm sorry, Rob. Any other time would be OK. But I'll be working most of the weekend . . .' he let it hang.

'No problem,' said Rob. 'I understand. Sorry to have called.'

'Don't be silly,' said Matt, 'don't apologise. Take care, yeah? We'll speak soon.'

Rob hung up. Matt stared at the phone for a few seconds, wondering if Rob would call Imogen. It would be awkward, but it wasn't as if they'd see much of him from now on.

He prodded the dishwasher a few more times before trying the coffee machine. He produced a rather dubious-looking latte before approaching the kitchen door, through the utility room. The door opened to the side of the house but looked hardly used. The lock was rusted and jammed, and would require replacing altogether. Rather dissatisfied at his DIY failures, he settled on the sofa, not planning to move until Imogen returned.

As he was about to close his eyes, his phone vibrated again. He pulled it out of his pocket. Rob again? No. A text message. He recognised the sender.

He stared at the notification for a few seconds before deleting it, unread.

Imogen

Nancy's invitation had caught me a little off guard, but it would have been rude to decline, and I was keen to make my first friend in the street. I'd seen her watching me from her garden as Ash and I strolled back from the village. I was slightly in awe of her house – it was perhaps the best in the street, with neat flowerbeds bursting with colour and a lawn that could double as a golfing green. On her driveway sat a gleaming yet dated Mercedes saloon. It looked like it belonged in a classic car showroom.

She'd introduced herself by leaning over the front fence, beckoning us towards her. I smiled and we diverted off the path on to her driveway.

Nancy White. Friendly in a grown-up, *we'll look after you*, kind of way. She couldn't have been much older than me, perhaps mid-forties, but she dressed older – refined. Matt would call it old-fashioned, frumpy. She looked at me like she actually wanted to know me. Her expression froze slightly when Jake started barking, but I held him tight against me, keeping him from one of his exuberant presentations of affection, even tighter when Nancy's daughter strode out of the front door. I double-took, such was the contrast to her mother. Long blond hair with a Lady Gaga T-shirt, tiny ripped denim shorts and clumpy purple Doc Marten boots at the end of slender legs. Her face was pale and clammy, her skin almost white. She strutted halfway down the path and stopped when she saw us, giving Ash and me the briefest of smiles before disappearing through the back gate.

For our coffee date, I left Jake behind, and the polite relief was evident on Nancy's face when she opened the door. She looked at me with the calm demeanour of a mother looking at one of her brood, sweeping Ashley and me inside, ushering us through to the rear of the house. Her house smelled of citrus, light, warm and relaxing. I caught a whiff of something else as we passed the stairs, cleaning products, bleach. I hoped she hadn't cleaned on my account.

We went through to the kitchen-diner. The doors were open to the garden and the summer breeze wafted in. Nancy hugged me, kissing me softly on each cheek. She wore a perfume I recognised, from Calvin Klein.

'I like your scent,' I said.

'Ah, it's Ruby's,' she said. 'Don't tell her, but I sometimes sneak some. Only on special occasions.'

She laughed. I was flattered. A special occasion, it seemed.

Nancy took the cake box, placing it on the worktop next to a baking tray covered in bright cupcakes. They were pink and yellow, the icing still glistening as it set. The sight was too much for Ashley, who stared at them like a hungry puppy.

'Would you like one?' Nancy asked.

Ashley nodded furiously.

28

'How about two?'

Ashley's eyes widened in delight.

'Pick whichever ones you like,' said Nancy. 'And why don't you take them out to the garden? I've set the rug on the lawn with some of Ruby's old figurines – I don't know what you call them . . .'

Ashley stared through the open door.

'Sylvanian families!' she shrieked.

Nancy beamed as Ashley grabbed a cupcake of each colour and ran off. I watched Nancy's face. The face of an experienced mother. The face of someone who cared until they were worn out, then cared some more. We said nothing about my shop-bought cake, and for that I was grateful.

'I'll bring you out some lemonade,' she called, before turning to me.

Nancy was slim, her hair cut into a neat bob, her make-up subtle. Her eyes were tired but resilient, her face locked in a smile which looked real but practised. I knew the look because I'd spent a good deal of time perfecting it myself. Part of the façade we all wore in order to survive life's troubles. It gave me an immediate sense of connection. An affinity.

'Tea?' she asked.

'Yes, please.'

While Nancy busied herself, I spied a wall full of photos. I walked over to take a peek.

'Wow,' I said, pointing at a portrait of Nancy holding a brace of pheasants, with what looked like a shotgun slung over her shoulder. 'Is that you?'

Nancy glanced over. She smiled. 'Many years ago,' she said. 'I was a proper country girl, back then.'

The scene was alien to me – we didn't hunt much in London, unless it was for the last slab of Manchego cheese at the Waitrose deli counter.

'Still do it?'

'No,' she said, her smile fading, 'not any more.'

We sat on wicker chairs on the patio, watching Ashley play for a few minutes. The silence was comfortable, although I prepared myself to start asking the usual questions; the *get to know you* questions. She got there first.

'What do you do, Imogen? You look like a professional woman.'

I smiled, more inside than out. 'I'm a nurse.'

Nancy's smile wavered, ever so slightly. It wasn't uncommon. Many people got nervous in the presence of doctors and nurses.

'Geriatrics, mainly,' I said. 'But I'm not working at the moment. Maybe in a few months I'll go back to it.'

'Ah,' said Nancy. Her face relaxed again. She reached over and filled my cup from the teapot. It was fine china.

'Do you miss it?' she asked. Her eyes were sympathetic. She already knew. Nursing is a vocation, part of my identity. Without it, and the routine that went with it, I already felt a part of me was missing, a huge chunk carved out. I was still a nurse, but without any patients.

It was temporary, I kept telling myself. In the new year I'd approach the local hospitals, public and private. There were always thousands of nursing vacancies – it was a job for life. I could go back when I was ready. When we were ready.

I nodded. 'Yes. But . . .'

'But you did what you had to do,' said Nancy. 'I understand. You moved for Matt's job.'

Matt's job. Of course. Standing in her front garden, when I'd introduced myself, that's what I'd told her. Blurted it out, like I had to give an excuse for moving into her street.

We watched Ashley. Listened to her small voice carry across the air. Marvelled at the sight of such a bundle of love and enthusiasm. My bundle.

'It's a lovely age,' said Nancy. 'Once they hit the teens, they lose this magic.'

'How old is Ruby?'

'Fifteen,' said Nancy, 'with enough hormones for the both of us.'

I laughed. Ash bounced up from one end of the rug and jumped to the other.

'I wish I still had that much energy,' said Nancy.

'Me too.'

'So how are you settling in?'

A great question. I didn't know her well enough to give her the truth, but my eyes would betray me if I said all was rosy.

'So far, so good,' I said, honestly. 'It's going to be a big adjustment.'

Nancy nodded, leaning in. 'You look tired, Imogen. Forgive me for saying so.'

She topped up my tea again. I noticed she hadn't touched her cake. I'd devoured mine and would be quite happy to eat hers as well.

'I'm fine,' I said. 'Tired, yes. Weary. But fine.'

Nancy nodded. 'Moving to a new house is stressful. It places all sorts of strains on your body and mind.'

I nodded. Our eyes met.

'Does Matt look after you?'

An odd thing to say, like she'd seen into my soul and plucked at the splinter.

'Of course,' I said, instinctively. I barely knew the woman. 'He's my husband.'

I wanted to tell her more. It should have felt awkward, but her eyes were genuine. I desperately thought of something else to say.

'Are you married?' I asked.

'I was,' she said. 'He's not here any more.' Her expression suggested it was a no-go area. *Not here*. Gone? Divorced? Dead? I didn't dare to ask.

Nancy stood abruptly; her eyes left me. 'I must get you another cupcake,' she said.

When Nancy returned with the tray, I helped myself. Ashley looked up expectantly, and I shook my head with a smile.

'Where is Ruby?' I asked, changing the subject.

'Upstairs,' said Nancy, settling back into the chair. 'She hasn't been so well today.'

'Oh, I'm sorry. What's wrong with her?'

Nancy took a deep breath, letting it out slowly. I thought I saw her eyes well up. She fingered the fabric of her skirt. 'Well ...'

I'd touched something. 'You don't need to explain. It's none of my—'

'Don't be silly,' said Nancy, shaking her head, looking up at me. 'I know we've only just met, but I have a feeling we're going to be good friends, Imogen. Of course I'll tell you what's wrong with Ruby.'

Nancy talked and I listened, with shock and increasing sympathy as she described what turned out to be the centre of their lives – not a minor ailment, as I'd naively assumed, but a debilitating and chronic illness. I got the feeling she held a lot back, but it became rapidly obvious that describing such sickness in one's offspring is not an easy task. Ruby had a blood disorder. A hereditary condition. Fatal? I had no idea, and didn't ask. Fluctuating symptoms and both of their lives turned upside down.

No, she didn't need to tell me, but I was glad she did. It felt like a bond, a hook she'd cast towards me to see if I wanted to be part of her life. I nodded my acceptance.

My problems paled in comparison, or at least, faded – they couldn't be erased that easily. Nancy insisted that we didn't dwell on it. She'd adjusted and Ruby's life was her life – their mother–daughter bond even closer as a result. They lived through the illness together, fought together. Nancy laughed that they'd probably die together, but I struggled to laugh with her.

'You don't have to say anything,' said Nancy, clearly seeing and sensing my discomfort. The tears had gone and her beaming smile was back. 'We're neighbours – it's useful that you know about Ruby, but please, I don't want you treating her any differently. She's a teenager. An innocent one. I want her to stay that way, at least for a little longer.'

I reached out, took her hand, gave it a squeeze. I saw her eyes flicker before she turned away, taking the teapot, arranging the cups, busying herself once again.

Matt

The weekend disappeared. Monday morning was cloudy and grey, so Matt headed into Guildford to pick up more supplies. He drove the long way home, through the village, slowing along the main road, past the village hall and an old church whose flint wall ran alongside the kerb. A family waited to cross and he stopped, watching the two young children bounce across the road, their parents waving to him as they followed.

He still couldn't get over how small the place was. Two pubs, four churches, a village hall and a gin distillery, which was a peculiar thing to have in a village of fewer than one thousand residents. Imogen liked gin; Matt didn't.

He sped up, turning towards their estate, fumbling for the key fob.

The black gate slid across and Matt eased the car forward. It gave an odd sense of protection, like entering a new country, with its own rules and laws. A community isolated by a single fence and a locked gate. A security company waited on the end of the phone, but as far as Matt knew had never been called. There was nothing that would warrant such security, inside or out. Everyone was safe, locked in, protected from the village bogeyman.

An elderly couple at the entrance to his road watched him pull in. He opened the car door and gave them a wave. They nodded politely but turned back to their conversation, not offering any indication they wanted to meet him or say hello. Matt smiled to himself as he unloaded the car, thinking that those were exactly the kind of neighbours he liked.

He carried the bags into the kitchen. The plumber's estimate still sat on the worktop. He'd left before lunch, taking just twenty-five minutes to condemn the boiler. He assured Matt he'd be in touch with a quote for a complete replacement of the heating system. In the meantime, use it, but don't touch it. If it fell off the wall it would cost considerably more in emergency work.

Matt had filed his advice away, deciding he wouldn't ruin Imogen's day by announcing the first huge bill for their otherwise perfect house. She'd gone into the village with Ashley to buy some accessories for Ashley's bedroom, promising not to rush back. She'd said that if Matt wanted to start painting the dining room, she wouldn't mind in the least.

He slipped on his painting jeans and a grubby T-shirt before heading to the shed. The air was fresh and warm, the sun breaking through the morning cloud. He stretched, feeling the kink in his back from so much lifting and moving over the last few days. He twisted, casting his eyes over the back of their house, then over to Nancy's. As expected, it was orderly, neat, a flowering wisteria snaking between the windows and up to the roofline.

The curtains were drawn in all but one window, where a young woman stood with her back to the glass, a towel around her body. She was pulling her hair back, fastening it into a ponytail. Ruby, he presumed. It must have been her bedroom, and Matt was just about to look away when she turned and saw him looking up. He raised his hand in an awkward wave. She smiled and waved back, pausing a moment before disappearing out of sight.

'Matthew?' The voice startled him so much he dropped the keys. He retrieved them from the grass, already overgrown and unkempt, and found Nancy staring through the trellis at the top of the fence. She was wearing a summer hat, tied under her chin. Sensible. Prim. She couldn't be much older than him, but it was like something Imogen's mum would wear.

'Nancy,' he said. He fumbled with the keys, tucking them in his pocket. 'Lovely to meet you.' He peered through the trellis. 'Even if only through the fence.'

Nancy laughed. 'Likewise.'

Matt glanced back up at the house. Nancy followed his gaze.

'It's a lovely day,' she said. 'Keeping busy?'

'Painting,' said Matt. 'There's a lot to do.'

Nancy nodded. 'Are you helping?' she asked.

'Helping?' said Matt, thinking of Imogen in the village, probably drinking hot chocolate with Ashley in some gastro café. 'Yes,' he smiled. 'I'm doing my bit.'

'Good,' said Nancy. 'Imogen and I had a wonderful chat yesterday. You have such a lovely wife.'

'Thank you,' said Matt, 'we—'

'She looked quite peaky,' continued Nancy. 'She mentioned how stressful the move was. Is she OK?'

'I . . .' Matt cleared his throat. 'Yes. I think so. We're both very busy,' he added. 'Things will calm down in a few weeks. Imogen's fine. Thank you for asking, though.'

Nancy sighed. She pointed at the garden. 'It needs a bit of work, doesn't it? It grows so fast at this time of year. I don't know how you'll manage it.'

Matt stared at the vast lawn and shrubbery. She was right – not that it was any of her business. This was why he wanted to leave the neighbours to Imogen – Matt had no intention of maintaining a running dialogue with somebody who picked him up on such things. He sighed, biting his tongue, thinking of Imogen. *Be nice*, he heard her say. *While you're at work, I have to live around these people.*

'Do you have a gardener?' he asked, renewing his smile.

'I do most of it myself,' she said proudly. 'I have a man you can call, though – if it gets too much.'

'That would be useful,' Matt said. 'Thanks.'

Nancy matched his smile and upped it. 'We wouldn't want Imogen tiring herself out doing it.'

A few seconds of silence passed. The birds started singing in the tree behind him. Perhaps they sensed the awkwardness.

'Imogen tells me we're coming around on Thursday,' he said, changing tack. Imogen had been quite emphatic about the date, although Matt hadn't paid much attention to the reason. 'A fundraiser?' Something about Ruby. Imogen had told him some of the details, but seemed keen that Matt talk to Nancy himself, introduce himself, get to know her. This was his chance.

'Yes,' said Nancy. She cleared her throat. 'I told Imogen about it all . . . it's for Ruby's medication. She has a rare illness. We're seeking new treatment.'

'Oh,' said Matt. He glanced again at Ruby's empty window. She was sick, that's right, Imogen had said something. Heredi- tary, chronic. 'Oh, God,' he said. 'I'm so sorry.'

37

'Don't be sorry,' said Nancy. 'She's had it all her life. It's hard, but we manage. The struggle is for the newest medications, hence the fundraiser. There are some stem-cell treatments coming out of America which might help.'

Matt nodded. He'd covered a stem-cell treatment for Parkinson's disease not so long ago for an article. An old friend was working at King's on a research project and had asked if he wanted some inside knowledge. It was a fascinating area, although he could hardly claim any expertise on the subject.

'It sounds like a very worthy fundraiser,' he said, wondering whether it would be polite to ask Nancy about the illness. But she must have told Imogen – he'd ask her later. 'Count me in.'

Nancy's smile reappeared.

'And for what it's worth,' he added, 'I think it's criminal that these experimental treatments aren't available on the National Health Service.' He thought back to his Parkinson's article. 'Have they turned this one down nationally? Have you tried a different hospital? Sometimes the area you live in makes a difference.'

Nancy seemed to stiffen again. 'The NHS can't help us, Matt,' she said. 'We've been there and tried it.'

Matt nodded. 'Sorry,' he said. 'Of course you have.'

A sick teenage daughter to care for, all on her own. It must be awful. He tried to imagine Ashley in the same position, the stress and anguish it must put a parent through. It didn't bear thinking about.

He had an idea.

'I'll tell you what,' he said, 'I'm not sure if Imogen told you, but I'm the new editor at the *Guildford Press*.'

Nancy nodded, smile fixed.

'I don't start until next week, but perhaps I could open with a piece on Ruby – nothing intrusive, we don't even need to interview her, but something to raise awareness.'

Nancy started to shake her head vigorously, her hat wobbling. 'No, I don't—'

'We'd pitch it carefully,' he said, 'drive it home to the NHS and our local MP that we need more than platitudes and prayers for people in this country with life-long conditions.'

'No,' said Nancy, her voice raised, her smile gone.

'I . . .' Matt put his hands out. 'Just an idea. If you—'

'Absolutely not!' said Nancy. The strength of her voice was startling. The birds took off from the trees, scattering in shock. Nancy's hands shook and she held them together under her chin until they steadied. She lowered her voice. 'You mean well, Matthew, but no. A fundraiser is one thing, but I won't have Ruby's private life exposed, not in that way.'

'I . . .' He watched Nancy's expression and managed to cut himself off. He'd gone too far. In his desperate attempt to be what he thought was neighbourly, he'd pushed it too hard without any thought for her privacy. He didn't know a thing about these people, what they'd been through. For all he knew they'd been burnt by the press before.

Imogen was much better at these conversations. Where was she when he needed her?

'I'm . . . I'm sorry, Nancy,' he said. 'It was a silly idea. Forgive me.'

Nancy breathed out, making an obvious attempt to calm herself. She smoothed her hat, fingering the cord, shaking her head. 'No, no,' she said. 'It's OK. You must think me terribly rude. I . . . Look, I've got to go. It's time for Ruby's medication. Please excuse me.'

She turned. Matt let out a breath.

'I'm sorry,' he called again. Had he put his foot in it already? Imogen would kill him.

Nancy turned back. She held his gaze for a few moments. 'You're very welcome at the fundraiser, Matthew. As neighbours, please. New friends. Not reporters.'

Matt nodded. 'Of course.'

Nancy smiled again as she walked away, but it was strained.

A little bewildered and embarrassed, Matt busied himself in the shed, taking longer than necessary, ensuring Nancy was back inside. After he'd gathered the sandpaper, dust sheets and an assortment of brushes and rollers, he perched on the workbench, watching a spider wrapping an unfortunate butterfly in its web. It worked fast; the delicate insect stood no chance, and death was quick.

He gave it another minute before emerging, equipment in hand. He threw a quick glance at Ruby's window, but her curtains were drawn. The poor girl, he thought, picturing her again, her pale skin and white-blond hair, towel around her small body, sick and vulnerable in the prime of her life.

He tucked his head down and headed towards the house.

Imogen

'Mrs Roberts, Ashley, lovely to meet you both.' The head made a point of checking her watch as she ushered us through from reception.

We were late. After lunch, we'd started painting in the garden, challenging each other to draw each other's favourite animals.

'Do we have to go?' Ashley had said, holding her first one up, a yellow and black splodge of a cheetah.

'Yes. This is the last chance before the holidays.'

'But I'm not starting for ages. You said so.'

I did. A place had become available starting in the autumn term, but the head had suggested that Ashley visited at least once beforehand. Today was it – a half-hour tour of the school. Matt had declined to join us, insisting he had to prepare for his first day in the office.

'Don't you want to see it first? You might meet some of the other children – make some new friends.'

Ashley shrugged. I could see her bottom lip quiver.

'Maybe,' she said.

I put down my brush and shuffled over towards her, squeezing up against her legs. I'd tried, but not hard enough, and I felt a fresh wave of guilt. In the rush to move, to get away from London, I hadn't properly considered how hard it might hit Ash. She was resilient, but not stupid. Though Matt and I had tried to hide the circumstances of our departure, she would have picked up on the stress. Four-year-old minds are like sponges, and Ash wouldn't have been able to help but absorb the emotions flying around, the whispers, the panicked hugs, even the make-up sex where we locked our door and tried to be quiet. The pretence that yes, everything was OK, but we couldn't stay.

But Matt seemed better. More himself. More like he used to be. He wasn't checking his phone every few minutes, at least that I could see.

He didn't start work until Monday, and he seemed to be looking forward to it. Our official position: redundancy – a wicked confidence-killer, and not something I've ever experienced in my line of work, but I've seen it devastate people, families, marriages. Matt did his fair share of sulking and sniping, blaming everything and everyone until he got around to me. And I supported him, didn't I? I thought of the solution. Me. It was my idea that he apply for the job in Guildford. Killing two birds with one stone, although I don't think he saw it like that.

My family weren't happy: why was Matt's job more important than mine? If the positions had been reversed, would we have made the same move? Would Matt have left his friends and family for my nursing job? They never asked him, of course they didn't. Thank God. It was too late, and what could it possibly achieve? It would plant a seed that would always grow, pushing through into every argument, every bad day, every off comment.

It's funny how you avoid talking about these things – for fear of what it will create, or unearth. For fear it'll disturb your carefully balanced existence.

He knew it. We both knew it. Yet I stood by him.

'It's OK to be nervous,' I said to Ash. 'I am. But nerves and excitement are sometimes hard to separate. It's the same feeling, with a twist.'

Ash dabbed a few more specks of grass at the cheetah's feet. She nodded.

'I reckon once you see the school, your nerves will spin the other way.'

'Promise?'

'I promise.'

But I'd also promised not to be late, and here we were.

'I'm so sorry,' I said to Mrs Glanville as I walked the corridor, trying to keep up, feeling like a naughty child. 'I was stuck talking to the renovators.' I don't know why I lied, and I had a sudden panic Ashley would pipe up and tell Mrs Glanville we'd been painting wildlife. Luckily, Ashley's attention was diverted towards the brightly coloured walls, covered with the pupils' artwork and photos of the school trips.

'No problem at all.' Mrs Glanville's eyes softened. I guessed her to be around sixty, with a round, understanding face. 'Moving house is hard work.'

I nodded, while she started the tour, walking at a rapid pace, explaining the basic layout of the school, the names of the classes, the important dates I needed to remember. I found myself drifting, agreeing with everything she said. Primary school was a wonder, wasn't it? A protective bubble of innocence, trying so hard to keep children focused on the important

43

things – keeping the big bad world at bay for so long. I glanced at Ashley, wishing she could remain this age forever.

'So do you want to go in?'

I came out of my reverie and focused on the door in front of us. Maple Class, written in Comic Sans. 'Oh. Yes, of course.'

We entered the classroom and Ashley's new teacher turned towards us.

My heart fluttered. Only for a second. It was the hair. And her age. Newly qualified? They turned them out so young these days. Perhaps it was the warmth of her smile, the exuberance that marked Generation Z out from the rest of us.

The recognition came and went. The smile, the hair, the body. It wasn't her. Obviously, it wasn't her. And yet it triggered a sick feeling, irrational and pointless.

'You must be Ashley,' said the teacher. She shushed the wide-eyed group of children sitting cross-legged on the floor and extended her hand, first to Ashley, then to me.

'I'm Miss Boucher.'

I squeezed my eyes together and pushed the stupid thoughts away.

'I'm Imogen,' I said, trying to match her smile. I listened as Miss Boucher described her class, pausing frequently to answer an extended hand or to quieten a couple of lively boys at the back. Ashley asked a series of questions about the Egyptians, the hieroglyphics circling us on the walls. I waited quietly, watching Ashley's face, letting her be the judge.

It didn't take long. There was the twist, her nerves evaporating and happiness taking their place – all I needed to see in her little features. Which is all primary school children should ever aim for. Ashley had decided to take change in her stride,

44

not thinking too deeply about the negatives. She focused on new things as opportunities to be explored, rather than risks to be agonised over – the wonder of an Enid Blyton adventure, setting out into a brave new world.

What happened wouldn't define us now. And it wouldn't define Ashley.

We thanked Miss Boucher and left, escorted back to reception by a polite girl called Jade. Ashley skipped along beside me.

'I can't wait to come here,' she said. I saw in her eyes it was true. No worries there. I needed to take a leaf out of Ashley's book.

Time for me to start skipping through life again.

There was absolutely no reason not to.

Matt

Matt's new office in central Guildford overlooked the river and the park, a stark contrast to his previous desk in London which overlooked a busy road. Sure, it was only a regional paper, but it was enough.

Monday morning. Matt still had paint under his nails, but his brain was engaged. He sat with Shelley and ran through the finer points of the business, getting a sense of the office politics, the priorities of the day, and the creative freedoms of his department.

This was a job he should enjoy, be comfortable in. A place he could avoid drama and focus on what he was good at. There was a small hiccup with payroll, but Shelley promised she'd sort it out. Matt did the sums, wondering what would happen if his new salary didn't land in the bank account by the first of next month. Trouble, that's what.

'You OK?'

Shelley paused, took a swig from her mug, which said 'World's Best Editor' on it, and closed the lid on her laptop. She peered at him, her body draped over the chair, with an expression of humorous impatience. Close to retirement age, Matt guessed, with tangled grey hair, Shelley looked like she'd never stop working – a whirlwind of a woman who seemed to relish stress and hard work. During his tour of the office she'd barked orders front and sides without waiting to see who accepted them. She'd got where she was by knowing what she wanted, and taking it.

'I'm OK,' he said. 'Just . . . it's all a bit alien.'

'It's not the city.'

Matt shook his head. Not being in the city was a good thing. It was the whole point. He hadn't expected first-day nerves, but they griped at him low down, his stomach fluttering in protest.

'I'm happy it's not,' he said, trying to force some conviction into his voice. 'Time for me to focus on some regional issues, proper human stories. I can avoid the city dross – all chasing the same crap, spending more time on spin than journalism.'

Shelley looked impressed, nodded. He'd obviously hit the right note. He wished he meant it.

'Good,' she said. 'But don't get too intense on your first day, yeah? Meet the team, do some background reading.' She heaved a stack of back issues on to his desk. He stared at them in surprise. 'I like paper,' she said. 'But it's all online if you prefer. Your passwords are all . . .' she looked around his desk, 'somewhere. Check with IT.'

He chuckled. 'Yes, boss.'

Shelley snorted as she stood up. 'Let's take a break. I'll give you the afternoon. We'll do this again tomorrow?'

'Sure thing.'

'And Matt?'

'Yeah?'

'Relax! It'll be fun here. I promise.'

Matt did his best, and spent his lunch break reclined in his chair, staring out of the window, reflecting, wondering how to make his mark here. His job wasn't to chase big stories, he had journalists for that, so his contribution needed to be focused – aim for that mug of Shelley's. Don't stop until you have it.

His mobile vibrated on the desk. Sliding it over, his good mood faded for a second. A text message.

You there?

Matt stared at it for a few moments.

I'm at work, he replied, staring across at the park. A pair of swans alighted on the surface of the river. They fussed for a few moments, scattering the other birds, staking their claim to the water and to each other.

The phone buzzed again.

Why are you being like this?

Matt felt his face flush, his temper rising.

I don't have it! he replied.

He dropped the phone to the desk. He could turn it off for the rest of the day, give himself some peace. It was a few minutes before the next message came through.

Bullshit.

Matt switched the phone to airplane mode and put it face down on the desk. He made a coffee then settled down with some background reading as the afternoon waned. His mood began to lift after a few hours as the rest of the office started to pack up for the day. He returned a few waves and smiles as people passed the glass wall of his office.

He closed his research and started browsing the web. He had a few things he wanted to catch up on, and the office might be a better place than home to do it.

Shelley poked her head in. She was carrying a laptop bag and a pile of folders, balancing them as she held the door open with her right foot. 'New Church Road?' she said, frowning, 'in Albury?'

Matt raised his eyebrows, puzzled. 'That's where I live, yes. Why?'

Shelley smiled. 'It rang a bell,' she said. 'A story a few years back, can't remember what about.'

'My road was in the news? This paper?'

Another frown. 'Not sure. It'll come to me.' She made to close the door, hopping backwards, trying not to drop anything.

'Oh, the reference came through,' she said.

Matt's heart skipped a beat. He smiled. 'I hope it was glowing?'

Shelley shrugged. 'Who knows? I didn't read it. It's filed away with HR. Checkbox exercise. Still, at least you're officially employed. We can pay you now. Should be in your account on the twenty-seventh.'

Matt struggled to contain his relief, the tension releasing in his shoulders, his back. Even his jaw felt slack.

It was done.

Shelley peered across at his screen.

'You're an influencer?' She laughed, more of a cackle.

'Oh . . .' Matt tried to minimise the Instagram window, but Shelley had already marched across his office. 'A what?'

'Who's *that*?'

Matt was a little taken aback by what some might consider

an invasion of privacy, but he supposed it was her office, her company, her computer.

'Just an ex-colleague. Seeing what they're up to.'

'From *CityPress*?'

'Yep.' Matt felt his heart flutter. This particular person was still at his old publisher, and still doing very well by the look of things. He wasn't checking up, not obsessively, just ... well. He tried to swallow his bitterness away.

'Wow, they live it up there, don't they?' said Shelley. 'You'll miss that party life here.'

Matt found the mouse cursor and closed the window, shaking his head.

'No,' he said. 'It was fun for a bit, but not any more. I'm over it.'

Shelley shrugged. 'I could do with a wild party or two,' she said wistfully. 'Just me and a bottle of prosecco, perhaps a couple of Instagram models to keep me company.'

She smirked, withdrawing from Matt's desk, kicking the door open again.

'Night,' she said. 'See you tomorrow?'

'Of course,' he replied, closing the Facebook and Twitter windows that Shelley hadn't seen, before shutting his machine down for the day.

Matt's commute home took twenty-five minutes, a dream compared to the cross-London commutes he was used to, when a couple of miles turned into delays, train cancellations and diversions. The country roads were peaceful, tree-lined and smooth; his old Volkswagen wafted along and Matt sank into the seat with mixed feelings about the months ahead. He tried to convince himself that the job would be good, the office was good. Minor hiccups aside, it was going to work. It had to.

He smiled as he drove into their cul-de-sac, into the peaceful security of the neighbourhood. He slowed, taking in glimpses of the other houses, open garages and garden rooms. He wondered if on a road like this, you could leave your front door unlocked at night. He wondered if the neighbours did. He wondered if Nancy did.

The curtains were open as he pulled into the driveway. He spied Imogen through the window, holding a sheet of paper against the wall.

He slammed the car door and grabbed his bag from the back seat, his gaze dropping to the ground. He saw small piles of bush trimmings scattered along his side of the fence. He sauntered over, kicking some of them. It was buddleia. He glanced towards the house. Sure enough, their side had been trimmed back level with Nancy's fence, the trimmings thrown over for him to pick up later.

Matt sighed. He guessed he'd be sweeping the garden tonight. Or he could leave them. Or throw them back. He'd mention it to Imogen later. She could deal with her new friend.

He stepped into the hallway and shut the door, dropping his bag on the floor.

'Through here,' Imogen called. He headed into the living room at the front of the house. Imogen held a colour chart against the chimney breast.

'Is it too yellow?' she said. She was wearing jogging bottoms and a crumpled T-shirt, her hair tied back. It didn't look like

51

she'd even showered yet. Matt squinted at the card showing twenty almost identical shades of white.

'No,' he offered. 'It looks just right.'

'Sorry,' said Imogen, shaking her head. She dropped the card on the coffee table, approached Matt and gave him a kiss on the lips. 'How was your first day?'

Matt slipped his arms around her and on to the small of her back, pulling her closer. She hesitated for a second before relaxing, putting her lips on his. They lingered, tongues teasing, bodies pushing against each other. Imogen pulled away first.

'Good, I take it?' she said, raising her eyebrows. Matt watched her smile, matching it, reaffirming everything would be OK. The problems were minor, leftovers, annoyances to be ironed out – they would disappear with time.

He had to keep remembering she took his side. She believed him. She always did, and it must have been hard for her to do so. Other people might have failed to find the strength – to believe the marriage was worth it. But not Imogen.

Not his Imogen.

'I love you,' he said. 'Yes. A good first day. Weird and new. I don't quite know what I'm doing, but I'll be fine.'

'Excellent,' she said. 'In which case I can start phase two.'

'Phase what?'

'I know we said we wouldn't change this room, but seeing as we're doing the rest, I thought we'd replace the fire surround? Maybe strip the floor?'

Matt's smile faltered.

'It's OK,' she said, 'we can use the contingency fund.'

Matt swallowed. 'We've spent a lot,' he said.

'I know,' said Imogen, 'so what's a few hundred more?' She laughed. 'Come on, what are savings for if not to spend on things like this?'

Matt knew exactly how much was left in their savings. He supposed he could move more money on to the credit cards, move cash into the current account, then into the savings. It would buy him a few months.

'Plus the credit card is clear, isn't it?' said Imogen, as if reading his mind. 'We only put the mover's fees on it. I don't mind stacking up a bit of debt to finish the house.'

Matt's throat tightened. He kept his smile fixed. A minor bump. A minor issue. This didn't need to be a thing.

But Imogen's face fell.

'We don't have to,' she said. 'I thought you'd be pleased.'

'I . . . I just like it the way it is in here,' he said, casting his eyes at the stained and scratched wooden floor. Imogen made a point of staring at the fireplace. Matt would have put up with it for years, but Imogen was right – it was rather offensive and didn't fit the house at all.

'Really?' said Imogen. She seemed to deflate, but then frowned, pulling herself up, crossing her arms. 'But maybe I want to do it anyway.'

Matt wasn't sure what to say. His heart hammered at the thought of Imogen logging on and checking the joint savings. It wasn't empty – he wasn't that stupid – but there was a good deal missing. He might explain it away if he had to. He just hoped he wouldn't have to.

'What's the problem?' Imogen narrowed her eyes.

He had to end this conversation.

'Nothing,' he said. He forced a smile. 'It's a good idea, let's do it. I was being grumpy, that's all.'

Imogen continued to eye him suspiciously for a few moments before her face relaxed.

'Excellent,' she said, grabbing his shirt, pulling him towards her. She planted another kiss on his lips before breaking away and heading out of the room.

Imogen

The doorbell rang. I smoothed my dress and opened the door, calling out to Ashley.

'Nancy, hi.' I ushered her in. No sooner was our first afternoon tea date over than we'd arranged the next. Nancy was exactly what I needed; I realised it as soon as she probed into my health, my wellbeing, my reason for being here. Her situation also aroused my nurturing instincts; her poor daughter, Ruby, was struggling through a nightmare most of us could only imagine.

Ruby: a stone of unnatural beauty. And she *was* beautiful, in the glimpses I'd caught, a fiery contrast of teenage rebellion and vulnerable child, not quite one or the other, but poised, ready to unleash her mark on the world, if only her health would allow.

Nancy's description of Ruby's illness was passionate and emotional. The clinical details, those which I'd naturally approach first, were missing, but I understood it was Nancy's way of coping. Her narrative for her life, and Ruby's, was phrased in a routine of treatments and recoveries, sickness and seclusion. A life of steady suffering. When I asked about her medical care, Nancy closed me down. Ruby's care was her burden, and hers only.

She would not hear of my offer of help. A friend was what she needed. Not a nurse.

I liked her even more for it. No ulterior motive, just a connection.

Nancy had a small parcel under her arm, brown paper wrapped with a ribbon.

'For you,' she said. 'Careful, it's fragile.'

'Oh, thank you,' I said, surprised, handling it with care as we walked through the house to the garden. I'd laid out a tablecloth on the rusting metal table, offering Nancy the least wobbly chair. A new garden dining set was also on the *things-to-buy* list.

'Matthew not here?' she said, as I tugged at the ribbon. Should I have bought her a gift? Was this going to be a regular thing? I wished I'd thought of it.

'He's at work,' I said, noticing Nancy sit back, more relaxed as a result. It made me smile. The idea that Nancy wasn't warming to Matt felt good, in a perverse sort of way. She wanted to be my friend, not his, which was fine by me. I kind of liked it.

The paper fell away, and the brightly coloured box revealed its contents.

'Oh, Nancy!' A bright blue china teapot with white polka dots. The box was from one of the village stores, locally made. She knew me already.

'I hope the colour is OK,' said Nancy, frowning. 'If it's not right, I have the receipt.'

'It's perfect,' I said truthfully. 'It was made for me.'

Nancy beamed. 'I thought you needed cheering up.'

I stared at the teapot, the comment catching me. Was I not the picture of cheerfulness? Was my perfect façade, in fact, flawed?

I looked at her. How could she see it?

56

'It has cheered me up,' I said.

Nancy's smile turned sceptical. 'I'm a little older than you, but not much. I can see when things are tough.'

My turn to frown. This was what proper friends did, wasn't it? I just thought I was better at hiding it; *it* being nothing except my leftover stress, my process for handling everything.

But it had to stop. I'd drawn a line under it. I believed him. What he did, or rather, what he didn't do. The initial embarrassment had been replaced with fatigue and sympathy. He'd been through a lot. We both had. And this was what we'd decided was for the best.

Now we had to deal with it, and move on.

'We're both very happy with the move,' I said, smiling, willing my face into the correct expression. 'You're right, Nancy, leaving everything behind is exactly what we did, but we did it with our eyes open.'

Nancy listened. I could see questions in her eyes, but she held them. I took the pot inside and filled it with boiling water and, to my shame, tea bags, writing *loose leaf tea!* on the notepad by the kettle. I rushed back out with it and two mugs on a tray, spilling a little through the spout. Nancy smiled as I set it down.

'It *has* been exhausting though,' I said. 'More than I'd anticipated. I must look terrible. Old.' I put my hand to my face. I could almost feel the skin stretching, the bags under my eyes drooping to my cheeks. I wondered how many grey hairs I'd sprouted these last few months.

Was I still young enough? Matt always told me I'd failed to age, my skin forever youthful, full of glow and radiance. He commented on my body like I was still in my twenties, teasing me, urging me to wear the sorts of clothes I did ten, fifteen years ago. He never gave me any reason to suspect I looked old to him.

Well, hardly any reason.

I poured the tea. I should believe him. I did look young, dammit. I worked out, and was already back to my jogging – taking a few laps of the estate in the early mornings, putting my new running shoes to good use. I ate OK, mostly I got lucky with my genes. My mum still looked fifty, even though she was pushing sixty-five. Luck, that's all it was.

But I knew the day would come, and I dreaded it. Perhaps it already had. One day I would morph from *young, hot* Imogen into just Imogen. The wife. Matt would suggest I wore something longer, something more covered-up. Had that day already passed? Was Matt just trapped in his cycle of flirtatious requests out of habit, embarrassed to admit those days were gone?

'You look young, radiant and wonderful,' said Nancy. She grasped the mug with both hands. 'But you also look tired and worn out. Your body is telling you something, Imogen. You risk becoming ill, and I can spot it because, well, I spend my life watching Ruby's symptoms – rising and falling.'

Nancy sipped at her tea, her expression fraught with concern. 'It must be hard to see it yourself,' she said, 'as a nurse. But I see it. Trust me, Imogen. You need a break.'

Nancy put her mug down, pulling out her mobile phone from her pocket. It buzzed in her hand. It was another thing that surprised me, for no rational reason. Nancy seemed too . . . *in control* to need a phone. I imagined her having a large, fifties-era rotary corded phone, which she'd take calls on and issue instructions through on Saturday afternoons. I smiled at the thought. She raised an eyebrow and answered.

58

'Yes, darling,' she said. 'No, I'll come home.' She nodded several times. 'Uh-huh.'

I politely avoided eye contact, but Nancy made no move to leave the table, or lower her voice.

'Stay in bed. Keep the bucket next to you. I'll bring the sachets up with me.'

Another pang of sympathy. A mother talking to her chronically ill daughter. I glanced around for Ashley, listening. I could hear her small voice drifting through the house and out of the open door. Healthy and happy. I was lucky.

Nancy ended the call and put her hands on her lap.

'Duty calls,' she said. 'I'm so sorry, but I need to dash.'

'Of course,' I said, standing, putting the mugs back on the tray, both still full. Next time I'd do it properly.

Nancy stood. She paused, reaching out, putting her hand on my shoulder. 'Imogen,' she said, 'I'm here for you. I wouldn't want to judge Matthew's priorities, but I believe you need a little extra TLC right now, and you're not getting it. Men don't see these things, but us mothers do.'

Her touch felt like a mother's. My mother's. I tilted my head towards her hand, feeling my insides tingle with affection. The fact she saw my trauma, but didn't ask what it was, was the most perfect caring of all. That she saw the tension with Matt, and took my side without question, was the icing on our new relationship.

'I'll take care of Ruby,' she said, 'then I'll give you a call. We'll do this,' she indicated the tray, 'again.'

The last thing I wanted was to be a burden, but Nancy seemed to take it in her stride. It felt quite nice. No, it felt *really* nice.

'Thank you, Nancy,' I said, holding her hand against my shoulder. I had a sudden burst of optimism, the summer days spreading out before me, not bleak like before, but full of friendship; the exploration of a new relationship. The excitement of fresh conversation and a clean slate. 'I'm pleased I met you.'

Nancy smiled and nodded, her eyes peering even deeper into my soul. 'I can help you, Imogen,' she said. 'I'll look after you. Don't you worry about a thing.'

Matt

'You ready?' said Matt, waiting for Imogen at the bottom of the stairs. She was fussing in front of the mirror.

'Do I look OK?' she asked.

Matt examined her from head to toe. She wore a flowing blue dress which hugged her waist, paired with expensive D&G shoes she never wore for fear of scuffing them. 'You look great,' he said. 'As always.'

Imogen looked as if she was waiting for more. He wondered what to say. She pinched her cheeks and her neck. 'Do my glands look swollen?'

He leaned in. Her neck looked normal. 'No.'

She huffed, pulling at the skin beneath her eyes.

Matt frowned. 'Do you feel OK? We can stay at home if you like.'

'No, no. We must go,' she said. 'It's just tiredness.' She didn't seem convinced, turning around in the mirror.

'If you feel ill, we'll stay.'

'I don't *feel* ill. I just look it.'

'Says who?'

'Can we stay at home?' Ashley stomped along the hallway. 'I don't want to go anyway.'

Imogen broke away from the mirror.

'We're going,' she said. 'Come on.'

Nancy's invite said six. Matt picked paint and filler from under his fingernails as he slammed their front door, dragging Ashley behind him, who was not impressed at the idea of an evening with the new neighbours. He could already hear the other guests next door, the low din of conversation, the clinking of glasses and cutlery.

'I still think we should have brought Jake,' said Matt, casting his eye over their front garden – the grass needed mowing and more shrubs were already straying over the fence.

Imogen shook her head. 'She's not a natural dog person. Let's wait until she's used to him.'

'He'll bark if he hears us in Nancy's garden.'

'We'll nip back and check on him. He'll be fine.' And he would be. Jake loved their garden, and Matt had wedged the door open on the old garden shed – Jake had taken it as his second home, sleeping there in the warm afternoons. Matt had left a blanket and one of his toys on the floor. Besides, his bark was friendly, soft, just letting the world know where he was, should it need him.

The door swung open before they had a chance to knock. Nancy beamed at Imogen.

'We're not early, I hope?' said Matt, holding out a bottle of Chablis, unsure what was appropriate for a fundraiser. Nancy took the bottle, glancing at the label.

'Thank you, Matthew.'

'Matt, please,' he said.

Nancy screwed her face up in concern. 'And you're OK?' she asked, extending her hand, gently touching Imogen's forearm.

'I am,' said Imogen, her eyes darting to Matt and back to Nancy. She nodded.

Nancy stared at Imogen for a few more concerned moments before stepping back, ushering them into the hallway. 'Come on through,' she said.

The inside of Nancy's house was as pristine as the outside, with a mixture of old and new, expensive furniture and polished hardwood flooring. A large dresser in the hallway held several photographs of Nancy and Ruby at different ages. Matt peered at them as they passed. He thought as Ruby got older, she smiled less, but that could just be teenagers. A large framed picture on the middle shelf showed her with shorter, bobbed hair. It suited her.

They continued into the kitchen, which was full of other guests, crowded into the back of the house, spilling out through the French doors on to the patio. There was no music, just huddles of twos and threes, people making quiet conversation. Matt couldn't see any other children around. Ashley's face fell.

'Is this a wake?' he whispered to Imogen.

Imogen nudged him sharply in the ribs. 'Not funny!'

Matt remembered Ruby had a chronic condition. 'I didn't mean it like *that*,' he said.

'Be nice,' she hissed.

They smiled their way into the garden while Nancy excused herself, taking the Chablis with her. Matt spied a table at the edge of the patio covered with spirits and wine. He edged over and helped himself to two glasses of Pinot and an apple juice.

'I'm bored,' said Ashley as he handed her the glass. She sipped the juice through a straw, pulling a face.

'Me too,' he whispered, still not sure what the event entailed, and too exhausted for socialising. All he wanted to do was slouch in front of the TV. 'We won't stay long.'

They both looked at Imogen for inspiration, who huffed, hands on hips.

'We're here to support our new neighbour,' she said. 'To mingle, make friends, et cetera. Please *smile*.'

She huffed again and grabbed Matt's arm. He let himself be led around the garden, shaking the hands of dozens of people whose names he instantly forgot. He noticed more guests arriving through the side gate and wondered if he might escape through it, but Imogen had a firm grasp on his arm as she led him across the patio, back into the house. She'd spied new faces in the kitchen – neighbours they hadn't yet met. Matt deposited his empty glass on the kitchen worktop while Imogen talked. The wine had gone straight to his head.

Imogen seemed happier as they mingled, her natural nerves fading. Matt was happy she was happy, and agreed with her assessment. The village welcome was most unlike his experience of moving into London. People here were genuinely interested in Matt's family and job. They made offers of drinks, and dinners, and country walks. The landlord of the Fox and Hound promised them a free bottle if they planned a night out. The village seemed a pretty normal place.

'Everyone seems nice,' said Imogen, breaking away from a small group. She glanced at him. There was still a small, worried smile on her lips.

'You'll fit right in here,' Matt assured her, 'although I don't understand how we're raising money.'

'She told me a bit about it,' said Imogen. 'They've created a

JustGiving page. You know, the charity website where people can donate online? Tonight is to tell the neighbours and village about it, and to ask for donations.'

It made sense, although Matt's offer of a newspaper story would have been much more effective. There was a limit to how much money they could raise in one small village.

They explored the front of the house, but it was empty. Matt peered into the living room as they passed. It was sparsely decorated, with two chesterfield sofas facing each other in front of a grand fireplace. A grey-haired man stood in front of it, studying something on the wall.

Matt narrowed his eyes, studying the old guy for a few moments. Then he smiled. It was their other next-door neighbour – the old chap he'd seen from his bedroom window on their first night, minus the bathrobe and the cigarette.

'Hi,' said Matt, stepping forward. 'I'm Matt, number thirteen. Just moved in.'

The old man nodded, extending a hand. His handshake was timid. 'Chris,' he said. 'Number eleven. Nice to meet you.'

'This is Imogen and Ashley,' said Matt.

Chris's eyes lit up. He nodded. 'A pleasure,' he said.

'So sorry I haven't popped round,' said Imogen. 'We've been so busy. How about a coffee or tea some time?'

Chris nodded. 'Sounds lovely,' he said.

Matt glanced at the fireplace, and the object which had held Chris's attention – an antique shotgun with a carved wooden stock and short, gleaming silver barrels – hanging above it.

'Nice,' said Matt, who'd never examined a real gun up close before. He felt a small surge of interest, primal, raw. He stepped closer.

'If you say so,' said Chris. 'Must have been George's – Nancy's husband.'

'And he . . .?'

'Passed away several years ago,' said Chris.

Matt nodded. At least that was settled, although he felt a renewed rush of sympathy for Nancy and Ruby. Luck didn't get much worse than a deceased husband and a chronically ill daughter. He glanced over to Imogen, who looked shocked, a little upset. It was clearly news to her, too. She swallowed.

'You were friends?'

'Friends?' Chris appeared to consider the question for a moment, before shaking his head. 'No. Not friends. We never met.'

An awkward silence followed.

'Do you think it works?' said Matt, pointing at the gun.

Chris stared at it. His face twisted. He looked angry, his jaw trembling at the sight of the thing. He didn't answer.

'Are you OK?' said Matt. He glanced at the gun and back to Chris. An old war memory, perhaps?

Chris examined the gun for a few more moments before tearing his eyes away. He pulled out a handkerchief and dabbed his forehead.

'Fine,' he said. 'I'm fine, but . . .'

He didn't look fine. Distracted, worried, more like. His eyes searched Matt's face, darting to and fro. He shook his head, dabbing his face again before pushing the handkerchief into his sleeve.

'It's nothing,' he said. 'I really shouldn't . . .'

'Shouldn't what?' Matt glanced at Imogen, who gave a small shrug. 'Can I get you a glass of water? Something stronger?'

'There you are!'

A shrill voice from the doorway. Nancy poked her head in, examining them all for a moment. She put her hands on Ashley's shoulders.

'There are some chocolate muffins on the kitchen worktop,' she whispered to her. 'Freshly baked. Do you want to go and grab one?'

Ashley nodded furiously and ran off down the hall. Nancy waited until she had gone. Her eyes rested on Chris.

'I didn't see you come in, Chris,' she said. 'Are you OK?'

Chris nodded, his eyes downturned. 'I'm fine, thank you, Nancy.'

Nancy turned to Imogen. 'Poor Chris. Since Catherine died, he's supposed to take it easy. That means no partying!' she laughed. 'Isn't that right, Chris?'

Matt looked at Chris, who didn't respond. He shuffled his feet, not returning Nancy's smile.

Nancy walked over and put her arm around him. 'It was so kind of you to come. I'll tell Ruby you were here, but please, go home and put your feet up. It won't be loud tonight, I promise. We're wrapping up in an hour or so.'

Matt noticed she pulled one of her winning smiles, but it was only in her lips. Her eyes were fixed on Chris's face, who appeared to consider arguing, but then nodded in submission.

'You're probably right,' he said, in a small voice. 'I'll get going.'

Nancy ushered Chris swiftly into the hallway and out of the front door. He said something else to her, what sounded like an apology, but Matt didn't hear her reply. She shut the door and strode past them.

'I'm announcing the fundraiser,' she said. 'Shall we gather in the garden?' She walked off without waiting for an answer.

Matt peered into the hallway after her. 'What was that about?' he whispered.

Imogen shrugged. 'You heard her. He's not well. I could see it myself.'

'He seemed agitated,' said Matt.

Imogen shook her head, looking sad. 'He's old. He was standing in here on his own, not mingling. Nancy was probably right.'

Matt was dubious, but Imogen's nurse's instinct was better than his.

'I didn't know her husband had died,' said Imogen. She looked distraught.

'We hardly know her,' said Matt. 'We don't know anything about any of them.' He lowered his voice. 'It's the way I prefer neighbours, on principle.'

Imogen didn't smile at the joke, her expression hardening. She looked about to reply but bit her lower lip instead. 'Come on,' she said, 'let's find Ash.'

Matt looked for the bathroom before joining the others. The downstairs toilet was occupied, so he headed upstairs. Nancy's house was larger than theirs, with a different floor plan, and he found himself creeping along the landing, tentatively poking his head in each room until he found it.

He washed his hands and face, lingering longer than necessary in front of the mirror, examining the growing bags under his eyes. The fatigue was taking its toll, and despite the friendliness of the other guests, he still just wanted to curl up and relax. He stared at the bathtub, wondering how comfortable it might be, imagining the scandal if he was found asleep in it.

The house was quiet and he figured everyone must already be gathered outside. He tiptoed towards the stairs and nearly tripped over Ruby, who was perched on the top step, chin on her knees.

Her long blond hair was down today, and she wore a black T-shirt with tiny denim shorts that contrasted with the pale skin of her legs. Her face was clammy, her skin almost white in the early evening light. Ruby looked every bit the sulky teenager, although he guessed she had a good excuse for it.

She looked up at him, raising her eyebrows, offering a small smile.

'I think the party's downstairs,' she said. If she was in a sulk, it didn't sound like it. Her voice was warm and genuine.

'Yes,' said Matt. 'I was just using the bathroom.' He pointed along the landing. 'I'm Matt, by the way. New neighbour.'

Ruby nodded. 'I know. Your wife and my mum are new best buddies.' She smirked. Nancy had been at their house nearly every day since they'd moved in. Matt smiled.

'She's friendly,' said Matt, not wanting to appear rude. 'Your mum. It's nice.'

Ruby shrugged. 'So's your wife.'

Matt thought about what to say, feeling a little tongue-tied. 'How are you feeling?' The sort of question you'd ask an adult if you knew they were ill. In this case he wondered if it was appropriate.

Ruby shuffled over on the step, stretching her legs out. She had bare feet with dark purple nail varnish. One of the nails was chipped and she reached down to pick at it.

'I'm OK,' she said. 'Weekly top-up today.' She pointed to her mouth, sticking her tongue out. 'I expect I'll be throwing my guts up later.'

69

'Sorry,' said Matt. 'Must be awful.'

She shrugged. 'You get used to it.'

She looked up at him, her green eyes piercing. An awkward silence followed. Matt shuffled on the step.

'So, a fundraiser?' he said. 'Shouldn't you be out there?' He indicated the garden.

'I should be,' said Ruby. 'You're right.' She smiled and let out a long breath. 'But being ill gets you out of a lot of things. Even your own fundraiser.'

Matt laughed. 'I guess this sort of gathering isn't your idea of a party,' he said. 'Ashley wasn't too keen either. Although she's only four.'

Ruby turned to him, twisting her body on the step. Her T-shirt hung off one shoulder. 'That's cute,' she said. 'I might have some old toys around somewhere, in the attic perhaps. I can find them.'

'Thanks. We weren't sure how many other kids live on the street.' Matt leaned against the bannister. 'Not that you're a kid,' he added.

'I wish I *was* still a kid,' she said. 'It was easier, back then.'

'Easier?'

'All of this. New treatments and stuff.' She huffed, tucking her chin back on to her knees.

'Does your mum throw a lot of fundraisers?'

She shook her head. 'No. Every once in a while. I don't think she likes to ask people, but . . . I guess we need it.'

Matt nodded.

'I bet you're sick of new treatments? Hospitals?'

Ruby shook her head again. 'No, not really – Mum does it all here, at home.'

'Your mum treats you?'

Ruby nodded.

Matt was intrigued. The burden on Nancy was huge. He couldn't resist asking.

'Forgive me, Ruby, but what is your condition?'

Ruby frowned, looking up at him. Her face looked so young in the light.

'Sorry,' he said. 'That was rude of me.'

'Not at all,' said Ruby. 'But, it's like ... complicated. It's a blood disorder. It makes me tired all the time, sick on some days. I get headaches. It's an inherited condition. My dad. He ...'

'Shit,' said Matt, the word escaping before he could catch it. He mentally kicked himself for not putting two and two together. Her dad had died of the same thing. No wonder Nancy behaved the way she did. She faced losing her daughter in the same way.

He pinched the bridge of his nose, shaking his head. Of all the ways to put your foot in it. 'I'm so sorry.'

Ruby smiled again. 'Please,' she said. 'You weren't to know. It's fine.'

Matt admired the maturity of her response. He guessed a condition like that forced her to grow up fast.

'So ... we're looking for new treatments. All the time. Mum tries everything, but some are expensive.' She shrugged. 'I'm not sure I'm worth it.'

'Don't be crazy,' said Matt, 'of course you are. You're young, with your whole ...' he struggled to finish the sentence. 'So much opportunity,' he tried. 'If there are treatments out there, you deserve them. I'm sad you have to raise the money yourselves.'

Ruby shrugged again. Matt felt he should offer something

else, something more profound – here was a young mind struggling with the most cruel and fundamental issue in her life, and all he could offer was platitudes – exactly what he'd told Nancy the health service shouldn't do. In the background he thought he could hear Nancy's voice, a murmur from the guests, and the faint, excited desperation of Jake barking in their garden.

'What do you do?' Ruby asked. 'I mean, as a job. Mum said Imogen was a nurse, but she didn't mention what you did.'

'I'm a newspaper editor,' he said. 'It's why we moved – I've taken a new job in Guildford.'

'Like a journalist?'

'Similar – journalism is how I started. Now I manage the stories we run, make sure we're being accurate, fair and unbiased.'

Ruby stared at him, her eyes widening. 'That's *totally cool.*'

Matt was surprised. Being called cool by anybody was rare. From a trendy teenager, it was astonishing. He smiled at Ruby's reaction, remembering the early stages of his career, when Imogen used to look at him like this, the rapt fascination in her face as he talked about his writing, her eyes lighting up in the same way, her body twisting towards him with anticipation.

He missed it.

'What sort of stories?'

Matt stopped himself from giving a passionate speech about the role of the modern press and the stories he ran. He also stopped himself from complaining that Twitter always got there first, that the press had been relegated beneath the many rumour and opinion factories of the Internet – facts weren't important unless they had a following of one million users and wore a bikini. He didn't mention any of his growing resentment towards the press and the world in which it operated. He reserved this for drunken dinner parties and it almost certainly was not cool.

'Anything we think the public have a right to know,' he said, 'or might be interested in. There's good news, bad news, everything in between.' He paused. 'The last big story I ran was about a public figure linked to an arms company – selling weapons to dodgy regimes.'

Ruby looked in awe.

'Wow! I'd love to do something like that,' she said. 'One day. If I graduate.' She sniffed. 'Home-schooling doesn't expose you to much. We hardly leave the village. But I read a lot. And write.'

'Then you've got the essentials,' said Matt.

He paused, wanting to offer something more than just words.

'And I'm sure I could sort out some work experience, if you're interested? Perhaps spend a few days at the paper – shadow a journalist for the day. Sound good?'

Ruby's jaw dropped. 'Honestly?'

Matt nodded. He thought he could swing it, provided Nancy approved. It could be fun.

'Sure,' he said. 'It's the least I can do.'

Ruby's smile was enough. It looked like a ray of light had burst through her.

'Amazing, thank you, Matt.'

Matt put his hands up. 'Don't thank me yet. It's hard work. You might wish you'd stayed at home!'

Ruby shook her head, her expression darkening ever so slightly, her jaw clenching.

'I'd never wish that,' she said. 'Never.'

A sudden rush of noise from downstairs suggested the end

of Nancy's speech. Voices and footsteps approached the hallway and front door.

'Crap,' said Matt. 'I missed it.'

'Me too,' said Ruby. 'That was the idea.'

Matt pushed himself away from the bannister.

'Yes, but I'll get in trouble,' he said, laughing. 'It was great to meet you properly, Ruby. I'll see you again soon, yeah?'

'No doubt,' she said. 'You live next door.'

Matt laughed again and nipped down the stairs, turning at the bottom to give Ruby a last smile. She returned it, gave him a thumbs up and headed back along the landing. He pushed through a number of people making an early exit, finding Imogen and Ashley in the kitchen.

Imogen narrowed her eyes. 'Where have you been hiding?'

'I nipped home for a nap,' he said. 'It was lovely.'

Imogen punched him on the arm. 'Well, Ash has a stomach ache and Jake is still barking. I think it's time to go.'

Matt nodded his agreement. 'Did you find out what we're all doing here?'

She nodded. 'It was kind of emotional. Nancy is doing an incredible job of holding things together here. Poor Ruby. Such a lovely girl. I said we'd donate what we could.'

'So it's a *give-what-you-can*, online?'

'Yes. I think these events are a call for help and I, for one, am happy to.'

They made their exit. Ash's stomach ache seemed to miraculously disappear once she was home, and Jake gave them all an apologetic wag of his tail before settling on the living room rug.

Matt stayed in the kitchen, preparing dinner, reflecting on the unique predicament of their new neighbours. He, too, was happy to help, if he could win Nancy over a little. He worried he'd screwed it up with his offer of a press story. Hopefully she'd forget about it in a few days and he'd get a second chance. There was no story here, just a recent tragedy and an ongoing challenge. Imogen seemed to warm to Nancy, and Ruby was charmingly polite, well-mannered and a delight to be around. She was a credit to Nancy, despite the situation, and there was already an opportunity for him to help her, in his own small way.

Living here could be, in Ruby's words, *totally cool*.

Nancy

Nancy wiped the kitchen worktop, giving it an extra spray of antibacterial solution before letting it air-dry. The vacuuming was finished; the surfaces were spotless. Her house was almost back in order. She frowned, glaring through the window. Why did people leave wine glasses on the patio and not bring them inside – or better still, wash them and put them in the cupboard themselves?

She couldn't relax until the garden was clear, the chairs tucked under the table, the rubbish emptied into the bin. It was another half-hour before she untied her apron and hung it on the back of the kitchen door, pausing for a minute to catch her breath. She did so hate having a house full of people, strangers with their germs and their grubby hands all over everything. It was a necessary evil; something she was forced to put herself through every once in a while.

'Ruby?' she called. Silence. Typical.

'Ruby?'

Nancy stomped along the hallway, pausing to adjust three photos on the wall that had been knocked out of alignment.

Above them, an empty picture hook remained. It had once held a wedding photo of her and George, removed after his death. Ruby kept asking to put it back, but so far, Nancy had resisted. She wasn't ready to look at him again, not yet.

Up the stairs. Ruby's door was closed – no lock, she wasn't allowed one – and Nancy pushed it open.

Ruby looked up at her from the bed, mouth open in protest.

'You could knock?' she said, her challenging tone causing Nancy's mood to sour further.

'You could help,' said Nancy. 'This evening was for you, not me. I've been cleaning for hours.' She glared at Ruby then scanned her bedroom, noting the underwear on the floor, the towel scrunched at the end of the bed. A half-drunk glass of strawberry smoothie rested on her bedside table.

'I was going to,' said Ruby, putting her book to one side. The sassy look was gone, replaced with a small frown. 'But I felt a bit dizzy after everyone had left, and the nausea is quite bad this evening. Leave some tidying for me – I'll do it tomorrow.' She sighed, stretching out her legs, leaning her head against the pillow. She closed her eyes.

Nancy also took a breath, watching her daughter – her gorgeous, precious daughter. Ruby was maturing by the day, her childlike features disappearing in a whirlwind of teenage growth and hormones. The last couple of years had transformed her. Her little girl was now an adult, her body and mind straining at the confines of her life.

If only her body was strong enough to take it.

Nancy felt her eyes welling up. She took a sharp breath, sitting on the edge of Ruby's bed.

'It's done now,' she said, in a softer tone. 'You relax. I'll fetch you something for the nausea.'

Ruby opened her eyes. She bit her lower lip and reached out to touch Nancy's hand. Nancy recognised the apology and gripped her daughter's fingers, squeezing them tight.

'Was it successful?' asked Ruby.

Nancy shrugged. 'I don't know yet. Most of the neighbours are generous. We'll get something. It'll be enough.' She damn well hoped so. Money didn't grow on trees, and it sure as hell didn't come from her measly widow's pension.

Ruby nodded. 'You know I don't mind,' she said. 'We can stop the treatments for a bit. Try something else, something cheaper. If money's an issue.'

'No,' said Nancy, patting Ruby's hand. 'We've come this far. I'm not giving up now. The treatments are working.'

'You think?'

Ruby had suffered more stomach issues on this last batch, it was true. But overall it was working. Nancy was sure of it.

'I know it's tough,' said Nancy. 'But you are looking better. You look perkier.'

'Really?' Ruby's eyes lit up a fraction.

'Really,' said Nancy. 'You look beautiful. Look at that hair of yours – healthier than mine. And your skin is perfect. I *wish* I'd had skin like that at your age.'

Ruby's smile widened. Her teeth were starting to dull, the whiteness of youth tarnishing. Nancy made a mental note to increase the concentration of whitening agent in the toothpaste. She couldn't bear the thought of Ruby being embarrassed about her teeth.

'It's a shame nobody sees me.'

Was that sass back again? Nancy frowned. No, just frustration. Nancy couldn't blame her. Friends had fallen by the wayside – home-schooling didn't encourage close friendships. Boys were a hurdle they hadn't crossed yet, and Nancy intended to keep it that way for as long as possible. Ruby's body might be mature, but her attitude to such matters was hopelessly naive and adolescent.

'When you're better, dear,' she said. 'When you're better.'

Ruby's smile faded. She gave a small nod.

Nancy stood up. 'I'll get you a drink,' she said, letting out a sigh. 'Did you talk to anybody at all tonight?'

'I did, actually.'

'Oh?'

'Matt, from next door.' Her smile returned. 'We sat on the landing earlier and had a long chat – he's a journalist.'

Nancy sniffed. 'On the landing?'

'He was looking for the bathroom. He said I might be able to do some work experience with him. At the paper in Guildford. Wouldn't that be cool?'

Nancy nodded. She'd told all of the guests to stay downstairs. Upstairs was out of bounds. That meant she needed to clean the upstairs bathroom as well.

'We'll see,' she said, pulling Ruby's door closed behind her.

She stomped into the bathroom, pulled on her rubber gloves and grabbed the bathroom cleaner, spraying it liberally all over the basin.

Imogen and Matt, she thought, as she cleaned. A curious couple.

Imogen needed a friend; Nancy could see it the second they met. The poor woman acted like she'd had the wind knocked out of her, desperate and lost. Nancy would never be so rude as to pry, at least, not immediately, but Imogen's vulnerability spoke to her in volumes, whatever the cause.

She'd already decided to take Imogen under her wing, give her a friend she could rely on – a neighbour in the true sense of the word. It wasn't as if Nancy couldn't do with one herself. The relentless routine of nursing and home-schooling meant Nancy, like Ruby, had few friends these days. Imogen seemed interesting, with hidden depths – a project to be explored. It would do her good. It would do both of them good.

Matthew, on the other hand, was a somewhat strange quantity. His attitude had irked her, his prying into her business too close to the line. Nancy prided herself on her ability to read people – and Matt triggered something she couldn't quite put her finger on.

She frowned, scanning the bathroom, grabbing the hand towel and throwing it into the laundry bin. She gave the rail a wipe and stared at the floor, knowing she must clean it before bed, or she'd never sleep. The thought of a stranger sneaking around her house riled her in a way she couldn't describe. Why was privacy such a difficult concept to understand?

She sighed, calming herself with a deep breath. She'd give him the benefit of the doubt, just this once. Everyone deserved a chance. New neighbours could become good neighbours, and good neighbours were something to be cherished.

And Nancy was nothing if not a good neighbour.

Imogen

Matt thought I didn't know about the money. I don't routinely check all of our accounts, but I do when I'm in shopping mode. Researching my renovation ideas led me to notice that the savings account was several thousand pounds lower than it should be. Or where I thought it should be.

It wouldn't have been a big deal. I let Matt move our money around because he liked controlling it and I couldn't be bothered. There was so much money going in and out of our accounts during the house move, I couldn't keep track if I wanted to.

Matt knew I didn't really worry about money, having grown up in a wealthy family – the safety net of my parents always just a phone call away. It didn't mean I was extravagant, or that I didn't know the value of money and the value of hard work – I was a *nurse*, after all. I didn't spend our money thinking it was limitless, but I also didn't have the legitimate worry many families have – living hand-to-mouth, wondering what would happen if the next pay cheque didn't arrive. Having no safety net – that was something to keep you awake at night. I thanked my lucky stars.

The money wasn't a big deal.

Except Matt had the opportunity to tell me where it had gone, and he didn't.

So that made it a big deal.

Ash held my hand and skipped next to me. We'd started at the top of the high street and walked halfway, having no particular aim for the day other than exploring and talking and perhaps treating ourselves to a hot chocolate at the café on the corner.

The shops in the village were delightful. A little bourgeoise, according to Matt, but this was a village in Surrey, so what did we expect? Every trinket and hand-crafted ornament you could imagine adorned the chalk-painted reclaimed shelving of several window displays, interspersed with enough antique shops to fill the village houses ten times over. Not a single useful thing in any of them, Matt would have said. I disagreed.

I wasn't buying, but I noted a few items, for when we were ready. For when I had a new fire surround and polished wood flooring. For when the money turned up.

The sick feeling grabbed me again. I had a suspicion where Matt had funnelled some of the money, but not *that* much. I stopped myself thinking too hard about it. Self-preservation, perhaps.

If I trusted Matt, I didn't need to know, did I? And if I didn't trust him, what was I doing here?

I grabbed my phone out of my bag.

'Why don't you run inside?' I said to Ash, standing in the doorway of a shop that had an array of wooden clockwork toys in the window. A sign proudly stated that all the toys were vegan-friendly, including the paint. Matt would roll his eyes. I smiled. Just my sort of shop. 'Pick something out?'

I found my mum's number and dialled. I waited the usual

ten rings or more – she would never have her mobile phone to hand, always hurrying across the house to retrieve it from her bag or kitchen drawer.

'Imogen, darling!' Hearing my mum's voice gave me a rush of warmth, of security. A bond that would always be there. Stronger than any disagreements we might have had.

'Mum,' I said. I paused. We'd spoken at length about the move out of London, but not much since. Mum had offered the lifeline – anything I needed, she'd grant. If it came to it, Ash and I could move back with them – they had plenty of room.

'Everything OK, darling?' she said. 'I meant to call you on Saturday but I got distracted with your father – he's hurt his back again. His own fault, I should add.'

'I'm OK,' I said, already feeling comforted at her voice, at the status report of Dad's usual list of minor illnesses. This was normal. This was how it should be. 'Just touching base.'

'The house is OK?'

I stared through the window at a clockwork woodpecker, its head repeatedly banging against a bright red post.

'The house is great,' I said.

'Matt's OK?'

There it was; her tone slightly off. What should I say? Matt took a load of money from our savings and I don't know what he's done with it? Ask him, she'd say. A reasonable response. No secrets – that was what we'd agreed, wasn't it?

'Matt's fine,' I said. 'We're all fine. It's nice here. When are you coming for dinner?'

Mum paused. I could imagine her shuffling through the hall, her face twisted in thought.

'Then I'm very pleased,' she said. 'And we'll come for dinner whenever you like, if I can drag your father away from the golf course for more than an hour.'

I laughed. 'Enjoying his retirement?'

'Of course he is, but that wasn't why you called?'

Mother's intuition. My turn to pause. Why did I call? To have another outpouring of worry? To get Mum on my side? But she was already on my side, always would be. And there were no sides. Just the past.

'I called to say hi,' I said. 'No other reason. Honestly, Mum. I'd tell you otherwise, you know I would.'

My mum cleared her throat but decided not to push it.

'Then I'm delighted,' she said.

Ashley knocked on the glass door, beckoning me inside the shop.

'And now I'll go,' I said. 'Ashley says hi, too.'

'Give her a squeeze from me, Imogen,' said Mum. 'Love you.'

I hung up, wishing I felt better, annoyed at the flurry of emotions that persisted, wishing I'd shared them. But Mum would over-analyse and start to worry when there was no need for it. Not any more.

I opened the door and smiled as Ash held up a collection of toys, almost dropping a painted elephant on to the floor, catching it at the last minute.

'Come on,' I said, grabbing her hand and the toy. 'Let's spend some money.'

Matt

No updates today. Matt flicked through a couple more apps before staring out of the office window, losing his vision as the heat turned everything into a haze.

The *Press Gazette* article still glared at him from the monitor. He should ignore it. A breaking story – an undercover investigation into tax avoidance by the UK's biggest online retailer. It would win respect, not to mention sales. The story should have been his; the name in the article should have been Matt Roberts. But it was just another in a long line of successes from his old life, his old employer, his old *team*, continuing without him.

Led by the person responsible for all of this.

Matt left his office and headed towards the communal kitchen. A few staffers hung around the fridge, looking up as he approached. He hadn't made the effort to meet everyone yet, and got a few shy smiles as the kitchen emptied.

Books and papers were scattered on the worktops next to a stack of flyers for a local book-reading event just around the corner from the office. Matt picked up one of the flyers, smiling.

He and Imogen had met at a book-reading at an independent bookstore in Shoreditch. Both there alone, both first-timers. The reading had been awkward, the author a talented writer but a terrible public speaker. He stuttered and stumbled through the passage, then tried to disappear immediately afterwards. Matt found himself standing next to Imogen in the queue for the book signing, staring at the empty desk where the author was supposed to be. They got chatting and ended up going to the pub next door instead. Matt fell head-over-heels for her that night, and apparently, she did the same. They returned to the same bookshop once each year for a date, and Imogen had even invited the owner to their wedding.

Matt folded the flyer and tucked it into his pocket, smiling at the memory. They had been young, full of expectation, with none of the baggage that mid-life brings.

'Matt Roberts?'

A sharply dressed woman drifted into the kitchen, grabbing a soft drink from the fridge. She turned to look at him, a flash of brown eyes, widening before narrowing.

'That's me.'

'Laura, PR manager,' she said, keeping both hands on her drinks can, opening and taking a swig. Laura looked only a little younger than him. She had an intense, piercing stare.

'I'm the new—'

'Editor, I know,' she said.

Matt smiled.

'How are you settling in?' asked Laura. She looked around for something, grabbing a handful of paper towels from the dispenser.

'OK,' said Matt. 'I haven't quite got my feet under the desk yet.' He winced at the cliché, finding Laura's continued gaze unnerving.

'You came from *CityPress*,' she said. Not a question.

Matt felt his throat dry up a little. These moments were to be expected. The rapid deconstruction of their life in London would leave a few scars, and this was just one of them. It was no secret, but he wondered how she knew.

'It's a big company,' he said. 'I did my time there.' He laughed. Laura smiled, small and forced.

'I know,' she said. 'I have a couple of friends there. Press PR is a small world.'

Matt nodded. A flutter in his chest, joining the unease in his throat.

'Word gets around,' she said.

There. She said it. Matt felt his face flush. He needed to close this down.

'I don't know what you heard,' he said. 'But we're publishers, aren't we? We know there are many versions of the same story.'

Laura cocked her head; her smile widened. 'I suppose there are,' she said. She nodded to herself, turning away from him. 'I suppose there are,' she repeated, facing the sink, rinsing her hands under the tap before drying them with the paper towels.

Laura dropped her can in the recycling bin and walked by him on the way out. It may have been his imagination, but he thought she gave him a wider berth than necessary.

Matt turned to watch her stroll away, the thud of his heartbeat deafening. He was rattled but forced himself to remember it didn't change anything. So what if some random woman thought she knew his life? What had happened wasn't a secret. He might have been painted as the villain, but Imogen believed his account, and that's all that mattered.

Everyone else could go to hell.

Matt's natural inclination was to hide in his office and stew on it. Instead, he forced himself across the open-plan array of desks, introducing himself to the rest of the unfamiliar faces. He met three of the editorial apprentices, all full of ideas, and struck up a heated debate in the design team about paddle boarding on the Thames – no, he wouldn't want to drink it, but it *was* possible to paddle without falling off every five minutes.

It was enough to get him through the afternoon, a bounce in his step that didn't leave him until the end of the day. It wasn't until he reached his car and his mobile rang that the sinking feeling returned. If it wasn't one thing it was another, and this particular thorn wasn't going anywhere fast. He perched on the bonnet, facing the sun, watching the screen for several seconds before answering.

'I said you need to give me more time,' he answered, trying to keep his voice firm. 'And some space.'

He heard a sharp intake of breath. 'And then what?' came the reply. Soft, feminine, yet with the familiar manic edge. 'You'll let me down again? You're full of it, Matt.'

'It's all I can do.'

'I don't believe you.'

Matt bit his tongue. He wished he didn't care, but he did – about this person more than most. He still managed to fail her.

'I'd give it to you if I had it.'

'Perhaps you need more of an incentive,' she said.

Matt slid off the bonnet, turning away from the sun. He didn't like her tone. This didn't sound like the usual empty threats. 'What do you mean?'

'I mean you promised me money. And now suddenly it's all gone. Where did it go, Matt?'

Matt swallowed; he lowered his voice. 'You know very well where it went.'

'But Imogen doesn't, does she?'

The sun lost its heat in an instant; a chill rolled down his back. The haze increased all around as his vision tunnelled.

'You wouldn't dare,' he whispered.

'You sure?'

Matt paced across the car park, startling a pair of seagulls feasting on the remains of a sandwich, the filling scattered across the tarmac. They watched Matt cautiously, daring him to proceed.

'She knows,' Matt lied. 'I told her. You can't do any damage. Sorry.'

Laughter flooded the line. 'Oh, Matt. You always make me chuckle. I know everything about you, Matt. *Everything*. Don't bullshit me.'

She was right. Matt would need to be careful. 'It's true,' he said, his stomach sinking with each word. This was not the right thing to bluff about.

'Then I'll call her and check.' The manic edge again.

'No!' he shouted, scaring the birds into flight. A passing elderly couple turned, offering him a disturbed glance before hurrying on their way.

'No,' he repeated. 'Please. I'll get you your money. Don't tell her.'

Silence. Several moments passed. The gulls returned, sensing a quick end to the battle.

'I'm sorry, Matt,' she said. 'By the end of the week, yeah?'

It was Matt's turn to laugh. 'You've got a fucking nerve,' he said, but the line had gone dead. She'd hung up.

Nancy

Nancy heard Matthew's car pull up. She watched him from her front bedroom window, slamming his car door, pausing to massage his temples with both hands before heading around the side of his house.

She hoped he might be headed into his back garden to address the growing mess that was his boundary – the clematis had sprawled over everything and required at least weekly trimming. She shouldn't have to ask, and she didn't want to burden poor Imogen with it – her new friend was looking more fatigued by the day, and Nancy was sure she'd need to intervene. A little TLC, that's all Imogen needed, and it was such a shame her own husband seemed too preoccupied to provide it.

'Dinner soon,' Nancy called, walking past Ruby's bedroom door towards the window on the landing that overlooked the rear gardens.

'OK,' came the muffled reply.

Nancy sighed. 'Are you dressed?'

'Nearly.'

Ruby had barely kept anything down today, staying in bed

for most of it. Nancy had prepared some fresh chicken soup – a few nutrients, some protein to put on those skinny limbs of hers. A fresh batch of smoothies was chilling in the fridge. She'd feel much better by tomorrow, Nancy was sure of it.

She stood back from the window, out of view. She could see Matthew pacing back and forth on his lawn, half-heartedly throwing a stick for that dog of theirs, shaking his head.

She wondered if Matthew let Imogen do all of the work at home, returning only to play with his dog and eat his dinner. Nancy knew many men lived their lives like that, an ignorant existence of all take and no give.

She sniffed, folding her arms. Matthew remained standing, slouched, staring into the distance, reaching up to put both hands behind his head. The dog ended up pawing his leg, dropping the stick on his foot.

Nancy's phone vibrated in the front of her apron. Puzzled, she pulled it out, relieved to see who was calling.

'Yes,' she answered, turning away from the window.

'Nancy,' came the young voice, 'your prescription is ready for collection.'

'Thank you,' she said. 'I may be a few minutes late, but please wait for me.'

'Sure thing.' A pause.

'What?'

'Well, I just need to let you know – one of your items is going up in price. The cost from our medical suppliers has risen. I have no choice but to pass that on to you. Is that OK?'

The voice wavered. What if it wasn't OK? Nancy huffed. 'Do I have a choice?'

'Umm.'

'I thought not. Very well.' It came out sterner than intended, but she ended the call and dropped the phone into her apron pocket. It was a good job the fundraiser was starting to pay dividends. Not a huge amount – just over a thousand so far – but enough for a few months, after which she'd think of something else. She always did.

Nancy turned back to the window, peering out, slightly shocked to see Matthew staring up at her house. His posture had changed, head tilted to the side, his lips curled into a small smile.

Nancy shrank back. It took a few moments for her to work out which window he was staring at, and when she did, it sent a tiny shiver down her spine.

She took a breath. 'Ruby,' she called, louder than necessary.

She heard a thump, footsteps, Ruby's door opening.

Ruby rubbed her eyes. 'What?' she said, standing in the doorway. She was partially dressed – black shorts and a crop-top, her hair tied up.

Nancy stared at her for a few seconds, running her eyes up and down her daughter, forcing her expression into a smile. 'Dinner time,' she said. 'Go down and lay the table?'

Ruby rolled her eyes and stomped off.

Nancy turned back to the window, face against the glass.

But Matthew had gone, the garden was empty. Even the dog had slipped away.

Matt

'Do you think she's well enough?' Matt repeated, scanning the menu. The pub was bustling and every table was occupied. He recognised Bhavna and her husband Hari, who they'd met at Nancy's fundraiser, sitting a few tables across. They offered a polite wave and returned to their dinner. A waitress paused on her way past to refill their glasses.

The Fox and Hound was within walking distance, a proper gastro pub with a reputation that carried further than the village limits. It was Friday, and Matt had booked it on impulse, an attempt to iron out the growing worries, the background anxiety that failed to budge.

It had taken him a few days to calm down. PR Laura had stayed away, which meant he could at least focus on sorting out his other issue. He would find the money. It wasn't impossible. And it wouldn't derail everything else.

Imogen had been quiet all week. She put it down to tiredness and a stomach bug, apologising but keeping her distance, a noticeable shift from the weekend of their move. They'd gone from acting like frisky newlyweds to passing ships in the night within two weeks. They needed a course correction, and Matt thought a night out would be a good start.

Ruby had arrived at seven, after what she described as a brief disagreement with her mother, delighted at the thought of earning £10 per hour to sit and watch TV. Imogen let her in, admiring Ruby's bright pink lipstick and even brighter boots. She looked much older with make-up. He wondered how he'd cope when Ashley entered that stage in her life.

'What if she suffers from blackouts or something?' he said.

'Then Nancy would have said so,' said Imogen. 'Ruby will be fine. She has both our numbers. Nancy's just next door.'

Matt nodded. He needed to stop worrying. About that, at least.

'What are you having?' Imogen asked.

'Steak. Or the sea bass,' said Matt. 'Or the risotto.'

'Helpful, thanks,' said Imogen. It got a smile out of her.

'Or whatever you're having,' he said.

They'd both toyed with going vegetarian for a while now, pushed by Imogen's insistence that it was only a matter of time until the world went vegan. Matt didn't disagree, but if the next generation was vegan, then surely his generation should make the most of it? He was the last of the meat eaters.

'Oh, I thought I'd go ahead and order the materials for the living room,' said Imogen, taking a sip of her wine. 'I got it discounted. We should be able to do the whole lot for under three thousand.'

Matt kept his eyes on the menu. Just another three thousand.

'You have ordered it,' he said, not looking up, 'or you're planning to?'

'I have,' she said. 'I stuck it on the credit card. You can transfer the money from the savings account, or whatever it is you do.'

She smiled, a little too widely, taking a gulp of wine this time.

Matt forced his breath all the way out, resisting the physical urge to hyperventilate. It wasn't a problem. He'd figure it out before the payment was due.

He watched Imogen. She seemed more distracted than ever, glancing around the pub, hardly making eye contact. He'd hoped for one of their regular dates where they'd eat too much, drink too much, make each other laugh until they embarrassed themselves, then stagger home, collapsing on to a bed or whatever soft surface was closest. It was their standard date format – it never seemed to get old. It might at least help him forget everything else, just for one night.

Except Imogen already looked like she wanted to go home, and not for the fun bit.

'Did you see what Nancy did to the garden?' he said, keen to change the subject.

Imogen smirked, rolling her eyes. 'You mean trimming our hedges for us? Yes. I thanked her, don't worry.'

'That's not . . .' Matt bit his tongue. 'I don't think she likes me. Do you get that impression?'

Imogen shrugged. 'Nancy has been nothing but nice to us. To me. Perhaps she feels awkward around you. Big deal.'

'I . . .' Matt wasn't sure how to reply.

Imogen shook her head. 'Forget it.'

The waitress took their orders. Matt chose steak, Imogen the pasta. Straight to main courses. Was this a race to finish and get home? Matt's mood sank. They'd barely spoken all week – again, his fault, but dinner was the time they talked about their feelings, their fears, their happiness. It was what they did.

'Have you spoken to your mum?' he asked, deciding to cycle

through topics until he landed on one that Imogen wanted to talk about.

Imogen shook her head.

'Claire? Siobhan? Any of your friends?'

Imogen shrugged. 'A few texts here and there,' she said. 'We've only been gone two weeks. People are busy.'

'Nancy doesn't seem to be,' said Matt. He couldn't help it. He tried to smile, make it into a joke, but Imogen's expression said he'd missed the mark.

Imogen met his eyes. She looked tired, excusing herself to go to the bathroom. Matt slouched in a trance, people-watching, slowly draining the bottle of wine. The waitress arrived with their food.

'Have you heard from Liv recently?' said Imogen, returning to their table.

Matt had been hoping not to think about his sister tonight, let alone talk about her. Discussing Liv was not likely to lift either of their moods.

'No,' he said. 'Not since before we moved.'

Imogen nodded, casting her eyes away, drifting across the pub. 'You should speak to her more. Family is important.'

Matt paused at the comment, before tucking into his meal. His stomach sank a fraction more.

He topped up their drinks and ordered another bottle. They drank and the conversation relaxed, the alcohol doing its job. Matt talked about Shelley and the new team. He talked about his short commute. He talked about the first editorial pieces he'd be running. He talked a lot, and he drank far more than he should have done.

He stared at the fireplace in the corner. Unlit, mid-summer, but piled high with logs in the grate. He couldn't wait to come here when winter fell, tucking in against the flames, losing himself in the dancing heat. He shifted his gaze towards Imogen. She'd been nodding and smiling while he talked. Had she drunk as much as he had? He wasn't sure, but he'd forgotten what they were talking about.

'So, what's Ashley's school like?' he said. 'Did you meet her new teacher? What's she like?'

Imogen paused mid-mouthful, staring at her plate for a few moments before draining her water glass and rummaging in her handbag for some painkillers. She popped two in her mouth, washing them down with Matt's water.

'You OK?' he asked.

'I have a migraine coming on,' she said. 'It just hit me. Can we go?'

'I . . .' Matt glanced at the desserts board on the wall, puzzled at the sudden onset. Imogen's migraines normally came on gradually, caused by too much stress or too little sleep. What had he said? 'Of course. I'll get the bill.'

They ambled home, hand in hand. It wasn't the wild evening Matt had been hoping for, a far cry from how they used to do it – Imogen would seduce him after a night out, tease him with that glint in her eye, send him into a frenzy with a flash of skin. Were they moving past that stage? Perhaps he was imagining things – his vision was swimming and he insisted on two laps around the estate before heading home.

With a marginally clearer head, he pushed open the front door. They both crept through to the lounge. Ruby was stretched out on the sofa, feet on the armrest, pink fluffy socks poking over the end. The TV was on low; Matt recognised the true crime series about serial killers.

'Are you awake?' he said.

Ruby shuffled into a seated position.

'Oh, hi,' she said, blinking, stifling a yawn. 'Yes. Just about.' She rubbed her legs.

Matt checked his watch. Quarter to eleven. They'd been out longer than he'd thought.

'Was Ash OK?' said Imogen.

'Not a peep out of her,' said Ruby. 'I checked on her every hour, as you asked.'

Imogen smiled. 'Thanks. You've obviously got the touch.'

Ruby shrugged. Matt swayed on the spot. Imogen yawned.

'Well, sorry not to be sociable, but I'm going to go to bed,' said Imogen. 'This migraine is getting worse. Finish your programme, Ruby, if you're watching something. Matt will make you a drink – tea, coffee?'

Matt looked at Imogen. Straight to sleep, then. So the wild bit was definitely off the menu.

'No, thanks,' said Ruby. 'Honestly, I should get going.'

'OK,' said Imogen, 'well, thanks again.' She waved to Ruby, rubbing Matt's arm as she passed him.

'Night, Mrs Roberts,' said Ruby, watching as Imogen left the room, the stairs creaking as she headed upstairs. Ruby blinked a few more times then stood, looking expectantly at Matt, a smile on her lips.

'Ah, of course,' said Matt, rummaging in his pocket. He pulled out his wallet. Four hours. 'Here you go,' he said, passing her the notes.

'Thanks,' she said, stuffing the cash into her shorts pocket. She shuffled through to the hall, her pink socks skidding on the wood. She pulled on her boots without doing the laces, tucking them in the sides. 'Did you have a good evening? It's a nice restaurant.'

Matt nodded, thinking he'd had much better nights out. 'It was OK,' he said, deciding to leave it at that.

Ruby smiled, reaching up to open the door. She struggled with the catch and Matt reached to help, his hand brushing hers.

'Sorry,' he said, pulling at the lock. 'There's not a single door in this house that opens properly.'

Ruby laughed. It was pitch-black outside, their front garden overshadowed from the streetlights by the overgrown trees and shrubs. Even with Nancy's efforts, it was still shrouded in darkness. Matt made a mental note to fix the porch light. A few mosquitoes buzzed around the doorway. A cat cried out from across the street.

'It's creepy out here,' said Ruby, peering around to look at her house.

Matt agreed. 'Come on,' he said, slipping his shoes back on, sorry he hadn't already suggested it. 'I'll walk you to your door.'

Imogen

I wished we'd had a normal night out, a drunken, debauched food-fest followed by sex on the kitchen floor, or wherever we'd staggered to. We were very compatible in that department – it was the one thing that still set us apart. We'd always been a romantic couple, remembering the little touches – the words, the kisses, the moments. A glass of wine already poured. A cup of tea by the bed. A spontaneous night of excitement, a movie at midnight. Matt once bought me surprise theatre tickets for Valentine's. A show called *Blood Brothers*. I'd bought the same tickets, same show, for the same night.

But last night I just couldn't summon the motivation. There were too many thoughts bouncing around my head, a fresh surge of a trauma I thought I'd dealt with. That's the thing about trauma: its effects can be latent, sneaking up on you just when you thought everything had turned out OK. Triggered by the most unlikely of conversations – such as the mention of Ash's young teacher.

Young, fit, energetic. A professional career woman. Wasn't that what Matt liked?

Everything that I am, or should be. And will be again.

I dragged out my pretence of a migraine for most of the morning, although with it existed a very real nausea, a hollow feeling in the pit of my stomach that had been coming and going for a few days now. Probably a bug, or stress, or both. I took a couple of antacid and made a decision I should have made weeks earlier. My mum was right. I searched for Angie's number on my phone and sat in bed to make the call.

'When can you start?' Angie's first words to me. My favourite recruitment agent, one who'd got me the best placements and the best money during my early days temping. She always had my back.

I laughed. 'I'm not sure. But sooner than I'd planned.'

'You said after Christmas. Something changed?'

What had changed? My unwavering confidence in my new life? Already? No. Not that. But the realisation that, despite the pleasure of a new house, a new friend, and a village that many people would give their right arm to live in, I feared being trapped as a village housewife, stuck with my past bouncing around in my head.

The excitement of the move was over, and I needed to face the fact that things weren't perfect. They could be, but not yet. Taking back a little control was what I needed – my career was part of my identity, and I needed it returned to me sooner rather than later.

'Not really,' I said, 'but I like to have a plan.'

Angie coughed. 'Someone with your experience, Imogen, you can take your pick. How far are you willing to travel?'

I thought of Ash, her new school, my commitment to do the school run, morning and afternoon. Could Matt get away from the office to do some of them? Perhaps, perhaps not. And what about half-terms, inset days, holidays – the things my mum and dad had always covered in London?

'Not far,' I said. 'I don't suppose there's anything in the village. Maybe this side of Guildford?'

I heard Angie tapping away at her keyboard. 'Lots in Guildford. A couple in the surrounding villages, private care homes. How far is Westcott from you?'

I'd never heard of it. 'Send me the details?'

'Will do.'

'Oh, and maybe just keep it to yourself?'

'Who would I tell?'

'I don't know.' I laughed, thinking it a ridiculous request.

'Mum's the word,' said Angie. 'So you'll be sneaking out in your nurse's uniform to this new job? Down the drainpipe?'

What would Matt say if I told him I wanted to go back to work early? Nothing, probably. Matt had always supported my career, pushed me towards promotions, never even hinted that he'd prefer me to stay at home. He wasn't that guy. The delay was my idea – in the frantic rush to get Matt's career back on track before anything else happened, I thought it best to get him settled, get Ash settled, scope out the place before venturing into the big bad world again.

So what if I decided to bring that forward? He'd support me. He always did.

It was why I loved him so much.

'I want to get the right thing before I announce it,' I said. 'That's all.'

'No problem. I'll gather what I can find and email it over in the next few days. Call me when you're ready?'

'Sure.'

I placed the phone on the bed and felt a small surge of confidence, fighting its way through the background simmer of angst. I still wanted to talk to Matt about the money, but I also wanted it to come from him. Was it worth making a thing of? Should I push it until he broke and told me? I had a hunch — based on years of small amounts being siphoned off — fifty pounds here, a hundred there. I had an inkling where it might have gone. But this was different. The amount was different.

I dressed and tidied up, grabbing armfuls of laundry, pausing on the landing to watch Matt in the back garden. He was struggling with our old hedge trimmer, precariously balanced on a garden chair, trimming the border with Nancy's house. A good hangover cure, I thought, judging by the way he was huffing and sweating.

I'd been fast asleep by the time he came to bed last night — it wouldn't have surprised me if he'd had a nightcap and watched some old horror film into the early hours. He certainly wasn't himself this morning when he slid out of bed and snuck downstairs.

But the more I watched my husband, the more my confidence increased. He was one of the good ones, despite his many flaws. We *had* made the right decision, moving out here, and although it might take a little more effort than I'd anticipated, I would make it work. I owed it to myself, and to my family.

Matt paused, wiping his brow, glancing up. I smiled and waved, but I don't think he saw me. His gaze was further across, towards Nancy's house. He peered up at it, shading his eyes against the sun.

After a few moments, his face broke into a smile, and he returned the wave. He must have seen me after all.

Matt

He'd promised himself he'd never speak to her again. The architect of his demise. As he'd told PR Laura in the kitchen, there could be many sides to a story. And the truth depended on who was telling it, and who was listening.

Matt sat in his study, door closed, spinning his phone around in his palm, willing himself to put it down and think of something else. But the red text on his computer monitor showed what the world thought of his other ideas. *DECLINED.* He'd been refused two credit cards in the last hour, and suspected he wouldn't get any more issued until he could demonstrate more than a minimum payment on the existing ones.

Unlike Imogen, he had no rich parents he could call on, no city banking friends who'd lend him a few grand, no questions asked. Matt had nobody he could ask for money, no safety net, no bail-out. Even the banks recognised the growing financial risk that was Mr Matt Roberts. He had nothing left, and he was desperate.

The threat he'd received, however remote, had the potential to topple his carefully built future before it started. He couldn't risk it.

Yun was the mentee he'd tried very hard to forget. The bright young team member who looked up to him, who gave him that look of youthful wonder and fascination he craved, and who'd destroyed his life – and then kept right on going, if Instagram was anything to go by, if Facebook photos had any bearing on the real world.

His mind wandered to the months they'd worked together. The memories were raw, dangerous, but he did recall the final words she'd left him with: she had asked for his forgiveness ...'*If there's anything I can do.*'

He hadn't offered forgiveness. He'd refused to give her what she wanted, to let her off the hook. There were some things that couldn't be forgiven.

But Matt's principles were on shakier ground now. He was not above saying what needed to be said if doing so put a few thousand quid in his bank account. He wasn't too proud to forgive her, or say that he did, even if she deserved nothing of the sort. It's amazing what being broke will do to a man's pride.

He swallowed, nipped into the hallway to check that Imogen and Ash were in the garden, before closing the door again. He dialled.

'Matt!'

'Hi, Yun.'

'I ... I wasn't expecting to hear from you. Hang on.'

Matt heard footsteps at the other end. He cleared his throat.

'It's nice to hear from you,' said Yun, silky smooth. A voice people lost themselves in – and she knew it. 'How are you?'

'Rebuilding my life,' he said, failing to hide the bitterness in his tone. He swallowed, trying to compose himself.

Yun sighed. 'That's not fair.'

'No? You tried to wreck it.'

'I . . . I didn't mean for any of that to happen. Besides, you did it to yourself. Look, if you just called to have a go at me—'

'No, no. Wait,' said Matt. 'I didn't. Sorry.' *Damn.* Why was he the one apologising? 'You know what you did,' he said. 'You can't pretend it was nothing.'

A pause. He imagined her playing with the ends of her hair, tilting her head, pretending to think about it. But her voice, when she spoke, was surprisingly genuine.

'I know, Matt,' she said. 'And I am sorry. I said so at the time, and I meant it. I still am. But it doesn't change anything.'

'No, it doesn't change anything,' he repeated softly. The damage of a story like Yun's couldn't be undone.

'And I do care that you're OK,' she said. 'I know that won't mean much.'

She was right. It didn't mean anything. But he wasn't calling to shout and scream, much as he wanted to.

'You said if I ever needed anything,' he said, getting to the point. 'When you walked away. When I last saw you. Did you mean it?'

A sniff. 'Depends what it is. I can't change what I said.'

She *could* change what she said. She *wouldn't*. There was a rather big difference, but perhaps she was too young to understand.

'I need money,' he said, feeling the hit to his ego like a physical kick in the gut. 'Not much. Not for someone like you. I wondered . . .'

'Money?' Genuine surprise. 'What for?'

'What for?' Matt struggled to keep his voice level. 'You know very well what for. Because of how much I spent.'

'Wow,' she said. 'I didn't make you spend it – not on me anyway. You were having a good time.'

'That's not true.'

'What, that you were having a good time?'

'No, that I didn't spend the money on you!'

'Christ, Matt. Give it a rest. Fine.'

'Fine?' Matt's pulse quickened slightly. 'Fine, you'll give me the money, or fine, you're the reason I'm broke?'

There was a pause. Matt hoped he hadn't pushed his luck. Then she spoke again. 'How much are we talking? I could lend some money, perhaps – to a friend. To someone who wasn't trying to get it as an admission of guilt or something.' Then, in a smaller voice, almost innocent, 'I really didn't know you couldn't afford it, Matt. How was I supposed to know you were broke?'

'You—' he said, then clamped his jaw shut, not trusting what might come out next. It was his own stupidity. Somebody as wealthy as Yun would never understand those who lived hand-to-mouth, who struggled to pay their mortgage, who didn't have a trust fund to fall back on. He spoke to her through gritted teeth.

'As old friends,' he said. 'Perhaps as a friend who owes another friend. You *do* owe me, Yun. You must see that.'

A long sigh on the end of the phone. He knew her reluctance wasn't because she couldn't afford it. Her Instagram profile no doubt revealed only a fraction of her spending and partying, and although her father kept a tight rein on the family money – one of the wealthiest families in London, if the rumours were correct – this could be easily hidden as a one-off to a friend.

'How much do you need?'

Matt had already arrived at a figure in his head, enough to

take care of both his savings and the blackmail. Enough to see him clear for a while.

'Ten thousand. A loan. I'll pay you back as soon as I can.'

Another sniff. 'Ten? Is that it?'

Matt felt his face redden. He should have asked for more. 'I don't have it.'

'Tough times,' she said. 'OK.'

'OK?' Despite his anger, he almost wanted to reach out and hug her. 'You will?'

'I will,' she said. 'Text me your account details. I'm out of town for a few days, so I'll sort it out when I get back, but . . .'

'Yes?' Matt sensed a catch.

Her voice softened again. 'I may have been in the wrong, Matt, but so were you. Surely you know that.'

Matt stared at the desk, across at his wedding photo, Imogen's perfectly sculpted hair and a smile that would last a lifetime. He lifted his eyes up, looking through the window as the sun broke out through the clouds, bathing the lush gardens in warmth. It all felt safe again, wrestled back under control.

'Thank you, Yun,' he said. 'You'll get it all back, I promise.'

He heard a small sigh. 'It was strangely nice to hear from you, even if it cost me ten thousand pounds. Take care, Matt.'

Matt hung up, thought for a few moments, then typed out a brief text message:

I've got it. You can have your money. Give me a week.

Imogen

'Are you saving some of those for Daddy?' I asked, watching Ash try to swallow what was in her mouth, failing, nodding her head instead.

'I like it here,' she said, with a gulp.

'You do?'

'It's pretty. There are more flowers here than around our old house. Do you think we can camp in the woods?'

'Woods?'

Ash pointed back the way we'd come, down the high street. 'There were woods. Near the path behind those shops. Evie's mum always said you're not allowed to camp in the parks in London. It's not safe. Is it safe here?'

I smiled, wondering how long it would be before she'd make a new best friend. Hopefully on day one of school.

'It's safe,' I said, having no idea which woods she meant, but assuming the countryside of Surrey was free from predators. 'But we don't have a tent.'

Ash shrugged. 'I don't mind,' she said. 'If it's warm we don't need one. We might see hedgehogs!'

I laughed, watching her shove more candy into her mouth, before taking her hand. As I did so, a sudden wave of nausea hit me. I stopped in my tracks, taking a few slow breaths, leaning on the wall. The sick rose in my throat but I managed to force it down, rummaging in my bag for the bottle of water I'd brought with me. How many days had I been feeling sick for? Over a week? Two?

'What's wrong, Mummy?' Ash tucked her packet of sweets into her pocket.

'Nothing, baby. But I think Mummy needs to go home and sit down.'

'You can sit over there,' she said, pointing to a bench.

I managed a smile. 'I need a comfy chair. Plus I need to nip to the chemist. Sorry.'

Ash reached out and held my hand, trying to support me with her tiny body, her head barely reaching my midriff. She was a caring soul. She led me back towards the shops, walking as slowly as she could, turning every few steps to check I was OK.

I held my breath in the queue, listening to the screams of the baby in the pram in front of us, watching it being wheeled back and forth with increasing speed. The young mum looked anxious, the bags under her eyes describing her current routine perfectly. I offered her a small smile but I couldn't sustain it. I thought she might cry, but I was in no position to stay and console her. The bile stung the back of my tongue. Vomiting over her wouldn't help things.

I grabbed the paper bag and rushed out, Ashley skipping to keep up, oblivious to my suffering. I checked the time. Three p.m. Matt wouldn't be home for hours – not that he'd do much when he did get back. He'd never quite mastered sympathy for minor ailments – of which I wasn't sure this was one – and tended to overreact by finding his own physical symptoms and describing them, as if that balanced out everything. Voilà – we're both cured. He'd have made a terrible nurse.

We made it home, and the exertion had helped – the nausea faded and fatigue set in. I put the kettle on and let Ash watch some telly. Once she was absorbed, I tiptoed upstairs and locked myself in the bathroom.

I peed into the sample pot. If you're a nurse, you do these things. I could have peed directly on to the test, but then I might not have any pee left for the second one. Or the third. I'd bought three to be sure. The probability of three false positives was low enough to convince me. One test would be enough for any normal person, but I remembered well from Ashley's pregnancy that I'm not normal at this stage. My rational nursing brain disappears into a state of *What the fuck? You must be joking?*

I stared at the white box.

I counted.

Shit.

I unwrapped the second test. Dipped it in the pot. Closed my eyes and swore. I counted to sixty then opened them.

Blue line number two.

How did that happen?

So I can probably guess how it happened. We'd been having sex, lots of sex – once we'd decided to move and it was all over. I hadn't been keeping track.

I laughed. It just came out, a splutter of disbelief. I unwrapped the third test, swished it around in the pot then threw it straight into the bin. I stared at the bin for sixty seconds before retrieving it.

112

So that was settled.

Matt and I were having a baby.

A thousand thoughts presented themselves before fading. A few urgent ones remained.

Morning sickness was a new one on me. I hadn't suffered much during Ashley's pregnancy, though I knew the feeling. This was something else – like the torrid fury of a norovirus, but kept under the surface. The hot rushing of nausea almost overwhelmed me to the point of hurling my breakfast at anybody in the vicinity, then it would fade as quickly as it started.

This would not be fun.

A thought struck me – I wondered if this was what Nancy had seen, her wise eyes piercing through. Had she known before I did? My nursing brain once again told me it wasn't uncommon. Experienced mothers could see it in others.

I felt a stab of guilt. It should be my mum watching me, seeing the change, delicately dancing around it until I realised myself. I should be in London with her, seeing her on my days off, complaining about tiredness, complaining about my body, listening as she promised everything would be OK.

And Nancy had bought me a teapot. My first baby gift. She'd mothered me as she plied me with tea and delicious cakes. I should be thankful. Nancy had stepped in where there was no one else.

I pushed the thought to one side. Thinking of baby gifts took me too far along the journey, to a stage I wasn't ready for. This was . . . what was it? Big. Massive. Wonderful.

The answer?

What would Matt say? He'd be delighted, I knew it. He always talked about baby number two, more than I thought about it, to be honest.

I was a little tender; my stomach had yet to swell. Standing side-on it was still flat, my runner's stomach firm and unwavering. Seven weeks? Eight? The more I stared, the more I felt a growing anxiety, a loss of control.

I could feel the walls closing in, a spike of panic. I'd need to call Angie back; tell her I wasn't available after all. The thought made my heart sink.

Pregnant. Trapped. But at the same time, biology was my friend. I could still feel a warm, fuzzy tingling of excitement. That spark – I remembered it from Ash's pregnancy – the electrifying mix of pure joy and pure terror at the thought of another life inside me, another heartbeat, another mind developing within.

Matt would be over the moon, and I would tell him as soon as I was ready. So maybe tomorrow, maybe next week. Maybe in a few weeks when I couldn't hide it. Maybe he'd notice himself, and he'd poke me in the side, and I'd say, 'This is all your fault, Matt Roberts!' We'd stare at each other, draw a line under everything; I wouldn't ask about the money, because he'd put it back, because we'd need it for the baby.

And we'd march forward into our new chapter.

Surely that's all that mattered?

Perhaps it was the morning sickness again, but a twinge of nausea hit me with the thought. A small cramp of unease. I swallowed it and went to find Ash. It was time for hot chocolate and a cuddle on the sofa.

Matt

Matt stared at the ceiling, enjoying the warmth of the duvet in that moment of waking, the haze of semi-consciousness, tainted only by the thought of having to get up.

The shadows were changing as the summer faded, the weeks dragging through the summer holidays, the sun that little bit lower, the threat of autumn looming. The light danced across the bedroom wall through the cracks in the blinds, exposing him to the new day.

It had been two weeks, but Yun would be true to her word. As soon as it landed, he'd shift it into the savings, replacing what was lost, pay a couple of credit card bills, then take care of the other matter. Neutralising the threat, at least for a while. True, her threat this time had been outrageous, hurtful, *deceitful*, but she'd forget it as soon as the money hit her account. She always did.

'You're awake?' Imogen stretched out next to him, letting out a deep sigh.

Matt reached over, resting his hand on hers. Imogen was coping well. Whatever nerves she'd harboured about the move seemed to be fading with the new routine. She still missed her friends and family, and seemed to have picked up a bug she couldn't shift, but otherwise . . . yes, things were improving, like he knew they would. The last couple of weeks had been great.

'I could do with a few more hours,' he said.

Imogen snorted. 'It's Friday. You can sleep tomorrow. Oh, and try to be home on time today, yeah? You've been getting later and later this week. I thought you said the office cleared out at five?'

Matt shrugged. 'There's always stuff to do,' he said, sliding lower, rolling towards Imogen, cuddling against her. He slid his hand around her waist. She'd put on weight. Not a lot, but a definite layer – no doubt caused by the endless cookies and muffins. He didn't mention it. He never would.

'How long have we got?'

He felt her tense up. She pushed herself away.

'You've got to be in the office in an hour, and Nancy's coming round.'

Matt sighed.

There was always Nancy.

He bit his tongue, maintaining his smile, staring at the ceiling for several minutes while Imogen slid out of the bed and headed for the shower.

They prepared for their days, separately.

Friday raced by. It had been a fun week, but the work experience he'd managed to wrangle for Ruby was now coming to an end. On Monday, Ruby had looked so pale he'd almost turned back, but she'd pleaded to continue, promising not to tell her mum how ill she felt if he let her stay. On Tuesday she'd improved immeasurably – they even visited the McDonald's drive-thru on the way home – this time Matt was sworn to secrecy. Every new day saw an improvement, her confidence boosted, her intelligence and curiosity shining through – showing some of the more experienced staffers a thing or two. They lunched and they chatted – today she looked bright and healthy, like a regular employee, her casual clothes replaced with a neat pencil skirt, blouse and low heels. She'd accompanied Matt to a couple of meetings, one across town, and impressed Matt with her maturity and attention to detail. She was bright, on the ball, and Matt could tell she'd go far, given the chance.

He wondered what awaited her after the home-schooling finished, if she'd be well enough to continue into higher education. The thought of her getting sicker, giving up on her studies, was hard to accept. He couldn't help but think of Ashley. It filled him with sadness.

He whistled, turning the air con up a fraction. It would be a hot weekend, the high-pressure weather front refusing to budge from the south of England. He slowed the car as they approached a junction, turning towards the passenger seat.

'So you had a good time?'

Ruby turned and beamed at him. 'The best,' she said. 'I had a terrific week. I'm sad it's over.'

'I had great feedback from the team,' he said. 'They said you could go back out with them anytime. With me anytime. There are always more stories than we can possibly cover.'

Ruby grinned. 'Awesome,' she said. 'So awesome. And I'd love to. I can't wait to tell Mum. About the stories.'

Matt nodded. 'She didn't seem so keen at first.'

'I know,' said Ruby, 'but it's on the year eleven syllabus. I told her it was your offer or I apply for work experience with a load of random companies. She preferred I stay with you. I guess she trusts you.'

Matt raised his eyebrows. It was Imogen she trusted.

'But I did OK?' she said. 'My work. Everything else?'

More than OK. Her enthusiasm was energising. She listened, hung on his every bit of advice, nodded in all the right places. The week had flown by.

'You were a perfect employee,' he said. She smirked, letting out a small chuckle.

They drove on in silence, the sun exploding through the clouds, sudden and welcome. Ruby rummaged through her bag to find her shades. Matt realised he'd forgotten his, squinting at the road ahead.

'And you're feeling well?' he asked. 'It hasn't been too much?'

Ruby shrugged. 'I'm not going to vomit in your car, if that's what you mean.'

He laughed. 'That's exactly what I mean.'

'I'll sleep a lot this weekend,' she added. 'Five days out of the house will take its toll, and I *am* exhausted. Mum will keep me in bed.'

Matt nodded, wondering what he'd get up to over the weekend. The forecast was good. He wondered if this was Ruby's future. A few good days followed by a bedridden recovery.

'Did she tell you about my idea?' he asked.

'What idea?'

Matt outlined his idea for the news article. Ruby's eyes lit up, but then she looked upset, frustrated. Nancy obviously hadn't said a word. 'It's a good idea,' she said. 'Mum keeps everything so damn private . . .'

'She's protective,' said Matt. Now that he'd raised it, he felt compelled to give a balanced argument. 'She's doing what she thinks is best.'

Ruby huffed. 'I guess.' She turned to him. 'Thanks for thinking of me, though. I appreciate the offer.'

Matt smiled. They drove through the village, approaching their road. The gate slid open.

Matt peered ahead, wondering if Imogen could see them. He'd never tell Ruby, but Imogen hadn't been keen on the work experience either. He could guess why – she didn't want to risk upsetting her new best friend by aggravating Ruby's condition. Heaven forbid they'd do anything to disappoint Nancy. But Matt's offer was there, and Ruby, despite her sickness, had won the argument.

'I'm going to drop you home and head to the supermarket,' he said, pulling up short of his house.

'Oh, I'll join you again, if that's OK?' said Ruby. 'I could do with grabbing some more things.'

'Sure?'

Ruby nodded. 'It's nice shopping without Mum.' She smiled. 'Besides, I like the drive.'

Matt grinned. He slowed the car to make a U-turn and spied Nancy in her front garden, gloves on, secateurs at the ready. She looked up as they approached, putting her hands on her hips. She called to Ruby and waved. Her gaze seemed to rest on Matt, although with the sun streaming through it was hard to tell.

Ruby huffed. 'Too late,' she said, undoing her seatbelt. She turned to him as she stepped out of the car. 'Thanks, Matt. This has been awesome.'

'I agree,' he said.

★

119

Matt pushed the trolley with one hand, holding his phone in the other, running through the list Imogen had sent him. There were plenty of small shops in the village, and while Imogen preferred to shop locally, there were some items only the supermarkets stocked.

Wine wasn't one of them, but he found himself in the aisle anyway, sliding a fifth bottle in with the others, wondering if he was drinking too much.

Imogen had cut down; she was hardly drinking at all. Were they ever heavy drinkers? Not really, not as much as certain friends, which allowed them those delightful moments of middle-class judgement – there was always somebody who consumed more wine than you did. Perhaps it reflected their new life out of London, a more sedate existence. Or maybe it was something else.

With the trolley full, he headed to the tills. The fresh flower stand caught his eye and he paused, selecting a huge bouquet of white and pink gerberas. A flashback to their wedding. A church full of colour. Imogen would love them.

'How are you today, sir?' The young assistant smiled, her braces reflecting the harsh overhead lights. She waited for an answer before picking up the first item.

'I'm great,' said Matt, staring at the flowers as they began to shudder along the conveyor behind the wine and cheese. Such a simple gesture; he should do it more often, not just when he was in a good mood.

'Can I help you with your packing?'

The last time he'd bought Imogen flowers was in London. He'd been working long hours for weeks and felt guilty about not seeing her. He'd promised to take her out on pay day, but the team had persuaded him to go out and celebrate instead.

He'd told Imogen he was working late again, and on the way home he'd grabbed a bunch to ease his conscience.

He'd bought gerberas then, too. It was the only flower Matt knew she loved. She must like others too, but why risk it?

'Sir? Can I help you pack?'

Matt looked at the girl. She'd stopped again. Her eyes darted between his face and his shopping, which was stacking up at the far end. He stared at the flowers for another moment.

'No,' he said, returning her smile and taking a carrier bag. 'I'm good, thank you.'

Matt loaded the car and reversed out of the narrow space. The car next to him had parked at an angle and he struggled to manoeuvre around it. He went back and forth several times, inching his way out. Frustrated, he gave the car a little too much throttle and it lurched backwards. He felt and heard the crunch at the same time.

'Shit,' he whispered, staring into the rear-view mirror. He'd reversed into another car. It was parked, empty, and he climbed out to check for damage. His own bumper was fine, a minor scrape, but the other car had a dent in the front bumper and a cracked headlight. At least a few hundred pounds to fix. He leaned against his car and scanned the car park, looking for the owner, feeling his face flush. A few other shoppers were loading their bags. Nobody looked in his direction.

He lifted his gaze, checking the building and streetlights. There didn't appear to be any security cameras; the supermarket windows were masked with advertising. The car alarms hadn't triggered. Nobody had seen him.

Matt crouched, checking the dent again, picking a fleck of silver paint out – paint from his Volkswagen.

He flicked it on to the ground.

Still nobody looking.

The blood rushed to his cheeks as he climbed back into his car. His heart raced as he started the engine and hammered in his chest as he sped out of the supermarket car park, on to the main road.

The house was quiet. Matt carried the shopping through to the kitchen and began unpacking the bags. He spied Imogen and Ashley in the garden, sitting on the picnic rug, playing with an array of cuddly toys. Imogen lay on her side, propped on one elbow. She was wearing the yellow summer dress she'd bought in Majorca the summer before. The sight of it conjured a brief memory of lying on a beach with Ashley pouring sand over his feet while he read a book. He smiled, yanking open the French doors just enough to squeeze through.

'For you, my love,' he said, swishing the flowers from behind his back.

Imogen sat up, causing several animals to fall over.

'Hey,' protested Ashley.

'They're ... lovely,' said Imogen, taking the flowers and placing them to one side.

Matt sat next to them both, crossing his legs, rearranging the animals into neat rows. His heart rate still hadn't settled.

'You're late again,' she said. 'You've been to the supermarket every day this week.'

Matt shrugged. 'I keep forgetting things,' he said. 'Besides, you needed some flowers.'

'Thank you,' said Imogen, tilting her head, shading her eyes from the sun. 'Are you OK?'

'Of course,' said Matt. 'Why?'

Imogen frowned. 'You look red. Your cheeks are all flushed.'

Matt shrugged. 'I just carried all the shopping in. It was heavy, that's all.'

Imogen sat straighter. 'You sure?'

'It's hot,' Matt protested, feeling his heart starting to race again. His face burned. 'I'm fine.' He stood up. 'I need a shower and a cold drink. You want one?'

Imogen narrowed her eyes, studying him for a few moments.

'No,' she said. 'We're fine. As long as you are.'

Nancy

Nancy stirred the thick liquid until the medication had fully dissolved. Ruby was still like a child in so many ways. Refused to take her medicine unless it was mixed with strawberries and sugar and served in a tall glass with a straw. But Nancy didn't mind. It was endearing, and it let her cling on to the early years for a little longer.

There would come a time when Ruby would want to grow up, to leave home, to have a career, a boyfriend – all those normal things she dreamed of. That would be the most difficult conversation of all, when Nancy had to break it to her – that she might never leave, that her condition might never allow it.

But Nancy would be there for her. Always. However difficult it might become, Ruby would always be her little girl.

She traipsed up the stairs and knocked at Ruby's bedroom door, balancing the tray against the bannister. Sometimes her daughter deserved her privacy.

The door swung open and Ruby turned away, slumping on to the bed, leaving Nancy to struggle with the tray.

'You're looking worse,' said Nancy, watching her daughter

carefully – for a reaction, for an argument. 'I knew it was a mistake.'

'It wasn't,' snapped Ruby. 'I had an amazing time. The best week I've *ever* had.' She turned away, crossing her arms and legs. A proper madam, thought Nancy.

She put the tray down. Her initial refusal to let Ruby go on work experience had turned into a blazing row the week before. It wasn't just Ruby's health; Nancy felt distinctly uncomfortable about the thought of Ruby leaving the house with a man she hardly knew – a man who triggered an uneasy sensation whenever she spoke to him. She swore those eyes of his were layered, hiding something.

She'd refused, but Imogen had changed her mind. She'd started talking about her own work experience when she was Ruby's age, how it had given her such a boost, a feeling that she could achieve anything, that she could be equal to anyone, a professional woman with a career to be proud of. She'd recalled how it had made her try harder at school. How it had even made her respect her own mother a little more.

Faced with such a passionate onslaught, Nancy had relented. She suspected her worries were based on nothing more than an instinctive dislike for men of that age – the age George had been when their marriage began to hit the rocks.

'Yes, you've said that,' she replied now. 'And it's rather hurtful, that the best week in your whole life was a week without me.'

Ruby pulled a face, the grumpy, apologetic expression she reserved for when she didn't have the energy to keep fighting.

'Whatever,' she said. 'He said I could do it again, whenever I like.'

'Did he now?' said Nancy. 'Well, we'll see.'

125

'Why shouldn't I?'

Nancy sighed. 'I didn't say you shouldn't, just that we'd see.'

'Which means *no*.'

Nancy took a breath. Ruby's behaviour certainly hadn't improved as a result of spending the week working. If anything, she appeared to respect her mother less. She was arguing as her equal while at the same time stomping around like a toddler.

'I'm still your mother,' she said. 'I'm the adult in this house. I make those decisions, not you.'

'Excuse me? I'm an adult, thank you.'

Nancy cast her eyes around the room, at the remains of Ruby's lunch, at the scattered clothing. She smiled at the pink gingham bedspread, the small frills on the pillow that Ruby had owned since she was nine years old and still refused to part with. She ran her finger along the windowsill, holding it up for Ruby to see.

All it prompted was another shrug.

'When I'm a famous journalist I'll hire a cleaner,' she said with a smirk.

Nancy knew when it was time to break away, to give her adolescent daughter time to reset and remember who cared for her night and day – who held her hair while she was throwing up, who wiped her brow with a cold flannel when the shivers took her. She was soaring at the moment, but she'd plummet soon enough – Nancy knew that for a fact – and she would be there to catch her.

'There's plenty of time to grow up,' said Nancy, taking the empty tray, leaving the smoothie on her bedside table. 'For now, enjoy your childhood.'

Ruby pushed the door closed behind her.

'I'm more grown up than you know,' came her muffled response, her insistence on the last word.

Nancy let it go.

Nancy opened the patio doors and enjoyed a few minutes of fresh air, the sun beating down. She paused, listening intently to the cacophony of birdsong. There – a wren, if she wasn't mistaken; a tell-tale machine rattle towards the end of its call. She scanned the trees at the end of the garden, but knew she had no hope of spotting it at this time of year. The branches were thick with foliage, perfect for being heard and not seen.

She cocked her ear. The chaffinches had been particularly raucous of late. Nothing yet. Perhaps later in the day.

A more human sound broke the natural noises of her garden. She recognised Imogen's voice in a heartbeat. Nancy sidled towards the fence, instinctively ducking down below the line of the trellis – there were a few gaps, and she hated the thought of Imogen seeing her prying.

It was one side of a conversation – a telephone call. Pretending to tend to one of her roses, Nancy cocked her head, hearing snippets and whispers.

'It's not that,' said Imogen. 'We've been through this, Mum.'

The voice faded, and Nancy felt a pinch of jealousy. Not because her own mum was long dead, but because she had already offered herself as a friend and confidante. And she could offer something Imogen's mother obviously couldn't – proximity.

'He's been working.'

Imogen's voice was raised, stressed.

'Late. He has a lot to do in the office . . . No. It's not the same. I've told you.'

Nancy wished she were party to the call. She could offer herself as a trusted friend, suggest that her mother need not worry, because Nancy could and would look after Imogen. That she had already started.

'It's not about trust,' said Imogen. 'I *do* trust him, Mum.'

Nancy narrowed her eyes. And there it was. Her hunch had been right, her instincts, as usual, bang on the money. Nancy was wise enough to know that when a woman like Imogen talked about trust, it was because it had been broken. Certainly before, perhaps again. She'd known there was something off about Matthew. This proved it.

She kept listening, but Imogen moved on to Ashley and her schooling. Nancy heard the creak of a chair as Imogen settled down to talk. A chat with an absent mother, one who wasn't around to care for her daughter. One who couldn't possibly give Imogen everything she needed from afar.

Nancy stepped away, heading inside to think. Perhaps it was time to take a harder line, show her solidarity with Imogen. Show her that men like Matthew didn't get to make all the rules and then break them when it suited.

It was time to start properly caring for Imogen.

Imogen

It was such a lovely daydream, the heat of the sun casting my thoughts back to summers in Spain, the small villa in Puerto Pollensa with the cracked patio and warm pool. Was it two summers ago or three? Time was speeding up, these happy memories becoming more distant by the day. I opened my eyes to the sound of my phone ringing. I lifted it, checking the screen, pausing while my eyes focused. Unrecognised. Perhaps one of Angie's colleagues.

'Hello?' I answered.

'Imogen?'

It took me a moment to recognise the voice. I checked the screen again, shuffling up in the sun lounger, regretting it as my head swam with vertigo. Low blood sugar; it was past lunchtime.

'Liv? Is that you?'

'I lost my phone. This is a new one.' Her voice was as I remembered, frantic and hollow. She didn't say anything else. The line hissed.

'What's up, Liv?' I said. 'Are you trying to get hold of Matt?'

'He promised,' she said. I detected the tone in her voice, the slur, the volume. She used to call Matt in this state at all hours. He'd be at a loss, pleading with me to help manage his sister. But dealing with an addict at the end of a phone required training neither of us had.

I cleared my throat. 'Liv, are you OK? Where are you?'

'He promised me, Imogen,' she said. 'Promised. He always promises.'

'OK . . .' I really didn't have the energy to deal with this now, but at the same time I couldn't in all conscience hang up on her. Liv was damaged and high, or coming down from a high. I had to talk to her, allay whatever fears she was filled with and gently get rid of her.

I always told Matt he should take the opportunity to get closer to his sister, and yet he never quite managed. He always offered some lame excuse for not meeting up at Christmas and birthdays. It had been three years since they'd talked face-to-face.

Matt didn't burden me about his feelings towards his parents or Liv, and I knew not to ask. Conversations with his sister were infrequent but held in hushed tones, away from Ashley and me, away from the stability he'd found in his adult life. I understood. He needed to separate us, for his own sanity.

Matt had told me about his childhood, stifling and strict. He'd moved away at eighteen to university and to London in search of freedom, a place to get lost in the throngs of people who didn't know you, didn't judge you – didn't care either way. His sister Liv followed him, but then went north to find a life in Scotland, away from her spiralling self-destruction in the city. The pills still found her up north, but she survived. With his help. He'd squirrelled small amounts to her over the months and years, never able to say no, never able to admit what she was spending the money on.

'Matt always looks after you,' I said. Matt loved his sister and would never abandon her, helping her out when she needed it, even against my advice. Even when we couldn't afford it. They had a strange relationship, but she was one of the few people he confided in – more so than his male friends. They offered each other a strange kind of therapy, the kind only blood can provide.

Liv laughed. 'Oh, does he?' she said. 'Does he?'

'You know he does.'

'How is that big house of yours, Imogen? How is the country? Three hundred, Imogen. Just three hundred quid, and my fucking brother ignores me.'

I wound down my natural response. *Just three hundred*. And how much more after that?

'Like scum,' she continued. 'That's how he treats me.'

I took a breath. Liv was borderline delirious, her voice wild and uncoordinated. 'You know that's not true.'

'It's been days,' said Liv. 'Weeks. Ignoring me. Fucking ignoring me.'

'If you need to borrow some money,' I said, clenching my jaw against my growing headache, 'I'm sure we can work something out. I think we always do, don't we?'

'Work something out?' said Liv. 'Three hundred quid. That's all I asked for. He's happy enough to spend a fortune on his own life. He seemed happy enough flinging thousands at that slut in London.'

My heart stopped. I wasn't sure if I'd heard it correctly. The vertigo gave way to a steady thumping in my temples. I stood, moving out of the heat.

'What?'

Liv laughed again, high-pitched, manic.

131

'What?' I repeated. 'What did you just say, Liv?'

'So I thought I'd call you, instead. The darling wife of the darling brother. If he can't be bothered to help me out, perhaps you can.'

'You need to tell me what you're talking about, Liv.' My head was galloping. I winced against the pain.

'Wouldn't it be better for me to get the money? Wouldn't you prefer he spent it on me than her?'

'Liv!' I shouted, my throat hurting with the effort. 'What are you talking about? What do you mean?'

My stomach flipped anew. This was not in our story. This was not part of the explanation he'd given me. The uncertainties grew and multiplied.

'What do you mean, he spent money on her?' I said, forcing myself not to scream. 'Why would you know that? Why would you say it?'

I heard a sudden intake of breath. Liv panted, moaned. 'Shit, shit, shit,' she said, her voice transformed within seconds. Another familiar trait of hers: the drugs had finished talking, now the regret lumbered in to repair the damage.

'Liv?'

'Sorry. I'm sorry,' she said. 'No, nothing. I didn't say anything. He trusted me. Fuck. Fuck. Fuck.'

Her voice tailed off, the phone moving away from her mouth.

'Liv?' I shouted again, my sympathy over. I wanted to know exactly what she meant, how long she'd known. This drain on our money that turned out not to be the drain I thought it was.

I shouted again, but the line went dead. She'd hung up. I paused, dialled her back, letting it ring twenty times before I ended the call. *Shit*.

Liv was an addict and a liar. That wasn't vicious, just fact, and I wanted to convince myself I couldn't rely on her word. I shouldn't believe a single utterance from her mouth.

And yet . . . how could she make that up? Why would she? The revelation was as obvious as it was hurtful. If our money hadn't all gone to Liv, as I'd long assumed, then where had it gone?

The memories came thick and fast, the carefully crafted narrative exposed. I'd pored over it a hundred times yet never suspected this, because it didn't fit.

London. *That slut*, as Liv put it.

Imogen

Twelve Months Ago

I heard Matt creeping in through the front door, along the hallway. He'd pulled all-nighters before, but it was mainly evenings – brainstorming, workshopping, the inevitable drinks afterwards. The company was flying high, and Matt was climbing, managing a small team but with promises of a larger one. I suggested they should give him the salary to match his devotion.

Mostly, I was too busy to care, my shifts and social life keeping me entertained. I worried about Ashley, though. My parents were wonderful, and so was our childminder, but I wondered if something had to give. I wanted both of us to be spending more time with Ash before she grew up, went to school, didn't need us as much.

'In here,' I called, checking the clock, frowning. Nine-thirty a.m. He'd better have a good explanation for this one. As he staggered into the dining room, I almost dropped my coffee.

'Fuck, Matt,' I said. He stood there in his creased suit, his white shirt stained and his tie absent. Thick stubble adorned his face and neck, which wouldn't have looked so bad if it weren't for the blood-red eyes and bags beneath. His hair was greasy and wild, the thinning patches showing through. My usually attractive husband looked disgusting.

I could have let it all go, but I knew there was something else to explore. His eyes were red, but they were also full of nerves, darting between me and the floor, where his scuffed shoes shuffled to and fro.

'Are you OK?'

He nodded. 'Uh-huh,' he said, clearing his throat. It sounded hoarse, thick with mucus. Did all women know that look? The one that said *OK*, but meant far from it? A desperate, wild look.

'Do you want to tell me about last night?' I offered. 'All night, Matt. Really?'

He laughed. It was a little manic, but weary. 'We worked until late,' he said. 'Really late. Then hit the clubs. You know what Richard and Trev are like. They dragged me to the casino. Ended up at the Hilton on Park Lane. Can you believe it? Luckily I wasn't buying . . .' He tapered off. 'I texted you?'

I shrugged. He had texted me. A couple of times. Did that excuse it? Did he need excusing? He was a grown man trying to fit into a work culture too young for him. They partied a lot, and poor Matt struggled to keep up. Should I feel sorry for him, or was my contempt the correct reaction?

'Anyway,' he said, dismissing it, or dismissing me. 'I'm beat. Plus I need to be in the office this afternoon. I'm gonna grab a shower and couple of hours' sleep. OK?'

I shrugged again. Before he left the room, our eyes met. His were worried, but they darted away before I could read him.

'I'll bring you a coffee in a bit,' I said, as he crept away.

★

I heard about it from Kirsten later the same day. She heard it from Jemma – her partner, Bo, worked at the same company as Matt. Bo hadn't been out partying, but he hadn't needed to be.

It was all over the company.

Shock and disbelief; those were the first and, as it turned out, appropriate reactions on my part.

I got the rumour in bits, painful little fragments that I had to piece together.

It had been brewing for weeks. Everybody could see it – after the fact, of course. Nobody said anything beforehand. Flirting and favouritism, the usual behaviours. I could forgive that; after all, who of us hasn't flirted at work? Matt was pushing forty, Yun was twenty-one. Who cares? I said. As long as flirting was all it was.

Unless it was one-sided. And unless it led to something like this.

Coercion. That was the word they used. He coerced her, pressured her, this young mentee of his. She'd complained, not to a friend or two, but to HR. This was a thing. This was serious.

A wild night out. A wild night in. At a fucking hotel casino of all places, the tacky glamour fuelled by alcohol and recklessness. The team had dwindled to a few hardcore managers with expense accounts and plenty of private funds to fall back on – the old money of journalism still pretending it was the heyday.

She'd wanted to go home. That's what they said. What Matt had said to her, *exactly* what he'd said, was unclear, but somebody had heard a threat at the hotel bar, a promise of what might happen if she didn't . . . *It's just a bit of fun. Think of your end-of-year appraisal.*

I couldn't imagine Matt saying such things.

She'd arrived at the office the next morning, hungover and dishevelled, and gone straight to HR. A tearful confession followed. Partying. Drink. Drugs. A haze of sex. Then waking up in a hotel bed with her boss.

Matt Roberts.

I didn't want to.

There was no claim of assault. Not once. Not ever. But it didn't matter. The abuse of the manager–employee relationship was equally bad. The number of women falling into this bracket was a disgusting statistic, and I would not have tolerated it.

Except it wasn't true. I believed Matt, not her.

HR threw everything they had at it, dragging Matt before a tribunal within days, his conduct and behaviour dissected in minute detail, his surprise and protests hitting a wall of young women and their new ward – the tearful Yun, who could barely look Matt in the eye.

Journalism is a small world, and London even smaller. Matt had been marked, made an example of. He'd become a person everybody loved to hate, the seedy middle manager preying on a bright young employee, barely out of university, asserting his primitive claim over his female team members. They weren't going to let this one go.

His career in London was finished; his social circle closed him out. Matt was a pariah, and by extension, so was I.

I had a choice to make.

And I chose Matt.

After I found out, I called Matt and gave him the opportunity to come home and explain. All I had was rumour. I needed to look him in the eye and see the truth, whatever it might be.

He rushed home, sat me down, made us a drink and gave me

every detail he could remember, unprompted. He looked me in the eye throughout, never flinching, never wavering. He was stressed, tired, desperate, but his eyes gave me the window I needed.

He'd flirted. No denial. He'd been aware he was doing it. She'd reciprocated – the smiles, the eye contact, the occasional moments where he let his mind wander . . . That hurt. He felt guilty – horribly guilty – and stupid, but he'd thought it was harmless, friendly banter, part of a close team dynamic. He'd thought she did it with everyone – Yun was outgoing, a wealthy socialite with an Instagram profile shot entirely in swimwear. She was confident, attractive, and she knew it. But they were otherwise professional, target driven and bloody successful in their department.

The late nights and the partying hadn't changed that, but on reflection he knew it didn't help his case. But it had never been just the two of them, he stressed.

She was aiming high. Career-wise, she resented the decision to put her in at such a low level. She told Matt this, in confidence, and made a point of repeating it. She was insanely bright, and her ideas made a difference. It was Matt's team, but he had to admit she was enjoying success after success. And she made sure she told him.

He never thought much of it; never saw it as a threat. He didn't feel threatened.

Until that night at the casino bar.

He'd caught Yun snorting coke in the foyer. Matt had always been vehemently anti-drugs, having experienced it first-hand with Liv. He lost his temper, dragging her to the bar for water to try to sober her up. He started lecturing her, patronising her, telling her of the obvious dangers of inhaling such crap into her body.

She laughed at first, told him to loosen up. She threw her arms around him and told him that coke made her go all night, like a *fucking Duracell bunny*, in her words. Matt only told me this to emphasise the point – she was off her head.

Whatever flirting he might have been guilty of, Matt was not interested in sleeping with his too-young, barely lucid, cocaine-filled employee. He didn't believe she meant it. She couldn't even focus on him by that time, he said.

She teased him, slid her hand on to his crotch (a detail I probably didn't need, but the honesty was reassuring), and in what was the biggest mistake of his career, Matt turned her down. *He turned her down.*

He said it was like he'd poured an ice-bucket over her head. His rejection prompted a look of pure disbelief, of shock. Of a *do-you-know-who-I-fucking-am?* level of surprise.

I could ruin you in a heartbeat, Matt – her parting words as she stormed off, leaving Matt at the bar, with his anger and regret battling through his own alcoholic stupor.

Matt sat at the casino trying to sober up into the early hours. Then he came home full of worry.

And that's where I saw him, standing in our dining room, his bloodshot eyes betraying the shittiest night out he would ever suffer.

Even now, nearly a year later, I struggle to believe anything other than Matt's story. I was a MeToo advocate. I fucking hated the shared history of so many women of my generation. And yet I found Yun's story wanting, and Matt's story exact and compelling.

Matt had been the victim of a vicious, narcissistic bitch who threw a tantrum when she didn't get her own way. She resented Matt for rejecting her, and saw a sweet opportunity to get him out of the way and perhaps take his job in the process. She got it, too, almost straight after Matt left the building. Proof, no?

We protested. Nobody listened. They saw Matt as the sleazy middle-aged man. They saw Yun as the up-and-coming editor. And our wide social circle evaporated and we were left out in the cold.

We made plans to leave London shortly afterwards. I lived with our story and pushed my doubts to one side. They stayed there. Most of the time.

But they never quite disappeared.

In the dead of night, in the middle of a conversation, I would think of it. The detail I was never sure of; the timeline that didn't quite fit. I was good at ignoring it all, because I convinced myself I believed him. I had to, because I'd picked his side, and there was no going back.

But now, the spanner thrown in by Liv. The money. There was no room in the story for it.

It didn't fit.

Matt

Matt stood in the driveway, checking the scrape on the bumper. His stomach turned. Why had he driven off? He had visions of the police turning up, arresting him for criminal damage. But it wasn't criminal damage; it was a minor accident and he could be forgiven for not even realising he'd hit the other car.

He was innocent. A minor lapse in judgement.

'Something wrong?' The voice startled him. Matt turned to see Ruby leaning over the fence. Her eyes were sunken, her face pasty, although the rest of her looked tanned, her skinny arms folded across her chest. She stared at him for a few moments.

'Nope,' he said. 'Bad night?'

She nodded. Her eyes filled with tears. Matt paused for a second before walking over, pushing aside a low branch on the cherry tree. It was long devoid of blossom, its annual cycle almost over.

'I'm sorry,' he said.

She shrugged. 'Double dose. It makes me . . .' She coughed; her face went yellow. She paused, taking a few deep breaths.

'Perhaps you should be inside, in bed?'

'No,' she said. 'I don't want to stay inside. I can vomit just as easily out here.'

Matt offered her an awkward laugh. Such a stark contrast to the few days they'd spent together in the office. He wouldn't have even known she was ill, half the time. But right now she looked shocking, vulnerable, sick.

'Is your treatment over for today?' he said.

Another nod.

'Is it every day?'

A shake this time. 'It varies,' she said. 'It's whenever Mum thinks I need it. She monitors me, gives me additional doses when she sees my symptoms getting worse.'

'But . . .' He stopped. He shouldn't interfere. This was none of his business. Nancy was doing her best.

'But what?'

'Nothing.'

'Tell me.'

'I was going to say how well you'd been. When you were with me. You were bright, alert, having fun . . . I didn't think you were getting worse. If I'd known, I wouldn't have . . . I mean, I would have brought you straight home.'

A pang of guilt hit him. Had he done this to her?

Ruby closed her eyes for a second. A single tear escaped on to her left cheek. 'I did feel well. And I had a great time.' She opened them, looking at Matt. They were bloodshot, watering, but there was something else, too.

Something in her eyes made him uneasy.

'Ruby!'

She flinched at her mum's voice. Nancy appeared at the

doorway, striding across the lawn. Ruby dried her tears on her T-shirt, leaving damp creases in the white cotton. She hastened back from the fence a few inches, putting some distance between them.

'What are you doing out here?' Nancy adopted a shrill tone, speaking loudly enough for the rest of the street to hear. Ruby cowered under her mum's gaze, like a naughty child, not a mature teenager.

'It's my fault,' said Matt. 'I called her over. I wanted to say hi, check she's OK after her work experience.'

Nancy brought her hands close to her body. Her eyes darted over Matt, past him into the garden, back to Ruby. She pointed at her daughter.

'Does she look OK?' she said.

'Well,' said Matt, 'I guess—'

'Your work experience made her quite unwell. She's been very sick since she got home. You're correct, Matthew, this is your fault.'

'I'm fine, Mum, please . . .'

'You're not fine!' Nancy shouted, her face growing redder.

'Hey,' said Matt, 'look. She didn't do anything—'

'Excuse me?' said Nancy. Her hands were trembling, her tone icy. 'What business is this of yours, Matthew? This is between me and my daughter. My *teenage* daughter.'

Matt frowned. He rested his hand on the fence. What was that supposed to mean?

'Mum!'

'Go inside, Ruby.' Nancy glared daggers at Ruby, who backed away, head down, towards the house. She threw one last glance at Matt – apologetic, fearful – and stepped through the porch, into the house.

'Matthew,' said Nancy. She lowered her voice, leaning in. She hissed across the fence at him. 'Ruby is sick and needs to be left alone. I suggest you spend more time worrying about your own family and a little less time with pretty young girls.'

The words were like a slap across the face. He opened his mouth but couldn't find the words.

'I . . .' He was shocked at Nancy's tone. Her *insinuation*. She was outright hostile, her voice low, her stance furious. Even if he could have thought of something to say, she didn't give him the chance. She threw him one final glare before stomping off after Ruby.

The front door slammed. The birds took off in surprise. Jake barked from the rear of the house. Matt was left at the fence, picking a splinter of wood from his finger where he'd gripped the wood too tight.

Matt

Matt stewed, perplexed. He replayed the confrontation with Nancy over and over in his head. What did she think he'd done? He'd been having a normal conversation with poor Ruby, that's all. They'd spent all week together – should it be strange for them to talk at the weekend? Nancy was so over-protective she couldn't see how destructive her behaviour was, how damaging to Ruby. Her young mind would be absorbing all of this, processing it. She needed some freedoms from the captivity of her illness. That's all Matt had offered.

But, on the other hand, could he blame Nancy? How would he behave if the position was reversed? If his own daughter was sick, and he struggled to look after her, trying his best, when the neighbour butted in, picking sides in a family spat? He'd probably lash out, pick a hurtful comment and throw it at them.

And it did hurt.

Matt paced around the house, feeling the walls closing in, the summer heat suddenly oppressive, stifling. He opened the front door, taking a few deep breaths, venturing on to the driveway.

He risked a glance over the fence. It was all quiet, but he sensed the safety of his new home being eroded.

He should be able to shake it off, put it down to emotion and stress on Nancy's part. But the feeling wouldn't budge. A feeling of doubt, of fear, almost. He had to talk to Imogen, whatever argument it might cause, and ensure she was on his side. He needed her to back him up.

He went back inside, jumped up the stairs, two at a time. Their bedroom door was ajar. He could hear Imogen talking.

'I know,' he heard her say. 'I will. Love you, Mum.'

He tapped on the door, poking his head in. Imogen was lying on the bed, propped up on several cushions – the orange ones with tassels she'd bought in the village which were far too large for their bed – holding her mobile. She placed it down as he crept in, patting the bed next to her.

'I need to talk to you,' she said.

'Me too,' said Matt, seeing the strange expression on Imogen's face. Her cheeks looked rosy; her eyes were narrow, secretive.

'Me first,' she said, patting the bed again.

Matt swallowed his frustration, his jaw tensing. A headache started to form. He sat.

'What's up?' he said. 'You OK?'

Imogen nodded. 'I've been speaking to Mum. She's coming down next weekend.'

'OK.' Matt got on fine with Imogen's parents. They maintained a polite distance most of the time; Imogen and her mum were close, but lacked time together – the nursing frequently scuppered lunch plans and weekend dinners. They spoke on the phone once a week out of habit.

'She wants to check on me.'

Matt swallowed again. He thought Imogen had settled all of this with her parents. They had no need to check on anything.

Imogen rested her hands on her stomach. She rubbed it.

'The sickness is a little better,' she said. 'If only it was just in the mornings, like they say it should be.'

Matt's brain took a few seconds to catch up. He stared at her hands, both of them caressing the slight bump of her belly.

His mouth dropped open, before forming into a twisted smile.

'No way.'

She nodded. 'Yes way.'

'But ...' he said, thinking of all the stupid comments he could make, before settling on the first thought that had come to him, 'that's amazing!'

He meant it. Absolutely. Another child. Another *baby*.

'How?' Stupid question.

Imogen shrugged. 'The usual method.'

Matt shook his head, his grin widening. He eyed her stomach again. 'How long have you known?' He didn't mind, but was a little surprised.

'Not long.'

Matt raised his eyebrows.

Imogen sighed. 'It was all such a shock with the move and everything. I put it down to stress, I was late, a little sick ...'

'So how far are you ...?'

'Ten weeks or so, I think,' she said. 'I've got an appointment with the GP next week. I've just told Mum.'

Matt watched her. Now she'd said it, it seemed obvious. Her cheeks were rosy and plump, her body subtly different, not so much in shape, but in the way she carried herself, her posture – protective, proud. Glowing.

147

Matt let out a long breath. He leaned back on the bed, suddenly dizzy, staring at the ceiling. Imogen's face appeared above him.

'You're happy?' she said. Her eyes darted between his. Nervous; still nervous. Why wouldn't he be happy?

'Yes,' he said. 'I'm in shock, but I'm happy. Really happy.'

Of course she would be nervous. Everything they'd been through, the emotional wringer of the last few months. But he hoped he'd never given the impression he wanted anything other than the rest of their lives together. A growing family, a brother or sister for Ash, was exactly what they needed.

This was the line they could draw. It couldn't be any more perfect.

His mind raced, the excitement tempered by a thousand practical thoughts.

'What's wrong?' said Imogen. 'You seem . . .'

Matt released his frown. 'Nothing. I just . . . wow. There's so much to think about.'

Imogen nodded, eyeing him, studying him. 'We're going into this together, yes? The new chapter we wanted. Draw a line, et cetera?'

Matt nodded. 'Of course.'

She took a deep breath, rubbing her stomach. 'And there's nothing else I need to know? We're secure? Job-wise, financially?'

Matt nodded again, but this time his heart rate increased, his mouth dry. 'Yes. Nothing,' he said. 'Money's not a problem. I've moved a few things around. It'll be tight, but we'll cope.' He hadn't heard back from Liv yet, and it was possible her threat would dry up along with her stash. He'd told her he had it, but he'd wait until she called before transferring any money.

Imogen bit her lower lip. She opened her mouth to say something, then closed it, nodding.

'When do you want to tell Ash?' Matt asked.

'Today. I thought we'd get pizza and tell her over dinner. If I can keep any down.'

'She'll be excited. Won't she?'

'I think so,' said Imogen. 'It's hard to say at her age, but we'll focus on her – the importance of the big sister role. She'll have plenty of time to get used to it.'

Matt had almost forgotten what he came in to talk to Imogen about. But that could wait. His mood had lifted, the news far outweighing anything else. Nancy and her funny behaviour, however worrying, disappeared to the back of his mind. He'd ignore her for a few days and it would all blow over.

He had much bigger things to think about.

'We've got most of the baby stuff in the garage, haven't we?' said Imogen. 'It's all boxed up but we kept it?'

'Yes. Well planned.'

Imogen frowned. 'I was still on the pill, Matt. This is about as unplanned as it gets.'

She stretched out next to him, both staring at the ceiling for a few moments, before she turned her head.

'This is it, isn't it?' she said.

'What?'

'The new start. Whatever happened . . . I mean, nothing did, but what was said. It's all over now. We can focus. We'll be busy. No time for the past?'

Matt's heart thudded, punching through his ribcage. Uncontrolled, yet fleeting. It settled. He swallowed. It must have come out wrong. *Whatever happened.* He'd thought it was settled. He'd thought it was already over. The doubts were already gone, sated, extinguished. She'd promised.

He took a breath, sucked it all down, locked it away.

'Absolutely,' he said.

Imogen

It had been three days since I'd told Matt. I'd tempered my shock, my anger, and given him a chance, and he'd chosen silence. But I'd checked our savings account and the money was back. So where did that leave me? With my own choice to make. To focus on the past or the future. I couldn't do both in my condition.

I chose the future. For now, at least.

My mum and dad were over the moon, my close friends shrieked down the phone, and Ash was possibly the most excited of all.

'Can I share a room with her?' she'd asked.

'Her?'

'My sister. Can we call her Flo?'

'Flo?'

The reasons why were not clear, but Ashley's plans soon were. She even sorted a few toys ready, *hand-me-downs*, preparing for sharing. I admired her practicality, and her bundle of smiles provided a constant of calm in amongst the daily worries.

'I think baby can have the spare room,' I'd said. 'We'll decorate?'

Ashley's face fell.

'But we'll pick a name together?' I'd offered, stroking Ash's hair, hoping for another identical child. That wasn't right, I guessed, or fair, but it was partly true. If I could blueprint Ashley and roll out another, it would make life much simpler. More predictable.

I was dying to share my news, and today, I sat in Nancy's garden, the sun baking my skin. I shifted my seat, getting my head under the parasol. Nancy remained in the sun, tilting her face to the sky. Ashley was at home with Matt; he'd taken the morning off to work from home. I'd told him to call the plumber again – the boiler was playing up, no hot water again today, and I swear I could smell gas in the kitchen, the boiler rattling as it fired up. He promised it was on his list.

I was growing used to spending mornings like this, lazy drinks. Nancy tended to host – her fondness for Jake had yet to develop, and I didn't want to force him on her. She wasn't a dog person – everyone has their faults.

'So, out with it,' said Nancy, with a sly smile.

'Out with what?'

I was a little nervous about telling Nancy. Our friendship was so new and I didn't want to risk spoiling it. I wondered if she'd still be as enthusiastic about me if all I did was talk about babies – which was inevitable, to an extent. But I couldn't hide it for much longer. I'd heard the second shows quicker than the first, if you have my luck. I'd swapped my wardrobe for looser fitting dresses, flowing tops. I was lucky – my stomach was the only thing that had expanded so far. The rest of my body was waiting, perhaps until I'd told everyone.

Nancy sat forward on her chair, raising her eyebrows. A

cupboard door slammed inside and I heard footsteps. Ruby appeared at the door, pausing to examine us both before stepping on to the patio.

'Hi, Mrs Roberts,' she said.

'Hi, Ruby. You must start calling me Imogen.' I laughed.

Ruby shrugged. She was dressed for an afternoon in the sun: bikini and flip-flops; a book tucked under one arm, a drink in hand. I stared for a few moments with envy as she settled on to the sun lounger, flicking her shades over her eyes. I remember being that young, looking that young, wearing a bikini that small. How far from this picture would my body look in a few weeks' time, when my stomach exploded outwards and my thighs fattened in sympathy? My bum wouldn't even fit in this chair in a few months. I wasn't small with Ashley, and I had no reason to suspect baby number two would be any different.

'Are you OK?' Ruby flicked her shades on to her forehead. I blinked, conscious I was still staring at her midriff.

'Oh. Yes,' I said, averting my eyes. I blushed. 'Fine. Sorry.'

'Imogen has some news,' said Nancy, 'but she's being secretive.'

'Well, it's not a secret . . .' I said, even more nervous now Ruby was here, 'but . . .' I paused, not for dramatic effect, but due to the nerves. Each person I told drove it home. This was happening. 'I'm pregnant!' I said, my voice wobbling. 'Matt and I are having another baby.'

I stared down at my stomach as I said it. I'd subconsciously placed both hands over it in a protective embrace, smoothing out the dress, as if doing a big reveal. Ta-da!

'Oh!'

I don't know what I'd expected, but her tone caught me. It was . . . I don't know. I looked up. Nancy's expression was hard

153

to read. She peered at me; through me, at my stomach. I saw her clench her jaw, grind her teeth.

But in an instant, she changed. Her face broke into a broad smile. She clapped her hands together, then pushed herself out of the chair.

'Imogen! Dear,' she exclaimed. 'Such wonderful news. Come here.'

Nancy leaned over and held me tight, kissing me on the left cheek. Over her shoulder I could see Ruby, who was also watching, also with a curious expression.

She didn't smile at all.

'Congratulations, Mrs Roberts,' she said, before flicking her shades back down, picking up her book, turning to her page.

I swallowed. Perhaps Ruby didn't like seeing her mum hugging other people. Perhaps the thought of a screaming baby next door wasn't her idea of good news.

'Thank you,' I said, with a degree of uncertainty as Nancy let me go. She clapped her hands together again. Her expression was still odd, troubled. I'm not sure what I expected, but I'd hoped for more. Not gushing, like my mum had, of course not, but ... more enthused than this.

'Are you OK?' I said. Maybe I'd made a mistake telling her. Perhaps I'd misjudged our relationship. What if Nancy wasn't maternal and it pushed us apart? What if I'd got it all wrong? But she looked it, acted it. I was at a bit of a loss. My burst of happy news seemed suddenly subdued.

Nancy sat down, breathed out. She gave a small laugh, which surprised me, and shook her head.

'Forgive me,' she said. 'I am over the moon for you. I ...' She glanced again at Ruby. 'I always wanted two. I had Ruby

154

in my thirties, you know . . . I don't think my body could do it again. And then Ruby's dad left us. It wasn't meant to be.'

I felt a surge of relief, and sympathy. I reached out, placing my hand on top of hers. She was wearing her emotions on her sleeves, that's all. Most of the time she seemed so contained, stoic, almost – like the picture of her in the dining room with a shotgun in one hand and her kill in the other. A proud, independent woman who took what she wanted. But everyone has their delicate subjects. I'd found Nancy's.

'You're blessed,' Nancy continued, 'and my reaction was silly. I often get like this around lovely ladies with bumps. I couldn't contain it. I'm sorry.'

'No, no,' I said. 'Don't be ridiculous. Baby talk can derail the best of us.'

It might not have been the most eloquent response, but I wasn't sure what else to say.

'When are you due?'

'February, ish.'

'You're hardly showing.' Nancy cast her eyes to my stomach. I saw a flash of irritation, as if she should have known. This was a surprise to her. I'd got it wrong.

'How does Matthew feel about it?'

'He's ecstatic,' I said. 'Really pleased and—'

Ruby dropped her book to one side and slid off the sun lounger.

'I'm going to get another drink,' she said, heading back inside, pulling at her bikini strap on the way past, swishing her hair behind her. I caught a whiff of her perfume mixed with suntan lotion, and noted her half-full glass on the patio with a smile.

At fifteen years old, a conversation about pregnancy would have been more than enough to scare me off, too. But I hoped Nancy would be interested. I had a feeling I'd need her.

I waited until Ruby had gone, then lowered my voice. 'The tension you sensed when we first met,' I said. 'When you thought I was stressed?'

Nancy leaned in, narrowed her eyes.

'Well, you were right,' I continued. 'It's been a difficult move, a difficult time. But this,' I patted my stomach again. 'This is our future. Matt, Ashley, me and this bundle of baby.'

Nancy nodded. 'Of course,' she said.

'We couldn't be stronger,' I said, hearing the words; not quite feeling them. Not yet. But give it time.

Nancy smiled. She glanced at me. Unconvinced. Like when she'd asked if Matt looked after me properly.

'I *mean* it,' I said. 'I know I must have seemed a bit off when we first moved in, but it's over. Matt and I, we're ...' I patted my stomach again.

'Fixed?' she said.

I frowned. 'If you like,' I said. 'But I don't think we were ever broken. Not completely.'

Nancy shrugged. 'If you say so, dear,' she said. Her tone was motherly rather than patronising, but it bugged me. I wanted her to know Matt and I were OK. I don't know why it meant so much to me, but her doubts triggered my doubts, and I needed to be clear of them, if only for the baby's health. Stressed out Imogen was not healthy for either of us.

Nancy's mild dislike of Matt was charming, and I think I'd even encouraged it on occasion. Today, though, with my news, it felt a little too much. I was supposed to be celebrating these moments, but instead I slumped in my chair, wondering what had gone wrong, if I should make my excuses and head home.

I saw Nancy watching me.

'Let me get you another drink,' she said.

Before I could protest, she was out of her chair and heading inside. I tried to relax, moving my chair back into the sun. A bit of vitamin D might help; the hot sun on my face would give me a boost.

A few minutes later Nancy placed two tall glasses on the table, containing what looked like a smoothie, full of green flecks, topped with ice. I lifted one of the glasses and sniffed it. A multitude of flavours hit my nostrils.

'I drank one of these every day when I was pregnant with Ruby,' said Nancy. 'Full of vitamins and fibre.'

I raised my eyebrows and took a sip. It was bitter, but not unpleasantly so. I drank a little more, then drained a quarter of the glass. I wiped my lips.

'OK,' I said. 'I'm impressed.'

Nancy seemed pleased. 'A peace offering,' she said. 'And a reminder. I'll look after you. Whatever happens.'

Whatever happens.

It was an odd comment, on reflection, and if I'd looked more deeply into it, perhaps the next few weeks would have panned out altogether differently.

But I didn't. I was already drinking the rest of the smoothie, enjoying the cold sensation as it seeped down my throat. I relaxed for a while longer, appreciating the sun and the company of my quirky new friend.

I thought no more of it.

Matt

A persistent thumping noise invaded Matt's dream. He stumbled out of the bed, waiting a few moments for his eyes to focus.

'What the hell?' he said, checking his watch. Six-thirty a.m. Saturday morning. Post? It was a bit early, and they didn't normally hammer the door down.

'You get it,' said Imogen, pulling the duvet over her head, groaning.

Matt pulled on a T-shirt and jogging bottoms and shuffled towards the stairs. He heard another three thumps at the door as he descended. Jake started barking from the kitchen, and Matt hurried to close the hallway door. Another two thumps as he reached the front door.

'OK, OK!' Matt swung it open.

Nancy took two steps back. She was breathing fast, panting, one hand to her chest, the other by her side. Her face was red, angry.

'Nancy, what on earth—?'

'How dare you!' Nancy shouted, her voice echoing off the neighbouring houses. It took Matt by surprise. He paused; his eyes darted behind her. At the end of the garden path, Ruby stood in her pyjamas. She'd been crying, was crying, her face red and blotchy. She kept looking away, reluctant to be standing there. But then her eyes locked with Matt's. She was scared.

Matt turned to Nancy. 'What do you mean?'

'Don't play games with me.'

Matt shook his head, clearing it, Nancy's shrill voice dragging him into consciousness.

Nancy continued. 'Do you have anything to tell me, Matthew? About you and Ruby?'

Again, Matt looked past Nancy. Ruby shook her head. He frowned.

'What do you mean?'

'Mum, let's go,' said Ruby.

Matt heard footsteps on the stairs. Imogen appeared behind him in her dressing gown.

'Nancy,' she said. 'Everything OK? I heard shouting.'

Nancy's eyes filled with tears. 'Imogen, dear. I'm sorry, but I had to say something.'

Matt glanced at his wife, back to Nancy.

'Say what, Nancy?'

Nancy took a deep breath. 'Ruby was agitated last night,' she said. 'She often is. And during those times I sit with her, holding her hand. She tells me what's on her mind, what's spinning around with the anxiety. What she's been thinking. What's happened to her.'

'Nancy, I—'

'Last night she made mention of you, Matthew. Several times, in fact. When I pressed her, she clammed up. When I asked her again, she admitted it.' Nancy looked away, composing herself.

Matt kept one eye on Ruby. She was shuffling back, trying to leave.

'Admitted what?' said Imogen.

Nancy's face grew redder. She stared at Matt. 'What you did after you walked her home, from babysitting a few weeks ago.'

Matt took a breath. He reached out sideways, searching for Imogen's hand, but didn't find it.

'Are you denying it?'

'I'm not denying anything,' he said. 'I don't know what you're talking about.'

'After she babysat for you.'

'Mum,' Ruby called again. The tears had stopped but she looked distraught. 'Mum, I . . . just leave it.'

'What did I do?'

'You know what you did!' Nancy shouted again. 'She's fifteen, Matthew! You kissed her!'

Matt's mouth hung open.

'I . . .' He turned to Imogen. 'I did not! I mean . . .' He saw Imogen's face darken. 'No!' he said. 'I . . . I gave her a hug. *Thanked* her for babysitting. That's it.'

He spun, turning to Nancy. 'You've got this all wrong, I—'

'Oh please. Don't take that line.'

'It's the truth!'

'*We kissed.* That's what Ruby told me. *A proper kiss.* You don't say that when somebody kisses you on the cheek. She said you *held her.* Your hands . . .'

Nancy's voice was shrill and loud, screaming in his ears. He could hear nothing but noise, feel nothing but the stares of Nancy and Imogen. His face rushed with blood. His head spun.

'My hands?' he stuttered.

160

'You groped her! You had your filthy hands on my daughter, Matthew.'

Imogen stepped away. Her face was twisted in bewilderment, disgust.

'Imogen. Please,' he said. 'This is nonsense. Ask her. Ask Ruby.'

Imogen swallowed. She looked out at Ruby, who begged with her eyes. 'Mum!' She turned and ran off, her bare feet silent as she cut across her front garden, the door slamming as she stormed into her house.

A few moments of silence, a pause in the storm. Nancy stared at Matt. Imogen stared after Ruby, holding it together. Finally, she turned to Matt.

'Swear to me,' she said. 'Swear it's not true. It's a misunderstanding.'

'I swear,' said Matt. He grabbed Imogen by the arms, held her while he looked into her eyes. He needed her to believe him. 'I swear this isn't true. Whatever Nancy thinks, whatever Ruby said. It's wrong. It *is* a misunderstanding. She's a girl, for Christ's sake.'

Nancy laughed, harsh and short. 'I know what I heard.'

'Do you?' said Matt. 'Because Ruby didn't seem so keen on backing you up.'

'Maybe she's embarrassed,' Nancy said.

'Maybe because she made it up?' Matt suggested.

'Why the hell would she?'

'I don't know! She's your daughter. She's sick. I . . .' Matt stopped short of insulting Ruby. Whatever Nancy thought he'd done, the poor girl didn't deserve to be attacked. She suffered enough as it was. Perhaps it was her sickness, making her tell tales she shouldn't. The thought was disturbing. But with a mother like that, who could tell what twisted feelings she'd entertain?

Imogen stepped forward. She put her hand against the door frame, her fingers trembling. 'Nancy,' she said. 'Are you sure you know what Ruby said? Because you must have it wrong. If Matt swears . . .' She turned to Matt.

'I gave her a *hug*,' he said, 'to thank her for babysitting. Perhaps it was stupid. I didn't mean . . .' He closed his eyes, taking a deep breath, aware he was also trembling. 'I'm sorry if I caused an issue, Nancy. But what you're accusing me of is crazy. I didn't touch her.'

Nancy's face was still red, her eyes wet with tears. 'I'm sorry, Imogen, I didn't want to drag you into this—'

'Nancy, he's my husband.'

'And I wasn't sure whether to say anything . . . I don't want to hurt you, Imogen, and I value your friendship. But please, you can see why I had to say something. Why I had to confront Matthew.'

'Nancy, I . . .' Matt struggled to think. His chest thumped in protest.

'I think we need to have some space,' said Nancy, 'while I consider what to do. Ruby is fifteen, Matthew, as you well know.'

'But—'

'We can't leave it like this!' said Imogen. 'Nancy. We need to talk this through. With Ruby. This is a serious accusation.'

'I know,' Nancy said. She stopped, putting her hands to her eyes. She sobbed, her shoulders heaving. Imogen stepped out on to the path.

'No,' said Nancy. 'This wasn't your doing, Imogen. I need time. Just give me that.'

She backed away and headed down the path, making her way towards her house. Matt watched until she'd closed the door behind her.

Then he turned to face Imogen.

Imogen

I felt dizzy, sick, a sudden rush of blood away from my head. I put my hand out, steadying myself against the wall. Matt closed the door. He stood, facing it for a moment.

What could I say, except, 'What the fuck, Matt?' He'd sworn his innocence in front of Nancy, but I'd need him to do it again, ten times over.

'I know,' he said. 'What the fuck? She's mad. Didn't I tell you she doesn't like me?'

Matt looked angry, his face red, the vein in his forehead pulsing. 'You're flushed.'

'Of course I am,' he said. 'I'm furious. Confused.' He scratched the back of his head. 'Look, Imogen, I—'

'Swear? Yes, you said.'

He nodded, taking a few deep breaths. It had been a while since I'd seen him like this. His normal cool evaporating. But this time seemed different. Felt different. It wasn't the same situation at all. I had to remind myself of that.

'You need to tell me exactly what happened,' I said. 'Every step, every word. You know why I need to know.'

'Of course!' he said. 'I'll tell you. I . . . shall I put on some coffee? Let's sit. Talk about this. It's crazy, and I need you to know it.'

I nodded, following him to the kitchen. He made coffee while I watched his every move. He was agitated, sure, but so would anyone be, after such a confrontation. I kept my eyes on him until we were seated across from each other at the breakfast bar.

He shook his head slowly. 'There's nothing to tell,' he said.

Not the best start, but I let him continue, sipping my coffee, reminding myself to stop after a few sips – I had sworn myself off caffeine for the pregnancy, but still insisted on the first few mouthfuls. Terrible, I know, but right then I needed my head to clear.

'The night we went to the pub. I assume that's when she meant. Ruby has only babysat for us once.'

'Let's assume,' I said.

Matt huffed. His eyes darted, left and right. 'I was very drunk.' He put his hand out. 'This isn't the beginning of an admission, by the way, but I wanted to remind you. I'd had a lot to drink. You went to bed.'

'And you?'

'Paid Ruby. Then walked her home. It was dark.'

'She lives next door.'

'And it was pitch-black and spooky,' said Matt. 'And she's a fifteen-year-old girl, so I made sure she was inside her house, safely.'

I nodded, watching him. His face was changing to a normal colour, the vein withdrawing. He was being honest, as far as I could tell.

'I . . . She unlocked her front door, she turned to me and said thanks. I put my arms out and gave her a clumsy hug, like I might do with Ashley. I was drunk. It was a stupid thing to do, but I didn't *touch* her! I didn't *kiss* her. Christ!'

I kept our eyes locked as he said the words. No flicker, no darting.

'She closed the door and I came home.'

We stared at each other for several seconds. I thought he was telling the truth. I *thought*. Neither blinked. I took another deep sip of my coffee, pushed it away. 'But why would she say it?'

'Nancy's irrational,' said Matt. 'Stressed. Overprotective of Ruby due to her illness. She's lashing out.'

'OK, but why did Ruby say those things?' I wanted to believe him. I *so* wanted to believe him. But I needed to cover all bases.

'How the fuck should I know?' he said. The vein appeared again. Faintly. His face flushed a little before settling.

'I need to ask her.'

Matt shrugged.

'Why shouldn't I?'

'I didn't say you shouldn't.' Matt's voice upped an octave. 'I just think if she's sick and delirious half the time, goodness knows what she'll come out with.'

'She isn't delirious half the time, Matt.'

He sagged. 'I didn't mean that.'

'Then I'll ask her. I'll ask why she said you kissed her, and why she said you touched her.'

Matt tossed his head from side to side. He looked at me in desperation. Hurt? His behaviour was normal, not shifty or suspicious. I saw my husband struggling. And this time it was different. But he was the same. I felt a small surge of relief, subconsciously, rising up and settling my heart, my soul. As far as I could possibly tell, he was being honest with me.

'Ask her,' he said, in a small voice. 'Ask away. But whatever she says, I didn't do what Nancy says I did. I promise you, Imogen.'

I stared at him, our eyes locked, history replaying, keeping quiet what we knew mustn't be said.

'We have to go over,' I said. 'We need to talk to Nancy. And to Ruby.'

Matt looked reluctant. 'Now?'

'Today,' I said.

'Wouldn't it be better to ignore them? Stay away?'

I shook my head. Even if I believed Matt, I still felt hurt and confused. Nancy was my neighbour, my *friend*. I wanted to fix this, not to push her away. If she'd made a mistake, it was an innocent one. If it was down to stress, I wanted to help her. I could understand the overprotective nature of a mother and her daughter.

'I don't want to ignore her,' I said. 'If you say she made a mistake, it needs fixing. I'm not going to let it ruin everything.'

'Everything?'

'This,' I said, casting my arms around. 'This new life of ours, Matt. It includes the people around us.'

'She made a mistake,' Matt insisted.

'Then we'll fix it.'

Matt nodded. Stayed silent.

'OK,' he said. 'Whatever you need. I love you. I'll do anything you want.'

I noticed his hands were trembling too. I reached out. He took mine. It felt good, like we were in it together. Were we?

He looked at my hands for a moment. 'I'll have a shower,'

he said. 'Then maybe we can have breakfast, give Nancy time to calm down. We'll go over this morning, OK?'

He slipped his hands away from mine. I watched him walk off. I listened to the floorboards in the hallway creak under his feet, the stairs as he climbed them. I sat and I breathed, four in, four out, trying to quell the last remnant of panic, panic that had surged when I listened to Nancy at the door, and had now subsided. Not gone, but subdued.

Was it or wasn't it? The thought caused the nausea to rise. The morning sickness had been worse than ever in the last twenty-four hours. I'd even vomited in the night, the remnants of Nancy's vegetable smoothie spraying into the toilet bowl. Right now my throat burned for another reason, but I swallowed the bitter coffee-tasting bile.

No.

It was different. Completely different. The circumstances nowhere near the same. This was an underage girl, and before, it was . . .

I closed my eyes. A mistake. I saw a horrific vision of Matt, kissing Ruby at Nancy's front door. Would she push him away or . . .? I opened my eyes, disgusted at the thought. She was fifteen, it wouldn't happen. Didn't happen.

He was telling the truth.

I hoped to God he was.

Because I couldn't go through this again.

Matt

Matt slipped on his shoes. His heart raced. He watched Imogen through the crack in the doorway. What must she be thinking? Perhaps he should have known better. No, he *should* have known better. He didn't know why, or what she aimed to achieve with such an accusation, but this was Nancy's doing.

He'd tried to hold it together earlier but had almost broken down. Did Nancy know how horrific such an allegation was to a man like him? Nearly forty? A family man? Did she know what it could do to him?

He should storm around there with the same anger that had brought her here. He should shout, scream his innocence, make the street echo with the truth. She deserved it.

His gut turned, sinking, anxious. This wasn't a minor complaint; this was serious. Criminal? His mouth went dry at the thought, his heart flipping in panic. He could imagine the police interviewing him, asking him about all of his interactions with Ruby. *How often have you been alone together? What did you talk about? Did you make any suggestion you were attracted to her?* He could see their eyes, the eyes of the neighbours – of his family, his friends. He pictured himself in court, protesting his innocence to the judge, to Imogen, to Ashley.

How the fuck did this happen?

'Are you ready?'

Imogen looked beyond weary. She'd cried, Matt could tell. Not in front of him, but while he was dressing, or while in the shower herself. Her eyes were puffy. She'd tried to hide it with make-up.

'Shit.' Imogen put her hand to her mouth before flying into the downstairs toilet. Matt heard her vomit, coughing her breakfast up. He went to help her, holding her hair, rubbing her back until it passed.

She flushed the toilet.

'You look pale,' said Matt. For a moment, she'd had the same clammy look as Ruby.

'What do you expect?'

'I . . . is it worse than usual?'

Imogen huffed, appearing to think about it. 'Yes,' she said. 'Much worse. I'd hoped it would get better by this stage.'

'Shall I get you some antacid?' Matt kept several bottles at the ready, remembering it was pretty much the only medication Imogen allowed herself during pregnancy.

'No,' she said. 'Let's go.'

Imogen washed her mouth out, dabbed at her lips with a tissue. She called for Ashley, who so far had remained oblivious, playing in her room all morning.

'She'll have to play in Nancy's garden,' said Imogen. 'Keep your voice down.'

They waited while Ash skipped down the stairs to join them, then headed for the door.

★

170

Nancy answered with a stony expression, which broke only when Ashley said hello.

'Can Ash play in your back garden?' said Imogen. 'While we talk?'

Nancy examined Matt for a couple of seconds. She nodded.

'Come in,' she said, turning and walking away.

They endured several moments of excruciating silence while Ash was ushered on to the grass with toys and a drink, and Ruby was asked to come downstairs. Nancy put the kettle on, arranging the cups and teapot on a floral-patterned tray. She didn't talk until the water was in the teapot. She nodded to the dining table.

'Ruby has had a bad night,' said Nancy, 'and obviously an upsetting morning, but she'll join us.'

'Good,' said Imogen, 'because we need to hear from her. This confusion . . .'

Nancy shook her head.

'It didn't happen,' said Matt, seeing Nancy's dismissal of Imogen, of him. She was still certain of her accusation, but it had to end.

Ruby appeared in the doorway. Her T-shirt and shorts were hanging off her today, her skin pale. Her face was still red and her hair greasy. Such a transformation from the last time Matt had seen her properly. Ruby looked straight at Matt, before turning her gaze to her fingernails, which she picked at, making no move to sit at the table.

Matt glanced at Imogen, could see she was staring intently at Ruby, examining the girl, her eyes moving down Ruby's body, pausing. She turned to Nancy.

'I need to ask Ruby about what she said.'

'I told you what she said,' said Nancy. She remained firm and defensive, but Matt could see she was struggling. She liked Imogen, that much was clear, and this must be very difficult for her.

'But it's not true,' said Matt, staring at Ruby. Again, she caught his eye, holding it for a few seconds this time. 'Is it, Ruby?'

Ruby's face reddened. She shuffled her feet, staying in the doorway.

'Is it?' said Imogen.

Matt felt a little taken aback. Imogen said she believed him. But he had to let her ask whatever she wanted. And Ruby had to deny it.

Ruby shrugged.

'What does that mean?' said Imogen.

Ruby didn't say anything; her shoulders remained hunched, her head downturned. Matt felt sorry for her, but needed her to be clear with Imogen what a mistake Nancy had made.

'Tell the truth—'

'It's not true.' Ruby's voice was small, husky.

Imogen sat straighter in her chair. Nancy narrowed her eyes, her hand on the teapot handle. Matt heard his own heartbeat thumping in his ears.

'What?' whispered Imogen.

Ruby finally looked up. She stared at Imogen. 'I . . . it wasn't. I mean. It was a dream, OK? I had a . . .' Her face continued to redden; she looked pleadingly at Nancy.

'A dream?' said Matt. His face flushed. It was unexpected, but it made sense.

'I dreamt it. My temperature was high – it often is with my condition. I get these feverish dreams – I told you my dream, Mum, that's all. Then you got mad and started shouting. I couldn't stop you.'

Imogen let out a huge sigh. 'A dream,' she said. Her face broke into a smile, clear with relief.

Matt saw that Ruby was hurting, embarrassed, desperate to escape this inquisition. 'Then it's nothing,' he said. 'And Ruby, there's nothing to be embarrassed about.'

Nancy slammed her palm on the table. 'Ruby,' she said. 'I don't think that's correct, is it?'

Ruby nodded. Nancy's face darkened; she looked like she was going to explode. 'Is that your final answer, dear?' she said.

Again, Ruby nodded.

'And there's nothing else you need to tell us?'

A small shake of the head. Matt's heart still seemed determined to jump out of his chest.

'Then go back upstairs,' said Nancy, her voice icy.

They waited while Ruby shuffled off, up the stairs, listening for the sound of her bedroom door closing.

Matt kept his eyes on Imogen, judging her reaction, her journey through this. She looked more relaxed, almost sympathetic. Even after something like this, Imogen cared about why people suffered. She was staring at Nancy.

'I'm sorry, Nancy,' she said.

Why? thought Matt. It should be Nancy apologising.

'I think Nancy must be sorry too,' said Matt. He grabbed his teacup, needing to hold something, sipping at it, feeling his hands trembling with adrenaline.

Nancy shook her head. She smiled again, with her mouth, not her eyes. She was good at it.

'I could have gone to the police,' she said. 'I almost called them.'

Matt's hands shook. He put down the cup and it clattered

on the saucer. He watched Nancy. Wouldn't she have called the police if she were certain? If somebody had touched his underage daughter, that's what he would do. Wasn't that odd? She marched round and shouted, but nothing else? Surely that meant she *knew* it wasn't a real accusation.

He bit his tongue. He wanted to leave. What might she think of next? What might she try and pry out of poor, vulnerable Ruby upstairs, guilty of nothing but a tall tale, albeit the sort of tale that could destroy lives?

Nancy held her own cup, caressing the handle and the sides, staring at the hot tea as it swirled. Matt let the silence do its work. He gazed past her, at the wall of the dining room, where several more pictures of Ruby were framed. Different ages, different expressions. To the right was an interesting snap of Nancy, standing in a field of wildflowers. She wore a waxed jacket and high boots, but the light reflected off the glass and Matt couldn't see the details. A picture of an older couple was framed next to it – Matt presumed grandparents. There was something odd about all of them. It took Matt a few moments to figure it out. There were no photos of Ruby's dad, Nancy's late husband. Not one.

'I decided not to tell the police because of you, Imogen,' said Nancy.

Matt's attention focused back on the table. He frowned. This wasn't quite the apology he wanted.

'In your condition,' said Nancy. The anger seemed to leave her face; kindness took its place, a strange, serene expression. 'I thought of the hurt it might cause you.'

Matt huffed. 'Good job you didn't,' he said.

Nancy ignored him. 'I still value your friendship, Imogen,' she said. 'And I still intend to be there for you.'

'Oh, Nancy,' Imogen looked confused and tired. She was comfortable with the truth, but uncomfortable with how to deal with Nancy. She looked about to say something but instead pushed herself away from the table, putting one hand to her mouth.

'Please excuse me,' she said, running off. The downstairs toilet door slammed.

Matt cleared his throat. 'Morning sickness,' he said.

'I told you she needed to rest,' said Nancy. 'Your behaviour doesn't help, does it?'

She seemed reluctant to meet his eye, now Imogen was out of the room. She focused on the table.

'You know it's not true, Nancy. Don't you?' he said. He felt weary, his desire to attack Nancy fading. He couldn't find the anger he wanted. Imogen's calming influence, no doubt. She was good for him, even in situations like this.

'Do I know, Matthew?' She sniffed. 'Time will tell, won't it.'

Matt paused. What did she mean?

They heard the toilet flushing. Imogen appeared, pale and perspiring.

'We should go,' she said.

Matt and Nancy both stood to help her. Nancy got to her first. She gave Imogen a hug, whispered something in her ear. Matt strained to hear but missed it. Imogen nodded, offered a small smile.

'I'll see you soon,' said Nancy, making a point of directing it at Imogen and not Matt. Imogen called to Ashley, who jumped up from her game and hurried through. Imogen ushered her ahead. Matt followed.

They stepped over the threshold. Imogen was several paces ahead, along the path, when Nancy grabbed Matt's arm.

'It stops now,' she hissed. 'Do you understand?'

Matt opened his mouth to protest, but Imogen turned and Nancy let go of Matt's arm in the same instant.

'I need the bathroom, Matt,' said Imogen. She looked green, and hurried off down the path, consumed with her nausea. Ashley skipped behind, questioning her. 'Are you OK, Mummy?'

'Imogen and I are friends,' said Nancy to Matt, watching them both go. She crossed her arms, giving Matt a peculiar look. It wasn't hurt, or upset. Something more controlled. Her eyes were dry, sparkling.

'Remember that, Matthew. She needs me, now more than ever. And I'll be there for her.'

Matt

Matt left an array of drinks and snacks by the bed. He kissed Imogen on the forehead and closed the bedroom door, pausing on the landing, leaning against the cold plaster of the wall. He closed his eyes, drawing a few deep breaths, trying to calm the hammering in his chest.

Imogen had assured him she believed Ruby's statement; she believed him. But she was too tired to talk about it any more; she just wanted to draw a line under the whole thing.

He'd forgiven Nancy before, when she'd made the off comment in the garden, over the fence, about staying away from pretty young girls. He'd put it down to stress, to overprotective single parenting. He hadn't blamed her at the time.

But this morning she'd crossed a line from defensive to aggressive. What must Ruby be thinking, embarrassed in front of her mum and the two of them? It wasn't her fault, and yet Matt feared the thought of being around her. Should he alter his behaviour? Stop saying hello? Stop chatting over the fence? But that would be like admitting he'd done something wrong. To stop interacting with Ruby might prompt the rumours to start – *he got caught, now he's being careful.* Imogen would notice. Nancy would notice. She'd make a point of noticing.

So where did that leave him? He'd already arranged another work experience day for Ruby. Should he cancel it? Could he be trusted alone in a car with her?

'Daddy?' The sound of Ash's voice cut through his thoughts.

He pushed himself away from the wall. 'Yes, sweetie,' he called, entering her bedroom. She had a selection of books spread on the floor, ordering them by colour.

'Can I have a drink?' she said.

Matt walked over and gave her a hug, watching her for a moment, wishing for the simplicity of childhood.

'Of course.'

Ash looked up at him, concern in her eyes, her lower lip wobbling.

'What's wrong, beautiful?' he said.

Ash swallowed. 'Is Mummy OK?'

Matt squeezed her tighter. What had Ash heard? Anything? Nothing? She should be as excited about Imogen's pregnancy as they were – it was something to be overjoyed about. This time should be precious, stress-free, treasured, for Ash as much as him and Imogen. And yet Nancy had managed to stick a knife in the middle of it, slicing some of that joy away, never to be replaced.

His growing anger towards her was tinged with desperation. Confronting Nancy again might lead to further accusations. Amidst his resentment was a desire for her to simply stay silent. To hold her tongue. Whatever she thought, he needed her to keep it to herself.

His thoughts spiralled. Unwelcome. Debilitating. Desperate.

'Has she been sick?'

Matt winced, mentally kicking himself. Ash had a particular fear of sick – not just in herself but anyone around her. Imogen said it wasn't uncommon in children her age, but it would often upset her. Matt wished he'd checked on her sooner.

'Come here,' he said. 'Mummy's fine, I promise. Babies sometimes make mummies sick, that's all. She'll be fine in no time.'

He gave her a big kiss on the forehead, squeezing her tighter until her lip stopped trembling, to be replaced with a squeal and a giggle. She wrestled herself away and Matt stood up.

'Drink coming right up,' he said.

Ash nodded, the concern still apparent, though settled for now.

Unfortunately, for the rest of the day, Imogen stayed in bed, a bucket by her side, her sickness getting worse. Matt ran up and down the stairs, bringing water, towels, a change of clothes. He didn't remember her being like this with Ashley's pregnancy and suggested calling the doctor, but Imogen assured him she was OK – some women went through particularly bad spells at this stage. The stress hadn't helped, and for that, Matt apologised yet again.

'Go out,' said Imogen, late in the afternoon. 'The sun is shining. Go for a walk, for a drive. Clear your head.'

Matt was uneasy about leaving her. Her hair was wet with sweat, plastered to the side of her face. He tried to brush it off her forehead. The last time he'd seen her like this was during a nasty bout of norovirus a couple of winters before. She'd vomited for three days. Matt remembered washing his hands every half-hour, terrified of catching it.

'I'll be fine,' she said. 'I've been through pregnancy once

before, remember, I can do it again. Ash will be fine in her room. I can get up if she needs me.'

'OK,' he said. 'I'll go for half an hour. Then I'll make you some dinner.'

Imogen pulled a face.

'Broth?'

'Yuck.'

'Another drink then. Water.'

They both smiled. Imogen reached out and held his arm. 'Go,' she said. 'Stop fussing.'

Ready for some air, Matt opened the front door, an unpleasant dread hitting him as he stepped outside. The neighbours would have heard some of the shouting – did they know what had been said? Would Nancy tell them anyway? He found himself creeping to the car, sliding into the driver's seat, refusing to look at Nancy's house. He managed to reverse out of the driveway without looking, taking the first corner a little too fast, almost clipping a car headed the other way. He drove through the neighbourhood as fast as he could, keeping his gaze forward. He spied several people out of the corners of his eyes, but didn't turn. Were they watching him? Judging? He waited at the gate while it slid open, counting the seconds, before escaping on to the country roads.

Once out of the village, Matt opened the windows and turned up the radio, drowning himself in noise, attempting to clear the sounds of the morning out of his head.

Matt drove to Guildford and back, snaking around at random for forty minutes, letting his mind wander, before he headed home. Imogen had been right – his head was clearer, his mood lifting. His gut still twisted at Nancy's words, but he hoped it would fade. These things tended to.

The gate slid open to allow him back into the community, although the usual welcoming feeling was absent. He drove at a sedate pace along the connecting road, trying to appreciate the lush trees and shrubs, the sounds of summer, the fresh warm air. But the pleasurable feelings he'd come to expect from the new neighbourhood evaded him.

He pulled the car over and cut the engine, enjoying a brief moment of silence. The anxiety hadn't departed, but it was under control. Looking after Imogen and Ashley would consume the rest of the weekend, after which he could distract himself with work. This would all blow over soon enough.

As he tried to sneak back inside the house, he heard a voice to his right. The bushes in Nancy's garden rustled.

'Matt.'

It was Ruby, hidden between a camellia and a large evergreen. She stepped into the light, shielded from her house by the undergrowth.

Matt hesitated. He glanced past Ruby, to the windows of her house. Nancy would be inside. Watching them? It would be hard, given the angle, but Matt was sure she'd manage.

He turned and glanced at his own house. The front window had the blinds closed. Imogen would be in bed, Ashley in her room.

'I shouldn't talk to you,' he said, keeping his voice low. He stepped towards the fence.

Ruby bit her lower lip. Matt could see the embarrassment once again, the anguish in her face. Did she feel as awkward as he did?

'I'm sorry,' she said.

'Me too,' he said. 'What your mum said, it was . . .'

'It's just Mum. It's nothing.'

'She was pretty mad for nothing.'

'Please don't be angry.' Ruby frowned. 'You heard what I told her. That's all it was. I didn't know what I'd said until she repeated it back to me.'

Matt held his tongue. There was no use getting angry at Ruby. She didn't deserve it. Her face was reddening by the second. But, on the other hand, he needed to make sure she knew not to say it again. This might be his only chance.

'Do you realise what it could do to me?' he said.

Ruby shrugged, puzzled.

'You're fifteen, Ruby,' he said. 'You understand? An accusation like that? It's against the law. You're a child.'

'I'm not a child, Matt.' Her expression fell. 'You're just like her.'

'No, no. That's not what I meant. In the eyes of the law, you're underage. It would mean extreme consequences for me. If what you said was true.'

Ruby paused. She understood. 'Oh,' she said. 'Yes.'

'Then you can see why I'm worried about standing here with you.'

Ruby swallowed. She looked hurt.

'So we can't talk? I thought we were friends.'

'We are,' he said.

'Mum got the wrong idea. She's overprotective. Ever since Dad died . . . my sickness, you know. It doesn't mean we can't—'

'I *do* know,' said Matt. 'And I understand, to an extent. I sympathise. But this isn't a joke, Ruby. If your mum persists with

182

these lies, my reputation could be ruined. My life. My marriage. People don't forgive things like this. I could be prosecuted.'

Ruby nodded. She stared at him for several moments; her eyes welled with tears. She stepped back from the fence, out of her hiding place. In full view now, she didn't seem to care.

'Fine,' she said. 'I get it. Leave me. I didn't have any friends before you, and I don't need any now. Just sod off and go back to your family, Matt.'

'Ruby, that's not . . .' But Ruby had already stomped off, heading around the back of her house. He heard the wooden gate close with a rattle. He stood for a moment, thinking how much better he could have handled the conversation, before deciding to remove himself from the driveway.

Getting the blame now from both Nancy and Ruby. Brilliant.

At least they were mad at him for different things.

And at least Imogen was on his side.

Instead of heading inside, he decided to take a quick walk around the block to clear his head. Perhaps when he got back, Ruby would have calmed down, and they could talk again.

Nancy

Change was inevitable, the season poised to fade as if it knew, signalling the transition. The deep heat of summer was coming to an end. Nancy took a deep breath before slamming her bedroom window shut, hoping the whole neighbourhood heard it.

It was worse than she'd thought, or ever imagined. Was this a parent's darkest nightmare? There were plenty to choose from, but this was surely amongst the most troubling. Nancy knew what she'd heard; there was no mistake, no dream, no invention. Ruby might have withdrawn into denial, but how was she supposed to process such an event? Despite her protestations of adulthood, she was fifteen years old – an adult in so many ways, but not in the ways that kept you safe.

Ruby begged and pleaded with her not to say or do anything more. Nancy held her tongue, but made no such promise. She needed time to consider her response – she'd been truthful about that. A police investigation, while delivering what Matthew deserved, was not necessarily in Ruby's best interests. Her privacy would be shattered, their lives exposed. Her precious daughter, already struggling to grow up, would have the remnants of her childhood stripped away by strangers. Their carefully balanced existence, which Nancy had cultivated over the years, would be destroyed.

And there was Imogen. Dear Imogen, another innocent in all of this. A new friend – a *close* friend. Nancy's natural inclination to protect her had grown, not diminished, in light of Ruby's accusation. What would Imogen do without her help? How could she cope, in her condition, carrying a new life, while her husband destroyed the sanctity of their marriage without a second glance?

What Imogen needed was protection. She needed Nancy, now more than ever, and Nancy would not abandon such a fragile soul in her time of need.

Nancy headed downstairs, opening the front door, treading the path until she could look up at Imogen's house.

'Mum?'

Nancy turned. Ruby stood in the doorway, still in her pyjamas, hair in a loose ponytail.

'What are you doing?' she asked.

Nancy smiled. 'Nothing, dear. Why don't you go back inside?'

'Please, Mum,' said Ruby. 'You've got it all wrong. I told you the truth.'

'I know you think you did.'

'It didn't happen, Mum. A stupid dream. It's embarrassing, but nothing, I promise. Let it go, please?'

Ruby's face twisted in anguish, in panic. Nancy saw the turmoil inside her daughter, and understood her desire to make it go away by pretending it never happened – lock it in a box, throw away the key. But it was still there, still lurking. You never knew what might open the box, or when.

185

'OK,' said Nancy, walking back up the path. 'If you're sure, dear.'

'I am.'

Ruby stepped backwards, steadying herself against the door. She put her hand to her mouth, taking a deep breath, ready to vomit. Slowly crouching, she dropped her head lower, practised, keeping the blood flowing, warding off the dizziness. Nancy hurried up to her. It often came on like this – rapid and acute, hitting Ruby mid-stride. The change in medication might have contributed, and Nancy made a mental note to alter the dose, even it out. She didn't want Ruby fainting at the top of the stairs, or at the side of the road. Managed properly, her condition should be controllable, predictable.

Ruby managed not to vomit, her face turning green in the process. Nancy took one of her hands; it was clammy and hot.

'Why don't you rest for a few minutes, get a drink of water? Perhaps we'll go for a walk or something when your head has cleared? It'll do you good. The weather's holding. It's beautiful out here.'

Ruby bit her bottom lip, in between blowing out in small pants. Nancy smiled, caressing her daughter's shoulder. 'Go on. I'm coming in now.'

She checked her watch. A quick walk with Ruby to make sure she was OK, then it would be time to pick up her medication, something she was forced to do every few days. Nancy mustn't be late – the collection window was small, and missing it would mean she couldn't mix the proper dosage.

She watched Ruby head up the stairs, her small figure twisting with each step. The thought of somebody touching that sick, delicate body made Nancy's blood boil, a rage she hadn't felt in a long while.

She stared at herself in the hallway mirror, adjusting her collar, moving a stray strand of hair back into place. The police and authorities had no place in their lives, but at the same time, Matthew must pay for what he did. If her accusation wasn't enough, and Ruby insisted on denying it, then it was up to Nancy to prove it.

She must show Imogen what Matthew was like, reveal his true colours, uncover his sordid deeds. That was the only way to protect Imogen, to protect Ruby, and to restore balance.

She had no choice but to get rid of Matthew.

Imogen

I stared at the inside of the toilet bowl, watching the water flush away my breakfast. The porcelain was sparkling – I'd bleached it about three times over the weekend, and once again this morning. I could probably lie my face against it, safe in the knowledge it would harbour fewer pathogens than my bedroom pillow.

I raised my head slowly. It thumped, a deep, nauseating pulse. Dehydration, my brain and skull screaming for some hydration.

Lifting myself off the floor, I crept back to the bedroom, pausing at the door to listen for Ashley. I could hear her singing to the cuddly toys she'd lined up for the day, in mock classroom style. Getting excited about real school, she was practising the register and how to sit still for more than five minutes. Despite my nausea, I laughed to myself, wincing as it echoed through my head.

The warm water from the glass beside my bed slipped down my throat. I waited a few seconds. It stayed down. Good. I lifted my feet and lay back.

Morning sickness . . . possibly. A bug or food poisoning, more likely. Or perhaps both – a perfect storm. I hadn't mentioned the bug to Matt, because he'd panic and quarantine the house, Ashley and himself. I figured if either of them was going to get it, they would have by now. I cleaned everything I touched, and myself, several times a day, keeping my distance from Ashley and asking Matt to prepare her breakfast and lunch in advance, to save me having to exert myself.

Whatever the cause, it would run its course and I would recover. My mind was too full of other things to worry about a minor bug.

I'd replayed Saturday to myself more times than I could remember, looking for holes, gaps, inconsistencies. I'd been awake for most of the last forty-eight hours. In the dead of night, I'd stared at Matt, picturing his face as Nancy shouted at him at our front door. I'd pictured him again at Nancy's house. I'd watched Ruby. I'd watched Ruby watching Matt, and I'd watched my husband staring at an attractive young girl.

Ruby's explanation made sense. Perfect? No. But reasonable. Nancy's behaviour *was* erratic, and I thought I could see it in her eyes, the deep anguish she must feel on a daily basis. The hurt, the regret, the weariness of living with the hand she'd been dealt. I saw it as Nancy's error, but I couldn't blame her for it.

Of course I compared it to before. London already seemed like such a long time ago, another lifetime. But that woman was altogether different, the situation so unlike this, I couldn't make it stick.

The thing is, rumours can destroy lives too. They can turn groups into warring factions, family members into defensive cadres. They can turn entire companies against one person. The truth gets lost, not having time to get its shoes on before the rumour has sprinted around every office, every cubicle, infecting every willing ear – of which there are many in a large city press. A rumour is like wildfire in the savannah of the modern office. Matt didn't stand a chance. Not when it was *her*.

The nausea rose once again. I swallowed it back, closing my eyes.

Let it go, Imogen. Let it all go. It's not the same. Matt is one of the good ones, and you know it.

I started to drift off, that delicious feeling of *almost sleep*, transient, warm and embracing. But my phone had other ideas, and it jolted me awake, vibrating across the bedside table before thudding on to the floor, where it continued its dance.

It took me a few seconds to grab it and focus on the screen.

'Mum,' I said.

'Imogen, darling. How are you feeling?'

'You know death?'

'Don't be funny.'

I huffed, lying on my side, still hanging half off the bed after grabbing the phone. I actually felt a little better in this position.

'It's just the morning sickness,' I said, not wanting her to worry unduly. 'Nothing I can't handle. Are you still coming this weekend?'

'Well, that's the thing, darling. Your father's back, it's getting worse – he's such a fool. He can hardly move.'

'He needs to keep moving, though, Mum. Bad backs need movement.'

'I know, darling, but it's the journey. He can't sit in the car without yelping like a child. We'll have to wait – maybe in a few weeks?'

'I guess.' I'd been looking forward to seeing her, more than

I realised. Some motherly support. A shoulder to cry on, if the mood so took me.

'Is something wrong? You sound upset.'

I *was* upset. Tired, sick, full of angst. But if I told Mum, she'd race down here, leaving poor dad on his own. She'd quiz me, and I'd have no answers to give. I wasn't ready to share the events of the last few days. The thought of it horrified me.

'I was just looking forward to seeing you,' I said.

'Me too. We'll be there, darling, but not until your father can stand upright.'

I heard a bang at the front door.

'Do you need to get that?'

'Mmm.' I was quite comfortable face down on the bed. Another knock. I could shout at Ashley to get it, but she struggled with the lock. Besides, she was still too young to open our door to strangers, even in our secure little community.

'Yes,' I said. 'Call me?'

'I will. Love you, Imogen.'

'You too, Mum.'

It took me a while to push myself upright. I let my blood pressure adjust before standing and shuffling towards the stairs.

I opened the door.

'Imogen.'

'Nancy.' She looked markedly different to the last time we'd spoken. Her composure was back, her posture rigidly proper. Motherly, like she'd heard my phone call and arrived as a substitute.

'How are you feeling?' she said.

'I . . .' I wasn't sure what to say. Did we act like nothing had happened? That would be absurd.

'I know what you're thinking,' she said, pausing to adjust her skirt. 'And I must admit it was very hard for me to come over today. But I want to show you we're still friends. Whatever Matt did—'

'He didn't, Nancy.'

She paused, forcing her mouth into a smile. She held it for a few moments, but I made no move to back down. I couldn't do this, not if she thought Matt was capable of such things. It wouldn't work.

'OK,' she said, hands out in submission. 'I was angry. Perhaps I got the wrong end of the stick.'

I paused. 'You mean it?'

She took my hands in hers, nodding. 'I think it might have been an honest misunderstanding. I saw red. I'm sorry.'

There it was. That's all I wanted. Now I could welcome her in again. My relief was overwhelming.

'You reacted as any mother would,' I said. 'I don't blame you for storming around here.'

'I was just so . . .'

'Shocked?' I said. 'Of course you were.'

'And Ruby – she can be so . . . I don't know. Sometimes I think I hardly know her. Her dreams are . . . well, her business.'

'Teenagers.'

Nancy nodded. Her face softened. 'I feel like an idiot,' she said.

'Don't,' I said, grabbing her hand. We shared a moment; two mothers coming together in understanding. 'You'll come in?'

'I was intending to, yes,' she said, 'to look after you for the day.'

'Oh, that's so kind.' I wondered whether to decline, but to be honest I welcomed the company. 'I'll make you a drink.'

'No, you won't,' she said, eyeing me up and down. 'Forgive me, Imogen, but you look like hell. You're green. Go to bed.'

I sagged a little in relief, realising even this short conversation had worn me out. It was worth having, though. Peace after the storm.

'I'll make you something.' She waved her handbag at me. 'I've got some magic remedies in here. They'll help to rehydrate you, reduce the nausea.'

'You really don't need to—'

'Nonsense,' she said. 'It's what friends do. Now go.' She pointed at the staircase.

I shuffled up the stairs, pausing halfway. Nancy was already in the kitchen. I heard her filling the kettle, the clink of mugs and the cutlery drawer. I couldn't resist a smile. All was not lost. I still had my new friend. And she'd look after me, like she said she would.

'Does Ash need anything?' she called.

'No,' I called back.

'I'll make her some juice,' said Nancy. 'Is she allowed biscuits?'

I heard the tin open. 'Just one.' The thought of biscuits made my stomach howl. It was so empty, but I wasn't sure if it could handle one yet.

The blender started up, whirring away. Five minutes later, Nancy crept into the bedroom and laid out a tray on the bed. She'd made another of her smoothies – green liquid, this time in one of our tall glasses, next to a mug of steaming water with lemon and ginger. A plate with crackers and a bunch of red grapes finished off the feast.

My mouth watered. I was tucked up, duvet to my chest, a book by my side. I felt a little awkward, like a child. A slight pang of guilt – this should be my mother, again. If I was in London, it would be.

Nancy patted the duvet down, adjusting it at the corners, smoothing it over my legs. She stood back and watched me for a moment, then moved the tray a few inches towards me.

'Eat and drink everything,' she said, 'then get some sleep. I'll be back to check on you in an hour.'

She clasped her hands together, apparently happy with everything, and winked at me, before turning and leaving the room.

Matt

Matt stared out of his office window. Mondays used to be his favourite. He'd avoid the usual office depressives who wandered around groaning at the thought of another week. He saw it as the beginning of opportunity. A breaking story, an exciting lead. A chance to deliver something new. That was his rule.

Today he struggled to keep it. The desperate feeling, which had lurked all weekend, remained. They'd veered off already; his careful planning of a new life had been disrupted.

He yawned, checking the clock. Eleven a.m. He'd been awake most of the night with Imogen, whose sickness seemed to have reached a whole new level. She was dry-retching by 3 a.m., unable to keep even water down. She insisted Matt go into work, despite his protests that he should be by her bedside. She'd even refused the doctor, but had agreed that Matt could call if things hadn't improved within twenty-four hours. He gave her a bunch of useless advice about staying hydrated – *I'm a nurse, Matt, I know!* – but obeyed her wishes.

'Matt?'

Shelley's head appeared at the doorway.

He turned to her, struggling to focus.

'In the land of the living?'

'Yes. Sorry. Away with the fairies.'

Shelley smiled, but it was strained. 'I've noticed.'

Matt caught her tone. 'I'm sorry,' he said. 'It's the morning sickness . . . I'm not getting a lot of sleep.'

Shelley nodded. He'd told her about the pregnancy and about Imogen's persistent sickness – possibly spreading the baby news earlier than he should, but hoping it might give him a bit of leeway. She'd offered her congratulations and her sympathy, but Matt got the impression it was limited. Shelley didn't have kids and didn't seem too interested in his procreation woes.

'The review – you said it would be with me Friday?'

Matt nodded slowly. The review. The one he hadn't written yet.

'End of the day?' he offered.

She shrugged. 'It's your review, Matt. The sooner you do it, the sooner I can hand over part of the day-to-day business to you. It's what you're here for.'

Shelley was no-nonsense. He liked and respected her for it. But couldn't she relax it for a few days? If she'd known the weekend he'd had, perhaps she'd understand. Or perhaps she wouldn't.

She left, giving Matt a look. *The* look. The one that says your brief honeymoon period is almost over, and you'd better be ready.

He would be ready. This was only a blip. A stupid, interfering neighbour, who would hopefully crawl away and darken his life no more.

Taking a deep breath, he opened a blank document and started collating the information he'd need. Shelley would get her review, it would be great, and his work here wouldn't be in question. He spent the next few hours absorbed in his work. He took a few minutes' break at 3 p.m., picked up his phone and dialled.

'Hi, how are you feeling?' he said.

'Imogen is sleeping.'

Matt pulled the phone away, checked the screen.

'Nancy?'

'Yes. It's me.'

'What? Why have you got Imogen's phone?'

'I told you, she's sleeping.'

'But—'

'Imogen needed somebody to look after her, and seeing as you're getting on with your week as if nothing's wrong, I thought I'd do it.' Nancy's tone was icy, hissing down the phone at him.

'Now hang on a minute,' he said. 'I had to come into the office. Imogen said she was fine. I was planning on calling the doctor later—'

'No need,' said Nancy. 'I've already spoken to Dr Padhir – she said it was a gastro bug doing the rounds. Imogen needs TLC, nothing more.'

'And I suppose you'll give it to her?' Matt caught himself. Getting angry on the phone wouldn't help. But what the hell was she playing at? A couple of days ago she was accusing him of abuse, and now she was in his house.

'What do you want, Nancy?'

'From you, Matthew? Nothing. But Imogen needs me and

197

I'm her friend. I'll tend to her while she's sick, and I'll be gone by the time you get home.'

Matt struggled to respond. Was she serious? Was he that blind to their friendship? Were they *that* close? How could they be, after what she'd said?

'OK,' he said. 'OK, Nancy. If Imogen wants you there, there's not much for me to say, is there?'

'No, Matthew. There isn't.'

'Then I presume this means you admit you made a mistake on Saturday? This is your way of apologising? Your penance?'

'You'll presume no such thing,' she said, her voice lowering in volume. 'I said I knew what you'd done, and I still want you to stay away from my daughter.'

'It's a lie!' Matt shouted, checking himself, glancing through the glass at the office. One of his reporters raised her head, saw Matt staring and quickly lowered it again.

'Don't you dare shout at me, Matthew,' said Nancy. 'Never. I knew it from the moment I saw you—'

'What?' he said. 'What did you *know*?'

'I know Imogen deserves much better than you can give her. She was upset when we first met and she's no better now. I'm not going to let her suffer during her pregnancy because you're useless and can't be bothered to care for her in her time of need.'

'I—'

'This conversation is over. Just know I'm watching you.'

She hung up the phone. Matt stared gobsmacked at the screen. The . . . How fucking dare she?! Useless? He gripped his mobile and slammed it on the desk, not caring this time who heard.

His thumb hovered on the redial button. Did he want to

speak to her again, or speak to Imogen? Would she even *let* him speak to his wife?

Matt breathed out, his heart thudding, a distinct disquiet snaking from his gut and circling his chest. He couldn't leave the office, not until he'd finished Shelley's bloody report. It took him the best part of the hour to calm himself, trying to focus on his rather sub-par work, finishing it at 5 p.m. and emailing it off.

He grabbed his bag and coat. Walking back to his car, his head spun – confusion, frustration, and still the anger. Nancy hadn't changed her tune, and their conversation had left him with an odd, lingering sensation of unease. The emphasis she'd placed on Imogen's needs, his failures as a husband, her ongoing suspicion of him and Ruby.

Why not go to the police, if she was so sure? Because of Imogen, like she said? Or because she had no evidence? The thought still terrified him, but Ruby would tell an altogether different story, one that would exonerate him.

He drove home in silence, a dull stress headache starting to pound, distorting his vision, creating a swirl of anxiety from which he could see no immediate escape.

Matt

Matt stared at his front door, wondering what would greet him. He glanced across at Nancy's immaculate front garden, up at her immaculate house. All quiet. No sign of Ruby.

Further down the road, a grey-haired man stood on the pavement in wellington boots and dungarees, trimming his hedge. He glanced at Matt, tipped an imaginary hat to him, but immediately turned away, continuing his chores, paying no attention to his neighbour. Matt watched him for a few moments before opening the door.

'It's me,' he called from the hallway, somewhat tentative. Hearing no reply, he crept up the stairs. As he reached the bedroom, he heard singing, soft tones, giggling. He opened the door to find Imogen sitting up in bed with Ashley. They were watching a video on his laptop, singing along.

'Daddy!' Ashley put her hand up for a high five, keeping her eyes on the video.

Matt glanced towards the en suite.

'Nancy here?' he said.

Imogen shook her head. 'She left an hour or so ago.'

'She made me lunch,' said Ashley. 'Then I had four biscuits.'

Matt smiled and ruffled her hair. 'How are you feeling?' he said to Imogen.

Imogen shrugged. He could see she was exhausted. Her skin was pale and clammy. She placed her hands over her stomach.

'I felt a little better earlier. Nancy, bless her, made me some food. But it's still lingering. Poor baby, being thrown around every time I vomit.'

Matt glanced at Ash. 'Hey, how about you go and play in your room for a few minutes? I need to speak to Mummy.'

Ash nodded, tearing her eyes from the screen. She closed the laptop and scampered off.

Matt put his hand on top of Imogen's. 'Baby is OK?'

She smiled. 'It'll take more than a sick bug to hurt her. Or him.'

Matt nodded. He relaxed a little. The benefits of having a nurse in the family. He had to remember what was important right now.

'I called earlier,' he said.

'Oh, sorry. I must have been asleep.'

'Nancy answered.'

'Oh, good.'

'Is it?'

Imogen frowned. 'You know she admitted she'd made a mistake?'

That was news to him. 'When did she say that?' It didn't tally with the conversation he'd had with her.

'This morning. We had a heart-to-heart.'

'She said she was wrong? It was a lie? That she was planning on apologising to me?'

Imogen shook her head. 'I . . . I think she's embarrassed. Look,

201

this is her daughter, Matt. She overreacted to something and she's sorry, but please don't push her. She has a lot to deal with.'

'*She* has a lot? Christ . . .'

Maybe Nancy was too stubborn to admit to him she was wrong. Perhaps she just didn't like him, and for that reason still didn't want him near Ruby. Hurtful in its own right, but as long as the accusation went no further, could he live with it?

His eyes landed on the laundry basket in the corner of the room. It was stacked with folded shirts. Even the underwear was neatly pressed. He and Imogen never folded their clothes straight out of the dryer.

Imogen followed his puzzled gaze.

'Nancy,' she said. 'She insisted.'

Matt almost laughed with the absurdity of it. The thought of Nancy folding his underwear after what she'd said was bizarre.

He sighed, the stress fading a fraction.

'I don't get it,' he said, 'your friendship. I'm not trying to spoil it. But you can understand why I'm struggling?'

Imogen gave him a small smile. She patted his hands. 'I understand. And our friendship relied on her admitting she'd made a mistake. I took your side, Matt. You know that, right?'

Matt leaned in and kissed her forehead.

'So,' he said, pulling away. 'Do I need to call the doctor? Nancy said she already had, but . . .'

'No need,' said Imogen. 'Not today. I'll see how things go over the next forty-eight hours. Trust me.'

He put his hands up in submission. 'OK. Dinner?'

Imogen pulled a face.

'I'll make Ash something, perhaps bring you something later?'

Imogen nodded. She slid back under the covers, pulling them to her chin.

'Love you, Matt,' she said.

They held each other's gaze for a moment.

'Love you, too,' he said.

Matt cleared the dishes, allowing Ash some extra TV time while he sat at the kitchen worktop to keep an eye on her. He grabbed his laptop, noticing the battery was almost empty – he'd made the mistake of sharing his login, and now his laptop seemed to disappear frequently and get returned to him powerless and covered in crumbs. He'd get a second one when he had some spare cash – something that looked unlikely in the foreseeable future. Another pang of guilt . . . He pushed it away.

He fired up the browser, trying to count the number of days Imogen had been sick. He trusted her, and the GP, but was still a little concerned. She looked awful, hardly keeping any food down. How long could she go on like this?

He searched her symptoms, worried at the results. Most seemed to suggest a GP visit, especially when pregnant. It looked like nothing more than a gastro bug, but it was better to be sure. He'd nag Imogen again tomorrow, but it was her body, her call.

As he closed the browser, a pop-up appeared, filling the screen. Matt blinked, shocked. The window advertised a hard-core pornography site, a video playing in the centre.

He glanced up, panicking that Ashley may have seen or heard it. She wasn't allowed unattended on the laptop, as a rule, but he closed the window and checked the browser history, to be sure.

As he scanned the day's activity, his heart began to race.

He pulled the laptop closer and refreshed the list, confused at what he saw, the times and dates displayed next to the website addresses.

Several recognisable porn sites – he was hardly an addict, but knew what YouPorn.com was – along with a dozen or so XXX-titled websites. He paused, trying to be rational. This wasn't him, and unless he didn't know Imogen at all, it wasn't her either. They were far from prudes, and Imogen had admitted to watching porn before – who hadn't? – but not recently, and surely not in her current health.

He glanced at Ashley again, surrounded by her toys, watching a cartoon. Perhaps she'd done it by mistake – but wouldn't she have asked him or Imogen what it was? His heart thumped. Was this his fault? He'd never put parental controls on his own laptop. Why would he need to? *Because you share your laptop with the family, Matt. That's why.*

It wasn't just one site. He counted fifteen, and as he scrolled, his discomfort increased. The names of the sites were niche, specialist. Three claiming to be teen porn.

The last two: BarelyLegalXXX and SchoolGirlLovers.

Matt's hand shook. He stared at the URLs. What the fuck? He hit delete, one at a time, until they were all gone.

He sifted through the previous days and weeks – nothing. It was only today.

Was there anything else? He didn't know, and didn't know who to ask. He was reluctant to google it. When he'd finished, he closed the lid.

'Ash,' he called, 'can I ask you something?'

Ashley paused her cartoon and turned her head.

'Did you go on Daddy's laptop today?'

She nodded. 'With Mummy.'

'Not on your own?'

Ash shook her head. 'I'm not allowed. Mummy said so.'

Matt nodded, smiling. 'Good girl. You didn't sneak on here at all? I won't be mad, I just want to know if there's anything I need to keep open, perhaps something you were looking at.'

Ash shook her head again. 'I promise, Daddy. Mummy said I'm not allowed.'

'OK, sweetie. You can keep watching your cartoon.'

Matt paused for a moment before opening the laptop again. He found the virus scanner. That was the most likely candidate, wasn't it? He waited while the progress bar completed.

When it hit one hundred percent, he let out a huge sigh of relief. Bingo. The virus checker popped up three alerts. He didn't understand the details, but it recommended removing the offending software. He agreed, hit a few buttons, and watched as it announced the laptop was now virus-free.

Panic over. Weird, but explained.

He poured a glass of water and headed into the garden for some air, sliding the glass door behind him. It stuck, grinding to a halt, making a scraping sound. Imogen had pestered him about it – the rail was broken and the door kept jamming either open or shut. She kept complaining that, along with the broken utility door, the whole back of the house was locked in – she had to go out of the front door to get to the back garden. Not ideal for Jake, and rather unsafe for Ash.

He stared at it for a few moments. Before they'd moved, he'd looked forward to doing DIY around the house, fixing these sorts of problems. The doors, the loose floorboards, the boiler, which failed every few days before springing into life again, but would cost more to fix than all the money in all of their bank accounts combined.

But the problems he had right now were rather more pressing. The house could wait.

The unease persisted – too much going on, too much to process. He worried for Imogen, and he worried for himself. But he wouldn't let it fail. He'd come too far.

Way too far.

Imogen

I knew it before I saw the evidence. A distinct shifting, wrenching inside, not just my body, but my mind.

I sat beside the toilet bowl and waited for a few moments, the tears forming in my eyes, trying not to panic. What would I tell a patient? *Get yourself checked out. It might not be what you think.* Except I was almost certain. The cramping and pain were much lower today, the physical signs like a checklist. I ticked all of them.

I gave myself a few moments, a mere few breaths to settle the waves of anxiety and nausea that battled each other for dominance, oblivious to the host they were damaging so badly.

I vomited again, heaving until I was exhausted, slumping back against the wall. Matt would be home from work any minute. It had taken three calls before he picked up, flustered, distracted. I hadn't given him much detail, but enough to get him moving.

I heard the door slam. It was time to go. Pushing myself to my feet, I washed my face in the basin, cursing as the water ran cold. That fucking boiler again.

'Matt?' I heard the desperation in my own voice. I pushed open the bathroom door.

'Matt?'

'Yes?' he called up from the hallway.

'Something's wrong, Matt. With the baby. I think ... Please come up here. I need to go to the hospital.'

I called Nancy once I was dressed, despite Matt's protestations. I didn't want to drag Ash to the hospital and I was sure Nancy would oblige. She arrived within a few minutes, made up and dressed in her usual formal skirt and shirt combination. For once I didn't care what I looked like, my jogging bottoms and grubby hoodie hanging off my body, my trainers still muddy from a run a few weeks ago.

Matt and Nancy had a brief stand-off at the door before she swished straight past him, patting my arm. 'Go,' she said. 'Ashley will be fine. I'll make her lunch and take her to my place. Ruby and I can read with her. She can stay over if she needs to.'

I nodded my thanks and stood on the porch while Matt started the car, swearing under his breath, but knowing it was the wrong time to object. I left Nancy in the kitchen, and could already hear her tidying, emptying the dishwasher, placing the crockery back into the cupboards.

Matt ran around to the passenger door and flung it open. Our eyes met and I nodded. We drove the twenty minutes to the hospital in silence, my hands on my stomach.

We were in the maternity ward at the Royal Surrey Hospital for two hours, and then they said I could go home.

I'd need to go back in a week or so for a further examination. The process was clinical, exactly as I was used to. Except it had never happened to me before, and my stoic nursing persona disappeared in a wave of guilt and tears. The midwife held my hand. Her hands were soft and experienced.

One in five, they said, at my age. It was not extraordinary, and there was no reason to suspect it would affect future pregnancies. Future. As if this one was already in the past. Gone, no more than an entry in my medical record. A few words, nothing more.

I told them about the vomiting – the gastric bug that had lingered for over a week now with no relief. They checked my vitals again – blood pressure a little low. They couldn't rule out a connection between the bug and the miscarriage, but it was unlikely. Most probable was a severe strain of norovirus. Nevertheless, they took some bloods for analysis. They told me to see my GP to get the results and book further tests to rule out anything else.

I was given three leaflets on the way out. The top one was called *Following Your Loss*. The obstetrician said she'd write to my GP and inform them of today's event.

Today's event: I lost my baby.

There wasn't much else to say.

Matt drove. I stared out of the passenger window. He'd behaved as I needed him to behave – not asking stupid questions, or talking over me, or the midwives. He'd assumed the supporting role, sitting and listening, holding my hand at the right time, searching my face for signs he should do more or less. I could see the tears forming in his eyes, but he forced them away.

I wouldn't have minded if he'd cried. At least I could see he wanted to. It was reassuring – we were both in this together. We'd both had an element of our future ripped away in front of our eyes.

I'd called my mum while Matt went to fetch the car. She offered all the love I needed, but I stopped her short of driving down to see me. She meant well, but I knew she'd fuss over me – like any mother would – and Matt would be ushered to one side. I needed this to be just me and Matt, at least for now – we'd get through this like we got through everything else. It was important he got a chance to do this.

I reached over and put my hand on his forearm, feeling the slight vibrations through the steering wheel. He placed his other hand over mine, gave it a squeeze as we drifted along the country roads. The tail end of summer. The height of happiness, on any other day.

Yes, we were both in this together.

I pulled my hand away as a wave of nausea hit. I reached for the plastic bag I'd taken to carrying in my handbag.

'Do you want to stop?' said Matt.

'No. Let's get home.' I held the bag on my lap, feeling my stomach lurching and churning, the added stress mixing a perfect storm of gastric trauma. I had no doubt it would all come out as soon as we got home.

I leaned back, trying to get comfortable, closing my eyes, pushing my face into the side of the seat.

But then something unexpected hit me:

I froze, calculating. I took a deep breath, drawing the scent in through my nostrils. It wasn't my imagination. My stomach churned, the nausea surging, and I racked my brain for a rational explanation.

I could smell perfume.

I could smell Calvin Klein perfume on the car seat.

Matt

Matt stared at the shelves in aisle four, forgetting what he was looking for. His mind was close to mush, dissolving under pressure. He checked his list. Pasta. Penne. Spaghetti. Get the right brand otherwise Ash won't eat it. She'll know.

He'd been in the supermarket for almost an hour. Imogen was tucked in bed. Nancy had gone home without a word or so much as a glance at Matt. He'd heard her and Imogen whispering, but decided not to pry. He'd kissed Imogen, assured her he was there, whatever she needed.

Imogen had pushed him away. Her eyes were hollow, confused, her grief immediate and raw. It looked like she wanted to talk, but then she clammed up. She said she needed space, so he gave it to her.

He'd cried in the car. Not a lot – he didn't know how to, these days. But the reality hit him as he sat in a traffic jam, and he mourned the loss, feeling his own surge of grief, begging it not to overcome him. It was another level, different to anything he'd experienced before.

The anger circled, looking for a target. The midwife had said there was nobody to blame for what happened, but Matt wasn't convinced. Stress wasn't a factor – it said so in one of the leaflets – yet it couldn't help, could it? And Imogen's well-being had taken a hammering in the last few days.

Matt stared at an old man halfway along the aisle, struggling with a large tin of tomato sauce on the top shelf. He had a strange vision of the tin falling and hitting the man in the forehead, knocking him out cold. He frowned, stepping forward. As he got closer, he recognised him.

'Chris,' said Matt. 'Let me get that for you.'

'Damn shoulders,' said Chris, letting go and stepping back. 'I'm not as flexible as I used to be.'

Matt nudged the tin off the edge of the shelf and dropped it into Chris's trolley. A month's supply of pasta sauce in one tin, by the look of it.

'Thanks,' said Chris.

'It's what neighbours do,' said Matt.

Chris laughed. It came out as a wheeze, with a small cough at the end. 'You're from London, right?'

Matt nodded.

'I used to live in London,' said Chris. 'Hackney.' He looked wistful. 'But that was a long time ago.' He blinked a few times, peering at Matt. 'Are you OK?'

Matt tried to smile and failed. His shoulders sagged.

'Not really,' he said, and in a rare outburst, he proceeded to tell Chris what had happened, the trip to the hospital, the result. He realised he hadn't told anybody else yet, not even Liv. This old man was the first.

'Oh my goodness,' said Chris. 'I'm so sorry, Matt. Life's a cruel bastard sometimes. How is Imogen?'

'Holding up,' said Matt. 'She's stronger than me. You wouldn't catch her blubbing to strangers in the supermarket, for example.'

Chris offered a sympathetic smile.

'I didn't mean ... that you're a complete stranger,' added Matt. 'But we don't know anybody well yet. Apart from Nancy, of course.'

Chris's smile faltered. 'Nancy?' he said.

'Yes, and her daughter. My wife has hit it off with her. They get on like a house on fire.' Matt shrugged.

Chris narrowed his eyes. His face twisted in worry.

'They're friends?' said Chris. 'Already?'

Something in Chris's eyes bothered Matt. 'How well do you know her?' he asked. Chris hadn't appeared to be friendly with Nancy, based on the brief encounter he'd witnessed at the fundraiser, but he couldn't be sure.

Chris glanced both ways along the aisle. 'Quite well ... My wife knew her better. I—'

Matt's phone buzzed. 'Sorry,' he said, pulling it out of his pocket. 'Imogen, asking for more supplies.' He glanced up. 'Do you know where the nearest pharmacy is?'

'Along the street, halfway.' Chris's eyes darkened. He looked puzzled. Matt could see the perspiration forming on his forehead; his face was flushed.

'Are you OK, Chris?'

Chris stared at him. He seemed to come out of his trance. 'Matt, I—'

'Chris.' A new voice, shrill and unmistakable. They both turned to find Nancy standing behind them. Her trolley was empty. She fixed Matt with an icy smile before turning to Chris.

'Out again on your own?' she said.

213

Chris appeared to shrink on the spot.

'Why shouldn't he be?' said Matt, matching Nancy's stare, daring himself. 'What's it got to do with you?'

What were the chances of Nancy being here at the same time? True, there was only one supermarket near the village, but the timing was an incredible coincidence.

Nancy placed a hand to her chest. 'I look out for my neighbours, Matthew. I just worry, that's all.'

Matt glanced at Chris, whose eyes were downturned, his hands clasped together.

'He looks OK to me,' said Matt. 'What brings you out at this time, Nancy?'

Nancy ignored his question. 'I'm sure Chris doesn't want me contacting social services again,' she said. 'I know how he loves his independence, remaining in our road, in that big house, all on his own.'

Chris shuffled back, putting his hands on his trolley.

'It would be a shame if it all fell apart,' Nancy continued, 'so I look out for him, Matthew, to ensure that doesn't happen.'

'I see,' said Matt, witnessing the veiled threat, confused, but feeling his hackles rise. Chris appeared to be no more than a sweet old man. What did Nancy have over him? 'Sorry, Nancy, but I don't—'

'It's OK, Matt,' said Chris. 'Nancy's right. I should get home. Keep myself safe.'

Matt paused. He saw the warning in Nancy's eyes. She tilted her head, watching him, and his own predicament rose to the fore. Would sticking up for Chris provoke Nancy even further?

Hard though it was, he bit his tongue. 'I'll see you again soon,' he said to Chris.

Chris nodded, obviously keen to escape. 'Stay safe,' he added, as he walked towards the checkouts, his old legs shuffling the trolley forward.

Matt turned, but Nancy was already gone. All he saw was the swish of her skirt as she disappeared into the next aisle.

Matt's frustration increased on the drive home. He felt like he should have done more, stuck up for Chris, and yet he had no idea what was going on. It was possible Nancy was right, even though she had a harsh way of putting it. Chris *could* be vulnerable, prone to falls, a danger to himself. Was Nancy, in fact, keeping him safe?

As he pulled into the drive, he figured he'd have to leave it. He had too much going on right now to deal with Chris. Whatever his battle with Nancy, Matt would have to let him fight it himself. There was only so much energy to go around. Matt was almost out.

He took a couple of days out of the office. Imogen said she didn't need a nurse, insisting she wanted some space, her mood plummeting. Matt stayed in the study, trying to get some work done, failing to concentrate on anything for long enough to make a dent in it.

On the third day, he entered the kitchen to find Imogen on the phone. She padded towards him in her slippers, sliding on the bare wood. He reached out to her and she leaned in, gave him a brief hug, turning her head away from him as she passed.

'OK,' she said. 'Thank you for letting me know.'

She hung up and turned to him. Her face looked clammy, her hair clean but limp. She'd already lost a little weight in the last few days – he could see it in her face, her neck. His poor Imogen, suffering so terribly.

'That was the GP surgery,' she said. 'The bloods they took at the hospital were clear.'

'Good news,' said Matt, 'right?'

'Well . . . I was expecting it to show a common strain of something. This means I have to go and have further blood tests, to rule out anything more serious.'

'More serious?'

'I'm sure it's not,' said Imogen. She huffed. 'But they want to check.'

'When? I can take you now? Tomorrow?'

Imogen shook her head. 'It's not urgent. I'll go in a few days.'

Matt started to protest, but something in Imogen's expression stopped him. She walked through to the living room and slumped into the recliner, tapping at her phone.

'How are *you* feeling?' she said, without looking up.

Matt stood in the doorway, a little surprised. 'I'm OK,' he said. 'I'm more worried about you. You've been through a lot.'

'So have you.'

'I . . . well. Yes.'

'This business with Ruby.' She glanced at Matt, peering at him, her thumb still on the screen of her phone. She paused. 'Are you still angry?'

He nodded, a little unnerved at the way Imogen was staring. It must be tiredness, he thought, and she was barely eating. All these pressures battling with each other, and now the miscarriage to kick her when she was at her lowest.

'I'm angry,' he said. A few days had hardly cured him of that. 'Of course I am.'

'Scared?'

'Well.' It was a strange thing to say. 'I . . . no, I guess a little. To be honest I've hardly thought about it since . . .' He glanced at her stomach. 'There have been more important things to think about.'

Imogen followed his gaze. They both stared at her tummy, where their new baby should be growing. Imogen turned away, sniffing.

'It'll blow over,' said Matt. 'You said yourself, Nancy knows she's in the wrong. It's only a matter of time.' He said it without conviction. Nancy may have admitted it to Imogen, but she sure as hell didn't believe it.

'I hope you're right,' she said.

Matt stepped forward, perching on the arm of the sofa. 'Why? Has Nancy said anything else?'

'No,' said Imogen. 'Why would she?'

'I don't know. You seem . . .'

'What do I seem?'

Matt paused. 'I thought we were over it.'

'*Over* it?' Imogen dropped her phone to her lap.

'I mean we'd discussed it, exposed it for what it was – a *lie*. Nancy told you as much.'

Imogen's face became unreadable. Her chest rose and fell, shaking, upset.

'Christ, Imogen,' said Matt. 'Do you want to discuss it all again?'

'I don't want to discuss it,' said Imogen. 'I don't know what I want. I'm hurting, Matt. All of this . . .' She put her hand to her mouth. 'And this *fucking* nausea. It's relentless.' A tear escaped; she wiped it on her sleeve.

217

Matt nodded. He saw the turmoil in her eyes. Those eyes he loved so much, and hated to see hurting. How much could a person take in such a short space of time? Nancy, Ruby, the baby, the sickness. He wished he could go back to the first day they'd moved in, to do things differently, to undo whatever path had taken them this way.

Imogen remained slumped, spinning her phone in her hands. She looked at him. Their eyes met. He must have projected something, or perhaps she just knew him so well.

'Shit just happens,' she said.

He nodded. 'It does.' He smiled. 'And we've had more than our fair share in the last few weeks, haven't we?'

Imogen offered a small smile. Her eyes were still wet, but she relaxed a fraction. Whatever it was, it seemed to have passed.

'You know, I wish I'd never asked Ruby to babysit that time,' he said, sliding off the arm of the sofa. He meant it in a light-hearted way, and Imogen's smile widened, before disappearing altogether.

'What do you mean?' she said.

'I . . . sorry. Bad taste.'

Imogen stared at him for a few moments. 'I thought Nancy offered.'

'What?'

'To babysit. I thought Nancy offered, not the other way around.'

Matt chuckled. He shook his head, feeling his cheeks flushing. He waited until they settled. A strange detail to pick up on. Did it matter? 'Yes. Sorry,' he said. 'You're right. She did.'

Imogen didn't respond. She turned her eyes downwards, keeping them on her phone. She took a deep breath. 'Matt, what—'

'Daddy!' Ashley bounced into the room, leaping into his arms. He grabbed her and swung her into a hug. She planted a kiss on his cheek and nuzzled his neck.

'I'm hungry,' she said. 'Can we have dinner now?'

Matt glanced down at Imogen. She closed her mouth and nodded, staring at her phone, scrolling aimlessly, clearly annoyed with him, and about to tell him as much. It was a bad joke, on reflection. Perhaps it was best to give her a bit of space. He'd apologise later, when Ash was in bed.

'Sure thing,' he said, swinging Ash on to his shoulders. 'Let's go.'

Imogen

'I'm not sure, Imogen,' said Claire. 'I'm really not sure. Hang on a sec.'

I heard my best mate stomping around on the other end of the phone. Since our university days, she'd been my sensible friend, my confidante, and my go-to for all legal matters. I heard her pull the phone away to speak to Thomas, her two-year-old. I could imagine her juggling him in one arm while preparing her legal casework in the other, simultaneously maintaining a perfect home in the centre of London. Living the dream – as long as the dream meant working sixty-hour weeks at a city law firm. However, I couldn't talk. My nursing had often surpassed that count. We used to compete – see whose blood pressure was the highest at the end of the week. I smiled at the thought, despite it all.

I was conscious I'd been neglecting my friends. The ones I'd preserved after leaving London were still there – Siobhan was still in publishing and Cara was jumping from one art gallery to the next seeking meaningful employment, but their messages only surfaced memories of a time I wanted to forget, which wasn't fair, because they'd helped me move on. I responded, promising to call, to meet up, but the truth was I liked the space of Albury – the separation from my past. If that's what I had.

It was Friday afternoon. The week had passed in a flash, the nausea surging and waning, much like the grief. But wrapped around all of my thoughts were the disturbing tendrils of suspicion creeping out once again, snaking upwards, focusing my attention on things I didn't want to see.

I hadn't summoned the energy to challenge Matt again – to unstitch the freshly closed wound, to poke around one more time, *just to be sure.*

I couldn't talk to Nancy, not about this. She'd given an open offer to talk about the miscarriage, and I'd seen her a few times in the week for coffee, but not *this.* And I didn't want to talk to my parents. Claire was one of the few people I trusted not to say, 'I *told* you!'

I opened my mail while I waited. A letter from the doctor confirmed my blood test appointment for the following week. I'd surrendered, the persistence of my illness starting to worry me. It was no worse, no better, the nausea and vomiting becoming a twice daily occurrence, draining me for hours before relenting. I could handle all manner of minor symptoms, but this . . . this was something else. I had visions of a major diagnosis, something I'd missed for years. I needed to know, to put my mind at rest; to know if the miscarriage was caused by something more sinister than chance. I resisted searching online. A google diagnosis would not help my already fractured mood.

The next letter was from Ash's school. She started in a couple of weeks. I still needed to provide her birth certificate (which box would I find that in?), confirm hot dinners or packed lunch, and buy her uniform. I smiled at the small hedgehog in the corner of the paper. I wish all demand letters were so cute.

'Sorry,' said Claire. 'He's being a little shit today.'

I laughed. Claire was the most devoted mum I knew, yet she loved to describe her darlings in the bluntest of terms.

'But back to you. Listen . . .' I heard her sucking in her breath. 'I honestly don't know what to say. You say you believe him?'

My turn to pause. 'I do.'

'Hmm.'

I'd need to do better than that with Claire. She could smell a lie from fifty miles away, even over the phone. 'But it's gone no further?'

'The mother, Nancy, says she made a mistake.'

'And the daughter? The girl?'

'Same.'

'Then that's the end of it. Look, it's not my area, Immy. I can speak to my friend Kyle – he works at a specialist law firm.'

'No. Don't do that,' I said. The fewer people who knew, the better, however irrational that sounded. 'I wanted . . . I'm not sure what I wanted.'

'You wanted me to tell you you're not going mad for having doubts. You believe him. Great. But given the year you've had, you'd be forgiven for questioning it.'

'So am I? Mad?'

'No.'

She sniffed, kept her silence. Claire was good at silences. She always won.

'What would you do?' I said, knowing Claire would have strung up her husband and skinned him alive if she so much as caught a whiff of another woman. I sometimes wished I

222

had that in me. But then I pictured Matt, terrified, his honest face sinking at Nancy's accusation, the fear I didn't trust him.

And then I pictured him again, driving home. My head on the headrest. The one that smelled of Ruby's perfume. This wasn't just another woman.

Looking further back, I pictured him in London, broken and crying, convincing me of his innocence. My Matt, my poor Matt. Hung out to dry. I had believed him then.

'Ask him,' said Claire. 'Then ask him again.'

'I did.' This wasn't getting me anywhere.

'Look, Immy. Do you want my honest opinion?'

'Of course.'

'You will never be one hundred percent sure of the truth. In these cases, it's one story versus another, and neither matters unless an allegation is made. The truth is often lost in the noise. Blunt, I know, but that's it.'

'I guess.'

'One thing I will add: in Kyle's practice they make the fundamental assumption that women don't lie about these things. Sexual assault. You take it as the truth.'

'Sexual assault? Nobody said anything about rape, Claire!'

'I didn't say rape. And I mean . . . this girl, she's fifteen, right? If she says Matt came on to her, she's telling the truth. Almost certainly.'

I thought back to Ruby's face, her insistence, her embarrassment. I saw the way she looked at me, the way she looked at Matt. I swallowed, but the lump remained. 'She didn't,' I said. 'She flat out denied it.'

'OK then,' said Claire.

'OK?'

'Like I said. Nobody knows except the two of them. You'll never know for sure, and you can never be a hundred percent sure of the truth. If she says it never happened . . .' She left it hanging.

I felt deflated. Claire's ruthless rationality was perhaps more than I needed. I should have asked her to sugar-coat it.

'I'm not going to tell you to leave your husband, Imm.'

'I don't want to leave him!' My heart thudded. Divorces happened to other couples, not us. Besides, I hadn't come this far, left my life behind, to have a change of heart.

Not unless the foundations of our marriage had fundamentally shifted. Another flash – the money. Liv's revelation had turned out to be a puzzling blip – the money returned, but conveniently forgotten in the excitement of our pregnancy, now simmering again. How far had our marriage come off the rails?

'Oh, shit,' said Claire. 'Sorry, Imm, I've got to go. Thomas has poured his juice into my Vuitton bag. Little shit. That's coming out of his trust fund.'

'Thanks, Claire.'

'For what?'

'For being honest. It's what I need.'

'Call me whenever you want, Immy. I'll give you all the attention you need, in five-minute chunks while I wrestle with my fiendish offspring.'

I hung up and paced the kitchen, pausing to stare through the glass doors. They were jammed shut, as usual. I turned and headed upstairs.

Claire was right, but she couldn't help me. I'd said I believed him. And I loved him, *truly* I did. I'd defended him before, when the company turned on him, when his friends turned on him, when most of *my* friends did the same. I'd defend him again. But it didn't stop the doubt, or what the doubt might do to us.

For the second time in twelve months, I felt that desperate vulnerability, when all I held dear was at risk, when everything I thought was strong became shaky and insubstantial, held together by faith alone, ready to collapse.

And I had no idea which way it would fall.

Imogen

'I'll get that,' said Matt. He saw me struggling towards him with the basket full of laundry. I checked the time. Home by six, for a change.

'Thanks,' I said, following him up the stairs.

I was all at sea. Matt kept glancing at me. What do I say? When do I say it? *Hey, Matt, you know I love you, but can we just run over this Ruby stuff one more time? And while we're at it, shall we revisit the last twelve months?*

'You don't look so good,' he said.

No shit. Battling the virus from hell, and the mental anguish invading my every waking moment.

I sat on the bed and folded the underwear. Matt got changed out of his suit and sat across from me, taking his shirts and hanging them one by one.

'You should leave the laundry,' he said. 'I'll do it when I get home each day. You need to rest.'

'Nancy did this lot,' I said, in a daze. Dear old Nancy, my new best friend. She was finding this situation as difficult as I was, but she was keen to help me out, look after me. The cleaning was a strange touch, and I should object to her doing the family laundry, but I let her take over. I liked it, and she seemed to be most comfortable when she was busy, fussing around me. It was motherly, practical, and while my own dear mum was stuck at home with my clumsy, loveable father, Nancy did a good job of things.

Matt raised his eyebrows, but he said nothing. He pulled another white shirt from the basket, shook it out, put it on a hanger.

'What's that?' I said, staring at the shoulder, near the collar. A smudge of colour.

Matt glanced at the shirt. 'Nothing,' he said, going to hang it in the wardrobe.

'Wait,' I said, standing. I took the shirt from him. 'This.' I pointed to a bright pink smudge on the front of the shoulder panel. I rubbed my finger against it. Greasy. Crayon? Paint? Or the other thing.

Where had I seen that colour before? My heart sank and my stomach twisted. Bright pink. Hardly my colour.

Matt didn't say anything, moving away, grabbing another shirt.

'When's the last time you wore this shirt?' I said.

Matt shrugged. 'No idea. I have dozens of white shirts. What's on it?'

'Pink lipstick,' I said. It blurted out; the accusation clear. Matt recoiled, frowning, placing the other shirt on the bed.

'Uh,' he said, turning to me. 'What?'

I clamped my lips together, staring at him. He walked over, grabbed the shirt. Stared at the stain. He rubbed it with his finger, face creasing in confusion.

'I . . . don't know what it is.' He caught my expression. 'Imogen, this is ridiculous. These have just been through the wash.'

'It doesn't wash out.'

He continued to stare at it. 'So it's yours?'

I wanted to scream. 'When was the last time you saw me wearing bright pink lipstick?'

He shrugged. 'Ash? She plays with your make-up all the time. She also plays with the laundry.'

I blew out the exasperated breath I'd been holding. I could feel it building, all of it, ready to unleash. Had I got it all wrong? But what, exactly? What was this? Proof of what?

'The other day, on the way back from the hospital,' I said. I couldn't stop myself. It was coming out whether I liked it or not.

'Yes?'

'Your passenger seat. It smelled of perfume, Matt. Not any perfume, but Ruby's. Calvin Klein. Did you know that?'

Matt looked like a guppy, his mouth opening and closing stupidly. 'I didn't . . .' he said. His eyes darted. What was I looking for? He seemed confused, nothing else.

He stared at the shirt, then back at me. 'Ruby was in my car, several times,' he said. 'I drove her to work experience, from office to office. She's a teenager – she wears a lot of perfume. I . . . what can I say?'

I spun this around in my head. He was right, of course, but that was weeks ago, wasn't it? I thought back. Christ, I'd lost all sense of time with this illness. Shouldn't the smell have gone by now?

'It smelled recent,' I said, having no idea if this was true. What did I want to achieve with such a statement? Matt eased himself on to the bed, still staring at me in confusion. He blew his cheeks out.

'I don't know why,' he said. 'Smells linger on car seats, Imogen. Jake can make it stink for weeks if he's wet.'

I still had the shirt in my hand. It was such a cliché I already doubted it. Lipstick on his shirt. Perfume in his car. I could laugh. And yet he still looked innocent. He didn't look like he'd been found out. Not a trace of guilt. And suddenly I doubted all of it.

'You swear?' I had to say it. It came out in a pathetically soft voice. I held the crumpled shirt with both hands, close to my chest. The tears welled and I couldn't stop them.

Matt jumped up, put his arms around me. I let him, the warm embrace so comforting, so necessary.

'I swear on my life, Imogen,' he said. 'Whatever this is, it can be explained, but it's not what you think.'

I resisted for a moment, then sank my face into his chest. I had no idea what was true, but I was so weary it hurt.

'I know why this is hard for you,' he said. 'I know why you doubt me, and I forgive you. But I'm telling the truth.'

Matt held me for several moments before breaking away. He led me to the bed and sat me down, holding my arms, keeping me upright. I wanted to fall. So confused, and yet my husband was right here, holding me. His expression, his words, his body language. All so convincing.

'This place,' he said. He glanced around the room, gesturing out of the window. 'Perhaps I was wrong. We were wrong.'

'What do you mean?'

Matt sighed. He pulled the face that meant he was about to say something I didn't like.

'Only a small community could breed somebody like Nancy. I'm beginning to think I should have trusted my gut about village life.'

'But . . .' What was he saying? We'd looked at all our options, but the clock was ticking, the job was here. I'd wanted to stay in London, of course I had. But we agreed it was for the best.

'This wasn't Nancy's fault,' I said. 'You can't blame the village.'

Matt huffed. 'I'm just saying. She's always . . .'

'What?' I couldn't believe he was deflecting this on to her.

Matt shrugged.

'This didn't start with her, Matt.'

'What do you mean?' he said.

London, Matt. What the hell do you think I mean?

The tears formed again. I shook my head.

'Nothing. I don't know,' I said. I couldn't drag it up again. Couldn't bring myself to talk about it. And I think Matt knew it. The thing is, he had every right to be angry, and every right to not want to talk about it. As long as he didn't pretend we didn't go through *something*. He might have been innocent, but that didn't mean it didn't hurt.

I sagged, lying back on the pillow. My head was thumping and my stomach churned, a deep, nauseous hell I was fast growing used to. I turned my head away and closed my eyes.

'I'll make some dinner,' he said. 'Play with Ash; read to her for a bit.'

I nodded into the pillow.

The conversation was over. He'd ended it, neatly, like he always did.

Matt

The morning felt strained already. Matt perched on the stool, leaning in against the kitchen worktop as the laptop started up. Seeing Imogen so distressed was awful. He felt powerless. Impotent. Unable to even comfort her without inviting that look of hers, the one that meant her mind was also spinning, processing, wondering whether the man she stared at was being truthful.

But what else could he say or do to convince her?

The perfume in the car was easy to explain. Ruby had spent the week back and forth in it – five hot summer days, and she *did* wear a lot of the damn stuff. Perhaps he should have cleaned the car, but he didn't think it would matter. Cleaning the seats would have been more suspicious, wouldn't it?

As for the lipstick, he was at a total loss. He didn't know what shades Imogen wore, but assumed it was hers. If she insisted it wasn't, then it must have been Ash, poking around in Imogen's old make-up drawer, wiping her hands on his clothes. Or perhaps there had still been a smudge on her lips when she gave him a hug after work. What else could it be?

Combined, the perfume and lipstick painted a damning picture of him, one which he had no idea how to shift.

He huffed, closing the online banking screen and firing up Instagram. He browsed for a few minutes, unable to shift the tension in his chest. At this rate he'd need to go to the doctor again, ask for another prescription. It was short-term, he convinced himself. The anxiety would fade like the last time. Nothing lasts forever.

'You OK?' Imogen's voice startled him. He closed the browser and looked up at her. She was pale, but fresher than the day before. Her clothes were beginning to hang off her – she needed to put on the weight she was losing. 'Where's Ash?'

'In the garden,' said Matt, refreshing the laptop screen, clicking through to the *Guardian* news and sports pages.

Imogen poured herself some coffee and sat next to him. They stared through to the garden for a few moments; a tense silence.

'The doors still need fixing,' said Imogen, blowing over her coffee, taking a sip.

Matt nodded. He'd managed to jam them open that morning, then jam them shut again. He'd decided to lock and leave them, forcing everyone around the front of the house. A minor inconvenience, all things considered.

'I'll get to it,' he said, looking back at the laptop, scrolling without reading, wondering what Imogen's first thoughts of the morning would turn to. Was she in a different frame of mind today, or would they replay yesterday's conversation again?

'You seem a bit better,' he said.

Imogen shrugged. 'It comes in waves,' she said. 'I'm keeping down half of what I eat, so I won't starve ... but no, I'm not better.'

Matt placed his hand on her back, running it up and down, caressing her through the thin cotton fabric. He could feel her ribs, the line of her backbone.

'You will be,' he said. 'The doctor will find something in the blood tests. You'll be right as rain, soon enough.'

He had no idea if that was true, but it was as much to re-assure himself as Imogen. He didn't know how he'd cope if she was seriously ill.

Imogen gave a small smile. 'I hope so.' She put her cup to her lips, taking another sip.

'Oh.' She tapped the screen of the laptop. 'I need a recent photo of Ash, for school. And a copy of her birth certificate. You've got those saved on here, yeah?'

Matt thought about it. 'Yes,' he said. He closed the browser and opened the file explorer. He was quite obsessive about photo storage, filing by year and month, conscious that anything in the cloud could disappear in a flash, keeping it saved locally, in case of disaster.

'We'll find a nice one,' he said.

He found the directory and opened the photo browser.

It took a few moments to refresh, the most recent photos displaying as large thumbnails on the screen, appearing one by one. There were several from this week, filed away, ready for whoever browsed them first.

Matt stared at the thumbnails, time slowing as he processed what he saw.

He turned to Imogen. She stared at the screen, slamming her coffee cup on to the worktop. The cup cracked and her coffee began to seep across the surface. They both ignored it.

Matt watched in slow motion as Imogen grabbed the laptop,

pulling it towards her, opening the first image, enlarging it until it filled the screen.

It was a photo of Ruby, lying on a sun lounger in her back garden, wearing a tiny black bikini. Her face was turned away from the camera. Shades covered her eyes.

Imogen turned to Matt, then back to the screen. 'Matt,' she said, her voice small, trembling, simmering. She clicked on to the next photo.

Ruby again. Lying on her front, her unclothed body captured in high resolution, the photo zoomed in from afar. The angle of the photo suggested it had been taken from an elevated position. A second floor, with the garden hedge showing to the bottom right of the photo.

'I . . .' Matt was lost for words. His eyes darted all over the photo, perplexed.

Imogen clicked to the next one. Then the next. A series of photos – ten or more – of Ruby in her back garden. They'd all been captured apparently without her knowing – her face never once turned to the camera. Sunbathing, mostly, but sometimes standing, holding a drink. All in her bikini. All captured in quick succession.

Imogen paused on the next one. Ruby standing, adjusting the straps on her top, facing towards her own house. Shades off this time. This photo wasn't zoomed in so much, and it had captured a window frame in the corner of the picture, along with a windowsill. A small toothbrush rested on the sill next to a tube of children's toothpaste. It was Ashley's toothbrush.

These photos had been taken from Matt and Imogen's family bathroom window.

234

'Matt.' Imogen's voice was still trembling, but firmer. She clasped the sides of the laptop, her whole body shaking.

'Imogen,' said Matt. 'I have no idea—'

'Stop!' Imogen screamed. She jumped off the stool, shaking her head, holding the laptop in both hands. 'Don't you dare,' she shouted. 'Don't you dare deny this! What the fuck, Matt? What the fuck!' She hurled the laptop on to the floor, staggering backwards until her back was against the cupboards. She held her cheeks in her palms, staring at him with horror.

Matt jumped off the stool. 'I didn't! I don't! Imogen, listen—'

'You did! What the fuck? How can you deny this?' She pointed at the cracked laptop on the floor. 'It's your laptop, Matt. Yours.' Her face twisted with disgust as she paced in circles. 'Fifteen. She's fifteen. And you're taking naked pictures of her. Matt . . .' Her face broke, her lips trembling and her eyes filling. She turned away.

'After everything, Matt. I defended you. I swore to myself you were telling the truth.' She turned and lunged at him, thumping him in the chest with both hands.

'I fucking trusted you,' she screamed. 'You bastard. You fucking arsehole.'

She stood back, face red, angrier than Matt had ever seen her. He could do nothing but stand and take it, his own shock not yet releasing him. His mind had frozen in confusion, utterly bewildered at what he'd just seen. These were not pictures he'd taken, not pictures he knew existed. For them to appear on his laptop was incredible. Not his doing. But he struggled and failed to find his voice.

'Imogen, I—'

'No,' she shouted. 'No, Matt. Not this time. I want you out.'

The blood drained from Matt's face. 'What?'

'Out, Matt. I want you gone. I need you to leave.' She laughed, manic, hysterical. 'I was thinking about it last night. One more thing, I thought. Just one, and that would be it. I'm an idiot. A total idiot.'

'But, Imogen,' said Matt. 'This is my house. I can't leave. This is crazy.'

'It's not crazy,' she shouted. She paced around the kitchen, her fists clenched. 'You have photos of Ruby on your laptop.'

'And I have no idea how they got there.'

'Have you slept with her?' she said.

'*What?*'

'Is that it? Are you seeing her? Are you engaged in some sordid affair with a fucking teenager?'

'No,' Matt stuttered, trying to keep up. 'Of course not. I didn't take those.' He pointed feebly at the laptop. 'I didn't do anything. Imogen . . .'

'You're a liar, Matt.' Her eyes had hardened. Her stance was firm, her thin body trembling with rage as she faced him.

Matt stepped forward, tried to hold her, but she pushed him hard.

'No, Matt. No fucking way. You're not talking or hugging your way out of this. Like you always do.' The tears streamed again. 'Just go, Matt. I need you to leave us alone.'

Matt paused. His heart was thumping, his mind spinning. He hunted for a rational explanation but could find none, the evidence against him mounting, his defence weak and unprepared.

'Go where?' he said, his own voice trembling. Did she mean for a few hours or a few days? He couldn't comprehend time away from Imogen. They'd never been away from each other at all since they got married. What about Ash? How would they explain Matt's absence? How would she cope without her dad in the house?

What the fuck was happening?

'There's a B&B in the village,' she said. 'Stay there tonight, Matt. I can't . . . I can't even look at you.'

She turned and left the room, her feet racing across the hallway and up the stairs. He heard the bathroom door slam and lock.

Still in a state of shock, Matt picked up the laptop, holding it closed, the hinge snapped and the lid cracked from the impact. He held it close to his chest as he slumped against the fridge, forcing his breathing to slow, trying to quell the tremors; trying to understand what had just happened.

Because he truthfully had no idea.

Imogen kept away from him as he packed a small suitcase, his arms working on autopilot, slow and uncoordinated. He switched from confusion to anger and back again, unable to process the events, the escalation, Imogen's violent reaction and his marching orders.

He could refuse, and stay. She couldn't physically throw him out. But then what? Would she leave instead? In her state, would she take Ash and go? Back to London, back to her parents? How would he mend things from here, once her mum had got her maternal claws into her? She'd refuse to let him talk to her, see her. He'd be left pleading to a dead phone line, all doors slammed in his face.

And he worried for her health. Could she travel? She might collapse somewhere – at the wheel, on a train. He couldn't risk anything like that.

Which left him one route. He had to do as she asked. He had to leave his marital home while this mess was cleared up – while he figured out how to fix it and convince Imogen it was all lies.

He packed everything he'd need for a night away and a day in the office tomorrow, assuming he went. Would Shelley understand? What story would he tell her? He could call in sick, he supposed, which would wash for a day or so. But then what? He was already on thin ice with her, his performance hanging by a thread. To lose his job would just about finish him off.

He tiptoed down the stairs, glancing down the long hallway towards the back of the house, the light dancing in from their impressive kitchen-diner. What they always wanted. It had been perfect.

Should he call out? He'd already spoken to Ashley, clutched her to his body, told her he was going away for work.

'How long?' she'd said.

'Just a night or two,' he replied.

'One or two?' she asked.

'I don't know,' he said, drawing her close, hugging her so she couldn't see his tears.

Imogen didn't want to speak to him. Refused. 'I need space,' she said, before turning her back and letting him go.

The front door opened with a creak. He held his suitcase in one hand and a jacket in the other, pausing to take a breath, still stunned at the unfolding events.

And then, he saw her.

He should have expected it, but the sight of Nancy walking up his garden path still caused a shudder.

'What are you doing here?' he said, unable to hide his hostility.

'What do *you* think, Matthew?' she said, clutching her handbag to her chest. She stood to one side, allowing him to pass. Something in her expression unnerved him: her eyes sparkled, and her mouth was twisted in a vicious smile. She looked *pleased*.

'Has Imogen told you why I'm going?' he said.

Nancy's smile narrowed. 'I don't think she knows the half of it, does she, Matthew?'

'What do you mean?'

Nancy closed the space between them, leaning in so he could smell her. Perfume wafted over him. He knew the brand without thinking. The hairs prickled on his neck.

'Your shameful behaviour with my daughter,' said Nancy. 'She thinks it was just a kiss. But *we* know better, don't we, Matthew?'

Matt swallowed. What the hell was she getting at?

'We know it wasn't *just* a kiss, don't we?' continued Nancy, her voice hissing between them. 'I suspect you've done far more with my vulnerable, sick daughter. More than a kiss. More than a touch. Which makes you the sick one, doesn't it?'

'I ...' Matt stepped back, trying to get away from this vile woman, these vile accusations. 'How can you say such things? This is your daughter we're talking about. She denies all of it.'

'I say it because I know it's true,' said Nancy. 'You might have threatened Ruby into silence, and strut around here like you're the devoted husband, the kind neighbour looking out for others, but I know what's in that head of yours, Matthew.

I know what you've done, and Imogen has discovered it too. She's finally realised what a snake you are – a nasty, lowlife piece of scum. She's woken up to you, Matthew.'

Nancy stepped back and stiffened, her face shifting into her signature smile.

'But now she's rid of you. And I can help her get her life back. A proper life, without you. With me at her side.'

Matt shook his head, the biting comments sinking in. Nancy was ratcheting it up again, another level of threat, another level of accusation. But her comments were confusing – meticulously prepared, rehearsed . . .

'I suggest you go,' she said, watching him struggle. 'The police are just a quick phone call away. It would destroy you in a flash, something like this. Sleeping with a fifteen-year-old. Dear me. Would your own paper run the story, do you think? I could call them and ask?'

Matt's hands shook as he clasped his coat closer, lifting his case.

'What do you *want*, Nancy?' he said, his voice small and pathetic, his anger replaced with fear, anxiety and submission. How had she beaten him so absolutely?

Nancy tittered. She straightened her skirt, patting it against her legs. 'I want you to go, Matthew. That's all I want.'

She turned and strode to the door. Matt watched in a daze as she knocked. It opened a few moments later and he saw her embracing Imogen, before slamming it closed behind her.

Matt

The owner of the bed and breakfast introduced herself as Mrs Owens and gave Matt the key to his room. She didn't appear to recognise him. No questions, no conversation. For that, at least, he was thankful.

The room was modest in size, with a dresser, wardrobe and en-suite bathroom. Floral wallpaper glared at him, while the single window overlooked the main road heading out of the village to the south. A fridge and minibar were tucked under the small plasma TV on the wall. Tea-making facilities were balanced on top of a small cupboard.

The sight of it all added a veneer of depression to his mood – he had a sudden vision of a future like this, tucked away in bedsits and temporary accommodation, running from the allegations, chasing his family.

Hiding from Nancy.

His perfect family, collapsing in front of his eyes. And she had smiled at him, hateful and victorious.

Nancy.

He pictured her face at his house. The sneer as he walked away. The face of a protective mother. But that wasn't all she was.

He grabbed a bottle of wine from the minibar. Was it the worst possible idea? To drink, to try to numb the last few days, just a little?

It was late in the day, the evening drawing in, night beckoning. He'd driven for miles after leaving the house, heading straight along the country roads to the south, unable to find calm in the chaos, only returning to the village at nightfall, hoping the darkness would somehow hide the horrors of the day.

The red wine was cheap and vinegary, but he gulped it down regardless, feeling the small warmth in his throat, the beginnings of inebriation. He finished the first glass and poured another, pulling his phone out of his pocket.

He should call Imogen. Speak to her, try again. Tell her what nonsense this all was. Explain. But . . . how? What could he tell Imogen to change her mind? The sequence of events was damning, the evidence mounting.

Stepping towards the window, he pulled aside the curtain and stared out. Not much traffic at this time, the occasional headlights breaking through the pitch-black. The sky was clear and full of stars. He found Orion's Belt and followed it outwards, tracing the hunter's body across the sky. It brought back a memory from years ago. One of their first weekends away, drunk on a beach before jumping in a taxi back to the cheap hotel, Imogen too inebriated to walk. It had been a wild night, one he remembered well. He hadn't got much sleep, for all the right reasons.

But the happy memory further soured his mood. He sipped at the second glass, already feeling the effects. Leaving his suitcase at the side of the bed, he kicked off his shoes and lay out, slumped against the headboard. He flicked the TV on, lowering the volume.

What did Nancy think she knew? What did she suspect? And why was she pushing him out, while at the same time cuddling up to Imogen, keeping the police a distant threat to be invoked as and when she felt like it?

And the first accusation *was* astonishing. The night of the babysitting. It had caught him off guard, but he'd explained it away. Ruby had corroborated it. It should have gone away.

But then the perfume, the lipstick . . . the photos. How they had got on to his laptop mystified him. His laptop, which he'd left at home, with his login, access to his files, his photos.

Disturbed and damaged, Matt's head spun, Nancy's threat lingering in his ears. A strange calm took him as he considered the sinister final words of his neighbour. *I want you to go, Matthew. That's all I want.*

Her warped beliefs had created a whirlwind, and Matt's family were caught in it, unable to break free.

Matt was lost. He had no idea where to turn.

Imogen

Nancy held me in her arms as I seethed, guiding me into the lounge, on to the sofa, staying with me the whole time, her arms around my body as it trembled with shock and rage.

I told her what had happened; it came out in bursts and splutters. Every time I raised my head from her neck, a fresh wave caught me and I buried it again, like a small child into her mother's bosom.

'It's not your fault, Imogen,' said Nancy, her voice soothing.

She meant it. Although I wondered how much blame might fall to me.

'I should have seen it,' I said. 'I should have believed you.'

'But I didn't know myself,' said Nancy, 'not for sure. She's a tricky one, Ruby.'

I pulled away. It was a strange comment. We weren't talking about misbehaviour, a disagreement. We were talking about my husband. What he did.

'Nancy, this is your daughter we're talking about.'

Her expression didn't change. Jake barked from the kitchen. He needed to be let out.

'I know, Imogen. I know. But right now, Matthew has gone. Ruby is safe at home and you're safe right here. I can look after both of you, and together we'll figure it out.'

I watched her eyes; deep, full of compassion, full of hurt. She must want to kill my husband, yet she was focusing on me first.

'Will you go to the police?' I said. The thought still terrified me: Matt being arrested, questioned, accused of these acts. I didn't even know what the crime was, not technically. Would he be placed on a register? He'd lose his job for certain. My heart sank. What about Ashley? How could she grow up with the weight of that in her family? What would it do to her? My heart flipped as another panic grabbed me – would social services get involved? Would I be judged too? If I couldn't even see what Matt was doing in front of my very eyes, was I a fit parent for Ashley?

Nancy saw my panic and held me tighter.

'I don't know,' she said. 'But not today. This is not something I will rush into. Ruby is fifteen, yes, but I need to speak to her first, understand what she thinks has happened, get it clear in my own mind – how far it went, what damage has been done. She's a very fragile young woman, Imogen. The police would terrify her, and I can't risk anything affecting her health at the moment.'

I listened to her explaining this to me as if it was the most normal thing in the world, like she was mediating in a playground spat. I didn't understand, but I wasn't in a good place to judge; in fact, my judgement on anything was suspect right now. I assured myself Nancy would know best. It was her daughter.

But I still felt like I'd betrayed her.

'I need to talk to Ruby,' I said. 'Apologise . . . but . . . I also

245

want to ask her about it. Would that be OK? I need to, Nancy. I'll go mad if I don't.'

'Shh.' Nancy rubbed my shoulders. 'There's a time and place. Today is for you to calm down and get some rest. You're still ill, you've recently miscarried, and this isn't helping one bit. Emotionally and physically, you're worn out.

'Unfortunately, Ruby is also suffering – her condition comes in waves and today she's having a bad spell. She can barely get out of bed, as it happens.'

'Oh, I'm so sorry,' I said. 'I didn't think. This must be really hard for her too.' I said it without knowing what Ruby was going through, because I still didn't know what had happened, not entirely.

My Matt. Could he really have done this? After everything we'd been through. We changed our whole lives for a new start, we'd been expecting a *baby*, and it was over already. Doubt still lingered.

But how many coincidences could I allow? I could believe a misunderstanding; accept a few chance incidents. But all of them combined . . . How many would it take before I was forced to write 'I am an idiot' on my forehead?

'As soon as she's well enough, I'll speak to her again,' said Nancy. 'But not before.' She sat back and took a breath.

'The important thing is we women stick together,' she said, stroking her skirt, focusing on her lap.

Another odd comment, uncomfortable. It was already a strange sensation, being looked after by the mother of the daughter Matt had supposedly abused. Should I push her away? Did this invite more consequences, or help matters?

In truth, I had no idea, and not the energy to think

about it any more. Nancy was right: I was exhausted and ill. The day had taken it out of me, my eyes already sore and heavy.

Time. I needed time to recover and to think.

Nancy nipped home to check on Ruby, promising to be back. I gave her a door key, told her to let herself in.

I let Jake out into the garden and rang Mum, entirely unsure what I was going to say. In truth I just wanted to hear her voice. The first time it went to voicemail, the second time I hung up after three rings, suddenly panicking that once I opened the floodgates, I wouldn't be able to close them.

'Hello?' Mum's voice. The delightful familiarity coupled with a sinking feeling. Did I want to tell Mum everything? Could I? What would she do?

I paused, staring at my reflection in the hallway mirror. I looked tired, haggard, my eyes sinking gradually into my skull, bloodshot and stressed.

'Hi Mum,' I said.

'Lovely to hear your voice,' she said. 'How are you feeling? Is everything settled . . . you know, down there? Is Matt pulling his weight?'

The sinking feeling intensified. What was Matt doing? *I kicked him out, Mum. I think he's cheating on me with a teenage girl. An underage one.* Christ. Of all the things I talked to Mum about, I struggled with this.

'I'm . . .'

She was my mum. She deserved to know. And yet I couldn't face it. My face turned red in the mirror; my heart started hammering.

'Give me a minute, will you, darling?' said Mum. 'Your dad's calling.'

'Actually,' I said, taking a deep breath, 'I'll call you back. It's nothing, really. Just calling for a chat.'

'OK, if you're sure?'

'I'm sure. Love you, Mum.'

'Love you too, darling. Speak soon.'

I hung up, gripping the phone, feeling sharp and conflicting pangs of relief and guilt. I couldn't bear to tell Mum about this. How would I phrase it? How would I explain it when I didn't understand it myself?

Perhaps in time, when I'd figured it out. But not now. Not yet.

I went upstairs to sit with Ash, my feelings of guilt extending to her – my world over the last couple of weeks had been so consumed either with my health or with this hanging over me.

I crept into her bedroom. The little angel was on her bed, surrounded by her soft toys and every small figurine she had. We'd spoken to Ash together about my miscarriage. Her sadness had been more mature than I expected, directed at me, rather than herself. She wanted to know I was OK. The baby was a future possibility, but she had no way of framing it as reality, not yet. Once certain that I would survive whatever malady had caused her new sibling to disappear, she never mentioned it, returning to normal very quickly. I wish I could say the same, but I admired her resilience.

Without looking up, she said, 'It's school assembly. All the children have to sit quietly.'

I nodded. 'I see. Can I join?'

Ash examined me for a second. 'Perhaps as a teacher. You're too big to be a child.'

248

I took my place next to her and slipped my arm around her small body. I tugged her a little closer.

'Are you mad at Daddy?' she said.

I picked up a small bunny rabbit, stroked it and placed it down again. I never lied to Ashley. 'Yes,' I said.

'Why?'

'Because he did something I'm not happy with.'

Ashley nodded, in complete understanding. 'Did he say sorry?'

I laughed. It just came out. But such a simple question – it made me replay the conversations we'd had. Sure, Matt was sorry. But what was he sorry for? That was at the heart of everything, wasn't it?

'Not yet,' I said.

'He will,' said Ashley. 'Then you can kiss and make up.'

With that final statement, she announced assembly was over and the children could go off into their classrooms.

She was happy, safe in her own world. I couldn't ruin it. Could Matt?

I shuffled back on her bed while she reorganised everything, lost in her game. I pulled my phone out and held it tight. It was set to *do not disturb*, and the screen was full of missed messages.

One from my mum, one from Claire. One from Matt: *Call me, please.*

I stared at it for a few moments. Part of me urgently wanted to talk to him – to ask him again, repeat it, pull it apart. I'd made a mistake, surely? This was all nonsense, all a misunderstanding, all a crazy mix-up.

Except it wasn't. It had gone too far. Further than last time.

Matt

A growing desperation. That's what had brought him here. Matt had spent the morning simmering in his anxiety, forced to wait until lunchtime for the appointment. It had required a bit of negotiation at such short notice, but here he was. The air conditioning in the waiting room was broken, and Matt squirmed in the seat, legs stuck to his suit trousers.

Beacher, Jordan and Carnegie, a criminal law specialist in the heart of Guildford – far enough from the village to avoid any recognition or contacts, close enough to use if he needed them.

'Mr Roberts,' said the woman behind the reception counter, 'Mr Jordan will see you now.'

Matt was shown through to a small office. He wasn't sure what to expect, but perhaps a few bookshelves stacked with old legal texts at a minimum. There was nothing except a modern glass desk, an iMac computer, and several uncomfortable-looking chairs. It was hotter than the waiting room.

'Mr Roberts.' The young solicitor extended a hand, gave Matt's a brisk shake and sat behind his desk, indicating Matt take a chair facing him. 'My name is Stephen.'

Stephen wore a tailored suit and a crisp tie. His head was cropped to a buzz cut, his beard immaculately trimmed. He peered at Matt through thick, square-rimmed glasses.

'Thank you for seeing me,' said Matt, wondering if he was doing the right thing. There was no commitment – no crime – but this was sensible preparation, wasn't it?

Stephen opened a notebook and scribbled something at the top of the blank page.

'So, further to our conversation on the phone this morning,' he said. 'We deal with a lot of false allegation cases. We have a high success rate for our clients. Now . . .' He scribbled another few words. 'How about we start at the beginning?'

Matt took a breath, his hands trembling. This lawyer would be the first person outside of Nancy and Imogen to hear about it. Was that a mistake? Once it was out, did that make it real? He paused.

Stephen smiled. 'I understand your concerns,' he said. 'But everything we talk about is confidential. I'm not here to judge guilt or innocence; I'm here to offer you our specialist advice, should you need it. I think today we'll establish what, if any, case can be made against you, and go from there. OK?'

Matt nodded. He took a deep breath, feeling the sweat gathering on his forehead and under his arms. Couldn't they open the window? Get some fans in? He noticed Stephen's skin was dry, not a hint of sweat or unease.

'OK,' he said. 'Let me think.'

Over the next fifteen minutes, Matt described, in as much detail as he thought necessary, his recent house move and his introduction to his new neighbours. He detailed interactions with Nancy and Ruby, then proceeded to describe the accusation. He faltered when he repeated the words she'd used. He mumbled them twice, forcing Stephen to ask him to repeat himself.

Finally, he fell silent. Stephen continued to scribble his notes. He finished, pursed his lips, then sat back in his chair.

'I'm innocent,' said Matt. 'I . . . What if she goes to the police?'

Stephen nodded. He clasped his hands together and stared at his notes for a moment. 'Based on what you've said, in my experience, the CPS may not pursue it. The police would do their jobs, but if,' he consulted his notes, 'Ruby does not support her mother's allegation, but supports *you*, then given what you've said, it may end there. It might.' Stephen looked unsure.

'And if she doesn't?'

Stephen frowned.

'I mean if Nancy convinces Ruby to lie,' said Matt. 'I told you – she's controlling, obsessive. Not her fault, I might add. Deceased husband, chronically ill daughter – it's enough to make anybody overprotective.'

More nods from Stephen. 'If Ruby makes the allegation directly, it would be a different matter. It would be a more substantial case. Nancy's quirks, as you describe them, would matter a lot less. Do you think it's likely?'

Matt shrugged. He couldn't know what Nancy would do next.

'She's good friends with my wife. Still. She's probably around there now, drinking tea. Doesn't that show it's a lie?'

'It doesn't put Nancy in a good light,' said Stephen, 'but as you've said, it depends who is making the allegation. Although, as I said on the phone, it's not that straightforward, due to Ruby's age.'

252

Matt swallowed.

'In the case of a minor, which Ruby is, accusations can be brought by the alleged victim, or by another person on the alleged victim's behalf. Anybody can allege you did this, Matt. The police would be bound to pursue it.'

'So Nancy could make this up, even if Ruby is denying it, and I might get prosecuted?'

Stephen put his palms on the desk. 'Let's not get ahead of ourselves, Matt. There's nothing to do right now unless Nancy or Ruby takes it further. If the police arrest you, which they will if an allegation is made, you can call us – and we'll take it from there. We'd need to go through everything again, in detail.'

'I gave you the details—'

'Everything, Matt. Every word, every action. To defend you, I'd need to know *everything*.'

Matt's heart thudded. Being arrested at home, or even at work – what would that do to him? The blood drained from his face.

'I know it's scary,' said Stephen. 'And to be honest, I can't make the fear go away. I also need you to be aware of a couple of things.'

'Oh?'

'First, what I can say is if this goes further, an accusation of this type is hard to prove, with a very low conviction rate.'

'A low conviction rate?'

'Yes.'

'Well . . .'

Stephen shook his head. 'It's not good news, Matt, it's just fact. But second, a conviction is only part of it. An allegation like this is very hard to recover from, regardless. We also need

253

to consider how much this sticks to you. It might be dismissed at the police station, at a later stage, or it might go all the way to court. The damage might be the same at any stage.'

Matt stared at Stephen, the room cooling, the sweat increasing. 'What are you saying?'

'I'm saying allegations like this can be devastating to both the accused and their families. Reputations can be ruined and lives can be shattered as a result. It's not something we can stop, but it is something we can attempt to minimise. As I said, we have a lot of experience in this type of case. We will help you and your family, should the worst happen.'

Matt had to grab the arms of the chair to stop his hands shaking. His sweaty palms slipped down them. Stephen's words spun, collided, amplified as they settled.

He shook his head, leaning forward, feeling faint. 'Shit,' he said. 'Shit, shit, shit.'

'But as I said, if neither Nancy nor Ruby go to the police, or anybody else, that's the end of it. It might be over as quickly as it started, with an overprotective mum screaming her fears at the nearest target, which happened to be you.'

Matt pulled himself upright. He had to get out of there, get some air. This had been a mistake. He'd done it to give himself reassurance – that he wasn't going mad, that the professionals would be on his side. What Stephen had told him only made him more terrified.

He stood, extending a sweaty hand. Stephen accepted it, before wiping his hand on his jacket.

'Thank you for your time,' said Matt. 'I need to get back to work.'

It wasn't until he hit the pavement outside and gulped a

few lungsful of air that he started to settle. He leaned against the first cold brick wall he could find, convincing himself it would never happen. This would blow over. Everything would blow over.

It must.

Matt

Matt called in sick the following day, drove as far as the estate and parked up. He sipped a takeaway coffee, watching the end of the street, staring through the dirty glass of the windscreen.

His new house. His new road. Why didn't he just drive up, park in his driveway, open the door and demand to talk?

Fear, that's why. Nancy's parting words sent a shiver down his spine and turned his stomach in somersaults. The thought of it stopped him in his tracks. He saw the malice in her eyes, her knowledge of how deep her accusations cut.

But still, she held off from going any further. And still, he had no idea what she wanted.

An hour passed, then another. Time slowed. His bladder complained and he realised what a useless activity this was, staring at the end of his cul-de-sac, willing a solution to jump out at him. He'd resisted calling Imogen again this morning. She deserved her space, if that's what she truly wanted. But he couldn't help wondering how much of it was driven by rational thought, and how much by Nancy's lies.

He started the engine and spun the car around in frustration, heading out of the road and through the community gate. There was a petrol station further along the road and he used their restroom, buying another coffee at the counter on the way out.

He rested for a few minutes at the pumps, staring into the distance. A car caught his eye, the sun glinting off its roof as it travelled along the main road. Polished and well kept, a classic Mercedes, drifting over the tarmac with a familiar face at the wheel.

Nancy didn't see him as she passed.

Matt jumped back into his car. His first thought was to head home. With Nancy out of the way, he might talk to Imogen, get enough time to convince her. He imagined her opening the door, welcoming him in, admitting the mistake she'd made. They'd kiss, make up, put it behind them without further stress – perhaps leave the village for a few days, wait for things to blow over. Perhaps put the house on the market. Start again.

And yet, as he watched the car gain distance, the hunched figure of Nancy behind the wheel, he knew that wouldn't happen. Imogen had been clear with him, the hurt in her eyes evident. She wanted him out, and at this moment, he had nothing to offer except a rambling protest against her new best friend.

But it didn't mean he must stand idle. He had everything to lose, but needed something new, the missing piece in his current confused explanation of events. He needed insight into Nancy's motivations, her reasons for acting as she did. A snippet, a clue.

Nancy's life appeared to be consumed by Ruby's illness, a small bubble of honest suffering. But her behaviour, odd at first but now extreme, suggested something else; a different person lurking beneath. A different life, perhaps. One that needed to be explored, to see what might emerge.

It might be a bad idea, but it wasn't like he had anything else to do that day. Matt revved the engine, pulled out of the petrol station car park, and followed the silver Mercedes.

Was this what private investigators did? It was what journalists often did, and flashes of his earlier career peppered his thoughts. Small-time, maybe ten years ago, he remembered tailing a restaurant owner for three whole days, convinced he was employing trafficked underage workers from a local gang. It was exciting work, dangerous, but the reward back then had been a breaking story and the warm feeling of a crime uncovered. Two twelve-year-old boys had been taken into care, released from their modern slavery. The world put right, one story at a time.

But the positive memories evaporated as he slouched in the car seat, parked in a lay-by on the main road out of the village. He'd been following Nancy for the last thirty minutes, and this was her third stop. First was the florist, second the pharmacy. Now, a health food shop on the outskirts, bolted on to a garden centre. The car park was almost empty, so he reversed out and stayed in the road, wondering whether or not to leave the car. If Nancy came out while he crossed the road, she'd see him for sure. A public confrontation was not desirable.

It turned out to be the right decision. Just five minutes later, Nancy reappeared, carrying two heavy bags to her car. She placed them into the boot then made a phone call, talking animatedly into the handset for a few minutes before hanging up.

Matt wondered who she'd called. Did she have friends outside of the community? She didn't have a job, as far as he knew. Perhaps she was speaking to Ruby. The thought triggered a fresh wave of anxiety. What was Ruby doing right now? Was she as devastated as he was – accused of such things by her own mother? Or was she playing the innocent party, silenced by Nancy and told to stick to whatever story her mum conjured up?

His thoughts cut out as Nancy slammed her driver's door and pulled away. Matt sighed, started his engine, and followed.

They drove towards Guildford, Matt keeping at least three cars between them on the main road. It wasn't hard – Nancy's Mercedes was distinctive enough to stand out, whereas his black VW blended into the traffic with ease.

She stuck to the inside lane, taking an early exit before the city, heading around the west of the centre. Signs for the Royal Surrey Hospital loomed, and Matt had an uncomfortable reminder of a few days before, bringing Imogen on this same route. His thoughts back then had been as bleak, but more frantic, urgent. He knew why he was taking Imogen to the maternity wing. This time he had no idea.

Their destination became clear when the main hospital building appeared directly ahead. Nancy pulled into the public car park, but rather than take one of the vacant spaces near the entrance, the Mercedes cruised across and through a slip road under the building into another area, marked *Deliveries Only – No Public Access*. Matt followed, keeping an eye out for parking wardens and staying at a reasonable distance.

Out of sight of the hospital entrance, Nancy pulled her car into a hatched yellow area, near a set of shuttered doors. Matt couldn't go any further and slid his car into a collection area between two wheelie-bins. He turned in his seat, keeping his face low behind the headrest. He had a clear view of Nancy as she stepped out of her car. He saw her tap a message into her phone, then wait, leaning against the bonnet, resting her handbag on the gleaming metal.

A few minutes later, one of the doors opened and a man stepped out. He wore a white lab coat – not a doctor, perhaps a technician or lab rat. He was distinctive – a mass of dark curly hair covering his forehead, drooping down over his thick glasses. He was carrying a small holdall – a blue fabric bag.

They spoke for less than a minute before Curly handed the bag to Nancy. In turn, she reached into her handbag and passed him a white envelope. He tucked it into his coat, turned and walked off. The door closed behind him.

As Nancy turned, Matt's view was cut off as a refuse truck reversed along the road. The driver of the truck spied Matt's car and honked his horn. Not wanting to create a scene, Matt had no choice but to reverse out and head back the way he'd come. Circling the car park a couple of times, he pulled into a space near the exit and waited.

A few minutes later, Nancy's car drifted out from the slip road and cruised past him. He ducked below the windscreen as she passed, not daring to raise his head until she'd exited the car park.

Stepping on the gas, he lurched out of his parking space only to be trapped by oncoming traffic. It was two or three minutes before he was able to pull out of the car park on to the road.

He looked left and right. Nancy was gone.

★

Matt sped back along the highway towards the village, certain he'd see Nancy's Mercedes and pick up the tail. But she was nowhere to be seen, and as he slowed to enter the village, he accepted that she'd unwittingly given him the slip.

Parking on one of the leafy streets near the pub, he considered what he'd seen at the hospital, wondering what business Nancy had at the hospital delivery entrance, making an exchange with a member of the medical staff.

Ruby – it had to be. Imogen had said the NHS were not supportive of Nancy's treatment regime, so it wasn't unreasonable to assume she was forced to buy prescriptions or provisions via some dodgy back-alley route. Was this what the fundraising cash was for? It seemed very out of character for Nancy, but he'd clearly misjudged her from the start. She was ruthless, vicious when she needed to be. Securing drugs for Ruby wouldn't be beyond her, and if buying them from the hospital illegally was the only way, he didn't doubt she'd do it. The most frustrating thing was that Matt couldn't blame her. He'd do the same for Ashley, if he had to.

Deflated, Matt checked the time, figured it was a day wasted, and drove off. On autopilot, he headed through the village and into the estate, stopping when he got to the bottom of their road, the exact same place he'd started his day.

Except this time he saw a lone figure walking up the road towards him. She saw him at the same time, slowed, but kept walking.

Matt opened the door and stepped out, staying near the car.

They both stopped, wondering who would speak first. Matt broke the silence.

'What did you tell her?' he said, keeping his voice low, unthreatening.

Ruby bit her lower lip. Matt thought she looked better today, on one of her good runs. The summer sun had helped, her skin now carrying a reasonable tan. Only the bags under her eyes betrayed her illness. Her boots today had been replaced with trainers, her shorts with a denim skirt. Subtle changes.

She shook her head. Tears formed in her eyes.

'I'm sorry,' she said. 'I'm so sorry, Matt.'

Imogen

I missed him. Already. So much.

My phone remained on silent, do not disturb, do not provoke. Several times in those first few days I picked it up, wanting to hear Matt's voice. But I resisted, terrified at what it might conjure – the fear that I didn't know him at all. That my husband was a stranger, and perhaps always had been.

Day three without Matt would have been torture were it not for Nancy, my ever-present carer and friend. She'd even called my mum to reassure her, called the doctor to move my appointment – *you're in no fit state to have your arm stabbed with needles* – and played with Ashley for two hours while I slept.

I still hadn't seen Ruby. Nancy said she was confined to her bed, getting worse – it might be a week or so before she was strong enough to emerge. It frustrated me but I couldn't argue. Ruby's health was more important than my thirst for the truth – which I already knew, didn't I? Not *the* truth, but the details of it. The extent of my husband's infidelity, his criminality – the latter never failed to send shudders through my chest.

Because he was a criminal, wasn't he? Nancy said he'd kissed her, *touched* her. I had a collection of incriminating clues – lingering perfume in the car, photos and lipstick, but nothing more. Did I suspect the ultimate betrayal? I suppose I did, but the thought added an extra layer of nausea, even harder to shift.

My brief search on the Internet had revealed a world of nuance and confusion. A second call with Claire had confirmed that sexual activity with somebody Ruby's age was criminal under the Sexual Offences Act, classed as *sexual activity with a child* and carrying a weighty punishment. She asked what had happened, serious, demanding to come and see me. I declined, said it was theoretical, it had no basis in fact, just curiosity. She didn't believe me for a second, promising to call every day until I explained myself.

The very idea was so hard to grasp, but I forced myself to confront it. If it was true, he deserved everything he got. If it wasn't, his life might be over regardless.

Matt had already lost, but I wanted to know how far he would drag me and Ash with him. The sinking feeling was echoed in my stomach. I ran to the toilet and vomited, the familiar sensation dragging me even lower, my body failing, my mind unable to stop it. I washed my hands and face with cold water. The boiler was playing up again. Fucking great.

'How are you feeling?' Nancy drifted in with a tray, balancing my teapot and two mugs, a plate of sandwiches tipping precariously on one side.

I'd slept for another few hours. My head banged and I struggled to sit up.

'Worse,' I said, my nurse's instincts firing up. 'Nancy, how long until I can get a new appointment?'

'The doctor? Oh. Sorry, the person who takes the tests is away for a week. Italy, I think – Lake Garda. Lovely at this time of year, though a little hot. Anyway,' she smiled, 'we had to rebook again.'

I nodded, concerned. I'd lost count of the days, but a normal gastric condition like mine shouldn't last beyond ten days, regardless of cause. It was becoming persistent, chronic. 'Perhaps I should go to the hospital instead,' I said. 'I can get a full spectrum of tests there. Get them sent to the GP. You'd drive me, wouldn't you?'

Nancy clasped her hands together, her way of evaluating something.

'Of course I will,' she said. 'But I'll give the GP another call – see if we can squeeze you in with someone else. It would be a shame to traipse all the way to Guildford in your state.'

I frowned. 'Well . . .'

'But it's up to you, of course,' she said. 'Just say the word. Tomorrow, perhaps? Can I see how Ruby is in the morning? I hate to leave her for too long.'

I supposed I could get a taxi if all else failed. My body was struggling, but with it came a fog I'd never experienced before – a detached feeling that left me losing time. The day would pass in a flash; I'd look down and see a fresh tray of tea and cakes with no memory of Nancy placing it there. I'd find myself in pyjamas without remembering getting changed.

Fatigue, stress, grief – I knew all of those things caused such psychological issues. The mind is wonderful at protecting itself against further damage, shutting off certain faculties and giving the sense of floating through time. That's what it was, I was sure of it.

It was no less disconcerting, just because I could apply my clinical brain to it, but it did mean I was unlikely to need urgent medical attention – there wasn't much they'd be able to do. A few more days wouldn't hurt.

I nodded, my head feeling heavier by the second. Nancy passed me the tea. It was herbal, with a distinct earthy taste, a hint of ginger.

'Do you want some sugar?' she said. 'I often drink it with half a teaspoon. Good for nausea, so Ruby says.'

'No, thank you.'

'I'll leave you to rest, then,' she said. 'I'm popping home. I'll call you later to check in?'

I smiled. 'You're a star, Nancy,' I said. 'This must be so strange, awkward, *awful*, for you . . .'

Nancy shook her head and put her hand up. 'Enough,' she said. 'If we start talking about it, our minds will follow. I've said what I needed to say about Matthew. Rest, Imogen, and know that I'm here for you.'

I didn't have a chance to reply. Nancy swished out of the bedroom and closed the door behind her. I heard the front door open and close, then I listened out for Ash, who was watching TV in the lounge. She'd been watching too much lately, but school started the following week, so I didn't mind.

I drifted, enjoying the hot tea. Reassured by Nancy's unwavering support, I checked my mobile phone, flicking it off silent, swiping away the recent messages and putting it on charge by the bed.

Imogen

It was the dream that woke me. The bright lights of London, snippets of our previous life. I watched myself listen to the rumours about Matt, drifting above both of us as he told me his version of events. I saw the cup marks on the pine table in our kitchen, the chalk-painted chairs, one-offs picked from a charity shop. I watched a slightly younger version of myself take sides with my husband, because I believed it to be the truth.

But this time it jarred, and I sat up in bed, a burst of clarity through the fog.

I had her number. I'd got it from a friend on the day Matt came home in the early hours with guilt in his eyes. I'd been prepared to call her and have it out, but I never did, deciding it would bring nothing but more focus on Matt and me. She was a liar – I didn't need to call her to prove it.

But perhaps I should have made that call.

I reached over, dragging my phone on to my lap, scrolling through until I found her. I closed my eyes and dialled. She picked up on the fifth ring.

'Hello? You're coming up as unrecognised. Esme? Have you got another new number? Honestly, I can't keep track.'

'No,' I said. 'It's Imogen. My name is Imogen.'

A long pause, enough for Yun to cycle through her enormous list of friends and acquaintances and try to match it.

'Imogen? I don't . . . Oh.'

'Yes – oh,' I said. 'That's the one.'

A sniff. 'What can I do for you, Imogen?' she said. 'I thought you'd left London?'

'We did,' I said, with as icy a tone as I could muster, 'Matt and I. But you knew that, Yun.'

Another pause. 'Of course I did, but . . . you know.'

'What do I know, Yun? Do I know everything?'

A small grunt. I imagined her smiling at me, safe at a distance, thinking of me as nothing more than the wife of a blip in her past. But I wanted an answer.

'I'm sorry, Imogen, I've got to go. You really shouldn't—'

'I know about the money,' I said.

Another pause. Silence.

'You hear me?'

'I heard. So what? Ten K between friends.'

Ten thousand! Fucking hell. I struggled to keep my voice from trembling. 'What was it for?'

A laugh this time. 'You'll have to ask him about that. Look, I—'

'I'm asking you. What did he give you all that money for?'

'Give *me*?'

My turn to pause. 'He gave you thousands. What was it for?' I was aware my voice had tapered from assertive to pathetic in a couple of sentences. Was Liv in fact a complete liar? Was my gut wrong?

'I don't know what you're talking about,' she said.

'Yes, you do. It's a lot of money. What do you want with my husband? What *did* you want with him?'

'Honestly, Imogen? Nothing. Look, you need to talk to him. It's not a big deal.'

Not a big deal. Was it a big deal? I didn't know.

'Is this about sex? Was the money . . .?'

'You're asking if I'm a prostitute? Fucking hell, Imogen.'

Imogen remained silent, her heart thumping with anger, her head thumping with confusion.

'It might seem like nothing to you, Yun, but I have to know. I—'

'He wasn't paying me for sex, Imogen. Christ. I can't believe I even have to say it.'

'Then what—?'

'No. I've got to go. I don't know what story he spun for you. We both said what we had to. That's life, isn't it? One big story. Sometimes the details are up to us, sometimes they're not. I'm sorry you didn't get the details you wanted, but those are Matt's to tell, not mine. Just rest assured – there's nothing I want from Matt, except perhaps my money back. I'm in no rush.'

She took a breath. 'You seem like a nice person, Imogen,' she said. 'And I know I'm not perfect. I've made mistakes, and I'm sorry about how this all turned out for Matt, I really am, but—'

'You're *sorry*?' I could barely contain my rage. Our lives had been upended as a result of this woman's lies, and she was apologising like all she'd done was flirt with him in a bar. '*Sorry* doesn't cut it, Yun. You said that Matt coerced you. You accused him, made him sound like a rapist, an abuser. A *predator*.'

'Look, it's not . . .' Yun's voice wavered; she sounded less sure of herself now. 'I wasn't even the one who went to HR, Imogen. They started asking questions, and then it all sort of . . . escalated. I didn't mean for—'

'Stop. Just stop,' I said. 'I don't want to hear any more lies.'

Yun sighed heavily. 'Imogen, this – the money – it isn't what you think it is. You need to speak to Matt. You're happily married, and you deserve to be. Nothing that happened needs to ruin that. I'm sorry – I've got to go.'

She hung up.

I redialled, and it rang several times before terminating. I tried again. She'd blocked my number.

It was only as I placed my phone back on the bedside table, my head swimming, that her final comment made sense. *Money back.* She wanted it back. It dawned on me. Matt said he had 'moved some things around'. The money had reappeared in our account.

She'd given it to him.

Matt

Matt's room was sweaty, the open window providing only a whisper of morning breeze. He buzzed with a nervous energy as he dressed and headed into the village. His mind was whirring, calculating – trying to make sense of Nancy's behaviour.

He offered a small wave to Mrs Owens on the way out. She'd maintained a polite distance from him during his stay, and Matt wondered how many people in the village knew what had happened. Did Nancy's reach extend that far – would she want it to? She'd made a point of protecting Ruby's privacy before.

The one glimmer of hope all week had been a brief text message from Imogen. It was Ash's first day at school today, and he'd been invited to join them. *Because she needs you there*, were Imogen's words. She'd ignored his reply, his request to talk. Matt bit back the frustration, but it was good news. There might be an opportunity to talk at the school gates, to sneak away for a coffee.

Although he still had no idea what he might say.

He parked on the road outside the school gates, edging closer to the chaos. His mood plummeted as he spied Imogen across the playground.

She stood with her arm around Ashley – his gorgeous Ashley, proud as punch in her new uniform, pigtails bouncing and her smile immovable as she watched the throngs of other kids racing around, weaving in and out of parents and teachers who were shouting over each other, trying to instil some form of order to the excitement.

Matt hesitated. Imogen was hunched over, her hair pulled back, greasy against her pallid face. She looked thin – had lost weight even in these last few days, her dress hanging off her shoulders. He would have headed over were it not for the figure behind her.

Nancy, standing proud, her gaze spread across the playground, watching over his wife and child. Matt shivered, despite the sunshine on his back.

Everything inside him screamed to challenge her, to pull his family out of her clutches, to expose her for the witch she was. And yet, all it would take were a few choice words from Nancy in the playground, surrounded by the sort of parents who'd willingly destroy him, lynch him, if they heard what he'd been accused of. He couldn't let Ash suffer such embarrassment.

He froze in indecision.

'Daddy!' Ash had been watching the gate and now sprinted over, leaping into his outstretched arms. He held her tight, watching over her head. Imogen gave a small wave, her face vacant. She made no indication she wanted him to join them. Nancy was more obvious in her distaste – she scowled, putting one hand on Imogen's shoulder, making her position clear. It was possessive, unnerving. Matt swallowed away his anger.

The bell rang, shrill and loud. Imogen flinched. Nancy didn't blink.

The crowds began to separate according to size. Adults stepped back; children lunged forward.

'Is she your teacher?' said Matt, watching a young woman attempting to line up the smallest children, the reception class. She struggled as they broke away, herding them back again. Matt glanced over to Imogen, who nodded, pointing at the line, without so much as a smile.

'Yes,' said Ashley. 'Should I line up now?'

'I think so,' Matt said.

'Will you be here to collect me at home time?'

Matt smiled, giving her a kiss on the forehead. 'Maybe, darling,' he said. 'Maybe.'

'And you'll be home soon?' She paused, staring at him with the intensity only a four-year-old can summon.

'I hope so, sweetie,' he said.

Ash smiled before running off. Matt straightened up, feeling his lower back protesting. The mattress at the B&B was hard, his body struggling with the change.

Ash's line was led off into the building. She waved to Imogen all the way. Imogen waved back, her face locked in a smile which looked as if it required huge effort to maintain. It dropped the second Ash was out of sight. Imogen turned and walked away, Nancy sticking close behind.

★

Ashley's first day at school. A time for happy tears and celebration, yet all Matt could feel was the cold emptiness of watching his daughter leaving in one direction, his wife in the other. He wanted to call out, stopping himself at the last second, aware of several strange looks from other parents as he stood alone, hands on the top of his head, the desperation clear on his face.

Matt kept his distance but couldn't help following. It was a five-minute walk to his street. He kept with them until he saw Nancy disappear behind Imogen into his house. *His house.*

He pulled out his phone and typed out a text message – the same message he'd typed numerous times over the last few days: *I'm innocent. This is madness. Please can we talk?*

Imogen replied promptly: *No.*

Matt jammed the phone back in his pocket and spun on the spot; fists clenched. He counted to ten before kicking out at the low wall in front of him, instantly regretting it as the pain shot through his foot.

'Something wrong?'

Matt looked up, racked his brains for the name. Jon, or James? The thick-set man strode across his front garden, gloves on. Jon. Definitely. They'd met at Nancy's fundraiser, the one and only time he'd managed to meet people from the neighbouring streets. It seemed an age ago.

'Tough day already?' said Jon, his head and chest visible above the thick lavender growing over the wall. Neatly pruned, thought Matt, like all the other perfect gardens in this stupid village.

Jon smiled, but it was wary. The sort of smile that said *Please don't kick my wall.*

Matt blew out his cheeks. He didn't want any trouble, but

274

didn't want to stand in the street and talk. 'I'm sorry.' He pointed at the offending bricks. 'Yeah, that was silly.'

Jon shrugged, standing the other side of his wall, keeping his gaze fixed on Matt.

'Trouble at home?' he asked.

Matt paused. The question caught him a little off guard. 'No,' he said, 'why do you ask?'

Jon smiled, again, tilting his head. 'Your car hasn't been in the drive for a few days. You've been parked at the kerb, spying on your own house. You followed your wife home today and stopped here to kick my wall.'

Matt's mouth dropped open a fraction. He caught it, but the panic was obviously evident on his face.

Jon laughed, putting his hands out, palms facing Matt. 'Sorry, buddy,' he said. 'I'm a retired police officer. I can't help myself.'

Fuck. Matt's throat seized for a second before he managed to force it open. The blood rushed to his cheeks – he could feel his face getting hotter.

'You got me,' he said. Jon didn't know; couldn't know. Matt had to assume Nancy hadn't spoken to anybody, particularly not an ex-copper. Matt wouldn't still be standing here if she had – he'd be in a world of pain right now. More so than he already was.

'I . . .' Matt shook his head, thinking Jon would know a lie when he saw it. 'We've had a bit of a domestic,' he admitted.

Jon raised his eyebrows.

'Not *domestic*,' Matt said hurriedly, wondering what connotations the word might have conjured. 'Just an argument. The move has been so stressful. Imogen's wondering if it was the right thing . . .' All true, he thought. Was that enough? Could he go now?

Jon nodded, keeping silent. This was what they did, the fuckers. Silence drives the confession.

But not from Matt. Not today.

'I'm sorry for bringing it to your front garden,' he said, backing away. 'I've got to go to work, anyway.'

Jon nodded, keeping his smile. 'Take care, Matt,' he said. 'I hope you work it out.'

Matt turned, feeling Jon's eyes on his back as he strolled along the main street, back towards the village, keeping his stride steady and his head high.

He didn't dare look back.

Matt didn't relax until he reached the main shopping street, comfortable that nobody was interested in him, let alone watching him. He picked an empty bench on the edge of the village green and sat, angry at himself for cowardly following Imogen and Nancy, for being so scared of Jon when challenged, and then running away to sit on this small wooden bench, sweating in his suit, grasping at the mess he found no way of containing.

He lifted his head, feeling the sun on his face. The soft sounds of the village should relax him, defuse the stress and carry it away. His inability to enjoy even this angered him. Nancy was screwing every aspect of his life down to the smallest sensation.

It had to end, but Matt still needed more than a vague suspicion and a story he could never prove about Nancy buying medications.

He had a fleeting thought of calling social services. Matt

and Imogen had never challenged Nancy's dedication to her daughter, but perhaps her efforts were as mad as the rest of her. But the same spiral of events would occur – Nancy would repeat her accusation. The police would believe her over him. They'd ask Imogen. Matt would be sunk.

He cast his eyes up the street, his next thoughts aligning perfectly with the person he could see strolling along the road, two shopping bags in her hands.

She spied him and smiled, biting her bottom lip as she dropped the bags by the bench and sat next to him.

'Hi,' said Ruby.

Matt took a deep breath, shifting around in his seat. Ruby looked full of colour today, her skin deeply tanned, her face flushed. She crossed her legs and tugged down her denim skirt. Matt thought she'd put on a bit of weight – healthier, a good sign. Perhaps his reservations about Nancy's treatments were wrong. Perhaps.

'We shouldn't be talking,' he said, trying to keep his tone friendly. Ruby was innocent and getting frustrated at her wouldn't help.

'You say that every time we talk,' said Ruby, smiling. She tucked her sunglasses down the front of her top.

Matt huffed, glancing around, suddenly aware of everyone else. Were they looking?

Ruby followed his gaze. 'Fine,' she said. 'Do you want me to leave?'

Matt shook his head. 'No. No, look . . . I'm in a bit of a mess right now.'

'I know,' said Ruby. 'And I'm sorry.'

'It's not your fault,' he said, wondering if even starting this conversation was wrong; surreal, inappropriate. He wanted to scream it was all her mother's fault, but managed to bite his tongue.

'I've tried talking to Mum,' she said. 'She'll come around. Give her time—'

Matt snorted. 'Time? I've been kicked out of my house, Ruby. What she's saying about me . . .'

'Please. She's massively overprotective. She'll calm down, see her mistake. It'll blow over.'

'She's turned Imogen against me,' said Matt. 'My wife doesn't want to talk to me. Your mum . . .' Matt stopped short of talking about the other things. The lipstick, the photos on his laptop. It wasn't fair to tell Ruby about those.

Ruby nodded. She bit her lower lip again, shrugging.

Matt closed his eyes. How could he expect Ruby to understand? She was a teenager; she'd never even been in a proper relationship yet, fallen in love, made a commitment. She was in the infancy of all this – with all of it to look forward to. Her life was consumed with her illness and her exposure to such things was almost non-existent. He hated to punish the girl, but his best strategy at this point was to stay away from her.

'I need to get to work,' he said, standing abruptly, stepping on to the footpath.

Ruby looked up at him. He could see the hurt in her eyes. 'Are you walking down the hill?'

Matt nodded. 'I'm staying at Mrs Owens' bed and breakfast.'

Ruby smiled. 'Lucky you. In which case I'll walk with you.' She stood and picked up her bags.

Matt wanted to tell her to go home, to leave him be, but

she straightened up and beamed at him, slipping her sunglasses over her eyes. 'I could do with the walk,' she said.

Matt sighed. It was probably a bad idea being with Ruby, but at this point he didn't have the energy to fight it. 'OK,' he said, 'let's go.'

Imogen

The trip to school almost killed me. I insisted on going, not wanting Matt to do it on his own. Ash wouldn't have minded, but it would have led to a conversation I wasn't yet ready to have. I needed Matt to stay away a little longer, until I had time to collect my thoughts. To prepare my challenge.

'Go upstairs,' said Nancy, pulling my front door closed. 'Get in bed.' She smiled at me. 'Emotional, isn't it?' she said.

I can only assume she meant Ash's first day, not everything else, although I caught a hint of something in her eyes – a deeper understanding.

'Is Ruby around today?' I asked. I saw Nancy's eyes narrow. Only for a second.

'She went into the village to pick some things up for me,' she said. 'Her first day out of bed in a while. She'll be back later.'

I nodded. 'OK,' I said, climbing the stairs. Perhaps I could speak to her later, I thought.

'Would you feed Jake for me?' I called. 'He'll be happy in the garden for the day once he's fed.'

Nancy's smile thinned at the edges, but she nodded. 'I will.'

I lay in bed but struggled to sleep, despite being up half the night with nausea. It was a hurtful reminder of my morning sickness, except without the prize at the end, no pregnancy to make it worth it. I heard Nancy moving around downstairs, still cleaning, still preparing my snacks and lunch. Her patients had increased in number by one, but if anything she seemed chirpier, more full of energy than ever before. She hurried between Ruby and me with a matronly purpose I'd rarely seen outside of my old hospital wards.

Without the strength to question it, I nevertheless knew it needed to end soon. Nancy brought me tea, smoothies, a shoulder to cry on, and while I appreciated her efforts, I knew my health was beyond that. I needed a full work-up, tests on gut function, sample analysis. I expected to be put on a course of antibiotics and medications to reduce acid production – I needed to heal with the benefits of western medicine, not just hospitality.

I wasn't seriously worried, not yet, but I needed the damn GP appointment, which, despite Nancy's best efforts, seemed to be rescheduled every time I asked – the downside of a small village practice, I guessed, although it was frustrating. Nancy was right about one thing – I didn't have the energy any more for a trip into Guildford hospital. I figured a few more days at home wouldn't kill me.

But I needed my health, because my mind was in danger of breaking too. I was putting Matt off, but we did need to talk. About Yun.

I reflected deep into the night, unsure which path to take. It was a detail, a small imperfection in the surface, paling into insignificance following the truth about Ruby.

Or was it?

It wasn't about the money; it was the uncertainty that hurt me. Knowing, one way or the other, is enough to keep you alive, whatever that knowledge is. At least you can throw yourself in one direction, follow the path, decide whether to move on or not.

I could choose to let it go, knowing that Matt was an adult and that, whatever had happened in London, he had already paid for it ten times over – his career, his life, *our* life in London. Or I could push, nag, dig until I revealed every little detail. It isn't the size of the lie that matters, or the content. It's the fact it was created in the first place. That's what gnawed away at me.

Claire's words rang in my ears – *the fundamental assumption that women don't lie about these things. You take it as the truth.*

I closed my eyes. I drifted. My dreams, when they arrived, were far from pleasant.

I woke to the sound of voices. Short and abrupt – spoken in the tone of people who were trying not to wake someone.

The door creaked open and Nancy entered, holding a tray full of her usual offerings. My stomach rumbled at the sight; my mouth watered. I noticed a severe thirst as she set the tray on the side of the mattress.

'Who were you talking to?' I said, shuffling upright, taking the fruit smoothie and drinking half of it, hoping to God it stayed down.

Nancy's smile thinned a fraction. 'Ruby decided to pop by,' she said. 'I said you weren't up to seeing anyone, but she ignored me. I don't know what to do with her at the moment.'

'I'd like to talk to her,' I said. 'I have to, Nancy. I know it's awkward for you, but we'll have to do this sooner or later.'

Nancy busied herself around my bedroom, whipping out a duster and wiping it along the windowsill. She paused, staring out of the window. I saw her shoulders rise and fall with a deep sigh.

'Do you think that's wise?' she said, moving onwards, re-arranging my things on the dressing table, dusting under them.

I frowned. Nancy remained facing away from me. 'Wise?' I said. 'It's necessary, Nancy. We can't *ignore* this.'

Nancy turned to me. 'Ignore it? Is that what you think I'm doing, Imogen?'

Her tone was off, hurt perhaps. She smoothed the front of her skirt.

'No,' I said. 'I didn't mean—'

'Because you're right. *Awkward* hardly covers it. This is devastating for me, Imogen, and I'm not quite sure how to process it. I'm trying to be a friend. I'm trying to . . .'

Her voice broke and she turned away.

I placed my glass down and, with great effort, slid out of the bed, putting my arm around her. 'Nancy, I'm sorry. I didn't mean to be . . . well, insensitive.' I paused while the room spun, my blood pressure so low it struggled to keep me upright. 'This is an impossible situation for both of us.'

I held her for a few moments longer, feeling her trembling subside.

'Mum?'

The voice from my doorway startled me. Ruby poked her head in, then entered. I couldn't help but look her up and down, wishing she'd wear a few more clothes, or at least *longer* clothes. I stopped myself – she was a teenager, wearing exactly what teenagers should. I wore skirts like that when I was her

283

age. It didn't help the sick feeling, though, and the images of her in her garden jumping into my mind. The knowledge that Matt found her body attractive was a kick in the gut I didn't need right now.

'Are you OK, Mum?' she said.

Nancy broke away, patting me on the shoulder. She pulled her signature smile.

'Ruby,' I said. 'Can we—'

'I'm fine, dear,' said Nancy, cutting me off. 'Just a little exhausted. I thought I told you to wait for me at home?'

Ruby's expression dropped, sulky. She looked at me then glanced around my room, my bed. Her eyes fell on the tray, on the half-drunk smoothie, and I saw a strange expression on her face. Her eyes widened. She walked over, reaching towards the glass. She looked about to say something when Nancy rushed forward.

'Home!' said Nancy, grabbing Ruby's hand and ushering her forcefully out of the room. 'Come on, Ruby.'

I stood where I was, slightly bewildered, listening to their hushed voices as they stomped down my stairs. The front door slammed; there was a pause, a few moments of silence, before I heard footsteps coming back up.

'Sorry,' said Nancy. 'She's so disobedient at the moment.'

I watched my flustered friend, not wanting to interfere, but worried I was somehow to blame. 'It's really OK, Nancy,' I said. 'I could have taken the opportunity to talk to her.'

'She's not well enough,' said Nancy, shaking her head.

'She looked OK to . . .' I tailed off. It wasn't my judgement, not my place. I nodded. Time to change the subject for today. There was always tomorrow.

284

'Did you have any luck with the doctor's appointment?' I asked, diverting the conversation. I sat on the bed, staring at the tray, and the smoothie that had distracted Ruby so much. I grabbed the glass and drank the rest, my thirst still not quenched. My vision was starting to blur, the nausea raging.

I turned back to Nancy, who was staring out of the window again.

'That girl,' she whispered under her breath.

I pushed myself up and joined her at the window, followed her gaze. Ruby was undressing in their back garden, revealing her bikini underneath. She reclined on the sun lounger, sipping at a glass of water. She lifted her head and waved at us, before flipping her shades down and opening a book.

The visions returned. Matt's laptop. Picture after picture. I shivered, stepping back, lowering myself on to the bed. A sudden weakness took my limbs; they felt detached, numb. I shook my head, brought my feet on to the mattress. Time to rest.

I endured a few minutes of silence before Nancy clapped her hands together.

'I'll make us some tea,' she said, sweeping past me, grabbing the tray as she did so. 'And don't worry, I can collect Ashley from school if you're not feeling up to it.'

'Thank you,' I said, 'if you don't mind. And Nancy?'

'Yes?' Nancy turned at the door, her smile perfect and brilliant.

'I . . .' I wanted to tell her it was time for me to call Matt, to start the next stage, whatever that might be and wherever it might take me.

But something stopped me. I don't know what. I felt a little spooked after Ruby's visit, seeing them together. Perhaps it was a primal need to keep something small to myself.

'Nothing,' I said. 'It's nothing.'

Nancy nodded and left.

I waited until her footsteps had faded, then I reached over to my bedside table. My hand hit the glass but nothing else. I rummaged around, checked down the side, by the pillow. I even pulled the mattress up at the corner.

Nothing.

On the floor, my charger cable snaked out from the plug socket. I hadn't unplugged my phone, or at least I didn't remember doing so. I *did* remember plugging it in when we'd returned from school.

The room spun. I was getting worse. My limbs felt leaden and I lay back, feeling the tiredness sweep through my body, a rush of hot and cold, pins and needles in my hands.

I shivered again.

Matt

Matt stared at the monitor, willing the motivation to act on the steady pile of work accumulating in his inbox. Losing his job would be a further disaster for both him and Imogen.

Shelley dropped a takeaway coffee on his desk and crossed her arms.

'Do you want to talk about it?' she said.

What could he possibly say? 'No. There's nothing to talk about. A few issues at home, that's all.'

Shelley looked thoughtful. 'OK. I'll give you a bit more time. But we need to discuss things, Matt. Late in again today. It's not quite working out, is it?'

Her words created a fresh flurry in his gut. 'It will,' he said. 'I promise, Shelley. You haven't seen the best of me.'

'I bloody hope not,' she said.

'Ash's first day of school,' he added, swallowing, cupping the hot drink in his hands, closing his eyes for a moment. Shelley let out a long breath and turned to leave.

'Don't give up on me,' he said, as she reached the door. His voice came out as a whine, high-pitched. Mildly pathetic.

Shelley frowned. 'I'll book something for next week, Matt. We'll talk then. In the meantime,' she pointed at his monitor, knowing his work stack was growing by the day, 'prove me wrong.'

Matt nodded, knowing he'd struggle to do any quality work while Nancy dominated his attention. There was very little here that could help him, unless . . . Unless. Something popped into his head – something he should have thought of earlier.

'Shelley?'

His boss slowly backtracked, raising her eyebrows. He saw her expression and decided against asking her directly.

'The archives. Do I have full access?'

Shelley frowned. 'Err. Yes. Your login should get you in. Why?'

Matt thought for a moment. 'No reason. I might need to look something up.'

She rolled her eyes and Matt smiled, watching her leave for the second time. She closed his door a little harder than necessary.

Matt opened a new browser window and clicked on the link for the paper's archive database. He should have looked sooner, but it was only Shelley's pissed-off expression that had reminded him of it.

Once the database search screen had loaded, he typed in his address, keeping the date parameters within the last ten years.

Several pages of results displayed, but most of them were from the surrounding area – the village, the Guildford suburbs – minor crime reporting, many covering highways and forestry planning applications. Matt refined the search parameters, narrowed the dates.

There. Staring him in the face.

Six years ago. *Coroner rejects request for inquest.* Highlighted text, part of a longer report by one of the team at the paper. It was tagged as unpublished, which meant it never saw print.

Matt stared at the address: 15 New Church Road, Albury, Surrey.

Nancy's house.

Matt loaded the full article. It concerned a resident, George Rupert White, who passed away on the 15th January that year. He died peacefully in his home, but before the funeral, the local GP practice raised a concern. The medical details were vague in the article, but the cause of death was disputed. It was initially recorded as death from pneumonia – a secondary infection caused by a hereditary blood disorder – but the GP practice claimed they had no record of such a condition and logged the anomaly. The grieving widow (Nancy White) insisted they continue with the cremation, and in return, the GP practice filed a referral to the coroner. This action would stop the cremation and keep the body in the morgue ready for a post-mortem, should the coroner decide to open an investigation.

The reporter who penned the original article was new and clearly excited by the whole thing – a few paragraphs of conjecture followed, with few details – not even the GP's name. A suspicious death in sleepy middle-class Surrey was newsworthy, except within a couple of weeks, by the time the coroner opened the file, the cremation had already taken place. It seemed there'd been a mix-up in paperwork and the body had been released to the undertaker. The funeral went ahead, unreported, at a south Guildford crematorium, away from the village. The service was restricted to close family and friends.

The coroner decided against opening an investigation and

provided no comment to the reporter, who surmised that cause of death would be very hard to establish on a pile of ashes, combined with a lack of other concerns – the wife was an upstanding member of the village community and there was no police or other service involvement. The matter was closed. The reporter was disappointed.

There was nothing to report.

Then why did Matt have goosebumps? Why did his discomfort ratchet up a level?

He re-read the article, then combed the archives for anything related. There were no results. He extended his search to the web, trawling Google with Nancy's name, her husband's name. His road, his village. Nothing else presented itself. In reporting terms, without leaving the office, it was a dead end.

He slumped in his chair, struggling to see how this fit, what it meant. The editor had concluded there was no story worth printing.

Although, in Matt's experience, that didn't mean there wasn't a story.

The day marched on, and his workload stacked up. A sea of red emails stared at him from the monitor. He was at the point of giving up when his phone rang. He hoped Imogen had changed her mind, was ready to talk. But no.

The number on the screen wasn't Imogen's. He didn't recognise it.

'Yes?'

'It's me, Matt.'

It was her. Of course it was. She only popped up at the

most inconvenient of times – when he needed to think, when he needed to focus. When he needed to pretend everything would turn out OK, if he could just make it through the next twenty-four hours.

'Liv,' he said. 'You win. I'll transfer it today. Just ... I can't deal with you right now. OK?'

He heard her slow breathing at the other end, a marked difference from their recent calls. Liv's mood might be stable now, but her swings were spontaneous and hard to manage. A consequence of her addiction, mixed with her persistent and growing mental health issues. He always questioned his responsibility. Could he have protected Liv more as they grew up? He did his best, but he was the younger sibling. Their parents' deaths had created a perfect storm of emotions, which they each dealt with in different ways.

But even now, he couldn't bring himself to resent her. Liv was damaged. By what, only a lifetime of therapy might answer. Their childhood was stifling and unhappy, but times changed, and Matt had changed with them. He wondered if his memories were accurate – as with so much in your childhood, who knew what was real and what was manufactured by time and emotion? He'd never know the true answers to many of the questions bouncing around his head.

He'd promised himself he'd never desert Liv, no matter how she behaved. He was a resolute failure as a brother, but even blackmail couldn't stop him loving his big sister. If he had the means, he'd give her a shedload of money and set her up properly. Get her some proper help, rather than the erratic group sessions she hated so much. But for years all he'd managed to do was drip-feed money while struggling to provide any other type of support – a listening ear, a shoulder to lean on. He'd told Liv a lot of secrets over the years, trusting that she'd never tell. It became their thing – complete transparency, a family therapy bound by the certainty of blood. She became his shoulder to cry on, a sibling confessional. A place to put the secrets. All of them. The money became his penance.

'You were desperate.' Matt sniffed.

'But . . . I didn't mean to actually tell her. It was just a threat. I never planned . . . I'm so sorry. Is Imogen OK?'

Matt's stomach sank. He stared at the desk, clenching his left hand into a fist, pushing it into the wood.

'You didn't.'

'I'm *sorry*. I was having a bad day. You still hadn't given me the money. I never said anything before. The others, I—'

'I *texted* you,' said Matt. 'I told you you'd get it. You can have it now.'

'I didn't get any text,' said Liv. 'I didn't know.'

Matt glanced at the screen again. New number. Of course she didn't get the fucking text.

'What did you say? Exactly? Tell me, Liv. It's important.'

'I just . . . I said you spent it on her. You told me you did. All that money, Matt. I was desperate. I'm sorry.'

'Did you say anything else? Did you tell her anything else?'

'No. I was asking her for money. The rent was due, I didn't have any food – the social didn't pay out until Friday. It just came out, that you'd rather spend your money on her than me. Your own flesh and blood. It hurt.'

Flesh and blood. If Matt could give Liv a family of her own, he would. But her path had taken her far away from such an existence. She could barely keep any friends, let alone start a family, a career, a life. He took a few deep breaths.

'That's not true, Liv. I've given you money for years, every month, for as long as I can remember.'

'I know. I know! I said I'm sorry. What else can I do?'

Matt heard her voice break. He could picture the tears streaming down her face, her mood plummeting until she reached for something to fix it.

'I forgive you,' he said. 'Do you hear me? I forgive you. You didn't mean it, and it hasn't done any damage. Imogen is fine. We're both fine.'

Her small gasps slowed. 'You mean it?' she said. 'I didn't . . .'

'You didn't, Liv,' he said. 'None of this is your fault. It's mine.'

'You're sure.'

Matt leaned back in his chair, trying to calculate the damage, trying to gauge Imogen's reaction. She hadn't mentioned it – why would she, given what she thought of him now, given the lies Nancy was feeding her? Perhaps she would ignore it, and it would remain the insignificant detail that he knew it to be. Imogen didn't need to know this, because it didn't change anything about what had happened in London.

Matt

It hadn't taken much to find the reporter. Simon Shaw no longer worked for the *Guildford Press*, but he'd stayed local, changing career to a traditional fiction publisher on the other side of town. Matt looked him up online and decided to door-step him, waiting outside his office, holding his phone and a social media photo he hoped was recent. Simon looked trendy, intelligent – the sort of reporter Matt had once strived to be.

At 6 p.m. the office started to empty, the staff filtering out singly and in groups. Matt watched the younger ones with a certain amount of jealousy. That used to be him.

'Simon.' Matt hurried up to a man who looked pretty much identical to the photo. It seemed some people were honest on social media. Matt hoped it extended to his reporting.

'Hi,' Simon said warily. He slowed, but kept walking.

'My name's Matt. I'm the editor at the *Guildford Press*.'

Simon stopped, his face relaxing in recognition. 'Oh, hi,' he said. 'I . . . What can I do for you?'

'Can I buy you a quick drink?'

Simon checked his watch. 'I really shouldn't . . .'

'Just a quick one? I'm fascinated by an old article you wrote – a few years back. Never made it to print, but I think there was something in it.'

That got Simon's attention. Nothing baited a reporter more than genuine interest in one of their investigative reports, particularly if it never got published.

Simon nodded towards a pub on the corner, the Black Lion. 'A quick one, then.'

They settled in a corner booth. The pub was busy but not too noisy, with most of the patrons choosing to stand outside, enjoying the last of the summer air. Simon declined alcohol and Matt followed his example, depositing two sparkling waters on to the table.

'Which article?' said Simon, still wary, sizing Matt up.

Matt had printed it from the archives, and he slid it across the table. Simon scanned it for a few seconds before speaking.

'The old bag kill someone else, did she?'

Matt almost dropped his drink on the table, grabbing the slippery glass at the last minute. He glanced around the pub, then back to the young man in front of him.

'What?' He cleared his throat, playing with his glass for a few seconds, still in shock. 'What do you mean?'

Simon slid the print-out back across the table. 'Hardly my finest work,' he said. 'You're not head-hunting, are you? I'm not looking to go back.'

'No,' said Matt. 'Don't worry, this isn't a sales pitch. I'm trawling through local unfinished stories, looking for the serious stuff that got missed, swept under the rug, that sort of thing . . .'

Simon looked intrigued, but laughed. 'Not many of those in Surrey,' he said. 'I think that article was the only genuinely suspicious thing I ever saw. It's hardly serious organised crime though.'

Matt nodded. 'It caught my eye. What do you mean, kill somebody?'

Simon watched him. Matt wasn't sure if it was the desperation in his eyes or the shake of his hands, but Simon's smile faded.

'I remember it distinctly,' said Simon. 'And I don't know, is the honest answer. But there's more to the story than I covered in my brief – and now I look at it, *amateur* – report.'

'It was good enough to grab my interest.'

Simon shrugged. 'I always found it hard to document the sense you get on first interviewing somebody. Some reporters are great at describing that first emotional connection. I never quite nailed it. Anyway, this person . . .' He grabbed the report again, scanning through the first few lines.

'Nancy White?' Matt offered.

'Right. Nancy. She gave me the shivers. The heebie-jeebies. I wasn't even going in hard. But I wanted to know why the GP had kicked up such a fuss. I saw a possible euthanasia, with a heart-wrenching story behind it. I may not have been the most sensitive chap, given she'd just lost her husband, but the way she shouted at me. Well . . .'

Matt thought of the way Nancy talked to him; her icy tone, her ability to strike fear. He recalled her response when he'd suggested running an article on Ruby. He could imagine how she might react to somebody probing about her husband.

Euthanasia would explain a lot, he thought. 'Did you get anything out of her?' he asked.

Simon shook his head. 'Nothing except threats. She knows

the law. I had a certain freedom of the press, but I was treading a line. It's . . .'

'What?'

'She seemed genuinely full of grief, and full of anger. Not unreasonable, after losing your loved one to a chronic illness. She had a young daughter, after all. But her attitude towards the GP and the coroner was startling. She was outright hostile.'

'She blamed the doctors? That would fit with euthanasia.'

Simon shook his head again. 'She said it was nobody's business except hers. She was emphatic. The coroner had no business desecrating her husband's body – that was how she put it.'

'And you spoke to the coroner?'

'No. They won't speak to the press.'

'The GP?'

'Yes, but he was bound by patient confidentiality. However, he was so outraged he let slip a few things.'

'What things?'

Simon laughed. 'You're persistent, aren't you? Nothing I could use. Again, it was body language, emotion – what was *unsaid*.'

Matt raised his eyebrows.

'The GP suspected something,' said Simon. 'I don't know how, or what. But he forgot himself in front of me. Close to retirement; I think he was frustrated. He told me he'd call the police himself if he had any proof.'

'Call the police and tell them what? It was a mercy killing?'

'No . . . he wouldn't say, exactly,' said Simon. 'That's why my article was so bad. But I had this feeling. George White apparently died of some rare chronic condition, one his GP didn't know he had, and which he'd never received any treatment for, not from anywhere local at least – I had a few sources. It was weird enough for the GP to call foul play. I mentioned the euthanasia suspicion – even that would have made a story, albeit a more forgivable one – but I could tell from the GP's body language I was off the mark.'

'But he didn't say what the mark was?'

Simon sighed. 'His professionalism kicked in, which was frustrating for both of us, I think. He did let slip one thing, which I don't think I put in this article.'

'What?'

'George White had been for one appointment in the three years before his death. He'd had a routine blood test which revealed something odd, apparently. But the GP caught himself, muttered something about losing his pension if he couldn't button his mouth. I remember we were walking out of his surgery at the end of the day. He climbed into his car and drove off, told me not to contact him again.'

'An odd blood test? What was odd about it?'

'No idea,' said Simon. 'Given the man died of a blood disorder, it didn't seem strange to me. But ... body language, emotion. The GP was deeply frustrated. And there was nothing he could do about it.'

Matt stared at the table. He spun his glass around in his hands.

'I'm afraid that's it,' said Simon, checking his watch. 'I can see you didn't get what you wanted, but I've got to go.' He finished his drink and grabbed his bag, ready to leave. 'I might have one other thing for you, also not in the report.'

Matt looked up.

'The GP's name. Got a pen?'

Imogen

Daylight streamed in through the window. I could feel a breeze, could see the curtain shifting. The bedside table moved, floated, lurched out of reach as I grasped for it.

I pushed myself on to my elbows but stopped, the vertigo so extreme I couldn't move further. I tried to focus on the pillow, my vision flickering. Nystagmus – involuntary eye movements, repetitive, unpleasant. Worrying.

I closed my eyes. My phone. Where was my phone?

'Nancy?' My voice croaked. There was a glass of something beside the bed. I reached out blindly and grabbed it, hearing the liquid spill across the bedsheet. I drank – a hint of lemon, a bitter aftertaste.

'No, Mummy. It's me.'

I rolled over. Ash leapt on to the bed, her small body cuddling up to me.

'Hey, baby,' I said. It was better on my back, I pushed myself upwards, against the headboard.

'Are you feeling better?' Ash's big eyes looked up.

'Not yet, sweetie,' I said, holding my head still, trying

299

to keep the dizziness from triggering the nausea. 'Is Nancy here?'

'Yes. She's downstairs. I think her and Ruby had an argument.' Ash giggled. 'Ruby said some bad words.'

What time was it? The sun was still bright, but the evenings were drawing in. It couldn't be much past 7 p.m.

'Did Nancy remember to feed Jake?' I asked. I'd hardly paid him any attention these last few days, though his barking had settled, which was a good sign.

Ash nodded. 'I always do his breakfast, then Ruby and I do dinner,' she said. 'Every day. And Nancy does if we forget, though she screws her face up at the smell. Ruby quite likes him. She plays with him while you're in bed.'

I smiled, thankful. At least Jake wasn't suffering in all of this. Extra faces always excited him – he was probably having the time of his life.

'What were you dreaming about?' asked Ashley.

'Dreaming?'

'Yes. You were pulling a funny face. Talking. I'm not sure what you were saying.'

'Oh. Well . . .' I knew what I'd been dreaming about. The same thing I'd dreamt about for the last few nights, most of which I wasn't about to share with Ash.

'I was dreaming about my wedding day,' I said truthfully. 'When me and Daddy got married.'

Ashley's eyes lit up. 'Like in the photos, downstairs.'

I laughed. 'Yes, baby, those ones. I was very happy.'

Happy, but anxious, and that was what the dream was about. No surprise, given my current circumstances.

I hugged Ashley tighter. The smiles were genuine in the photos.

I'd hidden my nerves so well on my wedding day, managing to conceal the terror in my eyes, the jitters in my speech. The wedding *was* wonderful, but I compensated for my anxiety during our engagement by over-spending. My parents laughed at the increasingly ridiculous demands but paid for them anyway. They wanted me to have whatever I wanted, however absurd. 'You'll regret the things you don't do, not the things you do,' said my mum, stealing from Mark Twain, who I'm sure never meant wedding lingerie and ice sculptures, although I expect he would have approved (if perhaps been a little shocked at my choice of lingerie).

I wonder what Matt made of my mum's advice about regrets.

'Did you always want to get married? To Daddy?' said Ash. She kept her face tucked under my arm. I wondered what she sensed, whether these innocent questions were a sign of something more troubling.

The idea of marriage hadn't come easy to me. My family upbringing had given me rock-solid financial and emotional stability, and when I broke out of the family home and decided to shack up with Matt, it came as something of a shock. *Are you sure?* my body kept asking. My mind spun it around. Of course I was. *He's gorgeous, isn't he?*

Dating was fine. Living together worked well. There was always Mummy and Daddy. I could always ditch him and run back home. But my bubble-wrapped body still panicked at the finality of marriage, building up to my special day, when I swallowed three diazepam and felt like I was going to break down in fits and tears.

But I did it. Because I'm an adult, an educated and professional woman who didn't take any shit and never would. I could love Matt, commit to him.

Trust him forever.

I felt my throat swelling before I could answer, not trusting the words that might spill out – the tone or the uncertainty. I *was* certain about marrying Matt, and at the time my doubts were not about his fidelity or his character. Of those, I was as certain as anyone can be at the beginning of married life. But now, in retrospect . . . were there warning signs I missed? Is that what my dreams were searching for?

I squeezed my daughter and decided I needed to deal with my dreams before I shared them.

'I'm so sorry I couldn't pick you up from school,' I said.

'It's OK, Mummy. Nancy and Ruby were there. I like Ruby. She makes me laugh.'

Nancy *and* Ruby. My ever-present friend, and the daughter I couldn't help feeling animosity towards. I had to remind myself she was fifteen, a child, technically. Not to blame. But that didn't mean I had to like her, did it?

Poor Ash. I worried she'd been spending far too much of her time in her own little world or with Nancy, but she seemed to take it in her stride, and I needed the help. There were several after-school clubs on offer and I figured they might help. Music, construction club, forest school – Ash seemed keen and it would keep her happy and occupied. I hadn't called Matt, hadn't even texted him. Whatever he was guilty of – and I had little doubt of his guilt – this was firmly in my court. My failing. If only I didn't feel so awful.

'Good,' I said, wanting to ask a hundred questions about Ash's first day – her teacher, the other children, where she sat – but I couldn't find the energy, or the concentration to hold a conversation, let alone pay attention. I owed it to Ash to do this properly, when I felt better.

'Could you run and get Nancy for me, please?'

I waited, time drifting. The alarm clock by my bed – the John Lewis one Mum had bought me when I first started shift work – was gone. Had I moved it?

The sun dipped and the shadows lengthened. I heard brief bursts of noise – laughter and voices. The nausea became unbearable and I half-walked, half-crawled to the bathroom. Emptying my stomach helped a fraction, the drink tasting even more bitter on the way back up, but getting back into bed felt like a herculean effort. I slumped on my back, out of breath.

The door opened. The draft was cold on my face. I opened my eyes.

'Nancy?'

'Shhh,' she said. 'Relax, Imogen.'

'No.' I shook my head, trying to push myself up again. 'I need a doctor, Nancy. Please can you call one for me?'

'I did,' came the soothing reply. Then Nancy was on the bed, holding my shoulders, stroking the duvet as she pushed me back down. 'There's nothing to worry about,' she said. 'The doctor will be here as soon as she can.'

'Today?'

Nancy hushed me again. I found myself sliding down the sheet as she rubbed my arm, caressed my cheeks. 'Soon, dear. Soon.'

The pillow was so soft, so warm and welcoming, I sank into it. Nancy was here, and the doctor would be coming. Ash was safe. That's all I needed. I smiled at the blurred face in front of me. 'Thank you,' I said.

'Not necessary,' said Nancy, pulling up my duvet, tucking

303

it around my chin and cheeks in a protective and soothing embrace.

I closed my eyes and drifted, the spinning slowing until it was almost bearable. My stomach rumbled but the cramps lessened.

'Go to sleep,' said Nancy. 'This will pass. I said I'd look after you, Imogen. Trust me. It's what I do.'

Matt

The village of Godalming was a twenty-minute drive. Matt buzzed with confusion, a growing number of pieces jostling in his mind, but not connecting. He was chasing ghosts, suspicions that might lead nowhere.

But still, he must chase. Matt was exposed, vulnerable, running on fear. He needed to turn it around, find Nancy's weakness, her secrets. He needed to stop her, one way or the other.

And right now he was in no doubt there were secrets to be found.

Dr Harry Banks had retired five years ago, but it didn't take much to find his address online. Matt traced his medical registration through to a community group and a church website, which revealed a charity garden party, and voilà – a current address.

Matt paused a few doors along from the large detached property, cutting the engine, realising he hadn't prepared anything that might encourage a complete stranger to talk to him at this time of the evening about a historical, not to mention confidential, patient matter.

It was an expensive area, full of professionals and wealthy pensioners. He felt self-conscious parked in his old and dusty car. The streets were quiet, the sky fading to pink as the sun set, the gardens full of blossom. Another tranquil neighbourhood.

Matt's fingers danced over the screen of his phone. His texts to Imogen still went unanswered or came back with one-word replies. There was no way he could explain his findings via a text message. There wasn't much to say, either, but he dialled anyway, hearing it ring several times before it diverted to voicemail.

Please, he texted, *there's something going on. It concerns Nancy and her husband.*

He leaned his head against the side window, feeling the heat in the car building. He opened the door and stepped out as her reply came through.

Leave me alone, and don't drag her into this. Stop prying. Im.

Matt sighed, tucking the phone away. She'd signed off *Im*, a nickname used by her friends, never with him. He figured he was being relegated already. A deliberate punishment.

Very well. He'd continue to respect her space, but as soon as he had something more, he'd need to speak to her. Imogen's fears were based on the accusations of a woman who was not who she claimed to be. Matt intended to fix that. There was still hope.

'Can I help you?'

The voice caught Matt before he was halfway up the pathway. He turned to see an elderly gentleman closing his garage door on the side of the house. He dusted off his hands and looked up expectantly.

'Dr Banks?' said Matt.

'Yes,' said the man, stepping closer. He had a kind, weathered face and a stoop. His clothes were grubby with what looked like oil, smears on his shirt. He glanced down.

'Working on the car this evening,' he said. 'An MGB – rusted heap, I'm afraid. One day I'll get her started.' He laughed, putting his hands on his hips.

Matt smiled. 'My name is Matt Roberts,' he said. 'I'm from the *Guildford Press*.'

Dr Banks nodded, a small frown. 'A reporter?'

'No, editor,' said Matt. 'My reporting days are behind me.'

'But you want to talk to me?'

Matt nodded. He glanced around at the doctor's front garden. 'I realise this is a little odd, unorthodox, perhaps, but I was sorting through the archives, and your name was mentioned in an article, a few years ago.'

'My name? Concerning what?' The frown deepened.

'A suspicious death.' Matt decided not to sugar-coat it. He didn't have time. Either the doctor would help or he wouldn't.

As it was, Dr Banks raised his eyebrows and laughed. 'Suspicious? I think you've got the wrong man, Mr Roberts.' His laugh faded. 'Or a sick sense of humour.'

'A patient of yours,' said Matt. 'Six years ago. George White. You raised a concern – filed it with the coroner. You were ignored, Dr Banks, and I think they were wrong to ignore you.'

Matt couldn't have been any blunter, but it did the trick. Dr Banks's recognition was almost instant, his face losing its rosy tint. He rubbed his hands again on his shirt, glancing at Matt with curious suspicion. He gestured to a bench under an old cherry tree at the centre of the garden.

'My wife is inside,' he said. 'I'll give you two minutes. We can talk out here.'

Matt took a seat, taking out the printed report. He handed it to the doctor, who pulled a pair of reading glasses out of his top pocket and scanned through it. He grunted a couple of times, folded it and handed it back.

'Not exactly *Murder She Wrote*, is it?' he said.

'Could it be?' said Matt.

'I don't understand.'

'With more details, proof, a compelling witness?'

Dr Banks grunted again. 'I remember your reporter. Steven, or—'

'Simon.'

'That's him. He caught me on a bad day. Patient confidentiality is not something I take lightly, although I still remember how frustrated I was at the time. Never seen anything quite like it.'

'What do you mean?'

'I could still get in trouble for this, you know,' he said. 'I asked that my name not be used. I was very specific about it.'

'He kept it out of the report,' said Matt. 'He kept his word.'

'And then he gave it to you.'

Matt smiled. 'I'm not going to use your name, Dr Banks. But I'd be grateful for anything you can tell me.'

Dr Banks was clearly too intelligent for sweet talk, but Matt could see the frustration underneath – still there after all these years. He had been ignored, professionally, by the coroner, and that hurt a man in his position. The village GP was supposed to be beyond question.

'I think you were right,' said Matt, 'but I don't have the medical knowledge. What was odd about George's blood test results? What was your suspicion?'

Dr Banks took a few breaths, his face clouding. He looked about to speak when the front door opened. His wife stood in the doorway.

'It's going cold, Harry,' she said. 'Come on. Is that oil on your shirt?'

'Give me a minute,' he called to her, with a wave. His wife narrowed her eyes with an impatience that suggested Harry spent far too long in the garden and garage.

Dr Banks turned to Matt. He took a few deep breaths before shaking his head. 'I'm sorry, Mr Roberts. I can't give you what you want. My suspicions were overruled, and my anger was unprofessional. I should never have spoken to your colleague, and I shouldn't speak to you now.'

'Not even to expose a crime?' Matt had no idea what the crime might be, he was still grasping at straws, but anything he could use to get at Nancy was worth learning. The doctor was on the verge of talking, he could sense it.

Dr Banks sighed. He examined Matt's face for a few moments.

'A crime.' It wasn't a question. The doctor closed his eyes for a few minutes, then shook his head. 'Do you have anything else?' he said. 'Besides this report?'

Matt thought of what he knew about Nancy, of why he was pursuing this. He decided to offer one thing.

'His wife, Nancy White. I think she's buying medicine or something from the Royal Surrey. Off the books – not pre-scribed. From a lab assistant. It must be illegal.' Matt stopped there. He didn't want his following of Nancy to be widely known. Visions of his arrest were never far from his mind. His heart began to race at the thought.

Dr Banks's eyes widened. 'Medicines?'

Matt shrugged.

The doctor shook his head, eyes down. He chewed his lip, giving it some thought.

'OK,' he said. 'Do you have an email address?'

Matt pulled out a pen and scribbled it on the top of the report, handing it over.

The doctor nodded before standing, placing his hands on his lower back, stretching. He took the report and folded it carefully, placing it into his shirt pocket along with his glasses.

'I need to think about it, Mr Roberts. I'll be in touch.'

Matt

Matt waited.

The way Dr Banks's eyes had lit up when he mentioned the Royal Surrey – he knew he was on to something. He'd driven the same route, parked in the same spot, tucked in behind another car, and hunkered down in his seat. He'd stay for an hour, maybe two.

The sun beat down and he cracked a window, sipping from the warm bottle of water, eyeing the packet of biscuits on the passenger seat. His hunger could wait.

He'd done this for the last two days, watching his road, feeling hopeless and helpless. Nancy had failed to appear on both days, and his anxiety peaked; he knew this might be his last opportunity before he had to return to work.

Calling in sick again had been painful, and he'd have to face Shelley soon. But that was for tomorrow, or the next day. Right now he was lost in a mess of confusion and suspicion.

He'd mentioned to Ruby, catching her briefly in the street, that he'd seen her mother at the Royal Surrey Hospital. They'd talked; she'd looked puzzled, shrugging it off. Nothing to do with her, she'd said. He'd left it, but it bugged him even more. If Nancy wasn't there for Ruby, then why? Or did Ruby not know about it? He wouldn't put it past Nancy to keep her in the dark. She managed to twist every other part of Ruby's life; why not this?

Matt's luck was in. After less than an hour he saw the shiny Mercedes cruise out of his road, Nancy at the wheel. She glanced his way as she pulled out, but he was low in his seat as she turned left, his car well hidden. If she saw him, she didn't care – she kept driving.

His heart hammering with anticipation, Matt pulled out behind her.

She took the same route, swinging straight out of the village on to the main road towards Guildford. As before, she drove at a sedate pace, keeping to the inside lane. Matt stayed several cars back. His car was dusty from the lack of summer rain, dark and dishevelled – a little like its driver.

Nancy took the same exit as before, heading west, around the city centre, before turning in at the first sign for the Royal Surrey hospital. Matt followed, puzzled, determined to find out what she was doing. It was probably nothing, harmless, ridiculous even, yet Matt yearned for some window into her life, however small.

'What the devil are you up to?' he whispered, as Nancy indicated and turned into the car park.

She followed the same route as before, through the underpass into the medical delivery area. There she parked in the same spot on the yellow hatched area. Restricted, but not for Nancy.

Matt stopped his car and reversed back, not wanting to be stuck or exposed. He parked his car in an empty space and jumped out, creeping back through the underpass and taking position behind an empty ambulance, some fifty feet away.

Nancy waited, leaning against the bonnet of her car. Matt glanced at the building, wondering how many CCTV cameras overlooked this area. Probably none, he thought, the underfunding of the NHS not even stretching to life-saving equipment, let alone security.

He slipped along the side of the vehicle and manged to get a better view of Nancy through the ambulance windows. Tucked between the glass and a concrete wall, he was well hidden.

Nancy examined one of her wing mirrors, rubbing it with her thumb. She did the same to the window, stepping back to examine the bodywork. She stopped at the sound of a door against brick, the spring-loaded doors teetering open for a few seconds before starting their long sweep closed. She straightened and turned, smoothing the front of her skirt as the curly-haired technician approached her from the double doors. He pushed his curls away from his glasses and lifted the bag he was carrying on to the bonnet, unzipping the top. Nancy passed him a white envelope. The man took it and handed Nancy a dark package in return. Matt couldn't see what it was before it disappeared into Nancy's handbag.

They spoke for a few seconds, the man nodding, agreeing with whatever she said. He gave her a faux salute before stepping away, letting Nancy climb back into her car. A friendly gesture, or at least a non-threatening one. They knew each other; this was a regular meeting.

Nancy reversed before moving off, heading directly towards Matt, who stood away from the ambulance window, holding his breath as her car passed a few feet to his left. It would have been a miracle if she'd looked along the side of the ambulance as she passed, but Matt's luck was pretty much at rock bottom – he wouldn't have been surprised.

As it was, the car drifted off and out of sight.

Matt had no way of giving chase, but that wasn't his intention. He let out the breath he'd been holding and watched Curly, who had produced a cigarette and was leaning against the metal railings while staring at the screen of his phone, taking long drags, letting the smoke flow out of his nostrils and billow around his face into the breeze. He pulled out a set of earphones and tucked them in. A few seconds later his head started to nod in time.

Matt had a strange craving. He'd smoked for a few years in his early twenties, kicking it when most of his friendship group did the same. He'd hardly wanted one since, and yet standing here now, watching this stranger, he had to force several deep breaths to make the desire go away.

Curly was a fast smoker, no doubt used to short breaks – grab the nicotine while you can – and dropped the butt on to the ground in a shower of sparks, stamping on it as he headed to the door.

Matt timed it as best he could before breaking cover, sprinting across the concrete loading area. Curly disappeared through the doors as Matt reached them, the spring-loaded hinges a few inches from shutting him out. He jabbed his hand into the gap, stifling a scream as the sharp metal edge pinched his wrist.

Matt swore under his breath and paused, counting to ten before pulling the door open, wincing as the bottom scraped on the ground. He stepped into a quiet grey corridor and was immediately hit with the smell of disinfectant, carried by hot air from the vent overhead. Curly was thirty feet to his left, sauntering along, head still nodding to the music as his trainers squeaked on the lino floor.

Matt followed, matching pace, pulling out his phone, pretending to look at it as he walked. If Curly turned then Matt could keep walking, playing the role of an employee or a student. Perhaps a lost patient.

The corridor terminated in a T-junction. Curly turned right and disappeared. Matt hurried, noting the sign on the wall: *Pharmacy Aseptic Unit, Laboratory B.*

He was well out of the hospital wards. This whole area must be restricted, its security reliant on diligent employees such as Curly. To the right was another long corridor, stretching towards a double set of security doors. Curly stopped short, swiping his ID card against the wall before pushing open a door marked *Pharmaceutical Storage.* Matt hurried forwards, tailgating through the doors, relying on Curly's music and general sloppiness to avoid detection.

The storage area was huge, like a warehouse within a building, filled with floor-to-ceiling drug shelving units, organised in rows with a central walkway down the centre. The right-hand side held regular racks of medicines, ordered by an alpha numeric system with labels and warnings. The left-hand side hummed with the sound of dozens of refrigerated units.

Matt slowed his pace, ducking into one of the right-hand rows, trying to keep an eye on Curly, at the same time having a brief attack of anxiety. This was trespassing, no question, and any story about getting lost wouldn't cut it. He could imagine being restrained, arrested, trying to explain his presence here. If he mentioned Nancy it would elicit more questions; the police would talk to her; she'd tell them what she suspected.

His life would be over.

He could leave, should leave.

Curly turned into row ten. Matt closed his eyes, took a breath and crept forward until he reached row nine, trying to see what Curly was doing, but finding his view obscured by the towering rows of medicines.

He tiptoed to the far end of the row, peering around from the other end, near the wall. Row ten didn't contain the same ordered compartments as the previous nine. He'd reached the end of the medicines and now seemed to be in a materials and chemical storage area. He thought back to the sign in the corridor – *Aseptic Unit*. He knew from a recent article that the Royal Surrey had its own huge research department and manufactured many of its own pharmaceuticals. He stared at some of the unrecognisable labels, watching as Curly unpacked his bag. The technician opened a small container door and placed something back on to the shelf. He pulled out the white envelope from the bag and extracted a wad of cash, stuffing it into his jacket pocket. The envelope was crumpled and placed into the bag, slung over his shoulder.

Once finished, the technician abruptly turned and headed out of the row, back to the entrance, the squeak of his shoes echoing through the shelves.

Assuming he could exit the room without an ID card, Matt waited for a few more seconds before approaching the shelf that Curly had just left. It contained several sturdy-looking containers with individual doors. The labels were puzzling. All heavy metals, as far as Matt could see – mercury, lead, cadmium. The doors to the first three were smudged with fingerprints – recently opened.

Matt stared at the containers. At the limit of his scientific knowledge, he struggled to understand what Nancy would want with such things. He cast his gaze around the shelving, feeling a shiver – it was colder in here, the air conditioning whining in competition with the fridge units.

His initial suspicion, that Nancy was buying pharmaceuticals, didn't tally with what he'd seen – with what was on the shelf in front of him. Nancy was buying heavy metals, and God knows what else, for cash from a dodgy lab technician.

The thump of a door broke his thoughts. From the far end of the room he heard more footsteps, hurried and purposeful. They stopped, somewhere in the refrigerated area. He heard a few doors being opened, the hum of the fridges cutting, then re-engaging as the doors were closed. It hadn't occurred to Matt there might be more than one entrance to this room.

He bit his lower lip to stop the expletive, but carefully back-tracked along the row he was in, tiptoeing as best he could. He made it to the door before risking a glance back. Two lab techs – neither of them Curly – stood over a metal trolley, examining a collection of vials and boxes.

Neither looked up as Matt pressed the exit button and slipped out.

Matt

The next morning Matt parked further away, hidden from Jon's corner bungalow, tucked behind a row of cars. He checked his email a couple of times. Dr Banks knew something, and was perhaps wrestling with whether to share it, but Matt tried not to put too much faith into this line of investigation.

Euthanasia? Could that be it? Was Simon wrong about his hunch? Matt hadn't mentioned it to Dr Banks, worried it might cloud the conversation, hoping something else would reveal itself.

His anxiety fluttered. The pressure built, a ticking clock, every second taking his family further away, his way out of it becoming harder. His work was suffering – every aspect of his routine was fracturing, day by day.

A knock at his window startled him. He looked up. *Shit.*

'Jon,' he said, opening the window. He felt the blood rush to his face. 'Here I am again,' he said, offering his best fake smile.

Jon was wearing jogging bottoms and a gym top, a bag slung over one shoulder. He looked sympathetic, not angry. 'Are you OK?' he said.

Matt didn't know whether to nod or cry. He had a sudden urge to talk to Jon, to trust his earnest face, to tell him everything. He had to force himself to stay silent, screaming inside. *You're crazy*, he convinced himself. Of all the people to talk to, an ex-copper should be way down the list.

'I'm . . .' *Stay honest*, he thought. 'No, I'm not OK,' he said. 'I was actually . . .' he shook his head. 'I was trying to work out how to fix things.'

Jon leaned in, put one hand at the top of the door. 'Well, I'm not going to give you some clichéd marriage advice,' he said, 'but I should tell you that hanging around the streets like this can't possibly help. You look like an OK guy, Matt – trust me, I have experience – but this is a little weird, you have to admit.'

'She *is* my wife,' said Matt.

Jon nodded. 'But the neighbour isn't.'

Matt's heart stopped again, before returning at a thunderous pace, drumming into his ribcage. He couldn't possibly . . .

'I d–don't understand,' he stuttered.

'Nancy?' said Jon. 'I'm sure she's just trying to help. Following her makes you look desperate, which I'm sure you aren't, but still.'

Matt took a couple of seconds to realise Jon must have seen him drive off after her. Did this man spend his life watching the street? He hoped not.

'Yeah,' said Matt, his pulse dropping a fraction. 'They're friends. Good friends. I was hoping to catch Nancy on her own – have a chat, see what I can do to patch things up.'

Jon looked unconvinced. 'So you followed her in your car?'

Matt shrugged. 'Yeah, I know. Stupid. I kick garden walls, too.'

Jon's face broke into a grin. 'So you know her well? Nancy?'

319

Matt wondered how to answer. Truthfully. 'Erm, no. I guess I don't. You?'

Jon shrugged. 'Hardly at all,' he said.

Matt sagged with relief. If Jon and Nancy were friends, the panic might tip him over the edge. 'Oh,' he said, before a thought grabbed him. 'So you never met her husband, George?'

'George?' said Jon. 'No, sorry.'

Matt nodded. More relief, although finding out something about George from the neighbours would have been a useful piece of the puzzle.

'It was very sad – his death,' said Matt, probing.

'Dead? Ah, makes sense. I thought perhaps divorced.'

'It was quite a few years ago,' said Matt. 'Sorry, I assumed everyone around here would know. It's such a close community and all.'

Jon gave an amused frown. 'Where did you hear that?'

Matt paused. 'Isn't it? I thought the whole point of a private community like this was so everyone becomes close. Friends? Love thy neighbour, et cetera?'

Jon laughed. 'I don't know anyone,' he said. 'Which was exactly my retirement plan. The whole attraction of this type of estate is that you get your privacy. Nobody pries, nobody watches. Nobody cares who you are or what you're doing.'

Matt raised his eyebrows. Jon laughed again, a deep bellow. 'Correction. Except us ex-coppers who can't seem to give it up. I'm an anomaly. But I don't live in your street – if you kept your stalking to your own road, I wouldn't so much as twitch the curtain.'

Matt's growing realisation must have shown on his face.

'Oh, everyone is perfectly friendly,' said Jon. 'We'll get

320

together for village fetes, Christmas parties – Nancy's fund-raiser, for example. But I can count the times on one hand that happens each year. If you thought moving here would mean a close group of friends, I'm afraid you've got it entirely the wrong way around. The community means privacy, even from your neighbours.'

'Huh,' said Matt, as much to himself as Jon, who tapped the roof of his car with a smile and said he'd no doubt see Matt again soon, grabbing his bag and strolling towards his house.

Matt thought on Jon's comments, realising they made perfect sense. Apart from the brief gathering a few weeks ago, Nancy was the only person Imogen and Matt had spoken to. Everyone else had been polite but stayed away since. After the initial invites for drinks and dinners, there had been nothing. Everyone snuck back into their own lives.

Except one person.

Matt had been wrong about the village – or rather, his little part of it – the gated community. And that mattered. Nancy didn't have community here. She had privacy. She had *secrecy* – a place to hide and do whatever she wanted.

But what did she want?

The spinning doubt in Matt's mind.

The burning question.

Nancy

Nancy stared through the patio doors, gazing without focus towards the end of her garden. The grass was too long, the golden hops sprouting uncontrolled across the end fence. She hadn't even dead-headed the climbing roses on the trellis.

Her perfect routine was coming unstuck, and her lips trembled with discontent.

The phone rang for the third time, edging against her mug, the vibrations taking on a musical quality as the china joined the harmony.

She snatched up the phone.

'What?'

'Nancy. Err. You OK?'

'That's none of your business. What do you want?'

'Nothing. I . . . I just wanted to mention, I think somebody was watching us at the last pick-up. Following me, to be precise.'

Nancy sat up straighter in her chair, bringing her gaze inside the house.

'You there?'

'Yes,' she said, softening her tone. 'Yes. What do you mean? Who?'

'I don't know. Some guy. I think he followed me into storage. Then he ran away afterwards. It might be nothing. But . . . I might need to be a bit more careful for a while. Know what I mean?'

Nancy's left hand trembled in her lap. She gripped the fabric of her skirt to stop it.

'What did he look like?' she said.

Her lab technician described the middle-aged man in enough detail for Nancy to know exactly who he meant.

'Thank you,' she said, her voice trembling. 'For letting me know.'

'Should I—'

Nancy hung up, dropping the phone back to the table, barely able to control her outrage. *How dare he?* she thought. What gave him the right?

'Bastard,' she said, unable to control the hate, the contempt, spitting it out. She thought of Matthew following her, prying into her business once again, interfering in every way possible. What drove a man like that, a predator, an *opportunist*? Nancy had seen it before, but never this close, never witnessed first-hand the damage that a man like Matthew could wreak on a family. Even her George had been better than that. At least he kept it in his pants. But Matthew had violated the most precious part of her family, and now he kept on coming.

'What do you want, you bastard?' she whispered, staring at the phone.

'Mum?' Ruby poked her head through the doorway. 'Who are you talking to?'

Nancy shook her head, trying to wind down her anger, her frustration, but she could feel it in her chest, her neck, rising into her jaw. Ruby's innocent expression served only to fuel it.

She stood, bearing down on her daughter. Ruby looked up, puzzled, expectant.

'Why couldn't you just ...?' Nancy swallowed, stopping at the last minute, resisting the urge to grab Ruby's shoulders, shake some sense into her.

'What?' Ruby backed away, her face creasing with concern. 'What's wrong, Mum?'

Nancy paced left and right, shaking her head, trying to push it back inside. She failed.

'This is your fault!' Her voice filled the room, uncontrolled. It had to be said.

'My fault?' said Ruby. 'What's my fault? Why?'

'Look at you,' screamed Nancy. She grabbed Ruby's arm and dragged her into the hallway, pushing her in front of the mirror. Ruby tried to resist, pulling away.

'Ow, Mum, that hurts. What are you—'

'Have you seen yourself?' shouted Nancy. 'Your slutty little skirts, your whore's tops, breasts out for the world to see? You're bait to a man like that. What did you expect to happen? Tell me!'

Nancy stared at her daughter's reflection in the mirror. Ruby's face turned bright red; her mouth dropped open, quivering. 'I ...'

Nancy clenched her mouth shut, regretting shouting, but not regretting what she'd said. She'd held it in long enough, perhaps too long, and Ruby needed to know. This was the real world, where girls like her got eaten alive by men like Matthew Roberts.

Ruby's eyes filled up; the tears streamed down her face.

'I don't understand,' she said. 'Mum . . . What do you mean? That was . . .'

'What you needed to hear,' said Nancy, lowering her voice. 'What you've done, Ruby. It can't be undone.'

'What I've done? I—'

'Get out of my sight,' said Nancy, turning her back to Ruby. It was harsh, but it was what she needed. Tough love, to protect her. Always, everything Nancy did, was to protect her.

Ruby sniffed, sounded like she was going to reply, then ran off, thumping upstairs, her bedroom door slamming. Nancy remained where she stood, sucking in deep breaths, urging calm, the fear spinning in her gut, waiting for an opportunity to take control.

She strode to the back of the house, pulling open the door, sucking in several breaths of fresh air. She placed her finger on her wrist, checking her pulse, waiting for five minutes until it had slowed to a reasonable rate.

Was that too much? Perhaps, but her intentions were pure. Always. This was her daughter, *hers*. Nobody else's.

Nobody understood how difficult it was for Nancy, Ruby least of all. Her condition, the toll it took on Nancy's mind and body – her whole life devoted to caring for her, and her father before. Did anybody think she wanted to be like this? Neurotic, cold, routine to the point of military precision? Nobody *wants* to be like that. But how else could she cope? Flit around like a normal mum, pretending her daughter wasn't dying? Pretending that everything would be OK if she just chilled out a little?

Chilling out never protected anyone, and Nancy was un-wavering in her purpose. Having been dealt this hand, she was going to play it as best she could, even if it killed her in the process.

She'd thought Ruby was safe. She'd thought Matthew had gone, and that would be the end of it. But perhaps predators didn't give up quite so easily.

The wind blew through the trees, picking up, the first sign of autumn. She checked her watch. Oh God. Imogen. How long had she been left alone? Poor Imogen, another casualty, another patient in desperate need of Nancy's help. That poor woman would never survive without her. Like Ruby, she depended on Nancy now. Nancy was her lifeline, her protector.

There was plenty of time, but Nancy fretted, still unnerved by the phone call and what it signified. Her anger surged as she headed into the kitchen to collect her ingredients, throwing them into her handbag along with a carton of fresh fruit and veg, grabbing a clean apron from the cupboard before heading out of the front door.

In her anger she'd forgotten herself.

It was time for Imogen's medicine.

Matt

Artie's café was on the outskirts of the village, out of the bustle of the high street and less popular than the eateries tucked into the many village side streets. It was plain, quiet. Perfect for a secluded chat.

Matt waited at the back, near the bathroom. Not the best table in the café, but it was hidden from the entrance and the front window, which faced the main road to the south. He'd been there for half an hour when the door clattered open. He heard the quiet voice of his neighbour, asking if anybody was waiting for him.

'Chris,' said Matt, standing and offering his hand as the old man peered over the counter. Chris's eyes darted around the café before he stepped forward and extended his own shaking hand, before sitting.

'Coffee?'

'Please,' said Chris. 'Black.'

Matt waved to the waitress and ordered.

Chris had lived on their street a long time. Matt had considered their brief encounters while surveilling his road earlier – Chris had been shooed away by Nancy at their first meeting, again in the supermarket on their second. Matt remembered him as being timid, nervous, scared of Nancy. He'd dismissed it as a simple misunderstanding at the time, not giving it much thought since. That might have been a mistake.

'I appreciate you meeting me,' Matt said. 'And sorry I haven't . . . we haven't . . . been better neighbours, spoken more. I've been so busy.'

Chris smiled. It was genuine, but sad. 'You have a family,' he said. 'A daughter. You must be run off your feet.'

'Do you have kids?' Matt asked.

Chris's smile thinned. 'No. Catherine and I met too late for that. It wasn't meant to be.'

Matt stared at his plate. He never knew the correct response to a statement of that sort. Sympathy or simple acknowledgement?

'It'll become clear why I didn't want you coming to the house for this,' said Chris.

Matt nodded. He'd looked up Chris's number and called, trying not to give too much away, but failing to stop a brief outpouring of emotions and suspicions. Chris had gone silent, asked to be left alone. Matt persisted, pleaded, before mentioning how ill Imogen was. Chris had stopped mid-sentence, offering to meet Matt here, two hours later.

Chris sipped at his coffee, glancing at the menu. 'I'll order a cake, if you don't mind?' he said.

'Order anything you like,' said Matt, wanting to get started, but not wanting to rush him. On tenterhooks, he finished his coffee and ordered another.

Chris waited until he was halfway through a large slab of Victoria sponge before he began. Matt picked at a fudge brownie, beginning to wonder if this wasn't a wasted trip. Chris was old, confused. Dragging him into this could be damaging. The last thing Matt needed on his conscience was another victim.

'Catherine and I met twenty-five years ago,' said Chris. 'Both second marriages,' he added with a shrug. 'Both looking for love – something long lost with our spouses at the time. She was thirteen years older than me.' He said it with a sly smile. 'I was her toy boy, and in the early days, despite our mature years, we snuck around like naughty teenagers. It was fun, a breath of new life.'

Matt smiled.

'And we came clean pretty darn quick,' Chris said. 'We weren't interested in a sordid affair; we wanted love and companionship, or rather, to confirm it, officially and without fuss. It turned out my first wife had already found her new man, and we parted on good terms. Catherine's husband wasn't so understanding, but love will do what it wants. We moved in and got married within six months. We moved to Albury to retire together five years ago.'

Matt watched Chris's eyes, the way his face creased into smiles when he said Catherine's name. Pure happiness, or memories of it.

'Five?' said Matt. That ruled one thing out. 'So you never knew Nancy's husband, George?'

Chris's smile faded. He shook his head. 'I knew *of* him. But that was from Nancy, so who knows what he was really like?' He huffed and poked at the remainder of the cake. 'Can I order another drink?'

Matt nodded. 'Of course. Please – order whatever you want. It's the least I can do.'

329

'We moved in just after George died,' said Chris, blowing across the top of his coffee. Matt couldn't take any more caffeine and grabbed a jug of water, filling his glass, swirling it around his dry mouth.

'Literally two weeks after,' said Chris. 'It was awkward, but Catherine did the neighbourly thing, reaching out, offering sympathy. She loved the idea of a gated community – all those close friendships, the politics, the *gossip* . . . although most of that never happened. Once Nancy got her claws into her, we never made friends with anybody else. Catherine didn't have time.'

'Oh?' Matt had memories of his own first few days in the road. His rapid introduction to Nancy and Ruby. Jon's comments about the community. The downhill trajectory ever since.

After Nancy had sunk her claws into Imogen.

'Nancy was grieving,' said Chris, 'and Catherine was such a kind soul – she couldn't bear to see love torn away like that. So she offered her friendship and her time, calling or popping round every day.'

'So you and Catherine weren't exactly spending the quality time together that you'd planned?'

Chris shrugged. 'I didn't mind. I had a huge garden that needed tending to, and a study full of unread books. My lazy retirement wouldn't suffer. Catherine and I would have our time together once she'd finished the Samaritans bit.'

He took another large bite of cake, washed it down and leaned back in the chair. The wood creaked in protest. 'Do you think I could ask for a cushion?'

Matt called the waiter over, apologising and making the request.

Once Chris was comfortable, he folded his arms and continued.

'I don't know at what point it all changed. Perhaps there wasn't an exact moment in time. Perhaps Nancy knew all along when it would be, or perhaps it was all in my head . . . That's what they concluded, by the way. There's nothing you can pin on Nancy. Not for me. Not for Catherine. Maybe you'll have more luck.'

Chris cleared his throat. Matt dared not speak, silently urging the man to continue his ramblings. Pin what on Nancy, exactly?

'Catherine had a heart condition,' said Chris. 'Atherosclerotic disease. It caused angina but was well managed with medication. She shrugged it off – most of the time . . .'

Chris shook his head. Matt could see the strain in his eyes.

'One day it wasn't about Nancy any more. Do you know what I mean?'

Matt nodded slowly.

'It became all about Catherine. About her condition, her illness. That she needed to take it easy, rest more. I don't know . . . my initial pleasure at choosing to spend time gardening suddenly felt enforced. I became a stranger, unwelcome, impotent in looking after my Catherine, whose health seemed to deteriorate in front of my eyes.'

Matt's unease turned to a shiver. The hairs on his neck prickled as the words sank in.

'What do you mean?' It came out as a whisper, catching in his throat.

Chris didn't hear him. 'Nancy was at my house every day, only returning home to look after her daughter. You know her? Ruby? Of course you do. You must.'

The mention of Ruby threw him. He swallowed. 'I—'

'Well, then Nancy *turned*,' said Chris. 'Jekyll became Hyde. It might have been gradual, but I saw it in an instant.'

Chris's lips trembled and he reached for his drink. 'Damn,' he said. 'It's cold.' He looked expectantly at Matt, who waved to the waiter, pointing at Chris's mug.

'Please,' said Matt. 'What do you mean? What happened?' He considered his own moments with Nancy. Was it earlier? From the start? Or was it Ruby who triggered it?

'Turned how?' he said.

'I messed up,' said Chris, shaking his head. Matt saw the old man's hands shake, his fists clenching, turning white. 'I was meticulous at filling her drug dispenser. Her arthritis meant she struggled with the bottle tops. Sunday night, without fail, I dished them out – the beta blockers, cholesterol tablets, diuretics. Carefully counted and placed in the correct compartments. I did it without thinking. But I screwed up, and Nancy caught me.'

'Caught you?' said Matt.

'Catherine was OK, you must understand. It was a higher dose than she should have had, but I called the GP and he assured me it was OK. But Nancy was livid. I was shocked – I didn't know how to react, being shouted at in my own kitchen. My own home! She said I was useless, unfit to care for Catherine. Then she made the threat.'

Matt found himself leaning forward, edging closer. His shoulders were tense, hurting as he watched. Chris's words bounced around his head, nudging, scaring him . . . *the threat.*

'Social services,' said Chris. 'She said it was her only option. We'd need to go into care, or at least Catherine would. As a responsible member of the community, a *neighbour who cared*, she had no choice. I couldn't be trusted to manage Catherine's medication. What if something serious happened? What if her condition deteriorated and I missed it?'

Chris's shakes increased. He could hardly hold his mug without it trembling, the liquid bouncing off the sides, spilling over the lip. Matt reached out and pushed it gently down on to the table.

'What did you do?' he asked.

'What could I do?' said Chris. 'I was mortified people would find out, terrified she'd contact social services. This was my *wife*, and I'd failed her, betrayed her trust . . .'

'Her trust?'

'In my ability to keep her safe,' said Chris. 'Don't you get it? That was my role, and Nancy took it. I was forced to give it to her. I had no choice.'

Matt took a sip of water, feeling his throat constricting. His shoulder pain spread. His muscles twitched; a sense of dread crept across his chest.

'Nancy took over her care,' said Matt, watching Chris's distress, wondering how much more he could reveal without breaking. Matt needed all of it. Every last bit.

Chris nodded. 'She left the threat hanging,' he said. 'She even makes it now, on occasion.'

Matt remembered a flash of their conversation in the supermarket, when Nancy had interrupted, pounced.

'I was pushed away, pushed out,' said Chris. 'Nancy would arrive in the morning and wouldn't leave until late. Catherine told me I was making a fuss, Nancy just needed someone to care for after George's death. They were friends, getting closer. What could I do?'

Matt stared at him, feeling the café shrinking, hearing every word, not quite believing it.

Chris shook his head, his eyes filling up. 'She died six weeks later.' He stared at the cup in front of him, turning it in his hands.

'Six weeks,' murmured Matt. *Six weeks.* 'What was the cause of death?' he blurted.

Chris's bottom lip trembled. 'She died of a heart attack. It's . . . not uncommon in patients with her condition, but . . . it was unexpected. We were managing it so well, for years. Until . . .'

'Nancy,' said Matt.

Chris looked torn up inside, but again, he shook his head. 'Her medications were checked after she died. All present and accounted for. It was her time to go, that's all. The GP said as much.'

'But . . .' Matt had to ask the obvious. They had to stop dancing around it. 'You think Nancy had something to do with it. You think she somehow caused her heart attack?'

'I . . .'

'Why didn't you go to the police? Tell the GP?' It came out harsher than he'd intended. Chris looked at him, a picture of guilt and grief.

'I tried,' he whispered. 'But they dismissed me. The ramblings of an old man. They took blood tests but her drug levels were normal. It was a heart attack, plain and simple. And . . . I stopped asking.'

'Why?' But Matt knew the answer.

'You don't understand. Nancy convinced everyone,' said Chris, his voice cracking above a whisper, pathetic in its admission, 'including me. We talked many times in the days after Catherine's death. Nancy cried with me; her daughter Ruby cried. She said it was tragic, that she'd done her best to look after Catherine, but my only option was to move on. She never wavered, never failed to look me in the eye. She told me if anyone was to blame, it was me. And I believed her.'

'And you didn't push it? You suspected Nancy and you didn't do anything?' Matt thought of the mild hypocrisy of such a statement. But at least he was here, trying to do something.

'What could I do? I doubted myself, doubted my suspicions. And Nancy threatened to tell the police I'd screwed up Catherine's medication, that perhaps I'd done it on purpose. On *purpose*! Perhaps she was a burden and I was confused, wanted to ease her transition.'

'She accused you of euthanasia?'

'Not outright,' said Chris, 'but the threat was there. Catherine was gone. I was awash with grief and with no close friends to speak of. Not here. Not in the gated community where everybody is close, yet everybody walls themselves behind politeness and immaculate hedgerows. Everyone looked at me as the poor grieving widower, nothing more.'

Matt found himself reaching out. He put his hands on top of Chris's, felt the tremble, gripped them tighter, realising he was trying to stop his own from shaking.

'I was hopeless, don't you see?' Chris continued. 'I woke up one morning and decided I needed to remember Catherine for who she was, what she meant to me – all the wonderful years we had. I needed to forget my suspicions about Nancy and not antagonise her. I want to live out my days in peace, with my independence. And so I have.'

Matt's mind churned with the details, and the tragic nature of Chris's story. He could understand that feeling of helplessness, that there was no way out. Nancy gripped people in the vice of her accusations and held them.

'You had nowhere to turn,' he said. 'You were scared of what she might say, might reveal. Lies. Threats. She made you feel like you were to blame, that it all rested on your failures, your indiscretions. Your actions.'

'My indiscretions?' Chris had a brief flash of confusion. 'I suppose so. If that's what you call a genuine mistake. Because it was a mistake, Matt. Or . . .'

He sighed, met Matt's eye. 'To this day I swear I didn't mix up her drugs. At least . . . I don't think . . .'

It didn't need to be said. Chris's face confirmed it. The magnitude of his revelation struggled to hit home. Two deaths. George and Catherine. Unrelated at first glance, but both tainted – something wasn't quite right. Nancy in the middle of both of them. Matt felt a fresh stab of fear – this was far worse than he'd considered. This wasn't going to help him, or save him.

There was still one thing he needed to know. The one thing he'd never considered before, that in the last few minutes had surged to the forefront of his mind – a desperate and horrifying thought about what Nancy was doing now. Right now.

'Why did you agree to talk to me, Chris? When I called you. What changed?'

'Why?' said Chris, his eyes darting once more across the café. He pulled his hands away, clasping them together in front of him, and leaned in.

'Because of what you said about Imogen, Matt. About her health. Because Catherine's condition, her steady deterioration from a well-managed illness to the day she died ... all of it started when we met Nancy ... and all of it started with a gastro bug.'

Imogen

I woke, the lingering dream of my wedding day dissipating slowly, the anxiety and the wonder, savouring it for a few seconds. I stood in front of Matt and we said our vows, and in that moment, I kept telling myself: there was absolutely nothing to be anxious about.

But it faded, and the world came rushing in – my world of sweaty bedsheets, an acid taste in my mouth, a head full of cotton wool.

My visions of Matt shifted as my brain caught up. I saw Ruby in her bikini, waving at me from the garden. Flash forward from my wedding day to the here and now. Of all the changes I feared, none quite matched the reality.

Did he do it? Did he *fucking do it*?

I slid out of bed, the muscles in my thighs trembling, my blood pressure plummeting. I grabbed the bed frame and guided myself to the door, pulling my robe off the hook, wrapping it around me. A drink? Some food. It was time to leave the house. To face it all. I needed a doctor and I needed to speak to the object of my dreams.

It took me an age to get downstairs. The bang of cupboards drew me to the kitchen. Nancy glanced up from the island, startled. She tucked a box of cereal back into the cupboard.

How many times had I relived this scene? Groundhog Day, my very recent existence, stumbling out of bed to find Nancy in my house, Nancy in my bedroom, Nancy in my kitchen. It hadn't bothered me before, and it shouldn't now. I shook my head. What did I see in Nancy's eyes? I owed her so much, but with the guilt came an increasing sense of disquiet. Whatever it was, it disappeared in a flash as she beamed at me, hurrying over, helping me on to a stool.

'Imogen,' she said. 'How are you feeling this morning?'

I smiled, watching as she moved away before waiting for an answer, taking the kettle, arranging the cups. Rinse and repeat. How many drinks had Nancy made me over the last few weeks?

'You shouldn't be out of bed,' she said, without turning.

'I must,' I said. 'I'm going to the doctor today, and I'm calling Matt.'

It came out almost as a challenge. I needed to assert myself in front of Nancy, to be clear this was my house and my decisions. She turned to me, puzzled, and I immediately doubted myself.

Nancy nodded, lifting the teapot to fill our mugs. She brought them over and sat next to me on a stool (I always thought she looked too proper to perch at a breakfast bar). She turned to me and I saw her eyes filling up.

'Do you want me to go?' She whispered it, the tears starting to flow. I experienced a rush of sympathy, despite my misgivings.

'No,' I said. 'But . . . you shouldn't be here all the time, Nancy. I need to look after myself. My family. I need to face what happened.'

There. I said it. And Nancy's tears increased, flooding out of her, her chest heaving and shoulders shaking.

'Nancy, please,' I said. 'What . . .?'

What else, I guess. What else other than my husband and your daughter. That was enough to hurt us both for a lifetime, surely?

Nancy took a deep breath, sniffing, pulling out a handkerchief to dab her eyes and nose. She looked at me, a brief smile breaking through the cracks.

'I never told you about George,' she said. 'I didn't think it appropriate. I didn't think it mattered.'

Her chest heaved again. It was clearly an effort for her. I sat back, silent, waiting. I was curious to know what her late husband was like, and she'd never offered, in the short time we'd known each other. If she needed to share something, listening was the least I could do.

'Tell me now,' I said.

'He wasn't a well man,' she said, pausing, as if to choose her words carefully. 'Physically, you will know he shared the same devastating condition as Ruby, which was what ultimately claimed his life. But psychologically . . . that was his real problem. And it was my problem – I suffered more than him from it, I believe.'

'Suffered how?' I said. I found Nancy's quirks appealing, the result of her situation with Ruby, an eccentric single mum with a chronically ill daughter. She'd suffered, that was never in question. But it seemed there was a further dimension.

'His condition made him angry,' said Nancy. 'Or rather . . . he blamed his condition for his anger. I'm not sure that's the same thing.'

I waited, wincing at the thought of what might come next.

340

'He expressed his anger in several ways,' she said. 'And most often it was directed at me.'

I placed my hand awkwardly on top of hers. I noticed my own skin looked pale, my forearm thin and weak.

'I'm so sorry,' I said.

Nancy shrugged, but clasped my hand. 'Ruby never saw it, or at least, I don't think she did. I could always explain it away. A bump here, an accident there.'

My heart sank. 'Oh, Nancy,' I said. 'It must have been . . .' I didn't know. I'd never had this conversation with a friend before. In the wards I saw many women in this situation, in the thick of an abusive relationship. We had processes, referrals. We tried, even though we knew we'd only succeed with a few. What could I do? What should I say? I was in no position to offer Nancy therapy.

'It wasn't all of the time,' she said. 'Weeks would go by, months even. I felt normal – we had a normal marriage, as much as was possible with a chronic illness and an uncertain future. But every now and then he'd turn. Do something, say something. It was so out of character, and it broke me, mentally – I could handle the physical. It was just so unexpected. I really didn't think he was the person I'd married. That he was capable of such a betrayal.'

Despite the tragedy of her story, the words were not lost on me. My heart began to race as my own situation threatened to take control of my thoughts.

'I suppose you're wondering why I stayed?' she said.

I shook my head. 'Not at all.' I knew better than that.

'I questioned it, more than once,' said Nancy. 'But he was *ill*. He *needed* me to look after him. More than I needed him. You have no idea how hard it was for me, but I realised it was my calling. Despite his behaviour, I knew nobody else could care for him like I did.'

I doubted that was true, but the psychology of such a situation was complicated, the guilt she probably felt, the toll of the abuse. Ruby in the middle of it, with the same condition as her father. It was never simple, never easy.

'I had my escapes,' she said. 'The country club – shooting game. Don't look at me like that,' she smiled, 'it was an outlet. And he was a bastard. More than once I imagined his head at the end of the barrel.'

The language shocked me. I'd never heard her utter an expletive before.

'I hated him,' she continued, 'but I loved him. He made me realise what I was good at. It was my duty to care for him.'

Nancy paused. The tears dried as she breathed. Several deep breaths. She glanced at me; her face changed. I saw a flash of something, but my own eyes were watery. I dabbed them on my sleeve.

She remained silent, staring forward at the worktop. I replayed her words in my head. I hated myself for thinking it, but there was something a little odd about her explanation. It was ordered, almost a textbook case of abuse. It didn't quite add up to her devotion, her time and attention to caring for George in his final days.

But once again I reminded myself my judgement was increasingly suspect. I didn't know what was going on under my own nose, let alone in Nancy's marriage.

'Nancy, I—'

'I'm telling you this,' she said, her tone much calmer, but firm, 'because it gave me an insight I've carried with me ever since – a sense when I'm talking to a man who can't be trusted, who has another side to him, a devious edge. A man who doesn't care who he hurts or what damage he leaves behind.'

I narrowed my eyes. I hoped she wasn't going where I thought she was . . .

'I saw it from day one,' she said. 'I'm sorry, but I did. When Matthew introduced himself over the fence. I saw the way he looked at me, I saw the way he increasingly looked at *Ruby* . . .'

She left it hanging. I opened and shut my mouth. The transformation on Nancy's face was extreme, the sadness replaced with calculated anger. It dawned on me that she'd planned this conversation, the build-up.

'I recognised Matthew was a bad apple,' she said. 'I've been there, Imogen. I see the signs, know the looks. Matthew is rotten, and rot pervades everything, creeping into your core, killing you from the inside out.'

'Matt's never laid a hand on me,' I protested. 'It's not . . . It's not even comparable.'

'It's not about that,' Nancy spat back at me. 'It's about their desire to take what they want, do what they want. To hell with the consequences. I'm trying to protect you.'

'I . . . No. I'm sorry, Nancy. It's not the same.'

Was it? Was I mad? A shiver took me, a deep unease. This was not the conversation I expected to have with Nancy. How could her tale of abuse be used against Matt? Why would it?

Nancy's expression changed again. Her eyes narrowed, then relaxed.

'I can see we disagree,' she said, shuffling on the stool.

'We do,' I said. 'I'm not defending Matt, but this is . . . I don't know. I'm sorry about what happened to you, I really am.'

343

But I wasn't sure I believed it. That was the truth. I wanted Nancy to leave, but at the same time I couldn't kick her out after her outpouring of grief. I was confused, and for once, Nancy wasn't helping.

'I only have your best interests at heart,' she said.

'I need to speak to Matt,' I said, wanting to give her something, a promise that I wasn't forgiving him. Maybe if I turned it around. 'I'm ill. I can't take proper care of Ash like this. I can't be a burden to you like this.'

Nancy frowned. 'Is that what you think you are?' She shook her head, laughing. 'Dear Imogen, it couldn't be further from the truth.'

She turned to me, staring for a few moments, like a mother unsure what to do with an uncooperative child.

'Look,' she said, 'Ruby will collect Ashley from school later – she has music club today, yes?'

I nodded.

'Then I'll go home and give you some space.' Nancy turned her hands in her lap. She shook her head a few times, agitated.

'Nancy,' I said. 'What . . .' I was at a loss.

'He *did* it, Imogen. Even if it weren't for everything else . . .' Nancy didn't meet my eyes, her face screwed up in anger.

Everything else? What did she mean?

'I don't—'

'I'll come back later,' she said. 'I'll bring Ashley back in time for dinner, if that's OK?'

I nodded.

'There's something I have to tell you, but it can wait. Please don't speak to Matt in the meantime.'

'Why? What else, Nancy?'

She shook her head again. 'I wasn't going to tell you, not with your health the way it is. He has gone too far. He's been poking around where he shouldn't, trying to dig things up about me he has no business doing. It's a shame, but I'm not sure what else I can do. Promise me?'

I nodded, watching her agitation, her controlled anger. She simmered in a way I'd never seen before. 'I promise,' I said. I owed her that. I wasn't sure what she meant, but if she had something else on Matt, I needed to hear it, although I couldn't fathom what might be worse than what I already knew. I was dreading the confrontation with Matt anyway. I was dreading speaking to Ruby. One more day wouldn't matter.

I let Nancy out the front door. She walked off, not looking back. I took a few deep breaths, feeling a chill, the cold air hitting my lungs and causing me to cough. My head felt clearer, but my body still felt weak, weary of its continuing battle.

I shivered. The wind was picking up, the summer sky hazing over. Dark clouds hovered in the distance. A storm was lurking.

The air prickled with electricity as I closed the door.

Matt

Matt exited the café, pulling his jacket close against the wind. The summer sun had disappeared behind a wall of grey. The sky was heavy and oppressive. Matt stared up, his panic matched by the turbulent air.

He held his phone to his ear. He tried three times but she didn't answer. He texted.

I'm coming round — we need to talk. I'm not taking no for an answer. Please don't talk to Nancy until I get there.

Chris's words bounced around his head. Catherine's symptoms, Imogen's symptoms, the same relentless nausea and vomiting. It wasn't a coincidence. It couldn't be.

But why?

He dragged his eyes away from the approaching storm and ran across the street. He slid into his car seat and paused, hand on the keys. He had to go to the house. In any normal situation he'd be calling the police right now, laying out everything he'd discovered, the mess of suspicion and conjecture, letting them take control.

But it started to make sense, the pieces falling clumsily into place.

Nancy's actions towards him were beginning to have meaning. He could imagine himself in an interview room, describing it, day by day, the detective nodding and building their case. Nancy would be arrested, removed. Silenced.

But the cruel reality was far from that. The balance was not in his favour, and whatever Nancy was doing, she wouldn't go down without a fight. The police would want both sides of the story. They'd interview her. She'd kick and scream and do her best to take Matt with her.

And there was every chance she'd succeed.

He was trapped, impotent, his mind a mess of swirling guilt and fear. What had she done to Imogen? What was she *doing*? Was this pay back, for his imagined crimes? But it started ... when, exactly? When had Imogen fallen ill? Matt racked his brains but the events of the last few weeks all blurred into one. He'd been so consumed with his own predicament, he hadn't considered Nancy might have another target in her sights.

This wasn't even about him. It was about Imogen.

But why?

His phone buzzed in reply.

I'm OK. Feeling a lot better, actually. I'm up and about – sickness seems to be fading. I need to get my head together. Perhaps we can talk at the weekend? Im.

Matt clenched the phone, re-reading the message. His heart rate dipped a fraction. She was OK. For now. But she needed to know the truth, whatever scraps he held. She was in danger, and by extension, Ash was in danger. His little girl, oblivious and innocent, still the centre of Matt's world. He needed to be careful, but couldn't wait until the weekend.

I'm coming round, he texted. *Where's Ash?*

He started the car, putting the phone on the passenger seat. It buzzed in reply.

No! I told you we'd speak at the weekend. Leave me until then. Ashley is at school.

Matt swore at the roof of the car, switching the engine off. Imogen would listen, she'd have to. He wondered how long it would take to get the death certificate for Catherine, as proof. Proof of what, he wasn't sure. But it would show something. Too long, he thought. Days, at least. Chris didn't have a copy.

He could drag Chris with him, get him to tell Imogen what he suspected. But Chris would be reluctant, and Matt had already considered and dismissed it, for one very simple reason: he couldn't have anybody else party to the conversations, for fear of what might get said, of what might get leaked. Matt's reputation was hanging by a thread, the rest of his life dangling over the abyss. There were only four people who knew what he'd been accused of. Nobody else could know. Nobody, not even Chris.

Matt cried in frustration. Proof. He had no proof. Neither did Nancy, but they both knew she didn't need any. Her accusation was enough to destroy him. His accusation was flimsy and far-fetched. He didn't even know what he was accusing her of.

His phone buzzed again. Imogen. Please.

But no. It was an email. Matt almost swiped the notification away, then saw who it was from.

drbanks134@gmail.com.

Matt opened the email, enlarging the text, scanning through it once, twice, his heart rate increasing with each word, each line, until it thudded in his ears – a deafening drum roll, warning him of the impending storm.

348

Third paragraph, after several lines asking for discretion and secrecy, but an admission that Dr Banks would support a police investigation if Matt found a way to initiate one. The blood test results for a George R. White, taken on 6 July 2013.

Matt's heart galloped then stopped. His eyes darted over the key points.

Traces of heavy metals.

Cadmium. Lead.

Referred after presenting with symptoms of nausea and vomiting.

Cause of symptoms was concluded as stomach flu – norovirus was doing the rounds. No follow-up deemed necessary. *The patient did not present with any further symptoms.*

Shit.

Matt's heart missed a beat as the words sank in.

The wind howled around the car as he revved the engine, spinning the wheels as he pulled away, speeding through the village towards his house, his street – his wife and child.

The storm had already begun.

Imogen

I watched the wind whipping up from Ash's bedroom window, chasing the clouds across the sky. The temperature was dropping fast. I hugged my arms to my chest.

Our road looked smaller in the gloom and grey, less grand, the wisterias and camellias shrinking without the sun to boost them, the tarmac dull and lifeless. The window rattled as a gust hammered the front of the house. I glanced over towards Nancy's, thought of her strange behaviour earlier. I wondered if she was in the right frame of mind to babysit Ashley. Ruby would help, but ... well. It was Ruby. I didn't trust her one bit, awful as that sounded.

I'd get dressed, then go and fetch Ash from school myself. Give Nancy whatever space she needed to calm down before she revealed what else she thought she knew. I wasn't sure if I could take another bolt to the heart.

I heard a car, its engine revving hard.

Matt's old Volkswagen screeched into the road, pulling into our driveway.

The front door creaked open. I heard it slam closed, footsteps on floorboards.

'Imogen?' Matt called to me, his voice echoing in the hallway. I felt a strange sense of relief, and then a familiar surge of hurt and anger. Why did I feel safer now Matt was here?

'Up here,' I called, then sat on the bed, waiting. I guessed it was time. Time for us to talk – for Matt to plead and deny, and for me to get answers to the rest. To the unanswered.

Can I trust anything you tell me?

I pushed myself back against the headboard, trying not to exert my body. The dizziness held, the nausea hovered, but I took a few deep breaths. Matt would not see me at my most vulnerable. He didn't deserve that satisfaction.

'Imogen.' Matt entered the bedroom, rushed over, then paused, obviously seeing my expression. He looked like crap, his stubble uneven, his clothes creased. I smelled strong deodorant, but his body odour seeped through. A cliché of marital breakdown.

But his desperation masked something else.

'Where's Ash?' he asked.

We stared at each other. I couldn't hide my pain and resentment, and didn't try.

'At school,' I said. 'It's the middle of the day.'

He nodded, pacing back and forth, pausing at the window, turning to Nancy's, turning to Chris's.

'She made it all up,' he said.

I narrowed my eyes. Was he really going to rehash the same tired argument? It wasn't good enough. It wasn't the starting point. We had to go further. I wanted to do it my way, in my order.

'You can't just barge in here,' I said.

'I had to. You don't understand. It couldn't wait.'

351

I raised my eyebrows. True, I'd decided it was time to talk and I wanted to see him. But he didn't know. I hadn't told him.

'So it's all in my head?' I asked. 'And Ruby's?'

'No,' he said, turning. He grabbed the bed frame, leaning over, eyes wild. 'You don't understand. It's not that. It isn't even because of that.'

'I—'

'No,' he said. 'Your illness, Imogen. This sickness of yours. Her husband's sickness.' He paced again, shaking his head. 'His *death*. It's not an illness, Imogen. *That's* what she made up!'

His face broke into a frantic smile, teeth bared. 'It sounds crazy. I know. But let me explain. Please. Listen.'

I'd never seen him like this. Well, that wasn't entirely true. I *had* seen him in this state before. Almost. But back then his defence had at least been coherent. This time it was bizarre, but . . . it jolted my curiosity.

'I'm pretty sure my sickness isn't made up,' I said. 'I feel like shit, Matt. I have for weeks. If this is your idea of some weird excuse, it's lame.'

Again he shook his head. 'No, no, no,' he said. 'Just listen.' He gave me his most earnest look, tinged with a madness which began to scare me. 'Please?'

'Five minutes,' I said. 'Explain what you mean, Matt, or leave. I don't have the time or energy for more pathetic excuses.'

And so he began.

Matt talked, and I listened.

He laid out everything, then repeated it. He stuttered at first, struggling to present his case, what he'd been doing, what he'd discovered. He started at the end and worked backwards. As he

352

talked, I found myself tucking my arms closer around me, the nagging doubt growing into a solid lump in my throat.

After he finished his first, fractured account, I had barely taken in any of it.

'It doesn't make any sense,' I said, after the second barrage of information. 'What's her motive? Why would Nancy commit such a wicked act on her own husband?'

Matt looked at me. 'I don't know why. Only that she did.'

I turned it over in my head. A hunch formed, hazy, something I'd read about but never encountered. I wasn't sure it fit.

'Nancy's actions towards me,' said Matt, repeating his claims. 'Her first accusation and everything that followed. It was *engineered*, planned. She tricked us, both of us, to get me out of the household – out of the way and powerless to stop her. She wanted *you*, Imogen. Not me. Don't you see? I was a casualty. She wanted me out of the way.'

I struggled with where this was headed. Matt kept talking – the symptoms of heavy metal poisoning, his conversation with Chris, the repeated mention of severe gastric trauma.

The next realisation was like a sledgehammer to my fragile state. If I'd heard it the first time, my mind had blanked it out, not wanting to hear.

Ruby.

'The accusation, the photos, the lipstick,' said Matt. 'The story about the babysitting. Everything. It was all Nancy! It was all fabricated.'

He paused. I could hear him panting.

I closed my eyes, processing the information, turning it around, judging it for reason, for logic. I couldn't help but see Ruby for the first time, the pale young girl and the burden she carried. Her symptoms so close to mine, so glaringly obvious. Right in front of me.

Could it be?

Dear Ruby. The poor girl had suffered for years, and if Matt's long and fantastic tale was truthful, her own mother had done it to her, dragging her through years of suffering, all for her own malign purposes.

'Why?' I said.

'Ruby's blood disorder doesn't exist,' said Matt. 'It never did. It was all a creation of Nancy's. She and her father were poisoned, *are* being poisoned. Chris's wife . . . and now you.'

I shook my head. Too much. It was too fantastic. I was being carried along by Matt, but he wasn't giving me time to process it.

'Why?' I repeated. 'It makes no sense. Nancy, a murderer? It's crazy.'

Matt stopped. He frowned, taking a few deep breaths. He was hyperventilating, so caught up with the excitement of his theory.

I tried to counter it, focus on the rational. His story was bizarre and unbelievable. I watched him, suddenly worried. Who was fabricating a story here? What was Matt's state of mind at this point? His desperation was extreme. What could it possibly lead to?

'You said you had proof?' I said.

'I do,' he said, jumping over, pulling out his phone. He showed me an email. I read it through once, then again.

'I know it's far-fetched,' he said. 'I know it sounds crazy. But look. This is what they found in Nancy's husband's blood. This is what prompted this GP to call the coroner.'

'But you already said the coroner dismissed it.'

354

'Because George had already been cremated! Because Nancy is such a perfect upstanding member of an expensive housing community in sleepy Surrey! Why would they bother pursuing it?'

Matt paused, out of breath. He sat on the edge of the bed. I'd tucked myself into a ball. I held on to his phone, but I was stuck. Why would he invent this? Could he?

'There's one way of knowing for certain,' he said. 'Please, have a blood test. Ask them to check for the presence of these poisons – these heavy metals. Do that for me.'

I could have kicked myself, and was almost too embarrassed to tell Matt I'd been trying to go to the doctor for days, for weeks, trying for a blood test, although they'd never look for this. There was only one thing that had stopped me.

One person.

I closed my eyes. Was I really that blind? That stupid? I shivered again, the enormity of Matt's words hammering against the walls I'd carefully erected over the last few weeks.

If he was right . . .

Then it occurred to me.

'I don't need to,' I said. 'At least, I don't think I do.'

I used Matt's phone to search for the number of the maternity ward at the Royal Surrey, called the switchboard and asked to be put through to the consultant who I'd seen at the appointment for my miscarriage.

Matt saw what I was doing and looked questioningly at me. 'They wouldn't have tested for it,' he said. 'They need to be looking for it. Toxicity.'

I put my hand over the mouthpiece. 'They have my blood.'

'Still?'

I nodded. 'It can be kept several weeks refrigerated. At Royal Surrey maternity it's standard if taking tests during pregnancy to store more than is needed. I should be able to—'

The midwife came on the line. She told me the consultant was unavailable, but she might be able to help.

I created a quick cover story, the first thing I could think of.

'Wow,' said the midwife. 'From a restaurant? I've never heard of that before.'

'Me neither,' I said. 'The police will reorder the tests, of course, but I thought you'd already have my bloods and could run a quick toxicity test?'

'It's unorthodox,' she said. 'We should only run these tests on referral, or after an examination.'

'But I need to know if it was in my blood back then,' I said, the consequences beginning to hit me. I put them to one side, ran through my credentials, said I knew what they should look for. As soon as she realised I was a nurse, she became more cooperative, and confirmed they did in fact have enough blood of mine in refrigerated storage.

'These are some nasty substances to pick up from food,' she said. I heard her tapping the keyboard in the background. 'From a pasta carbonara? Jesus. What was the name of the restaurant?'

'I'm afraid I can't say at this point,' I said. 'They'll be shut down if it's true.'

Another few taps at the other end. 'Yes,' she said finally. 'We can run these here. I'll order them now – I'll file it under your original visit. Could be anywhere from twenty minutes to four hours.'

'Call me back on this number?' I said.

'OK,' said the midwife. 'Will do.'

I hung up.

Matt slumped back on the bed, his chest rising and falling in short, rapid breaths. I stared straight ahead. I was less than four hours from the truth, and yet I still couldn't judge what my reaction would be.

It was too much to process in one go. The idea that someone – my friend Nancy – had anything but the best intentions towards me was so alien. The suggestion she'd hurt me, and not just me, was incredible. If it was true, this woman was locked in a cycle of serious assaults, with two of them already ending in death.

I pictured Nancy, her kindness, the small, careful way she probed and coaxed my problems out. I confided in her, relaxed when she was around. I *trusted* her implicitly, more than I trusted most people. With my mum and my friends so far away, she was my go-to. I needed her, and the thought of her being torn away hurt. It cut me, deep down.

But almost as difficult to comprehend was Ruby's situation. I had been certain, beyond reasonable doubt. There was no way those coincidences didn't add up to Matt's infidelity – his criminality. But if what he claimed was true, they weren't co-incidences, were they? They were a carefully executed plan of incrimination by Nancy, of a sort almost impossible to argue or defend against.

But Ruby . . . she said it. Didn't she? No. I was getting confused. My mind was still a haze, my thoughts a mess. She didn't. She denied it. All of it. And so did Matt. Their stories were consistent; little good it had done them.

It was me who'd failed. Blind and stupid.

Except I wasn't. I had to remind myself that my suspicions were grounded in a pattern of behaviour. It wasn't baseless, and I wasn't irrational. Matt had done something and I'd extrapolated, drawn reasonable conclusions based on the data I had. I was a nurse, after all, clinical – I had to use the data in front of me, and the observations that enabled a diagnosis.

I'd identified an anomaly, that's all.

And for one of the inconsistencies, I still didn't have an answer.

'What's the time?' I asked.

'One,' said Matt, checking his watch.

I needed this if nothing else. Before the storm raged, I needed at least one ounce of truth.

'Before they call back,' I said. 'Before all of this gets serious ... more serious. Before we call the police ...'

Matt shot me a look, his eyes wild. He quickly tempered it, giving a small nod.

I paused. 'London,' I said. 'The money, Matt. Tell me the truth.'

I opened the drawer to my bedside table and withdrew the bank statement for Matt's account, which I'd grabbed off the doormat, folding it to the correct page, the page that listed a deposit for £10,000, from a Ms Yun Huang.

'Explain this, Matt.'

Matt's eyes widened then narrowed again. I saw him calculating, perhaps weighing his options. *Don't do it*, I thought. *Come clean. We have no room for more deceit in our lives.*

He nodded. Closed his eyes for a second, let out a breath like he'd been holding it for hours.

'You want to do this now?' he said. 'In the middle of . . . all of this? After what I just said?'

'We had a life ruined before all of this,' I said. 'And I need to know if it was deserved.'

He frowned. 'That's not . . . it's not about what I say. The blood tests will prove it. At least, I think they will. If they don't . . .'

I could see it wasn't an eventuality he'd considered. That my blood tests would come back negative. I guess that said a lot.

'You know why it's important, Matt. What you've told me is terrifying. I'm terrified. But I can't even see the future with this unanswered.'

He looked in pain, struggling with the memory.

'London,' he said, almost a whisper, like it was a decade ago, not last year.

'I know you went out drinking, clubbing – everyone knew it,' I said. It had come out at the brief tribunal, the gossip, the whispers amongst friends – more partying than work. He'd lied, but it wasn't a terrible betrayal. 'I'm not talking about that. I mean the thousands, Matt. Where did the thousands go? Why is this woman putting money in our account?'

Matt stared at me. His face was less manic, more controlled. Still a mess, but more . . . Matt.

'I know Liv told you,' he said.

I nodded. 'She did. Not that it matters who told me.'

I saw his face flush, only a little, but enough to know I'd hit a nerve. I didn't blame Liv, and I knew Matt wouldn't either. He loved his sister, and he'd even forgive her this.

Matt paused. 'So you know it was drugs?' he said. Almost a question, not quite.

I swallowed. No, I did not. But I held my poker face. I nodded.

Matt kept watching, but shifted on the bed, getting more comfortable. Drugs? After all of his lectures to Liv, to me! He hated what drugs had done to his sister; hated what they could do to a vulnerable mind – the toll they took.

'Yun was . . .' Matt started and stopped, obviously seeing my face twist at the mention of her name. I couldn't help it.

'I left it out because I was ashamed,' he said.

'Step back a minute,' I said. 'Yun took drugs. You told me she did. That was the whole basis of your argument.' *And your defence*, I thought.

Matt shook his head. He sighed. 'No. I mean yes, she did, but not only her.'

He looked at me with bloodshot eyes, the guilt clear as day. He nodded.

'You?' I said. That was . . . shit. Not what I'd expected. Not good, but not . . . 'You took drugs?'

'I feel stupid,' he said. 'I was stupid. Everything I told you was true – I flirted, I partied. I acted like an absolute arse. But I didn't stop at drinking, Imogen. I was far too naive to stop there. I needed to impress, to go wild. I . . . I was taking coke most nights.'

'Coke? You're telling me that's where the money went? Cocaine? Shit, Matt.'

He plucked at a fingernail. 'It got out of control before I could stop it—'

'Bullshit,' I said. My initial relief at his admission was fast turning to anger. He spent our money on drugs for him and this witch of a woman who'd tried to destroy him. Destroy us.

'It did!' he insisted. 'It's not a defence, it's a fact. The first time, I was so drunk I don't think I even knew I'd taken it. The second time was easier.' He shook his head again. 'It got easier. And the money . . . disappeared. I was spending hundreds every night.'

'On her?'

'On both of us,' he said. 'It was . . .'

'And the other thing? Tell me you didn't lie about the rest.' My heart raced. Was this it? Where it all crashed down again?

'No!' he said. 'I didn't sleep with her, Imogen. That was her attack. Everything I told you was the truth, except this. I hid it because it was—'

'An addiction?' I didn't care. As long as the other thing wasn't true.

'No,' he said. 'I'm not an addict. The lifestyle was the lure. The drugs were just part of it. We did argue that night. It's true – it's all true. I just left out the bit I was most ashamed of. It didn't change the outcome – wouldn't have done. It wouldn't exactly help my case, would it? If I'd accused Yun of taking drugs, then admitted I was coked off my head?'

My heart thumped, a little harder. The secrets, the lies. Could I take any more?

'How much?' I said.

He shrugged. 'Eight thousand . . . maybe a little more.'

'Eight thousand pounds?' I shouted. 'On coke! You fucking idiot, Matt.'

The shouting didn't quench even a fraction of my anger. All it did was kick off a headache, slow and dull. It matched my frame of mind.

'And you let me think it had all gone to Liv,' I said.

Matt did well to hide his surprise. 'I didn't think . . .'

'I'm not a complete idiot,' I said, feeling pretty close to one. 'I knew the money was gone. I assumed you were funnelling it to Liv, to feed her drug habit like you've always done. How stupid of me.'

'You knew?' he said. 'Why didn't you—'

'I was waiting,' I said. 'We're married. We trusted each other. I thought you'd tell me in your own time. It's not about the money, Matt. It never was.'

I slumped back, my head thumping against the bed frame.

Matt sat at the other end, picking at his nails. He looked defeated.

'I would have told you,' he said.

'Again, bullshit,' I said. I tried to muster more anger, but the bizarre thing was, I actually felt relief. I hadn't known what to expect, but this wasn't it. Drugs I could forgive, although I didn't need to tell him that. Not yet.

'But Yun. The money.' I tried to get my thoughts in order. 'Why would she give it to you? After what she'd accused you of?'

Matt took a deep breath, shaking his head. 'She feels guilty, I guess.' He shrugged. 'Maybe she wants to make it right.'

The mention of Yun still left a sour taste in my mouth, but it was necessary. This might be the line I had to draw under it all. It was a car crash, no doubt, but at least it made sense. I'd known he was hiding something – and now I knew what.

'Imogen, I'm so sorry. I've been an idiot.' My husband leaned closer, his head bowed. 'Please forgive me. I don't deserve it, I know I don't, but we can fix this. I know we can. For Ashley.'

I turned to Matt as his phone buzzed, vibrating into the duvet. He passed it to me.

The Royal Surrey switchboard.

'Yes,' I answered, grappling with the phone, jamming it to my ear.

'Mrs Roberts?' said the midwife. 'Are you sitting down?'

Matt was right.

He was right about everything.

Lead, mercury and arsenic. I made her repeat it several times. She invited me in, she said I needed to see a doctor without delay. I promised I would, then hung up.

Two thoughts struck me in that moment, as I dropped the phone to the bed. Both vitally important, but for very different reasons.

The first was fleeting. Clinical. Nancy had poisoned several people with heavy metals. Two of us were still alive. I was still alive. It niggled, and I couldn't figure out why, but gradual heavy metal poisoning doesn't give you a fever, not usually. It causes various hideous symptoms, but not a temperature. I didn't know why it was important, or why it jumped into my head at that moment, only that it was.

But it faded as the second thought lurched into mind.

This one was much clearer, a combination of fragments that had gathered in my consciousness, unbeknown to me thus far, but now obvious.

Nancy had poisoned her husband, her neighbour, her daughter, and now me.

And I knew why.

Nancy

S he held the phone in front of her, staring at the text.

Please don't talk to Nancy until I get there.

The screen faded, turning black. Nancy woke it up with a tap, entering the passcode she'd seen Imogen type in so many times. She'd taken it from Imogen's bedside, keeping it with her most of the time, placing it back on occasion. She didn't want Imogen looking too hard, tiring herself out.

She was getting sick of these messages, though; they worried her. There were secrets to be found, of course, but which did he know? What did he think he could prove? His persistence was in equal parts frustrating and infuriating. What she'd tried to reveal about *him* was enough to make any coward run and hide, and yet, he still kept coming.

To make matters worse, she'd done everything possible for Imogen. She tried her damned hardest to protect the woman from her own husband, getting involved as soon as she realised what he was like, making it clear what he was capable of, looking after her as her health deteriorated.

Sure, she had to nudge things along a little, but did the lipstick on his shirts mean nothing? Was the pornographic material on his laptop the behaviour of a normal loving husband? What doting father had lewd pictures of a fifteen-year-old girl on his family laptop, kept for his own personal gratification, to feed his disgusting urges, his animal desires?

Had it all been for nothing? Desperation engulfed her, something Nancy rarely felt – the sensation that control was slipping away, had already departed – leaving behind a lost battle, the wrong casualties, the wrong *sides*.

The truth remained.

Imogen wasn't stupid, but even her behaviour stank to high heaven. How many chances do you give a rat like Matthew before kicking it out of the house, out of your life? This wasn't the first time, Nancy was sure of it, and it sure as hell wouldn't be the last. Rotten to the core, that man. But Nancy had failed to reveal it to the woman who would no doubt suffer the most if he stayed around.

She cocked her ear. The tyres screeching outside could only mean one thing. He'd made good on his message and returned to the family home. She listened as the engine was cut, thought she could hear his footsteps as he ran up the garden path that he had no right to inhabit, pushing to open the door he should be locked out of forever.

Nancy dipped her head, allowing herself several moments to compose herself.

'Ruby?' she called, making her way into the hallway.

'Ruby?' Louder this time. Her patience was shot.

Ruby appeared at the top of the stairs. 'What is it?'

'We're going to pick up Ashley from school.'

'But . . . it's only midday. I—'

'Don't argue. For once, do as you're told. We're going to collect Ashley, then we're going next door. This ends today.'

Ruby's face dropped. 'But . . .'

Nancy glared at Ruby, shaking her head. 'Don't try me,' she said.

Ruby slid down the stairs and put her boots on, keeping her mouth shut as she laced them up.

'Get in the car,' said Nancy, giving her the keys. 'Wait for me.'

Nancy watched her daughter open the passenger door. She gave Nancy a worried glance before getting in, turning to face the road. Nancy headed into the living room to collect two items. The first, a small box from the dresser drawer. She checked it was full before emptying it into her coat pocket. The second, a rather heavier item, she grabbed with a practised hold and slung over her shoulder.

The time for civility was over, and it wasn't without a certain degree of damaged pride that she admitted this to herself. It had come to this with George, eventually, and Catherine. They simply couldn't see that Nancy was only trying to help them. They couldn't accept the *truth*. Consumed by their lies, Nancy had no choice but to make a stand, end the circle of deceit and dishonesty. Just as she must do now.

Matthew was back, and she had no doubt he'd weasel his way back in with Imogen. He'd brainwash her with his charm and his stories, his inventions about Nancy and her history, dragging her poor George into the frame, no doubt. And once he was settled with Imogen, playing happy families, he would come for Ruby again.

Matthew was here because he wanted Ruby.

It was as clear to Nancy as night and day.

Imogen

The disorder was named after an eighteenth-century German aristocrat, a literary figure with a reputation for tall stories. The irony was not lost on me. Never in my fifteen years of nursing had I seen a case, never had I properly researched the condition or its effect. As I stared at the NHS guidance on the syndrome, scrolling on the laptop, sitting on the bed, I experienced a plethora of mixed emotions – my heart sank and my blood boiled. I focused inwards, replaying my interactions with Nancy, her words, her language. Her motivations.

Munchausen Syndrome by proxy.

Not to be confused, said the literature, with Munchausen Syndrome, a rare psychological disorder where someone pretends to be ill or deliberately produces symptoms of illness in themselves.

The *by proxy* is important, and even more devastating in its effects. The psychological syndrome is defined as when a parent or carer, usually a child's biological mother, exaggerates or deliberately causes symptoms of illness in their own child.

Deliberately causes an illness.

I paused, couldn't stop the vision of Ruby's pale face springing to mind, her thin limbs, her tailored medication, her sheltered existence. Then I saw her strutting around in her skimpy clothes, looking at me, questioning me.

I shook my head. I'd got it all wrong. I'd got it *wrong*.

The literature stressed it wasn't limited to children. Anyone under the person's direct care might be targeted, particularly if they already had a health condition.

Anyone. Their husband. A close neighbour.

Fuck.

The mother or carer may induce symptoms of illness – for example, by poisoning her child with unnecessary medicine or other substances.

Fuck, fuck, fuck.

I read through a list of warning signs. *If your patient presents with any of the following . . .* I scanned, wincing, looking away. I was conscious of Matt looking over my shoulder, mentally ticking them off, as I was.

Patients typically have borderline personality disorders characterised by emotional instability, impulsiveness and disturbed thinking.

'My God,' said Matt. 'Do you really think . . .?'

Disturbed thinking.

Did Nancy know her accusations were untrue, or that her own actions were wrong? How much was she in control of her own behaviour? She might have seen the threat to Ruby as real. In her attempt to get at me she might have genuinely thought Matt was a threat, that he actually did what she thought he did.

She lived in a delusion, and in that fantasy, Matt had abused the most precious object in the world – her own daughter, who she could not stop herself from harming, to satisfy her unquenchable needs and desires.

Matt's explanation fit. Any lingering doubts were quashed. My idiotic husband, guilty of such betrayal, was innocent of this. Innocent of Ruby. I started to cry with relief, absurd as that sounded.

'I'm so sorry.' The words tumbled out. I stared at him, my eyes filling. I couldn't stop them.

Matt leaned in on the bed, crumpling next to me. He put one arm around my shoulders and held me tight.

'I could have been killed,' I said, before letting the other thoughts free. The horrible realisation that had struck me when I was on the phone to the midwife.

'She killed my baby.' I said it in a gasp. The truth, even more hurtful than the rest put together. 'It was her. It could only have been her.'

Matt gripped me tighter. He didn't say anything, he just stared at the screen.

'I . . .' What did I say? What did I do? There was only one option.

'Give me your phone,' I said.

Matt went to grab it. 'Are you calling the hospital?'

'No, the police.'

Matt's hand paused over his phone. It was still out of my reach, and he held it there.

'What are you doing?' I said. 'She tried to kill me. She's killing Ruby. We have to call the police. *Now*.'

At the sound of her name, Matt turned to face me. He blinked, screwing up his face.

'I know,' he said. 'And we will. But . . .'

'But what?'

'Listen,' he said, his tone softer, more controlled. My own nerves were crackling with energy.

'We need to think about this first, that's all.'

'There's nothing to think about,' I said. 'She's dangerous, delusional – what we've seen is a façade. Underneath she could be seriously unstable. You've read what it says here.' I pointed at the laptop. 'She could have a personality disorder. She might become violent, snap. We need the police here when we confront her. There's no telling what she might do.'

'I know, I know,' he said. 'But . . . do I have to spell it out?'

'What . . . Oh,' I said. 'But that's easy to explain. We've just said – she's delusional. She made it all up. The accusation about Ruby won't get taken seriously . . .'

As I said it, I realised it wasn't true. As serious as our accusation about Nancy was, she'd counter it with her own, and it was no less serious. I thought back to my conversations with Claire. The legal advice I'd managed to find online. As soon as Nancy pointed at Matt, it wouldn't matter what she was guilty of. Matt would be arrested anyway. And the battle from there would not be quick or painless.

'I . . . but what else can we do?' I had to remember that Nancy might be disturbed, but she wasn't stupid. She had known this all along. This was her protection, almost perfect in its deviousness.

'She did this to Chris,' said Matt. 'The same trap, the same prison of accusation.' He shook his head. 'Chris had no way out. So he let her be.'

'He let Nancy kill his wife and get away with it,' I said.

'He didn't know for sure,' said Matt. 'He never had anything concrete, and the risk was . . . well. His life. He risked losing his life as he knew it.'

I swallowed, my mouth dry, my head starting to thump with urgency.

'So what do we do?' I said. 'I can call Claire, get you a lawyer from the outset. Before the police even arrive.'

Matt shook his head. His eyes burned, bloodshot, his forehead beading with sweat. He risked looking worse than me, if that was possible.

'It won't make any difference,' he said. 'And it makes me look even more guilty – the police will wonder why I felt the need to get a lawyer.'

'Because she's crazy,' I said, but the words were hollow, not a credible defence. My panic increased, the revelation of the last hour sinking in, and the look in Matt's eyes as he broke the awful truth.

'She won't retract it,' he said. 'She'll repeat it, shout it . . .'

I could see his hands shaking, his face flushing.

'And then—'

I heard the front door slam open, hitting the stopper. Matt and I both froze. The sound of the wind howled through the hallway, up the stairs. The draft pushed open our bedroom door, chilling the air.

'Mummy?' Ash called out to us, her delicate voice carried on the air.

Matt turned to me. 'Ash?' he said. 'You said she was at school. How would she—'

The blood drained from his face. I didn't let him finish, jumping from the bed, staggering as my legs struggled to take the weight, my blood pressure plummeting.

I ran out to the landing, to the stairs, Matt following close behind.

Nancy was here.

Matt

Matt steadied himself on the bannister, taking in the scene below. The three faces looked up at him, a mixture of terror, confusion and fury.

'Ashley,' he said, as calmly as he could manage. 'Nancy, let her go.'

Nancy narrowed her eyes, taking her hand off Ashley's shoulder. Ash froze, looking sideways at Ruby, who pulled her away from her mother, ushering her along the hallway.

Matt swallowed, watching Nancy's other hand as it swung the handle of the antique shotgun into view. The one that hung above Nancy's fireplace – ornamental, functional? She cradled the barrel expertly across her other arm, smiling as Matt stared at it.

'It wasn't George's,' she said. 'I know you thought it was, but George never liked shooting. I, on the other hand, hunted regularly. Still would if I had the time.'

She shrugged.

Ruby stared up at Matt. She moved her head slowly, left and right, her eyes pleading.

'Don't look at her,' Nancy snapped at him. 'Don't look at

my daughter! And how dare you think I'd hurt Ashley? Young girls are more *your* thing, aren't they?'

Matt put one foot forward, stepping down. The staircase creaked as Imogen took the step behind him.

'I collected her from school a little early, by the way,' said Nancy. 'I called them on your phone, Imogen, hope you don't mind. They recognised the number.'

'Nancy,' said Imogen, her voice softer than Matt's, trembling but focused. 'Nancy, why did you do that? And why did you bring that thing to our house?'

Nancy laughed, the shrill, familiar tone cutting through the air. She pushed the front door closed, latching it.

Her smile dropped. She looked at the shotgun, frowning. 'I used to be something of a sharpshooter,' she said. 'Up at the club. Before. Before ...'

'But you don't need it here,' said Imogen, resting her hand on Matt's shoulder as she stepped past him. Matt followed. They stopped four steps from the bottom.

'Do you, Nancy?' Imogen persisted. 'Why would you need that here, amongst friends?'

Nancy's face twisted. She turned to Imogen. 'What else can I do?' she said. 'You were my friend, Imogen, and I valued you. But him,' she nodded to Matt without looking him in the face, 'he's a monster. I tried to show you, to protect you. But he's cast his spell on you.' Nancy shook her head again.

'Go,' she said, indicating the hallway, through to the kitchen. She moved the gun in her grip, keeping the barrels pointed downwards. Matt struggled with the sight of it in her hands, the way she cradled it like a baby. Nancy's quirks, those mannerisms he once found eccentric, then annoying, then worrying, had now revealed themselves for what they were – the symptoms of a profoundly troubled and dangerous mind.

In those brief minutes upstairs he'd read as much as Imogen about the condition that they suspected, although Imogen would understand it far better than he. A personality disorder? How much did it distort her view, her *understanding* of reality?

If Imogen was right, Nancy's motivations had never been normal, not in the time they'd known her. She'd been consumed by Ruby, but not for the reasons they thought. Her behaviour, which had generated such sympathy, even from him, was revealed as that of a disturbed psyche, one which had seen another target the minute they moved in – another vulnerable person in need of care. In need of Nancy's unique form of care.

Her hostility towards Matt was clear, and her accusations were all part of it. Did she really *believe* Matt had done those things with Ruby? Was she convinced, even while she set him up – smeared lipstick on his shirts, placed photos on his laptop? Were those acts detached somehow, part of a different Nancy, one who was convinced she must do such things to protect her daughter? She was blind to the heart-breaking reality – that she was killing her own daughter in the process.

He hadn't seen it, none of them had.

But Imogen was right: Nancy had never been pushed this far, and his actions, his investigations, were the final straw. She had snapped, and her unpredictability was their biggest threat.

'Go!' she repeated. Matt and Imogen both stumbled down the remaining steps. Imogen hurried through to get Ash, Matt close behind. They paused in the kitchen, huddled against the far side of the island. Ash ran to Imogen, who tucked her head against her chest, gripping her tight, ducking below the worktop.

Matt stood in front of both of them, shielding them as Nancy approached, blocking their exit back to the hallway. Ruby stepped in next to her, across to the dining area, shrinking against her mother's wrath, hiding against the wall, not daring to look up.

The utility room was behind Matt, the French doors straight ahead. Matt's stomach sank, wondering how long it would take to prise open either of the broken doors. The utility lock was rusted and needed a screwdriver to turn. The French doors were jammed fast. His fault, his mistake. But Nancy didn't know that. She had to assume they'd run at any second, try to escape. Or would she? What was the extent of her delusion?

Why had she brought them in here?

His eyes darted across the worktops, not knowing what he was looking for. A knife against a shotgun? No. A fight would end in disaster, even he could see that.

Nancy needed talking down.

The windows rattled in the wind. Matt's heart thudded, his breathing laboured as the lump in his throat swelled. Jake barked from the garden, running up to the glass doors, watching them.

'Nancy,' he said. 'Please. I think we need to talk. All of us.'

'It's too late for that,' said Nancy. 'I gave you your chance, Matthew. A chance to come clean.' She looked at Ruby, who stared at her hands, fidgeting. Her knees trembled, her small figure almost childlike in the moment, betraying her age. Yet Matt knew she was a different person away from Nancy – happy, mature, desperate for a normal life.

375

She was no child, yet she had no idea what her mum was doing to her.

Matt swallowed. Nancy needed to hear it again. There must be some way through; some fragment of sanity Matt could play on. He glanced behind him at Imogen. She supported herself against the worktop, face twisted in concentration.

Imogen needed to hear it.

'I know you think it's true,' he said, turning back to Nancy. He put his hands out, palms facing her, trying to look as non-threatening as possible – which wasn't too hard given Nancy's experienced grip on the stock of the shotgun.

She moved it, keeping the barrels tipped downwards. Could he lunge for it? She was six feet away, give or take. Could he grab it before she could raise it and fire? The thought caused a rush of adrenaline; his skin prickled with tension. But he froze in place – he had no experience of guns, no idea what Nancy could do, even if she were sane. In her current state, he couldn't risk the gun going off. He couldn't risk Imogen or Ash.

'You've been poking into my business, Matthew,' she said, fixing her glare on him. Matt tried not to waver, but her eyes were piercing, a madness he'd never seen. But it had been there all along.

'*My* business,' she said, 'and you had no right. Like everything else you did, Matthew, you had *no right*!' Her voice quivered with rage, barely contained.

'I had to,' said Matt. 'Because this isn't about me, Nancy. It's about you.'

'Liar!' she screamed, what was left of her composure crumbling. 'This is about you and my daughter. You sick bastard.'

The words were spat with such venom that Matt recoiled, wanting to step back, further out of reach. He shook his head, watching the gun, watching her arms trembling as she shifted it, moving it ever so slightly upwards.

'I know you believe that,' he said, struggling to look away from the gleaming silver barrel. 'But you're mistaken. You're wrong, Nancy.' He glanced at Ruby, trying to judge her mental state. She looked terrified. He needed her to deny this. Could he risk it?

'Talk to her. Talk to your daughter. Ruby. Please.'

'No,' Nancy screamed. 'You don't get to talk to her. Not after what you've done.'

Ruby remained silent but glanced up. Their eyes met. Hers were full of pain. Matt wished he could have done something sooner, realised what was going on, rescued her from Nancy's grasp.

'She'll tell you,' said Matt, keeping his eyes on Ruby. 'She'll tell you it never happened. Won't you, Ruby?'

'It's not just the pictures,' said Nancy. 'Not just the groping. Not just the kiss. Oh no.' She peered around Matt, towards Imogen. 'You thought it was just that, didn't you? And I protected you. I cared for you!'

'Nancy, I—' Imogen was struggling, Matt could hear it in her voice, the trauma, the doubt. She kept Ashley below the worktop, standing next to him.

'Sex, dear Imogen. More than once. More than a flirt, or whatever their disgusting conversations might've been. Your husband had sex with my fifteen-year-old daughter. I believe that's rape, under common law.'

'No!' Matt shouted. He couldn't help his own anger rising.

'You're a fucking liar, Nancy. You're sick in the head. You're making all of this up.'

The gun swung this time, and Matt's heart stopped ahead of his mouth. He'd never experienced such raw fear, seeing the cold barrels pointed at his chest. His words departed. Imogen hunched over behind him, placing herself in front of Ash.

'Wait, wait,' he said. 'Please, Nancy. I didn't mean . . .'

'Not in control, Matthew?' said Nancy, her voice icy. 'A strange feeling for you, I guess. Young women are much easier to manipulate.'

Matt took a small breath, watching Nancy flip from seething anger to apparent calm. He needed to keep her that way.

'Stop.' The small, timid voice of Ruby. She glanced at her mum then at Matt. 'I know now it was wrong, Matt,' she said. 'What we did. I'm sorry.'

Silence in the room, broken by a small rumble of thunder in the distance.

The windows shook in their frames as the wind howled, the earth taking a breath.

Matt watched Ruby's face, seeing how fragile she looked. How confused.

'Why are you lying, Ruby?' he said, his voice as calm as he could manage. 'Look at me. What is she threatening you with? She's ill, Ruby. She needs help. Please.'

Ruby gave a small shake of her head, but the confusion remained. 'I don't know . . . It's over. What do you mean—'

'You're damn right it's over,' said Nancy, smiling at Ruby with a wicked expression. 'So my daughter has found her voice, at last,' she said, keeping the gun in position, pointed at Matt,

378

her head tilted to one side. 'Then perhaps . . . perhaps we don't do this.'

This. Matt gulped. 'We don't need to do anything, Nancy,' he said. 'Ruby is confused, and so are you. You're not well. Put the gun down and we'll talk about it. How about that?'

Nancy laughed again, sending a fresh shiver through him.

'Mum?' Ruby tried.

'No,' said Nancy. 'I don't think so. We've done enough talking. I think I'll take care of this right now. We call the police, wait here for them.' She glanced at Ruby. 'Well done, love. That was brave. And you don't have to worry about this man any more. He'll be gone for good. Now stay quiet.'

'Nancy—' Matt needed to push it. Push Ruby.

'They'll have her testimony and mine,' said Nancy, turning back to Matt. 'That will be enough, whatever happens.'

He took another breath, deeper this time.

Still blocking their exit in front of the doorway, Nancy and Ruby stood between the dining area and the kitchen. Matt, Imogen and Ash remained behind the kitchen island, with no exit other than through Nancy. Matt's eyes darted again to the utility room door. Ash whimpered behind him, whispering to Imogen, who tried to calm her.

'I'm doing this for you, Imogen,' Nancy said. 'I told you, I knew what he was like. I could see it.'

'It's a fabrication, and the police will know it,' said Matt, knowing the reality would be less forgiving, his desperation matched only by Nancy's madness, her determination.

Nancy shrugged. 'So I'll make it public. Conviction or not, Matthew, you're done. I'll make a phone call to that paper of yours. You were keen to run a story on us, weren't you? This is juicier than what you had in mind. *Neighbour rapes teenager*, that should do it.'

Matt shook his head. 'Stop saying that.' His voice trembled, sounded pathetic even to his own ears.

'Ruby?' he called to her. 'Tell your mum. It's not . . .'

But Ruby shook her head. 'What do you mean, not well, Matt? Don't lie to me. Mum is only being protective. Mum, please put the gun down.'

Matt watched her, disbelieving. Was she really going to say such things, side with her mother? He realised, again too late, that he'd underestimated the twisted bond between them. A Stockholm Syndrome-type relationship. The abused and the abuser. It needed to be broken. He had to push, however much it might hurt – it was no worse than whatever Nancy was putting her through, or would continue to do if he let this happen.

He put his hands on the worktop, tried to calm the stampede in his chest.

'Your mum is very ill, Ruby,' he said. 'Mentally ill. Your sickness isn't real. You've been poisoned by her. All of your symptoms—'

'Liar,' hissed Nancy. She swung the barrel and cocked the hammer. Matt winced, unable to move. He closed his eyes, waiting for the click, the shot. It didn't come. He opened them, seeing the fury in Nancy's eyes but also the hesitation. There was only one way through this.

'It has a name,' he continued, seeing Ruby's eyes widen. He'd hit some recognition, some doubt in her mind.

'A mental illness,' he continued. 'It's not just you, Ruby. Imogen's been poisoned too. Look at her . . . she looks the same as you – nausea, vomiting, losing weight. This is your mother's doing. She needs help, Ruby.'

'No, no, no, no,' said Nancy. 'You don't know what you're talking about, Matthew.'

But Matt could see the panic as Nancy turned back to her daughter, and the growing confusion as Ruby processed his words.

'Don't listen to him, Ruby,' said Nancy, her voice increasingly shrill. 'He's poisoning your ears! It wasn't enough to take your body, now he wants to take your mind from me too. He wants to have you for himself, away from me!'

'Your dad, Ruby.' Matt was shouting now, he and Nancy both facing Ruby, the lynchpin of the room. 'Your dad – he died because of it. Your mum killed him, Ruby. That's what I dug up. I have proof. I'll show you. All of this is about your mum, Ruby.'

Ruby's face broke. She stepped back, holding her head in her hands. Matt could see her putting the pieces together. She looked at her mum, her breath coming in short gasps.

'Mum?'

Nancy shook her head. 'He's a liar, darling. Ignore him.'

'Look at her, Ruby,' said Matt. 'Is this normal? Think, Ruby. All of the years you've been ill. All of your symptoms. Think of your dad, Ruby.'

Ruby tilted her head, staring at her mum with a new intensity. Tears started to flow; her lips trembled.

'Mum?' she said, almost a sob. 'Please, say it's not true.'

'Of course it's not true,' snapped Nancy. 'It's madness. Listen to me, darling. Your treatment is hard, I know, but you're improving under my care.'

'My treatment,' said Ruby, shaking her head. 'My treatment . . . No, Mum. I don't always take it.'

Matt paused.

Nancy's smile faded; an icy expression returned. 'What do you mean?'

'It makes me so sick,' said Ruby. 'Sometimes I pour it in the sink. I have better days when I don't take it. I'm sorry, Mum. I . . . It makes me worse.'

'You don't understand,' said Nancy. 'That's how it works, darling. You take it. You hear me? You take your medicine! It's the only thing that will keep you safe.'

'The smoothie,' said Ruby. A fresh wave of tears. She paced back and forth, getting closer to Nancy.

Nancy narrowed her eyes. Matt watched her grip, her finger caressing the trigger guard.

'The smoothie you made for Imogen,' said Ruby. 'It was on the tray on her bed. It looked and smelled like the ones I have, the ones you put my medication in. The ones I always feel sick after.'

Matt heard Imogen's swift intake of breath. She kept Ash behind her, leaned around Matt. 'Ruby,' she said. 'I'm so sorry, but it's true.'

'The medicine is poison,' said Matt. 'I know where she gets it from.'

Ruby stepped towards Nancy. Matt could see her gradually taking control of herself. The timid child who'd entered the room was growing, processing the situation, the awful reality. It would be too much for her, but all he needed was doubt.

'Why?' said Ruby, standing close, in front of her mum, arms hanging by her sides. A beautiful picture of innocence and hurt, facing her abuser.

382

But Matt realised Nancy didn't know *why*. That was her illness. She knew *what* she was doing, but she could never articulate what drove her.

'Dad?' said Ruby. 'Tell me it's not true, Mum. Did you give him the same thing?'

Nancy paused, taking several deep breaths, studying her daughter with a cold intensity. Matt wanted to keep pushing, driving home the point, but Imogen held his arm gently, pulling him back. He glanced to his right and she gave a little shake of her head.

Nancy finally broke the silence.

'Your father was a wicked man. But he was sick, very sick. I looked after him, like I'm looking after you.' She turned to Imogen. 'And you.'

'You're not denying it,' said Ruby, glancing at Imogen. 'Tell me what you did to him. He had the same symptoms as me. Was he ill or not?'

'Your father was a bastard, Ruby.'

'Don't talk about him like that.' Ruby grew in size, standing taller, her face twisted with hurt. She faced her mother. 'Don't you dare. He was my dad, he loved me.'

'He loved himself,' said Nancy. 'That's all he loved. He never paid any attention to you.'

'Was he sick?' Ruby asked.

'Yes! He was sick,' said Nancy. 'But he deserved everything he got! He died of his illness. Just as you will. Just as Catherine did, and just as Imogen will!'

The shock of her statement forced the room to silence.

Matt reached for Imogen's hand, feeling Ash against his legs. Ruby stood in shock, gobsmacked, bottom lip trembling.

Matt turned, but was too late to see Nancy boil over, the realisation of what she'd said provoking some primal shift, a final ignition. A switch from the simmering delusion of the past years towards a final moment of madness. She hissed, the decision made, before raising the gun towards him.

'You bastard,' she screamed.

Matt didn't have time to move, could only watch in slow motion as Ruby lunged at Nancy, just as the shot was fired.

Imogen

I saw the barrel being knocked sideways, Ruby grappling it from her mother's hands. The sound of the shot hitting the side of the kitchen boiler was louder than the shot itself. The metal casing was punched through, the fixings shattering as the insides were torn from the wall.

I heard the hiss at the same time as the ignition – a high-pitched rushing sound which deepened into a thump as the escaping gas caught alight. The flames rushed out with the full force of the gas main, exploding up the wall and across the ceiling. The wall of heat hit us all – Matt staggered back into me and I shielded Ash as we fell. I couldn't help crying out as my shoulder hit the tiles.

I scrambled sideways with Matt, keeping my head low, squeezing Ash to my side. It took me a few seconds to take in what had happened. Our decrepit gas boiler had exploded with the force of the shot and was spewing flames, fuelled by a gushing source of propellant, surging upwards on to the ceiling and over the kitchen-diner. I could see the heat in the air as it hit the other side of the room. The curtains over the French doors caught alight, a faint blue flame that turned orange as it spread. I felt a fresh surge – the initial explosion from the boiler was matched by a second wave. Bulbs exploded overhead, the fire flowing over the ceiling in a terrifying blanket of heat. My hair singed and my lungs seared in pain. I heard a distant barking, frantic; Jake was still outside, thank goodness.

The air was thickening by the second, the oxygen sucked into the flames which were snaking across each surface, igniting everything they touched. I saw the door frame to the hallway catch, the paint already bubbling. Our only way out, and I could already see the wooden support for the staircase blackening as the varnish melted.

'Wait,' Matt shouted, peering through the smoke towards Nancy.

'There,' I said. The smoke and heat obscured my vision, but I could see both Nancy and Ruby – they'd been closer to the boiler and had been thrown sideways in the blast. Nancy lay on her back, but Ruby was crawling towards the dining table, dazed, taking shelter underneath.

'Out,' said Matt, grabbing me, pulling me with one hand, Ash with the other. He shielded me as we stumbled past the boiler, a furnace on the wall, dragging us towards the hallway. I kept an eye on Nancy as we passed. She was moving with laboured breaths, the shotgun still clasped in her hands.

The gun she'd tried to kill my husband with.

Three more steps; it felt like a mile. The heat was intense, the sound of the air like a tornado, consuming everything in its path. The door frame groaned and I glanced up, throwing my hands above me as the wood splintered, shattering, firing down flakes of burning paint and shards. Ash cried out, wrenching herself away from Matt. Her small body scrambled past me, back towards the kitchen window, behind the deceptive safety of the island.

'Ash,' I screamed. I could hear her cries. Her screams. 'Ashley!'

'Mummy!'

I spun around, but felt Matt's strong arms pulling me across the floor, my feet skidding as he grabbed my shoulders and hurled me through the doorway into the hallway. I slipped on the wood and landed heavily, scrambling to my feet as the flames surged across the ceiling, searching for air, searching for fresh fuel, searching for me.

'Matt,' I shouted, my voice faltering, watching as he disappeared in front of me, the smoke descending into a thick wall, reducing the visibility to a few feet. I struggled to draw breath in the acrid smoke and coughed, pulling my shirt up to cover my mouth, shielding my face from the heat.

'I'll get her,' Matt called back, already a silhouette in the smoke, crouching as he re-entered the kitchen. 'I'll get them.'

I backed away. I had no choice, the flames already licking at the walls, the paint darkening in its wake. I pulled open the front door, feeling the rush of air behind me. The ceiling cracked and fell in as more plaster shattered in the heat, the walls caving in protest. Our house was crumbling, fracturing in the heat, in the trauma, in the moment.

I staggered out on to the path, screaming for help, screaming for anyone. I reached the grass verge before collapsing to my knees.

My daughter and my husband.

My life disappearing in a storm of smoke and flames.

After

My stomach heaved. I coughed, hacking up smoke and soot, wheezing with the effort, my eyes watering in protest as the first body bag was zipped and tagged. The paramedics didn't look at me. I wasn't hurt. Not badly. I heaved again.

The stretcher caught on the kerb, the wheels snagging, lurching to the left before righting itself. The paramedics yanked it free, cursing as they pulled it on to the road.

Smoke billowed from the rear of the house. The firefighters ran in and out, unpacking more equipment, rolling hoses across the front lawn, shouting at each other with controlled urgency. The noise swept over me. I couldn't process it. Just another wave of chaos.

I resisted the urge to run to the ambulance, to jump inside and beg. My legs were frozen, rooted to the ground. The grief was overwhelming, the relentless build-up of the last few weeks seizing my every muscle.

A second stretcher appeared, a second body bag, wheeled more carefully, missing the kerb. The paramedics lifted this one easily into the vehicle. The bile caught in my throat this time. I coughed again, my saliva thick with ash.

I struggled to tear myself away from this moment, where time had stopped, a period of respite between the pain of before and the pain yet to come.

There was a roar as the first police car entered the road. It was followed by a second. They disappeared from view behind the fire trucks and the sirens stopped. The doors opened; slamming shut a second later. My heart missed a beat.

I'd expected to see them, but it didn't reduce the shock. Or the fear.

Three short months.

And it still wasn't over.

Now

St James's park is busy, the cool autumn air whipping around the bench and the playground equipment, lifting whatever detritus it can find, spinning it a few feet further on before relinquishing its grip.

I look sideways at Matt, tucking my coat under my legs, pulling it tighter against the chill. He stares forward with a fixed grin on his face, watching Ashley shriek with delight as she swings higher, kicking her feet with each pass.

'Careful,' he calls, but she's OK, and we both know it.

Ashley is fine, safe, unscathed. At least one of us is.

My recovery has been swift, physically, once the steady stream of poison into my body stopped. The doctors were shocked, the specialists intrigued, but the treatment was the same, and the lasting damage, they hope, will be minimal.

Psychologically, I may take a little longer.

It feels strange to be back in London, but the police investigation was rapid, and we were free to go.

Nancy's diagnosis was made post-mortem, from what little

evidence the police could gather, combined with my and Matt's testimony. Dr Banks was very pleased to give his account of the death of Nancy's husband, though less pleased when the issue of his confidentiality breach came to light. He'll go unpunished by the police, though the medical board might take a different view.

It only took a bit of probing before it all came out, Nancy's recent history and actions laid bare. Poor Chris was still too scared to reveal what he suspected, what Matt told the police, even now dismissing it and asking if he could remain in his house – the medical advisor suggested dementia had started to set in, probably a result of the consistent stress he put himself under, living in fear, one door away from the woman he suspected of killing his dear wife. His meeting with Matt had probably been his last lucid moment, a final attempt to put right the evil that had befallen his beloved Catherine. Nancy's guilt was confirmed, her punishment absolute.

The medical profession closed ranks. Nancy's diagnosis of Munchausen by proxy was never made while she was alive, never even suspected. She'd never suffered from so much as a cold and avoided medical facilities religiously – unless of course she was buying her poisons.

They found packets of heavy metals in her pantry, locked away, labelled and sorted. They found the lab technician, Curly, who faced a surprisingly minimal punishment for his part in Nancy's years-long battle. He had no idea, he said. He'd thought she was buying them for home-school science projects. Matt and I questioned the plausibility of this, but the police believed him. The truth was too fantastic.

The forensics team said the amounts were perfectly meas-ured to ensure a survivable level of sickness. I shivered reading the report – Nancy was meticulous in her dosage. She even had separate containers for Ruby and me, prepared weeks in advance.

It turned out I'd been poisoned from almost the first time I'd met Nancy. The first cup of tea, the first cake. Why she tar-geted only me and not Ashley was a mystery, until the specialist explained the core of her condition. It wasn't about assault or murder; it was about caring for a person she considered to be vulnerable. Someone who needed her. Ash didn't fit that cat-egory, but I did. I was vulnerable, still am, and Nancy saw it in a heartbeat. It's why I liked her so much. As soon as I hinted that all was not well in my household, I became her focus, her patient, her *target*. The shock of her death will endure for some time. She needed help, not a coffin.

But Matt couldn't help her.

That's what he said.

The tragedy of Ruby White hit the headline news and lin-gered there for some time. Even Matt's paper ran it, a local story with international appeal. Specialists from all over the country clamoured to review her story, her suffering. Ruby, like Nancy, was a picture of health in official terms – no GP complaints, no hospital admissions, no school nurse, no concerned teachers checking up on her. Not a single professional ever got a chance to cast their eyes over Ruby, to see if she was OK, to see if her childhood was within normal parameters, an expected product of a wealthy middle-class woman in Surrey.

Ruby had never needed treatment for anything, and yet her short life was one of suffering. Matt and I declined to be interviewed, declined to be part of it. Matt removed himself from the paper, and his new job in the process. But we'd had our experience of the White family, and it was time to move on. Again.

Blood tests on Ruby's body showed the same as me – just under a lethal dose, enough to eat away at us indefinitely. She would have gone on for years before organ failure or fatal nerve damage set in.

But she died of smoke inhalation before the fire service could pull her out. At the tender age of fifteen. Still a child. A vulnerable, abused child.

Matt couldn't help her either.

That's what he said.

We'd spent many hours in the interview rooms, Matt more than I. All I could do was describe my friendship and my slowly deteriorating health. I defended Nancy, as much as I could, but ultimately I was powerless. Perhaps that was true, perhaps not, but in my weakened state I don't see how I could have acted differently. I choose to not look too deeply into my conclusion, for fear of what it might bring.

Matt had a far more twisted story to tell, much of which I was hearing for the first time. As I listened, I realised he left out much of the finer detail. And a lot of the coarser detail.

Nobody else knew what Nancy had accused him of. Her string of accusations and attempts to frame Matt were hidden as he steered the focus away from him and towards me, and towards Catherine and George, the two people Nancy had killed. The police were happy to focus on that, and I kept my mouth shut. It wouldn't do to muddy the water. Nancy's delusions were heart-breaking and all-consuming, but her actions were what killed her.

I listened as Matt described how she'd come for us, once she realised what he knew, once she'd stolen my phone and read every message he'd sent. She'd snapped – the specialist said it was inevitable, her inner psyche unable to maintain its delusion under such a sustained attack. Her intentions at the back of our house that day still raise the hairs on my neck. Matt believes she planned to kill us all. I wonder, when I think of the anguish in her face in those final moments, whether she was just crying out for help. She believed it, all of it, and even in those last seconds of confusion, she thought she was defending the daughter she doted on.

The gun was a surprise to us, but not to the Surrey detective who plied us with undrinkable coffee and stale biscuits and forced us to run through the whole story again with him. *You wouldn't believe how many domestics in this neck of the woods involve a shotgun,* he'd told us. *More than one Surrey husband has been killed at the wrong end of one of those.*

Nancy the hunter was an odd thought, but perhaps rather apt, given her actions.

The details of that day were picked over many times. The fire service confirmed the dangerous state of our house – the lack of useable exits and the unserviceable gas boiler were a house fire waiting to happen. It would have taken far less than a shotgun blast to make the thing explode, they'd said. The fact we'd only just purchased the house was the reason they let it go, although what charges they could have brought against us remained vague. Owning your own death-trap property was not in itself a crime.

Nevertheless, two people had died, and we had survived. It was a weight we'd carry for the rest of our lives.

That was the official story. That was what I knew. And it was what Matt had told me.

Matt offered several accounts about how he tried to save Nancy and Ruby. How he dragged Ashley to the back, smashed a window with a chair and fled into the garden. Ash squeezed through a break in the hedge into Chris's garden. They found her an hour later, hiding in his shed, playing with a watering can, talking to a bumblebee that was trapped in the window.

Matt went back in for Nancy and Ruby, but the heat was too much, the smoke too thick. He tried several times, but failed, and hated himself for it. He cried as he told the firefighters on scene. They assured him he did the best he could, that without proper equipment it would have been difficult to get either of them to safety.

Difficult. Not impossible.

In the days immediately afterwards, Matt showed varying degrees of bitterness about the entire ordeal. It surprised me, at first. I asked him if there was some part of him that was glad Nancy had died. He seemed shocked, asking how I could suggest such a thing. She was a sick woman, he said, and she needed help. He wished he'd had a chance to give her that.

But his cheeks flushed as he said it. And I didn't ask again.

I didn't ask about Ruby.

The wind blows harder, the leaves flutter up on to the bench. Matt turns to me.

'She's happy,' he says, nodding towards our daughter, putting his hand across on to my lap.

I nod, keeping my hands in my pockets. My right one taps

the edge of my phone. Three unread messages from Claire, who I've been in daily contact with over the last week.

Since I made my discovery.

Since everything changed. Again.

I wonder what I would ask Nancy and Ruby if they were alive. I have so many questions about so many days, lost time, lost minutes and hours. A word here, a conversation there. It all adds up, but much of it is now buried, along with their bodies.

Claire's words repeat in my head, morning and night: *You will never be one hundred percent sure of the truth. You'll never know for sure.*

Except I did know, and the last few days have been the most difficult of my life, my tragedy this time playing out in secret phone calls and messages as I piece together the fragments I need.

The wonderful yet terrifying thing about modern technology is that it's gathering answers to the questions you haven't asked yet, and may never ask. It wasn't until a week ago, after we moved in with my parents – the house is being renovated before we put it up for sale – that I posed it.

It was Ashley, in fact, who triggered it. Funny how the actions of our daughter, the other innocent child in our saga, were the tipping point.

We still have the laptop. Matt's laptop. The one I threw on the kitchen floor after seeing the pictures of Ruby – pictures we now knew Nancy planted. It still worked, with a cracked screen and a dodgy space bar. Matt thought we'd thrown it away, but I kept it for Ashley, who loved to play her games and explore the world through online maps and the wonders of the Internet.

Matt never was tech-savvy. He left himself logged into every-thing, giving me a window into a digital footprint he didn't know existed. He didn't realise I had access to his main account, his email, his location – his *location history*. I should have checked sooner, ages ago, when my first niggling doubt resisted my attempts to quash it, but it only came to me when Ash and I decided to explore our old village from the comfort of the sofa. Ash showed me what was possible.

We found it funny, following Matt's phone history as he left the house, went to work, drove home. Repeated every day, except weekends, where the path deviated, and we tried to remember where we'd been – to the park or the shops or south for a country walk.

And then I saw a strange thing, curious. A route heading out into the country, then backtracking on itself. Going nowhere. It raised a smile on my face. It wasn't like Matt to get lost. I checked the dates, and I traced his path. And I found him somewhere he shouldn't have been.

I found Matt. Not at the supermarket, where he'd said he was. Not quite, but nearby. A secluded car park in the woods, each day after work. Only for a week. One week.

Ruby's work experience week.

What were you doing in the woods with her, Matt? What were you doing in a secluded part of the woods with a beautiful fifteen-year-old girl? Every day, for at least an hour, before you returned home. You always needed a shower after the heat of the office, I remember. Of course you did.

My smile faded in that instant, and so did a bit of my soul. I remember Ash calling to me, through a wall of white noise, as my brain rewound and replayed, stuck in a loop, kicking itself as it pieced it all together – all the little inconsistencies, the lies, the timings. The smell of perfume on the car seat – something Nancy would never have been able to do.

The anticipated shock, however, didn't arrive. Because I wasn't shocked.

I made a phone call or two. I was in a curious state, with a fixed smile and a fresh dose of anti-anxiety meds (which the doctor had prescribed me, to get over this initial difficult period).

Every village needs a gossiper, and I was lucky – Mrs Owens was the Albury gossip queen, and she also happened to own the B&B Matt had stayed in. I only asked how many nights he'd stayed and offered to pay any outstanding bills. She insisted on giving me the details of his movements, including the day she saw Matt and Ruby going into the room together, carrying bags of shopping. She wasn't wearing much, so Mrs Owens said. They reappeared a couple of hours later.

But that's how rumours start, she said, not that she'd dream of doing so, after her tragic death. But honesty is the best policy. She thought she should tell me. In case anybody else brought it up.

That day grew darker, and with it my reality. This time there was little doubt. I picked up one of my medical texts and checked my final suspicion. I knew what had bothered me about heavy metal poisoning. It didn't cause a fever, not usually. Not in me, and therefore not in Ruby. Nancy didn't realise – her knowledge of her own poison was scarily incomplete. But Ruby's admission to her mum, the one she blamed on her temperature, the one she'd said was made in the midst of a feverish dream ... There never was a fever. There never was a dream. The admission was true, all of it.

Ruby, the poor child, the *fifteen-year-old* child, had told her mother what had happened, how Matt had come on to her. How he'd groped and kissed her. It had troubled her and she'd reached out to her mother, confused, no doubt battling with her immature teenage emotions, an attraction to a man who gave her the sort of attention she'd never received before. An attraction that developed into something it never should have. A groomed and cultivated relationship with the man next door. A sinister betrayal and a criminal act.

And her mother believed her. Nancy believed her. And she told me.

But I didn't believe her. I didn't.

Claire's words, once again, screaming at me – *women don't lie about these things ... you take it as the truth.*

I'm sorry, Ruby. I'm sorry. I'll never forgive myself for not believing you, for letting him do it. You were right, Nancy was right. I failed you both.

I called Liv yesterday. We had a long chat, put our shared history to rest, told each other a few home truths. I told her about Ruby and she cried, hung up, called me back. Their sibling bond was strong, and born out of a damaged childhood. Where she found drugs, Matt found something else.

But it wasn't strong enough to weather this.

Liv told me what I needed to know. She said she owed me that. He couldn't pay for her silence this time. I thanked her. It was just another piece – a hanging thread that needed to be cut off. But a foundation for the rest.

London was not the beginning or the end. Matt's penchant for younger women started well before that. Not as young as Ruby, not until now, but heading that way. He confides in Liv because he needs to. Guilt? Perhaps. But also the confidence she'll never tell because she relies on him so absolutely. He told her about Yun – not what he told me, but another version. A version that included him sleeping with her in a casino hotel room, just as Yun had maintained.

I don't trust Yun, but something she said on the phone stuck with me. *I wasn't even the one who went to HR . . . They started asking questions.* They came to her, not the other way around. Yun's attack was not calculated.

Somebody saw something. Somebody reported it.

When Yun was called into HR, did she tell the truth and admit an office affair – or did she see an opportunity to save her reputation and take Matt's job in the process? Given how willingly she lent Matt the money, I'm inclined to think the latter. That she felt at least slightly guilty for her lies. But I might just be clutching at straws.

The truth? Who could say for sure? Both regretted it, both fixed it by telling their own accounts, creating fractures in their lives and others. So many versions of the same story. I admire Matt's ability to keep track.

Liv also told me about the girl before Yun – three years ago. A young intern, eighteen, I believe. A graduate who fled before it all came out; before it had a chance to damage her.

There were more, but I told Liv that was enough.

Matt's guilt was placed on Liv, and he moved on.

Or he thought he did. What he hadn't reckoned on was Yun screwing him up so royally. Or that Liv would spill his secrets.

What I do know, now, is the lengths to which Matt will go to convince the world he is innocent.

Did they both need to die in the fire?

Only Matt knows the answer to that question. But I think I know the truth.

The details. It's always in the details – the small, insignificant items that just don't fit. Stack them up, turn them around, and the story changes enough to make you question everything. They always come out in the end.

All the lies.

It took me a few days to process, to regroup, mentally, to find the courage to tell Claire, to prepare for the next stage.

The messages in my pocket, I hope, are to confirm exactly that. The divorce papers are drawn up, ready to one side. My statement is ready to go. My story. The story of Matt, my husband, and what he did.

'Ash is happy, Matt,' I say, shifting in my seat so his hand falls away from me. 'Are you?'

Matt smiles, stands up, brushes his trousers down. I look at his gorgeous deep eyes, full of love for me, full of his relief at how things have ended, full of secrets that will never be told.

As he walks off towards Ash, he gives me one last look. His eyes burn with something I've never seen before, a knowledge, a contentment. A freedom. But I see his cheeks. Bright red, flushed. Like they always are when he's lying.

Because my husband is a liar. A compulsive, relentless and persistent liar. A serial philanderer. And now, a sordid criminal.

Nancy was right. In all of her madness, she warned me. *Take what they want, do what they want. To hell with the consequences.* That's my Matt.

I don't think he knows any different.

I return Matt's smile and give him a wave.

Don't worry, I think. *I'll tell them. I'll tell everyone your secrets. Your lies. Starting tomorrow, Matt. Your story will be told.*

I'll make sure of it.

Acknowledgements

I want to thank a number of wonderful people who have helped to get this story out of my head and onto the page, particularly during these troubled times. I am writing this in the middle of the Covid-19 pandemic, which has devastated so many lives and families, and so my first thanks must go to the key workers – the health and government staff, the delivery drivers, the shop workers, and the many others who have kept life running as we know it – and enabled authors like me to keep writing.

My agent, Julie Fergusson, continues to be a brilliant friend and advisor on every aspect of my writing, shaping new ideas and squeezing the absolute best out of me at each and every stage, from idea to publication and beyond. She suffered through the early drafts of this book, patiently guiding me towards the final manuscript. Thank you, Julie!

A huge thank you to my new publisher, Headline, and the fantastic and energising bunch of professionals who work there. My new editor, Katie Sunley, has been so lovely and enthusiastic from the outset, offering her professional eye and keeping the whole process super fun and stress-free. Special mentions to

Emily Patience, Martin Kerans, Frances Doyle, Phil Beresford, Sarah Bance and Jill Cole – all of whom added their magic at each stage.

Thank you to the many crime and thriller authors I've had the pleasure of meeting over the last couple of years (Criminal Minds – you know who you are). They are a friendly, supportive group (and extremely talented) and I'm honoured to join the ranks. I can't wait to meet up in real life very soon.

A continued thank you to my wonderful parents, Brian and Mary, and my sister, Lucy (and Tim, Charlotte, Millie and Alice), for their encouragement, enthusiasm and kind words throughout.

Thank you to my amazing wife, Kerry, and my loving daughters, Isla and Daisy, who continue to provide the perfect home in which to write, offering patience, time and the motivation to keep going, even when we've been confined to the house for weeks of lockdown. My sanity is down to you guys!

And the final thank you is to you, the wonderful readers, tweeters, bloggers and reviewers, who take the time to remind everyone that the comfort of fiction is a constant, no matter what the world is doing. It's a necessary form of escapism for many, and even in these times it can make those moments of isolation bearable – a sanctuary when we need to escape into someone else's imagination. I hope I managed to provide that for you in some small way.